One Last Love

an Andy Shepard novel

by Denis Eucalyptus

Copyright © 2018 by Denis Eucalyptus

All rights reserved. No part of this publication may be reproduced, distributed or transmitted in any form or by any means, without prior written permission.

Limbic Lines Publishing
P.O. Box 131
Finley, California 95435
LimbicLines.com

This is a work of fiction. Names, characters, places, and incidents are a product of the author's imagination. Locales and public names are sometimes used for atmospheric purposes. Any resemblance to actual people, living or dead, or to businesses, companies, events, institutions, or locales is completely coincidental.

Scripture taken from the Holy Bible, Today's New International Version™ TNIV®.
Copyright © 2001, 2005 by International Bible Society®. All rights reserved worldwide.

Cover design by Stephanie Bell of Bella Designs

One Last Love: An Andy Shepard Novel/
Denis Eucalyptus. -- 1st ed.

Special thanks to:

Ginny Chavarria

Kirsten Barquist

Contents

Map of California's Gold Country _____ i
Forward _____ 1
Part 1: Andy Sings the Blues _____ 2
Part 2: Limping Into Heaven _____ 212
Postscript _____ 454
Note to Readers _____ 455

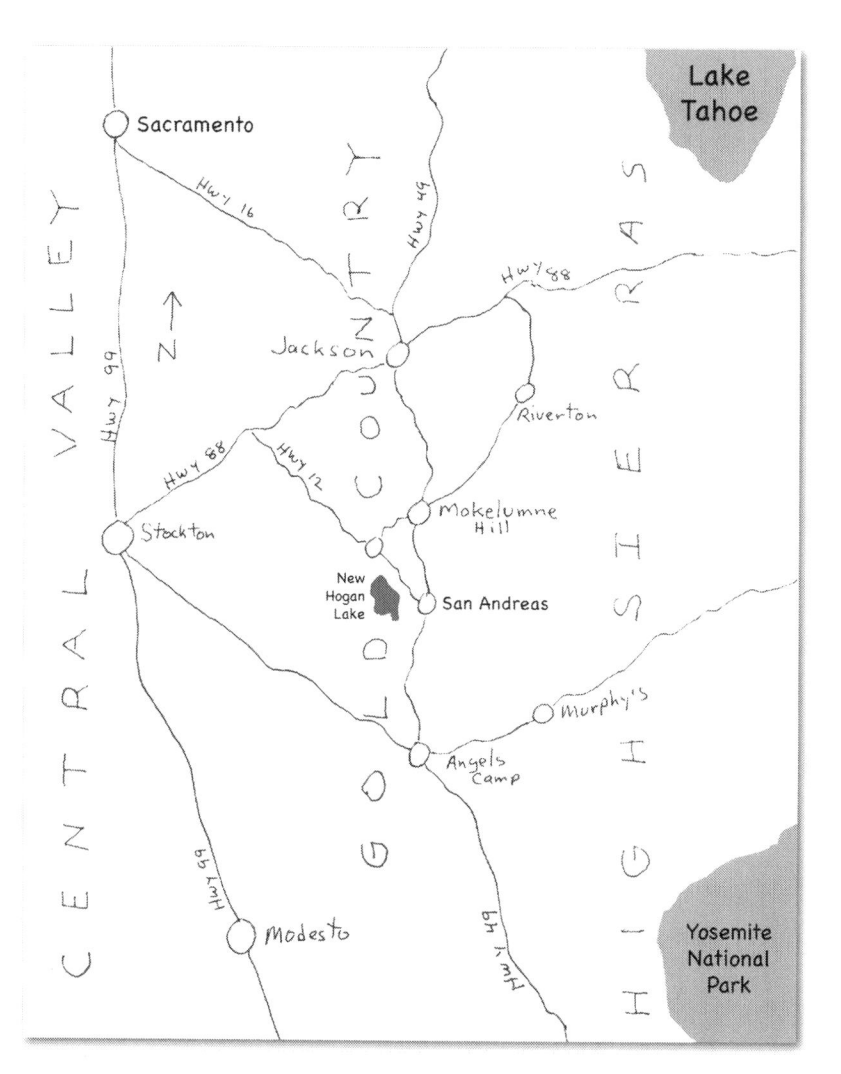

Map of California's Gold Country

Forward

An idea for a short story about a minister took on a life of its own and evolved into several Rev. Andy Shepard novels: *Hot Water – Holy Water*, *Spirit Driven*, *Desert Signs*, *The Ticket Home*, and *One Last Love*.

Although each novel stands on its own, here is a word about this story's context. *The Ticket Home*, which brings us to this story, tells of the end of Andy's marriage and pastoral career as he reluctantly gets pulled into a battle with the California Lottery and ultimately with an Indian Casino. In some ways he won and in some ways he lost. In the process he was able to start a philanthropic foundation with all the money that came his way. Now as the present story begins, Andy has suddenly retired.

One Last Love is told in two parts: "Andy Sings the Blues" which is narrated by Andy, and "Limping Into Heaven" narrated by Barbara, his lover.

I want to thank Ginny Chavarria for her generous help and encouragement with this whole series.

Part 1: Andy Sings the Blues

Chapter 1

My job as CEO of the Shepard Foundation lasted only a year – a long, painful, bumpy year. After I had resigned from my pastorate at the Riverton Church, and poured all the lottery money into the Foundation, and convinced five close friends to work for it, I quit. It turned out that they all loved the work, but we discovered that I made a lousy CEO.

Did I love the work? Not really. I believed winning the lottery was a God thing, and you might say I got a little obsessive about how to spend God's money. In my mind the money we granted had to be used in the right way. I felt we had to clean up the gambling money and make it count for something. Soon I found myself getting uncomfortable and a bit cranky with my friends when the programs receiving our grants did not fulfill my expectations. I suppose if I were honest with myself I would have to admit that the real problem was I did not feel good (and noble) working with gambling money in the first place.

It became clear to me: either lose my friends or quit. I quit, and my friends feigned disappointment, sighed a sigh of relief, and continued on their merry way.

I see now that it was really a transition year: from being a pastor to being a layman, from being married to being divorced once again, and from being an abandoned child to nurturing the love-center within me. What's more, I'm now a pensioner, and I am finding that it has its own transitional phase. Although I had the option to accept another appointment to pastor a different church, I couldn't bring myself to do it. Too much of my church work was hitched to my old neediness. And that wasn't all of it, my theology took a hit with the gambling drama. I now have too many questions without answers. I wouldn't know what to preach.

So, in my typical fashion, without much planning and preparation, I chose to become a pensioner. I prefer thinking of myself as a pensioner over being "retired." Retired connotes being tired and worn out, or old and useless. It brings to mind "retiring for the night," going to bed, to oblivion. But "pensioner" simply means that I draw a monthly check and I don't work.

"Work," I have to say it: I had no idea how much of my identity was tied to the work that I felt "called" to and "ordained" to by God…blah, blah, blah. Day after day I would get up and go to work. Work defined and structured my life, and (embarrassingly) gave my life the thin veneer of meaning. It now seems that I was trying to invent a life rather than live a life. After a few months of the lightness and freedom of being a pensioner, that paper person could no longer stand.

This, combined with the other transitions I was experiencing made me feel like an exhausted decathlon athlete facing one challenge after another. I was wobbling a bit as September moved Calaveras County into Autumn, and the green leaves that considered themselves so important and indispensable to the trees began looking dry and fatigued. Then a bit of grace came into my life: a cabin at Hogan Lake. I mentioned to Barbara Hanson, the manager of the historic Mokelumne Hill Hotel, Restaurant and Saloon, that I was looking for a place to rent. Over the years we had become acquaintances on a first name basis. She was on the short side, but looked taller in her cowgirl hat and boots. I guessed she was in her late forties. She had a medium build, but a bit wide in the hips. She had long dark hair that she wore loosely pulled back, and a generous smile that, like most women her age, was the key to her beauty.

Barbara was a divorcée and lived on New Hogan Lake, thirty miles from where I had lived on the Middle Fork of the Mokelumne. She had a ten-acre spread with a cabin that sat by the lakeshore. She had lived in the cabin while she built her horse barn, stables and corral. Then she had a manufactured house installed on the high point of her property. The cabin was fixed up as a guest house – but it turned out she had few guests.

Barbara said that she had stopped trying to rent the cabin, but since she knew me, I could come out and take a look. It was small and rustic but cared for. Inside, the furnishings were quite nice and the views of the lake and surrounding oak studded hills were beautiful.

"I'll give it to you, furnished, for a thousand dollars a month which I think is a fair rate," she said.

"It's a nice place Barbara, and a fair rate, but I need something a little more economical. I'll be honest with you I'm in a strange predicament. A month ago, as you may know, I was giving away millions of dollars from the foundation I created. And the Foundation will be doing that for years to come. But now, a thousand a month is a good third of my pension which is my sole income."

"Right. I tell you what, I have problems with my shoulder and I could use some help with the horses. Maybe we could work something out. How are you with horses, Andy?"

"Truthfully, I like horses – from a distance."

She nodded. I walked into the bedroom. It had an open beam ceiling and a large sliding glass door that looked out on the lake. I was falling in love with the place; and I felt an urgency to put some distance between me and my former life.

"Well, Andy, I don't know what I can do. I'm not anticipating any funerals that you could help me with – unless you could arrange one for my ex-husband." She gave a mischievous smile. "And I am sure as hell not planning any more weddings. So that's that."

On a lark I said, "How about a massage a week? It might help that shoulder?"

She looked at me with surprise, "Are you a massage therapist too?"

"Not technically, but I've had some training."

"How are you with feet?"

"My specialty."

"Man, my own resident masseur! That's tempting." She thought it over for a few moments. "Can you afford eight hundred?"

"Seven fifty would be more manageable."

"One hour massage every week?"

"And I'll provide the table."

"Deal, Andy," and she stuck out her hand.

As we shook on this special deal, I said, "And one more thing, I don't want the business of the Foundation following me here, so it would be a big help to me if no one knew where I lived or my phone number."

"No problem."

* * *

So I quit my work at the Foundation and moved into my new home – it is so easy to say those words but the actual experience was wrenching in a crazy-making way. Intellectually I knew the issues and pitfalls retirees faced, but the transition soon called into question the value of my whole life in a far deeper way than I expected. It was like the difference between knowing about earthquakes and experiencing an 8.5 teeth-rattler. The aftershocks still have me on edge.

During the first week, I drove down to Sacramento, and with my severance pay bought a massage table, a good sound system and a fourteen-foot sailboat. Who knew when I would be able to afford these essentials again?

After the first three massages, Barbara was noticeably much more relaxed with me and our arrangement. We did the massages on her turf. I kept her modestly draped during the sessions. I spoke only when she wanted to talk. She iced and heated her shoulder and neck before we would start, and then I worked that area and the related muscles, trying to give her some relief. She said there was some improvement. I also spent extra time on her poor hard-working feet. I covered them in hot damp towels for five or ten minutes before massaging them with almond oil. I used slow, medium-firm strokes that from time to time continued to move up her ankles and calves. She was very grateful.

The special deal I got on the cabin actually started on the fourth massage. She was lying on her belly and I had just finished her feet. I began working up the back of her legs. Then with long strokes, using both oiled hands together, I glided from her feet, up her legs, under the cover and up over her rear to the small of her back; then back down and finishing with her toes.

"Mmm, that's good," she said softly.

I did it again. She moaned a bit. "A little saddle-sore?" I asked.

"Maybe. It feels so good."

On the next long stroke, I let the cover fall to the side and continued up her back to her neck and shoulders, then more slowly back down following the contours of her little body. As my hands rode up over her generous rear she half moaned and half groaned. So I began to knead her butt like soft warm fragrant bread dough, including broad circles on the small of her back and firm strokes on the back of her thighs.

I was getting lost in the feel of her body under my hands as I worked to the sound of soft music playing, and I was almost startled when she said unexpectedly, "All right, Andy," and she began to turn to face me. I thought that I had somehow blown it; that the massage had perhaps become too sensual for her, and our deal would be off.

"But don't screw up and fall in love with me or I will have to raise your rent," she said as she maneuvered to her back, and smiled.

"Just a happy-ending, right?" I said, interpreting that come-on-boy smile.

"Exactly." Then with a softer voice, "You clean?"

I thought I knew what she meant. I wore loose cotton pants with a drawstring. By her side I let them fall with my briefs, and said, "No unprotected sex; in fact no sex since Joy left last year."
"Poor baby," she said and her hand wrapped around my erection and slightly pulled me closer to the table. She gave me a lingering inspection. "Nice, and clean. Me too." She gave me a slight squeeze, let go and said, "Honey, you feel like you are rearing to go, so let's bring me up to speed before you start galloping, okay?" Then she let her knees spread open. I leaned over her breasts and let my lips get close to a nipple until I could feel its heat. Then I kissed each as if offering a devotional prayer.

Chapter 2

I created a morning routine in my cozy lakeside cabin, a ritual that helped secure my sanity in this sudden dislocation of my life. The ritual would start when my aching back told me to rise. I hung my glasses on my face and shuffled to the glass door to look at Hogan Lake with its surrounding hills and trees. This was usually the most magical moment of the day. There it was, the world-earth and sky – looking back at me.

Some mornings it beckoned me as a lover, "Come, enter my intoxicating beauty and dance with me."

Some mornings it gave me a cynical smile, as if saying, "Who are you? You are a fly speck. You didn't even reproduce. I've been here four billion years, and you? You are a blink in time."

And some days the view didn't say anything, like the passing scenery that one glimpses while riding on a train; a view always different, but with no way to hear it or connect with it. A train ride is too fast and too noisy.

On the morning of the fateful phone call the world grinned at me like it knew a joke that I wasn't privy to. So I headed for the coffeemaker, the next stop on my sanity-saving morning routine.

I had bought the cheapest espresso machine I could find: A $39.95 Mr. Coffee at Walmart. I pressed the finely ground, darkly roasted beans into the small stainless-steel filter cup. The aroma was reassuring – my brain would soon be more functional. I measured the tap water and poured it into the pressure chamber – water that had recently been drawn from among the bluegill, carp and catfish. Though filtered, the water carried a hint of earthy fragrance which I was still getting used to.

I replaced the large screw cap that topped the little machine, tightened it the best I could with my morning hands, then turned the dial to build the steam and pressure. I poured milk into a large glass mug, filling it half full and then waited for the machine.

Here my ritual slipped into reflection: Do the Giants play today? What time? Should I pick more blackberries down on Calaveras Creek. Do I have enough to share with Barbara? Oh man, remember that houseboat trip on the Sacramento Delta with Carol and two other couples when we moored at an island and used black berries to paint our bodies. It seems like a dream now. What was that dream I had last night?

Espresso, dark and aromatic, topped with a creamy light froth, began to dribble into the small carafe. I let the brewing have a head-start, then turned the dial and started to steam and foam the milk in the mug. While I waited for the milk to reach 130 degrees, I noticed the etching on the mug, the logo of a retreat center where I used to go annually for continuing education for my noble, meaningful job so that my work would be more meaningful and important. Oh well, at least it was a cool logo.

I poured the bitter, strong coffee into the sweet, hot milk, then cleaned my honest little machine for the next day. I took the latte' back to my bed-with-a-view to continue my routine. Propped up with pillows, I first enjoyed the coffee and view – nothing more, nothing less.

* * *

I have stopped talking to God, that ridiculous habit so many people have. Even the Bible says that God knows what we're going to say before we say it, knows in fact what we're afraid to say; and what's more, knows what we know but don't know we know: our deep subconscious well of fears.

I knew this, yet I used to say that we still should talk to God because the practice opens us up to God; and good prayer is how we say yes to God. Which is somewhat true in Spirituality 101, but it soon becomes, you know, ridiculous.

John Denver used to sing of one "talking to God and listening to the casual reply, Rocky mountain high." Trouble is, like most people, I can cleverly let myself be convinced that God is saying all kinds of stupid things to me. This can lead to a tragic early death, like Denver. It's a form of arrogance.

So now, almost fully awake and propped up in my bed-with-a-view, I don't pray, I meditate. It's a practice not of talking to the Mystery, but of being with the Mystery.

Damn, Barbara's right, when will I stop sounding like a preacher?

* * *

My morning meditation usually gave me peace until almost lunch time before it inevitably got attacked and disabled. This day my inner peace was disabled by my bank statement. I was spending more than I was receiving. I had cut my expenses, if not to the bone, then nearly to the bone. I had actually made a budget. I kept track of my expenditures. Yet in these first three months of living as a pensioner I was still not living within my means.

For the first time in my life I began clipping coupons and checking prices at the grocery store. Now those L.L. Bean and Eddie Bauer catalogues were recycled before I even open them. I knew where the cheapest gas was sold. I learned to cut my own hair with fifteen-dollar electric clippers.

That sounds like a sad story, but it was the health insurance that was killing me. I wasn't quite old enough for Medicare. And of course, a rural church pension is -- not to complain -- modest. I had a little savings, the proceeds from splitting the home insurance settlement with the bank and my ex-wife. As I stared at my bank statement I wondered how much closer to the bone I could cut?

So was it just a coincidence that I was ruminating over my bank statement when I got the phone call? Lately I had been very suspicious of coincidences.

Recent events had convinced me that there were spirits and unseen forces interfering in my life -- and, I presumed, in everyone else's life as well. And although they didn't seem to want to do me harm, they certainly messed with my life in unpredictable ways: now I am a broke pensioner; the house I had planned to retire in was burned along with all my stuff; and my fourth (and I swear to God! my last) wife is long gone and learning to be a medicine woman, like her grandmother with the Miwok Indians. So I'm starting to get it, the loving home that I have forever searched for is not out there, it is in me. A good wife, a holy vocation, or a half-billion dollars would be just icing on the cake. My days are now about living without the icing – I'm a naked cake. But I think it is time for the hand of God to nudge someone else's life off their rails and let me roll along by myself for a while, thank you very much!

The phone rang.

"Hello?"

"Hi Andy, its Wade. How is life on Hogan's Lake? Haven't heard from you for a while."

Wade was a good friend; good enough to point out my inadequacies as a CEO while leaving the door open for friendship.

"Hi Wade. I'm still adjusting, but okay. How are you?"

"Too busy this Fall with our new clients, but otherwise fine. I miss you, guy."

"Oh really?" I had no illusions, I knew I almost killed the baby I brought to birth.

"You know what I mean, Andy. I miss seeing you as a friend and neighbor, and hanging out together."

"I know, Wade. I miss you too. Give me a little more time to get my feet under me. We'll go sailing or something."

"Let's make it soon."

"Could be."

"Hey, one of the reasons I'm calling is that I know a guy who wants to get married. Can I refer him to you?"

What did Wade want me to do, talk the guy out of it? He knew how I felt about marriage and doing weddings. I bit my tongue and let the question hang there.

"His name is Nathan Porter, and he was at our wedding and really liked how you tied the knot."

Wade and Marilyn's was the last wedding I performed, and the last one I ever wanted to do. My bank statement was still in my hand. Shit. How much could I charge? I took a breath and tried to find the residual of the morning's meditation. My bind was not Wade's fault. "I don't know, Wade. Have him call me. We'll see."

"Fair enough. Let's stay in touch, friend."

"Yes. See you soon."

I laid the statement down, picked up my harmonica, stepped out the slider and sat heavily in the lawn chair that faced the lake some fifty yards down a gentle slope. I began to play mindlessly. I had always wanted to learn to play a blues harmonica. I bought the instrument and an instruction book a month after I got the cabin -- but I needed a tutor.

After a minute I realized that the tune I was puzzling out was:

>Nobody knows the trouble I see,
>Nobody knows but Jesus.
>Nobody knows the trouble I see,
>Glory Halleluiah.

It was an old black spiritual. I couldn't remember the verses, but the chorus was good enough for practicing my blues riffs -- I was still finding my harmonica "voice," my own unique way of improvising on a melody. I suppose I was also still trying to find my unique way of playing out this role of retired minister.

There were two major ways people dealt with retirement. The first was keeping busy. With hidden pride many retirees will complain, "I'm busier now than when I was working. I can't get everything done."

How easy to fill the void created by retirement, fill it with meaningless chores, manufactured concerns and diversions. It's puzzling how people seem to take care of life's little tasks while working forty hours a week at their jobs, but when they retire they can fill their days to overflowing with shopping, cooking, cleaning, laundry, home and auto repairs, doctor and dentist appointments, yard work, paying bills, chatting on the phone, vegging in front of the TV, or now submerging themselves in their computer.

Keeping busy? To what end? To fill an empty life? What's the point?

The other related strategy is obvious: get another job.

I didn't want to fall mindlessly into either choice. I simply wanted to be awake to life. Whatever I did, I wanted it to be life-giving. I played this theme through my harmonica.

After twenty minutes I felt better and I got an idea. I went in and got my writing tablet and began to create a list of items: issues that make marriage almost impossible; a map of the gauntlet that Nathan and his beloved were going to have to run. It was an outline of the pre-marital counseling I wanted to give them.

My list ran for two pages, and the longer I wrote the angrier and self-righteous I became.

Suddenly I stopped. What the hell was I doing? I crumpled the paper and threw it out the open slider into the early fall sunshine; it bounced and rolled along the brick floor of the small patio. Why would I want to make myself sad by making a list of my perceived grievances?! And do I really want to assault this couple with my crap? The idea made my eyes tear up and I said out loud, "Man, am I a mess."

I walked into the bedroom and found my journal on the nightstand. I sat on the bed and opened it. It was nearly full. I had started it around the time Joy left. The first entry was about a ski accident I had that week, and the related dream. I had dreamed about an encounter with my deceased alcoholic father. I read my description of the dream and stopped when I got to the part where he asked me where I was going? I said I wanted to go home but that I didn't know the way. And to that he said, "Son, why are you making yourself so sad? The love you need is right there inside you. Wake up!"

Why do we have to keep learning the same lessons over and over again?

* * *

It was after 1:00 p.m. when I finished writing in my journal. I not only used the last four pages in the book, but I had to write sideways along the margin to finish my thoughts. This journal described my inner life of the last eighteen months, from the miracle of the lottery jackpots, to taking a leave of absence from the church and starting the Foundation, to my decision to step down as the CEO and walk away rather than lose five close friendships; and then finishing with my Summer-long adjustment to being a pensioner. And now this last entry, which ended with a love note to myself:

Dear Andy, yes, here you are faced with the same lesson again: you can be the love you want. Don't beat yourself up about the need to be reminded over and over. You rehearsed the idea of having a loveless life for a long while. It will take steady practice to see yourself differently. An honest look will show that you are doing a good job. Be kind to yourself, you are in transition. Keep writing.

I made a note on my to-do list to buy a new journal; but it wouldn't be like my old one which cost twenty dollars, a leather-bound beauty. The days of buying without looking at price tags are over. I was no longer a DINK -- double income, no kids. I would pick up a cheap spiral bound tablet instead.

I began making my favorite sandwich of potato salad, tomatoes (from Barbara's garden), onion and lettuce on whole wheat. Cutting way back on eating out had been the hardest part of staying within my budget. Perhaps when I began to draw my Social Security in a couple of years, it would be easier.

It was during these thoughts that the phone rang.

"Hello?"

"Hello, Rev. Shepard?"

"Yes."

"This is Nathan Porter. I got your name from a mutual friend, Wade Handly. My fiancée Cindy and I are planning our wedding and we were hoping you could do the ceremony."

I wasn't ready for this call and wouldn't be for the foreseeable future. A variety of responses jumped to mind:

I'm sorry Nathan, I haven't gotten over my last divorce yet, cool your heels and try me next year.

Mr. Porter, I'd rather do your funeral.

You're in luck Nathan! I'm offering a special packaged deal this month: your wedding, future marriage counseling, help with filling out the forms of your do-it-yourself divorce, and some follow-up grief counseling, all for only five thousand dollars, payable in easy monthly installments. Act now and I will throw in a pound of rice and a copy of the classic but useless *Women Are From Venus and Men Are From Mars*.

"Hi Nathan. Wade called earlier and spoke of you. Congratulations. Have you a date in mind?" I was buying time. I was so conflicted.

"Next month, October 31st."

"Halloween?"

"Yeah. I know that sounds bizarre, Rev. Shepard, but Cindy and I have both been through divorces and have some fears about getting married again. So we thought we would just put that out there and laugh in the face of this scary commitment. And Wade said that if anyone could help us it would be you."

I smiled. "Please, call me Andy."

"Sure. So are you available on October 31st, Andy?"

"Nathan, I'm retired. I don't even know what day it is today. But I'm sure it's fine. My fee is $350. Would that work for you and Cindy?" It was by far the highest fee I had ever asked for. If Nathan said no, I would be relieved.

"That would be fine."

Oh well. "Where are you planning to have your wedding?"

"In an abandoned old church building near the Mokelumne Hill Hotel. And the reception will be at the hotel."

I knew that building's story. The last congregation to use it, quickly declined when their pastor had an affair with the organist. Both got divorced. Classic. But I didn't think Nathan needed to know about those skeletons in its closet.

"Okay," I said, "Here's how it works. You and Cindy buy me lunch at the hotel and we will work out the details of the ceremony then."

"Sounds great. When?"

"When? Nathan, I'm a pensioner!"

"Well then, how about Saturday -- that is two days from today, Andy."

I laughed. I knew I would like Nathan, even if he was naïve enough to get married -- it's a universal cultural blindness.

"Great. See you there at noon," I said.

"Thanks. Good-bye!"

We hung up. I shook my head, picked up my harmonica and played the spiritual again, this time stumbling less and a bit more bluesy. When I got to the end of the chorus, I walked to the book case. The only books I had from my past, the ones not destroyed by the fire, were my resource books from the pastor's study at the church. I found a song book and checked the index. There it was. I flipped to the page and sang a verse:

> Sometimes I'm up, sometimes I'm down,
> Oh Yes, Lord!
> Sometimes I'm almost to the ground,
> Oh Yes, Lord!
> Nobody knows the trouble I see,
> Nobody knows my sorrow.
> Nobody knows the trouble I see,
> Glory, halleluiah.

Chapter 3

On the day of the phone call, I went sailing in the afternoon. The little boat was easy to beach, just run it up on the gravel shore, then pull it a bit up and out of the water, drop the sail and carry the sail to the cabin's covered patio. And it was easy to launch as well, just rig the sail and push off from the shore.

The only thing that was a challenge was dealing with the breeze as it negotiated the surrounding hills. Sometimes the wind tended to swirl and shift the boom to the opposite side of the boat unexpectedly. I imagine from a distance it appeared that I didn't know what I was doing as I tried to keep up with the wind changes (sort of like being a pastor of a church).

But by 4:00 p.m., when a steady afternoon breeze should have been coming up from the west, I was in the middle of the lake in the doldrums -- the sailor's term for no breeze at all. After sitting for some time on the placid lake, and after a swim and a struggle to get back on the boat with my forty extra pounds, I took up a new strategy. I looked out on the lake's surface for wind signs; there are zephyrs that from time to time blow on different areas of the lake's surface and the water in those areas will appear darker or ruffled. When I spotted one I used the rudder as a paddle and worked the boat toward the breeze. Then my sail filled and I moved along nicely -- but not for long on this day. So I sat in the doldrums again.

Then my phone rang. I hurriedly opened the twice-sealed double plastic bags to get to my cell.

"Hello?"

"Having fun out there?"

It was Barbara. I looked up toward the hills to where her house sat and waved at where I imagined she was watching.

"Sailing imitates life" I said, "You can't predict the winds of change, and plans are always tentative."

"I hear you, that's why I prefer horses," she said. "Got any tentative plans for dinner? I thought maybe we could have dinner up here before my massage."

"Are you sure it's wise to fraternize with the renter? It might make it awkward to evict me."

"I'm fairly certain it's not wise, but we should talk about Nathan."

I was confused, "So you know him?"

"Sort of, he's my son."

"Oh, Oh," I said. And a feeling came over me that God was messing with me again.

"It's a small county. But don't worry, you and I just need to figure out how to ride down this trail together."

"Okay. What time?" I asked.

"We better let the wind decide. Just call a little before you come up. Do you eat artichokes?"

"I love artichokes more than you."

"Uh, more than I do? Or more than me?"

I grinned. "It's going to be a long time before I fall in love with you, cowgirl. I don't even know how you cook your artichokes."

"You don't? I do it just like you, Andy. I rub them all over real good with oil and get them real hot until their petals sort of spread, and then gently work through the soft fuzzy part until I find the tender, succulent heart of the matter, and then I take my time to enjoy it thoroughly. And afterwards, like you Reverend, I give thanks to God from whom all blessings flow."

"Barbara, I think the wind is coming up!"

"See you soon, Masseur."

I eventually caught a fair breeze and I was back at the cabin by 5:30 p.m. The sun was low and showering the hills with golden light that in turn reflected on Hogan Lake like a colorful idealized painting.

I called Barbara and said I would be there in an hour. I showered and purposefully trimmed my fingernails to accommodate soft skin and tender orifices. I still had some time, so I decided to lay down for a power nap – or so I told myself, but who was I kidding? I was getting older and I was just bushed. The fifteen-minute rest did me good. I certainly didn't have the stamina I used to.

When it was time to go, I made another concession to my age. I took what I liked to call a booster pill. I didn't think I had erectile dysfunction, just that sometimes the wind filled my sails and sometimes it didn't. So my two dollar-a pill-generic Levitra from India took care of any possible frustration, and Barbara and I always reached the shore with a nice crashing wave.

* * *

Barbara was still cooking when I got there. Her home felt more substantial than many manufactured houses, and the floor plan was open and inviting as you entered through a large foyer. She had many western themed items and pictures but it wasn't cluttered. The large picture windows in the living room captured the expansive lake view that was now darkening.

I sat at the breakfast bar and watched while she put the garlic bread under the broiler. Then she tested the artichokes.

"I've never looked forward to artichokes as much as I do tonight," I said.

"I'm sorry if I went a little over the top on the phone, Andy."

"I think you still had a ways to go to the top. Sex is, at its best, a celebration of life, Barbara. My massage teacher was a wonderful older woman in Berkeley. One day she was giving a demonstration for our group and she had a nude young guy on the table. She was explaining to us how to do big two handed circles on the belly using strokes not too soft or too firm. She oiled her hands and with her exquisite touch she began the slow, rounding strokes on his abs."

Barbara drained the pasta, then gently added it to the pan of stir fried veggies. She knew her way around the kitchen.

"All were watching, wishing we were the one on the table, the lucky guy! Then one of her hands slightly brushed the top of his pubic hair a few inches below his belly button -- accident? I'm not sure -- and bingo, his cock was standing at attention.

"She turned to the group and said, 'Don't worry at all if you get a hard-on. It only indicates your orientation towards life: UP!'"

Barbara gave a laugh and said "That's great. So were there any happy endings in your class?"

"No. Sex is best when it is private, focused, and loving, don't you think?"

She removed the artichokes and put them in pretty blue and green bowls, then asked, "What does that mean to you?"

"Well, private infers respect, discretion; like having a secret garden, a special space that only the two of you share and tend together.

"And focused means mindful, paying attention, even when you are in ecstasy, you are in a duet, not a solo."

The dinner was ready. She motioned me to the table. We sat down and she took a big breath. "And loving?"

"It's what we do, Barbara. You give yourself to me and I give myself to you. You let me share in your joy and I let you share in mine. When sex is good for you, it tends to be good for me; and vice versa. It's caring, but deeper and more spiritual. You were so right today: Praise God from Whom all Blessings flow!"

She looked at me for a long time. I think I went over the top. This wasn't light dinner conversation, but it was the first time we had talked like this.

"Barbara?"

"Yes."

"We have the evening. Shall we lighten up and enjoy this good meal? Boy, it smells wonderful."

"Sure, but what shall we do when we get to the artichokes?!"

That did it; back to earth. We both laughed.

The dinner wasn't only delicious, but Barbara honored two suggestions that I made with the second massage: it is best to eat lightly and have no alcohol before giving or receiving a massage. So the portions were small and we drank iced tea.

"Nathan was so pleased when he called today to say he had found a minister who would go along with their crazy wedding plans," she said. "I seriously doubted that he would. I think he had already called four or five churches."

"I can imagine; there are so many rigid conservative churches up here. Sometimes the pastors balk at marrying off some of their own members who aren't saved or who are living in sin. And I bet the Halloween thing shocked them; devil worship and all that."

"That's what he said. Then his friend from his river rafting days gave him your name."

"Wade, he's on the board of the Foundation."

"Andy, I think it will be better if Nathan doesn't know about...."

I waited; I was curious how she would characterize our relationship.

"...about, you know."

I nodded.

"I told him today that you were my renter and a good guy; but that was all."

"That's good," I said. "It might be distracting as we stand at the altar if the groom knew the Reverend was…you know, with his mother." I smiled and I thought she slightly blushed. Even after two months of weekly massage and sex, and after my mini-sermon before dinner, she was still unsure about what she was doing with me. In that moment I decided that it was fine, and I shouldn't push it. But I did want to know something.

"Barbara, how do you think we are doing? Is our relationship working out for you?"

"Relationship?"

"I was going to say arrangement, but that's not the right word anymore. We have a somewhat unique relationship, and there's no one word to describe it. It's simple in some ways, but with us humans nothing is simple. I think it's healthy to try to keep things honest and open. So, how's our relationship working out for you?"

"Boy, you sure are a preacher, aren't you?"

I didn't think that was a compliment. Most people like their private thoughts to remain private, and resent anyone who pries. However, I think I was divorced four times because there was too little prying, not too much. But I had said enough. Either she knew I cared enough about her to ask, or not. Either she would trust me, or not.

"Our relationship is great! Private, focused and loving."

Her answer to my unspoken question was "not yet." And I had the feeling that private, focused, and loving meant something different to her.

"And you, Andy?"

"It couldn't be better," I said. In a way, it was the truth because it was all we were capable of.

I helped her clear the table as she talked about her part in arranging for the old, empty church which was owned by a local realtor. She was also taking care of the reception, working closely with Cindy, her soon-to- be daughter-in-law.

As I set up the folding massage table in the living room, and covered it with a clean sheet, and heated the bottle of oil and some small towels in hot water, Barbara picked out two CDs, started the music, and turned off most of the lights.

I sat on the couch for a while as she got herself ready in the master bedroom. I wanted to re-center myself and relax after our intense conversation.

Why did it feel so intense? Maybe I over-think things. Ironically I caught myself over-thinking again! Relax and enjoy the moment, I told myself; trust, remember you are not in control. You have given Barbara a dozen massages, but stay open to this unique, unrepeatable, magical moment. (I need a pep talk occasionally.)

Finally the thoughts slowed down and I was just breathing easily when Barbara emerged from the bedroom, walking slowly and looking right at me. When she got to the table she let her robe drop to the floor, like the drawing of the curtain for what promised to be a terrific third act.

She slid onto the table face down. We had dispensed with the draping in July, and I used the cover only when she needed warmth. I slipped out of my clothes and for twenty minutes I massaged her back, shoulders and neck. Then I moved to her feet and legs for fifteen minutes. Then I began the long Esalen-style strokes that went from toe to head and back down. Each time I came down I lingered on her ravishing, perfectly round bottom, improvising sensual kneading strokes while she would slightly raise her rear in response.

I was about to finish with her backside; I wanted to save some time for her front, particularly her face, hands, arms, and some more on her shoulders. I moved to the side of the table to finish her backside with firm circles on the small of her back, when I felt her hand reaching out for my already half erection. I moved slightly to give her full access.

"Andy," she purred, "how did I get so lucky?"

I almost answered: that's what they all say -- in the beginning. But there is a time and a place for honesty and openness. So I said, "I'm the lucky one." I was prone to jump into relationships that I believed to be my true soul mates and life-long partners; but now I didn't feel any need to have that fantasy. This was enough. The love was already inside me. I could truly give love to Barbara without expectation that she fulfill my life.

"Ready to turn over?"

"I'm ready for something a little different." She gave me a squeeze and let go. I waited as she took her time getting to a sitting position with her legs over the side of the table. She drew me to her with her legs around mine. "How about we forget the front side this time and go in and use my bed for…you know."

We had always used the table for love-making, usually with me in some creative standing position. This kept the notion, I suppose, that we were doing massage, albeit an expanded definition of massage. If we used the bed it was definitely making love, and the euphemism of a happy ending would be out the window.

"I don't know," I kidded, "I was so looking forward to massaging your hands."

"Oh, I think we can work that out, maybe using your other massager. It seems to be made for my hands."

"Oh yes, it's very versatile."

Then she leaned in and kissed me. It was the first time. Oh, I had kissed her pretty much everywhere, but I didn't remember our lips ever touching. She never invited a kiss on the mouth. In the beginning Barbara had warned me not to fall in love with her, and she implied she wasn't interested in giving her heart to me, or to anyone; and if things went in that direction I would have to find another place to live.

Did I believe kisses could be a sensual turn-on and nothing more? Like savoring other parts of her body with my lips and tongue? Or was each passionate kiss a heartfelt seal of eternal love?

Red flags went up. "I have to ask you something first, Cowgirl."

"Yes," and she kissed me lightly again.

I so very much didn't want to break the mood. Yet, moods come and go, but relationship mistakes last God only knows how long. So in a soft, but clear voice I asked, "Are you ready to fall in and out of love again?"

"Oh, no, Andy. You aren't falling in love with me, are you?" She still held me with her legs, but with her hands she gently took my face.

"No, not yet," I said. I took her hands in mine, "But the bedroom is your personal space, where you are just you: a strong, capable, beautiful woman. It is where you can be vulnerable and sometimes let your heart cry, where you groom yourself and get ready to face the world, where you know who you are.

"I believe you and I are reclaiming ourselves after getting seriously wounded. We need our space to do that. I'm afraid that sharing your bedroom is like giving up that precious space -- and giving away our hearts."

She thought for what seemed like a long time. I looked down at our hands together, thinking that I hadn't said this very well. Then she gave me a rare, shy, little girl smile, "You could have just said I was getting a little carried away."

"Always the preacher," I said.

"Damn, Andy, it's so fun getting carried away!"

"I know, Honey, I used to live for it."

"And I have died for it," she said in a more somber tone.

"I think so few people are able to make it work for a lifetime. Let's hope Nathan and Cindy can."

"Yes. So what do we do now?"

"Did you have a plan for the bed?"

"Yeah. I've never had a chance to lay on you."

"Okay." I let go of her hands and she loosened her legs. I gathered some pillows, a towel, the oil, and I spread the cover on the floor, then lay down facing up at her, "All yours."

She put on a wicked smile and playfully got down on her hands and knees. On all fours she approached the top of my head; then looking down into my eyes she stuck her tongue out, curling and uncurling the end. I met her tongue with mine. She explored it top to bottom, then deep in my mouth until I closed my lips around her tongue, so warm and alive, and sucked on it. She began moving it in and out across my lips. I raised my arms and cupped both her warm breasts in my hands and gave them their delayed massage.

Barbara then began her slow crawl over me, kissing my neck, then my nipples, then my belly, then my navel as she straddled me with her arms and legs. All the while the landscape of the front of her naked body passed before my eyes. When she moved a bit lower, I reached around with both hands and pulled her round bottom to where I could pleasure her. Barbara's full weight rested nicely on top of me. We moaned a duet. Time stood still. I was lost. But she had the audacity to ask from down below, "Sugar, is this too much into your personal space?"

Chapter 4

The morning I was to meet Nathan and Cindy to plan their wedding I got a death call. And since in my mind marriage and death are linked, I felt the phone call was rather ominous, and I wondered if God or the spirits or both were trying to prod me along again. I was on guard. The call was from Pearl, baby-faced Donny's grandmother, who said that her daughter Clarise had died of a massive stroke, and would I do the funeral. It seemed like a cosmic ploy, first a wedding and then a funeral; I just couldn't see what direction it was heading.

"I'm so sorry to hear that," I lied to Pearl, "but you should be calling the new pastor in Riverton."

"Reverend, you know how long it's been since we've gone to church. They sent us a letter last fall saying politely that because we haven't shown up they were dropping us from their roles."

I'd been tempted to send that letter myself until Pearl, a pioneer in Riverton, came into my office to plan her funeral. How surprising to hear that her daughter (the woman that Joy and I had tagged as "little Mussolini") had died before Pearl.

On the other hand, maybe not so surprising since Clarise always seemed on the verge of blowing a gasket.

"All right, Pearl. How are you doing?"

"I'm fine. It was just sort of a shock, that's all. Her son is here with me. He's taking it harder than me."

Amazingly Donny still lived with his mother and grandmother, his new wife and her toddler, a painful scenario that now seemed to have been resolved. Would the funeral be a celebration of Clarise's life, or her death?

"I can drop in this afternoon" I conceded.

"That would be fine."

"About 3:30 or so?"

"Yes. Thank you Reverend."

"Good-bye."

How many times in conversation have I made the Freudian slip of calling weddings funerals? That may sound like a ridiculous mistake, but from a pastor's point of view it's understandable, if not forgivable. They both require the pastor to meet with the family to prepare for a special ritual. They both bring the pastor into awkward contact with people not in the pastor's congregation. They both start with prayer and end with a blessing, and afterward there's food. The difference is that funerals and memorial services can be meaningful and healing, and provide an opportunity to deepen relationships; whereas weddings are most often just anxious, pretentious, expensive fluff, full of promises that seldom are fulfilled -- and thus there's a lot of drinking involved.

So for me, weddings are usually much sadder affairs -- and I get them mixed up. Now with both on my plate at once, I felt doomed. Surely I would embarrass myself with Nathan and Cindy.

These were my thoughts on Saturday as I turned from the long driveway onto the county road that skirted the lake. I noticed a white car parked on the road as I accelerated. With my convertible top down I waved as I drove past, thinking it was probably someone from the Army Corps of Engineers who ran the dam and kept an eye on things. A minute later I noticed the car in the mirror following me. But soon I was distracted by the beautiful old oaks and the views of the lake as I headed toward Valley Springs and then on to Moke Hill. I was looking forward to lunch at the hotel, it was one of my favorite places to eat, but now as a pensioner I couldn't afford it.

It's hard to imagine how many fortune-seekers poured over the Rockies or around the horn to get to the California goldfields, especially here in the Mother Lode counties that are squeezed between the great Central Valley and the High Sierras. Mokelumne-On-The-Hill, referring to the boomtown a mile up from the Mokelumne River, was just one of scores of similar towns, and was founded in 1850. In a few years the population swelled to over 15,000. In l851 a Frenchman saw his fortune in establishing the most elegant hotel outside San Francisco. The town has escaped the familiar fate of lapsing into a ghost-town because it was on the main north-south route, Highway 49. Now there were only a couple hundred residents, but the historic hotel still did a decent tourist business. And this grand old lady was doing a brisk business on this early fall weekend. It was only an hour or two from the central valley cities of Sacramento, Stockton and Modesto; and not that much farther from the San Francisco Bay Area. People were touring the gold country, antiquing, wine tasting, and gambling in the Indian Casinos. As I pulled up in front, I wondered where the white car was going when it slowed and passed by the hotel. For a while I even wondered if it was Nathan.

I always knew a wedding was going to be particularly difficult when the couple showed up late for their appointment with me, or stood me up altogether. But now as a pensioner and a reluctant officiate, if they thought a long conversation about the color of the bridesmaid's shoes was more important than meeting with the minister, then screw it! It would give me a good excuse.

But no such luck. There they were sitting at a table with Barbara when I arrived. They all stood up as I walked toward them. Barbara introduced me and then excused herself. They thanked me for agreeing to do their wedding, then we ordered drinks and I asked them to tell me something about themselves. They were thirty and thirty-one, and each had been divorced. They had no children and were both lawyers in Stockton.

Cindy worked in the Stockton D.A.'s Office. She looked thin in her beige pantsuit. She had shoulder length blond hair and gave me a confident smile that said, "I was top of my class, everywhere."

Nathan, Barbara's oldest, was a good-looking kid. He had short dark hair and a relaxed manner. He worked in a law firm doing tax and business law.

After we ordered lunch and our server left, Nathan asked, "So Andy, how are you getting along with the landlady?"

A small shock went through my nervous system that I hoped wouldn't show. I glanced up and met his eyes to see what his intensions were. "Fine," I said.

He gave a little grin. Then Cindy softly said, "She's peaking."

I slowly turned my head expecting to see her peeking through the kitchen doorway.

"I mean hormonally," she said with a chuckle.

I looked back at Cindy not believing my ears.

Nathan then explained, "My mom rents to single guys then pesters them until they end up moving out. But she hasn't had a renter for quite a while; then, when we learned that she had rented to a minister, I was, well, a little curious.

I was more than a little curious. There was no mistaking what "pester" meant, and this was not the story I was getting from Barbara -- or was I just not listening? Did I really need to be reminded again that I'm clueless about women? Apparently so.

"Well, let's just say we have an understanding that's working out for both of us," I said, then wondered if it was saying too much.

"Good," Nathan said. "I know mom can take care of herself, but I worry less knowing she's not alone out there. Now, the wedding."

"Yes," I said, glad to change the subject, "I'm wondering what would be appropriate for me to wear?" I thought this would give me a hint of what kind of wedding they had in mind.

They looked at each other trying to decide who would say what. Then Cindy said, "Uh, we had a couple of ideas, but it's up to you, of course. We thought either a Pope's outfit, or a Merlin the Magician costume."

"We're asking everyone in the wedding party to be in costume," Nathan assured me. "And of course we are also encouraging our guests to dress for Halloween."

"The groomsmen will have skeleton costumes," explained Cindy. "And the bridesmaids will be dressed as witches."

"And you two?" I asked.

"Vampires," said Nathan. "Blood sucking creatures of the night that change others into monstrous versions of themselves."

"Nice image of marriage," I said with more sincerity than they could know. "I think Merlin, perhaps. The Pope would be fun, but I try not to demean other denominations or religions. I let them demean themselves. But Merlin has some possibilities. He transforms things with his knowledge of how things really work -- the secret powers of the universe.

"You have both made a mess of relationships in the past (not that maintaining a loving relationship is easy). Indeed, that's the most misunderstood and delicate task in life. With Merlin tying the knot, he endows you with more than wishful thinking, he conjures up a spell, or you might call it a spirit, that transforms your bloodsucking ways. You receive a magical transfusion of grace: the ability to love with no expectations or strings attached. Then you can joyfully laugh through the pain of the past and your fears of the future."

I'm like a carnival attraction. You just put a quarter in my slot (or buy me lunch) and out comes a sermon, spewing wisdom for your life.

They just sat there holding their wine glasses, nodding. And when I was finished, Cindy said, "Andy, can you say that again, just like that at the wedding?"

"That's exactly what we want," Nathan agreed.

"Sure." I told them; even though I was not sure what I said. "I will if you agree to something as well."

"Okay," Nathan said without knowing how difficult this task would be.

"Would you hold hands for a moment?"

"Sure," Cindy said happily, taking Nathan's hand.

"Now, will you promise each other to research the concept suggested by the word 'grace', as thoroughly as you research a precedent in the law? And then write it across the top of the legal pad of your marriage every day so you see it there when you go to cross examine, when a part of you pushes for a conviction and judgment against the other, or when you are sketching out a strategy to get the advantage in a negotiation with your partner? Will you agree to let grace be the first principle of your marriage contract?"

They looked at each other and Nathan said, "I will."

Cindy gave him a sweet kiss and said, "I will."

"I now pronounce you husband and wife together!" I lifted my glass, "That wasn't so scary, was it?"

As they lifted their glasses with me, Nathan raised his eyebrows. He was looking over my shoulder, "Oh, Oh. Mom is peeking," He waved at her across the room, and the three of us laughed.

The lunch and the wedding planning went on for another hour. We mapped out the whole service and agreed that they would write their own vows. We set a time for the rehearsal and then toured the church with Harvey, the owner.

The church was a simple wooden structure built in 1884 after the original had burned down. It had probably seated a hundred and twenty, but it was hard to tell because all the pews had been removed. It had been refurbished a few years before when the last congregation had a bit of a renaissance as the people rallied with their new pastor to put on a new roof, fix the front steps and door, replace the heat pump, paint inside and out, and repair the old, gothic-style stained glass windows. The realtor/owner said they had borrowed to do the work, then after the pastor left in disgrace and most of the people went over to the Baptist church in San Andreas, the bank took over the building. Harvey picked it up for a bargain price. But after a year he had not been able to flip it, or even rent it.

When I stood in the raised chancel area and faced an imaginary congregation it felt so familiar and comfortable. It was coming up on two years since I had preached for real, but it felt as if only Sunday last. All those words, where did they land? Did they do any good? St. Francis told his followers to always and everywhere preach the Kingdom of God; and if one had to, they should even use words. I had used too many words.

Chapter 5

When I got behind the wheel of my little convertible VW bug, I breathed in the warm autumn air and gave a prayer of thanks that indeed, I hadn't embarrassed myself with a Freudian slip in front of Nathan and Cindy. Playing a CD of B.B. King singing the blues, I headed toward Riverton thinking of the old days of weddings and funerals. But when I reached the town thirty minutes later, other memories bubbled up.

I had not been back to Riverton since early summer when I quit the Foundation and left it for my friends to run. It was still doing business, but now it had a new name: The Shepard Foundation. It was ironic and misleading. I had hoped the six of us could work and live as a family; that was part of the meaning implied its old name Kindom Come. But I had to learn the hard way what usually happens when kin work for you: the normal disagreements and conflicting points of view in doing business become sticking points in the relationships.

And because the Foundation was my baby, I was overly attached to its operation and the work my friends were doing. The only way I felt I could let go was to step away. I suppose my friends felt they were honoring me by changing the name, but it made it sound like the funds they were granting came from me, which they most certainly did not. I thought it was obvious to all of us that the Lottery money just came through me, not from me. So driving into this town to plan a funeral, only filled me with the confusing feelings of a mourner, feelings I wished I could bury as well.

Soon I was drinking ice tea with Pearl and her grandson. She was eighty and looked to have been a hard-working woman. She was thin, and though her face was deeply etched, it still spoke of vitality. She was sharp in a folksy way.

Clarise had been her only child and Pearl had moved in with her years ago to help Clarise raise Donny. Then less than two years ago Donny married Joannie, and Joannie and her daughter moved into Clarise's house.

"Clarise didn't want a funeral," Pearl said. "I think she was leery about what people would say about her and she would have no control over it. So Donny and me, we just want you to help with a short graveside service when we bury her ashes – just family."

I nodded and looked toward Donny.

"Right," he said. "Just a prayer, maybe."

Well, there went my "little Mussolini" joke. For some reason this reminded me of a time when families could quietly send away a troublesome member to a far-away institution.

"Tell me how she died," I asked.

Donny glanced at Joannie who was keeping her toddler occupied and who hadn't said anything. Then Donny began, "Mom had been having a real hard time lately."

"Ever since Joannie and Katherine joined us," Pearl added in a tone that was sympathetic to Joannie.

"She seemed to be at Joannie a lot," he said, "over nothing, really. And Mom wasn't well."

"She put on over fifty pounds this year, I think," Pearl added.

"And she started smoking again," Donny continued. "The doctors had her on a lot of pills to try to calm her down. Then she lost her job a couple of weeks ago. She was really upset and angry."

"And you know Clarise, pastor. She was mad most of the time anyway," Pearl said matter-of-factly.

"Well yesterday, we were having some lunch and Katherine spilled her milk. Mom hit the table, stood up and was going to yell, 'God damn it', but all she got out was 'God…' then she sat back down; her eyes began to roll back, and foam started to cover her lips. She sort of slumped down into her chair and slid to the floor."

"She had stopped breathing by the time the ambulance came. It was real quick like," Pearl said nodding to affirm the mercy of it.

I had once thought that it would be good to die with God on my lips. I began to rethink that.

"So how are you doing, Donny?" I asked.

"You know, last night I tried to sort things out in my head. I think what I feel bad about is that she wasn't happy. She couldn't enjoy her grandchild or love the one that's on the way."

"Yes, that's a shame," Pearl said. "There is no use in dying over spilled milk."

I looked over at Pearl. Did she know what she had just said? Yes, of course she did, but there wasn't a wry smile in the room.

We set the graveside for the following Saturday to give time for the cremation. I prayed with them and then left. As I drove back to Hogan Lake I wondered what people would say at my funeral? Would I be there in spirit to hear it? Would they sing my favorite songs or drone through some meaningless ritual lead by someone who didn't know me? Who would be sad? Who would be happy? And who would be disappointed with my life?

And at that point, does it really matter?

That night I had a dream.

I was at a cemetery. There was going to be a funeral and I was in a small crowd of people standing around. The cemetery was stark, no grass, just gravel and a few trees. There was a school yard next to the cemetery and children were playing and laughing beyond the fence and not paying any attention until a big black hearse slowly drove up to the grave site. The funeral director asked for the pallbearers to come and help with the coffin. Nobody came forward as the wide rear door swung open on the hearse. I felt anxious as the funeral director began tugging on the coffin by himself, trying to pull it out. I was afraid he was just going to let it drop in the gravel. All the children were at the fence to see what was going to happen. The coffin slid out a bit with each tug, then crashed to the ground. The lid slightly popped open and all the children ran forward to see what was inside. They lifted the lid and it was empty.

The scene shifted and I was in a classroom; maybe I was the teacher. I was getting the kids to decorate the coffin that was now on a table. They had crayons and paint brushes and colored paper and glue and glitter. They were drawing flowers and birds and stick figure families all over the outside. And some of the kids were taking turns climbing inside and then popping up and yelling "boo!" to try to scare the others. They wanted me to take a turn. I said I wasn't ready.

It was six when I woke up out of the dream, and there was only a hint of daylight over the lake. The dream was still fresh, so I switched on the lamp and took up my new journal and wrote it down.

I considered my anxious feelings about no one helping the funeral director, and I related it to my experience of attending funerals as just one of the mourners. Talk about the blind leading the blind. No one seems to have any understanding or grace or insight, or even humanity to make the funeral a sacred moment. They fall back on ritual and custom; or worse, some ministers will take advantage of a captive crowd and clumsily try to evangelize.

But it was the children in my dream that I was most interested in. They were playing in the playground – always a good sign. Life should be seen more as a playground. And they were curious – another healthy sign – what would happen next!? What was inside?! And they were creative, drawing outside the lines, re-imagining the face of death with a riot of color and laughter.

I was about to reflect on the end of the dream where I said, "I wasn't ready" to play peek-a-boo in the coffin; but then I saw three horses mosey up onto my brick patio in the morning light that now colored the sky with an apricot wash.

"Oh shit," I said out loud, "The horses are loose." One big golden beast actually came to the window and looked in at me propped up in bed. Its eyes were so big and beautiful they stirred me. Suddenly, as if those school children inside of me took over, I said "Okay horsy, just a minute," and I slid out of bed, threw on a robe and rushed to the kitchen to grab three apples out of a bowl. I slid the door open, then hesitated. I had never been this close to a horse without a fence between us. God they were big. All three looked at me as if to say, "Well, you going to eat all those apples by yourself?" I stepped out. I held out an apple at arm's length. The golden one stretched out its neck and took a step towards me. When his lips parted and I saw those teeth I dropped the apple and considered retreating back into the cabin. But the paint came toward me as the golden horse gently picked up its apple. So this time I flattened my palm and let the apple sit away from my fingers, then reached out with it, "Okay, if you bite me," I said looking into his eyes, "it's the very last apple you'll get around here, no matter how much Barbara pesters me." The paint took the apple with its big soft lips before snapping it in half with those big front teeth – everything on these beasts was big!

The shiny dark horse stayed back but had his eyes on the last apple. "Come on you beast, its cold out here." It took two or three slow steps to me, its shoes clomping on the bricks which gave me an alarming impression of its weight. My bare feet would not stay still. I tossed him the apple and retreated inside to phone Barbara.

"Is that you Andy? What time is it?"

"6:30 a.m. Your horses came down to my place for breakfast and they are hanging out on the patio."

"Okay, Honey, I'll be down in a little while. And don't feed them anything, they bite."

"What!"

"Only kidding."

I made a latte' and sat where I could watch the horses. They just stood there, filling the whole patio, as if they were waiting for me to come out and play.

"I'm not ready," I said out loud. Then I closed my eyes. What did that mean in my dream? Not ready to get into a coffin – to die? Not ready to play peek-a-boo? What is peek-a-boo? It is a slightly scary fun game that adults play with small children, pretending to hide and pretending to startle. Is death a cosmic game of peek-a-boo? We seem to disappear, but lo and behold we surprisingly pop up again. Do we need funerals to make us believe we have "lost" a loved one so we can be joyful when they pop up again in some other place and time?

"I'm not ready," I began to say softly. "Wait a minute, I'm not finished. I'm not prepared." I relaxed and breathed and said it again.

"I'm not ready to retire and climb into that coffin."

"But its fun, Andy, come on."

"No, I'm not ready."

"Ooh, he's scared. Peek-a-boo!"

"No, it's like death."

"Look, Andy, we decorated it real pretty."

"Yeah, but it's still a coffin."

I opened my eyes. That's it, I thought: the hearse brought an empty coffin to a dead place, for me! Part of me thinks it's fun and games – time to lighten up. But another part feels like I'm dying – and I'm not ready!

I closed my eyes again and breathed and relaxed. Slowly I silently said, "I'm not ready; lighten up. I'm not ready; lighten up."

Then it came: I had already died. My old life was gone: jobs, marriages, homes, even my dog – gone, gone, gone. Now get ready (yes, you are never quite ready, are you Andy); get ready for what pops up, peek-a-boo!

I smiled. Of course! I saw that I had some work to do: I had to more deeply acknowledge and accept what was gone in my life; and at the same time let in a little more light and lighten up. Make room for some surprises. Peek-a-boo should be fun, damn it.

I heard Barbara's boots crunching in the gravel. I laughed. So what if Barbara is just peaking and pestering. Enjoy it.

She came around to the patio in back and said, "Okay kids, the party is over." Then she looked at me through the door, "Relax, Andy, it's safe to come out now."

"Careful, smart ass, those horses and I are good friends now. We are like apple-brothers."

"Oh yeah. Sure enough, there are some road-apples here on your patio to clean up before you have a fly problem."

I opened the slider, "Oh no, brothers! How could you?"

"Uh, Andy?" Barbara patted the bay on the neck, "this is your apple-sister."

"I knew that."

She gave me a grin as she slipped a halter on the filly.

"In fact," I said, "I think I am ready."

Barbara stopped and waited. Then finally said, "Ready for what?"

"To… you know. Learn to ride."

She smiled and adjusted the straps, "Honey, you already ride damn good."

"A horse, Barbara."

"Really?"

"Really."

"When?"

"How about today?"

"Aren't you going to church or something?"

"I already preached myself a sermon this morning."

"I don't doubt that. All right, cowboy. After my Sunday brunch shift, say, about three?"

"Great." Then acting bravely I stepped to the side of the golden guy and firmly patted his side.

Lord, he was big.

The next day I had trouble walking, so I put off Barbara's massage until later in the week. The only thing I could do that didn't hurt was play my harmonica. I may have been ready, but not for this. So to keep my sense of humor I worked up a song I called "My Old Bottom Blues":

> I thought I was ready
> But I was wrong.
> I thought I was ready
> But I was so wrong.
> So when I got off that horse
> I had to write down this song.
> I've got the old bottom blues,
> My old bottom blues,
> And I pray I won't have them for long.
>
> My baby she has a
> Sweet round bottom.
> Oh yes she has the
> Sweetest round bottom.
> But my skinny old butt
> Feels like I've been to Sodom.
> I've got those old bottom blues

> My old bottom blues
> But please don't tell my baby I've got 'em.

* * *

I was asked to only say a prayer at Clarise's graveside. Normally I could come up with a decent prayer extemporaneously. But if I was to usher in a sacred moment for this conflicted family, I knew this prayer had to be thoughtful.

In my morning meditation I asked for inspiration for the prayer. What came to me was that forgiveness is the main ingredient in the sacred bread of grace. The recipe also contains compassion, mercy, hospitality, generosity, and humor. But the Lord's Prayer implies that forgiveness is the most necessary ingredient to manifest grace. My prayer would ask for grace through forgiveness.

We met under a tree next to Pearl's family plot in the county cemetery. Indeed, it was only Pearl, Donny, Joannie, little Katherine, and myself. The cemetery workers had dug a small square hole, neatly cut into the earth. Next to this tiny grave was a low stand on which a heavy box of ashes was placed. Pearl had brought a potted plant of mums which she set next to the ashes.

I said we would begin with a minute of silence, giving thanks for life as we listened to the sounds of life around us.

Then I said, "Let us pray." I began with a quote from the Psalms:

> Oh Lord, you are compassionate and gracious,
> Slow to anger, abounding in love.
> You will not always accuse
> Nor will you harbor your anger forever;
> You do not treat us as our sins deserve
> Or repay us according to our inequities.
> For as high as the heavens are above the earth,
> So great is your love for those who know your awesome presence.

As far as the east is from the west,
So far have you removed our transgressions from us.

Then I continued, "From our hearts we thank you for your gift of grace, and for the gifts and lessons we have received from Clarise. We pray your forgiveness will flow through us for the failures in love that were experienced in this family. Help us release Clarise into your healing hands. And in this grace, bless us and bless her. This is our prayer. Amen."

After a moment, Donny and I together lifted the box and inserted it into the grave. As we stepped back I asked if anyone wanted to say a word. I let the pause stretch out a while and then was about to say the words of committal when Pearl cleared her throat and said, "Sweetheart, I am sorry I did not protect you sooner from your father. I didn't want to believe that he would bother you. Forgive me."

Tears came to my eyes. Then Donny spoke, "Mom, you drove away my father -- I never understood why -- so I didn't give you my love. Forgive me."

Now tears came down my face.

Joannie was wearing a very full maternity dress. Without a word, she left the stroller and stepped to the little square hole and managed to squat down. I thought she was going to place something in the grave. Then there was the rushing sound of liquid. I had a moment of panic, thinking she had just had an accident -- but then I realized it was no accident. As we waited for her to finish, Pearl and Donny didn't even blink. Then she stood, stretched her back, and stepped back to the stroller and said, "Clarise, forgive me. But you were a bitch." And she started crying.

We all cried. Donny took her hand. The two cemetery workers who were looking on, turned their backs. I took out my bandana, blew my nose, wiped my eyes, and said, "Even as we commit Clarise's remains here to the earth, dust to dust, ashes to ashes, we commend her spirit to you, our gracious

Creator, from whom we come and to whom we go. Amen."

Chapter 6

I suspect attending church as a former pastor is tricky for most clergy. When I was working as a pastor it was only on vacations that I had the chance to sit in a pew. I was always surprised at how hard and uncomfortable they were. One theory is that they were made to keep parishioners awake.

Nonetheless, pastors are not made for pews. We are more opinionated about theology than most worshippers, so when we hear what we consider bad theology, it jangles in our ears – phrases like: God will only give us the amount of hardship that we can bear (how great to blame hardships on God! Even so, then who the hell passes out the hardships that push us over the edge!?).

And pastors know too well the context of the scripture passages read in worship. We are sensitive to when scriptures are carelessly misused.

And it doesn't help, as we sit in the pews, that we can quickly spot emotional manipulation in worship (because we have used those tricks ourselves).

Plus, we over-identify with the pastor, their struggles seem so transparent. Thus, unfortunately it's rare for us to truly have a spiritual experience in church, except when we find an exceptional church. My solution was to go sailing Sunday mornings on Hogan Lake.

Some old timers still call it New Hogan Lake. It's a flood control reservoir that keeps the Calaveras River from frequently flooding the city of Stockton in the valley. Mr. Hogan, City Manager in 1930, was a hero for getting the thing built. But it was under built, and from time to time Stockton still flooded. So instead of calling it Hogan's Folly, the feds built a taller dam directly in front of the old one, creating a larger lake and saving Hogan's good name.

On this particular Sunday morning it was St. Hogan's Full Gospel Lady of the Waters Christ the Fisherman

Church. And I was not the only one in attendance. There were several other guys on the lake fishing while their wives were probably in the pews of another church singing something ridiculous like, "Nothing But The Blood of Jesus".

There was a perfect fall breeze coming across the lake making the low mid-morning sun sparkle in the rippling water. The grebes, cormorants, and mergansers seeking their daily bread, were charming company. I pulled in the main sheet, bringing the boom closer to the center of the boat which tightened the sail; and then I pushed the tiller so the rudder steered the boat into a position where the breeze was coming directly at the side of the boat – the fastest, most powerful position for sailing. The boat tipped a little away from the wind and I scooted my old bottom closer to the windward side of the small deck to keep the mast pointing straight up as much as possible, which in turn kept as much wind in the sail as possible and sent the boat zipping through the water. Not that I was going anywhere in particular; I just wanted to fly for the fun of it. I wanted to let the wind take me and move me. I wanted to feel its power (to a point!), to cooperate with it though knowing full well it was a wild force and a power greater than I.

You get the picture? Sometimes sailing is worship.

But I have from time to time experienced profound worship in church in a way only church can provide. Part of me still desired it; still desired being with other men and women who are humbly open to the Powerful Presence, the Mystery Within Creation, The Transformative Light of Love, and to experience it together in community, to feel the bond of spirit and not be alone.

Was this a fantasy? Should I give up the pursuit of spiritual community? Was I too jaded?

I was passing by a hill on the shore, the wind shifted suddenly. I pushed the tiller and the bow turned more up wind and the sail filled again. I picked up speed. Then the wind shifted again and before I could respond I was in irons: facing directly into the wind and stalled. I pushed the tiller hard away from me and held it there while the boat drifted backwards. Slowly the bow turned away from the wind and the sail popped full again. The boat tipped steeply, the mast dipped halfway to the water (water that would be uncomfortably cold). I quickly released the main sheet that held the angle of the boom. The trailing edge of the sail swung out to point down wind, and it lost its power so the boat rocked back upright.

Relieved, I took hold of the rope again and pulled the boom and the sail closer to me and we took off, momentarily under control, as is the case generally in life.

Heading back across the lake toward the cabin my thoughts returned to church. Then a Hindu story came to mind. Two fellows were walking down a street on a Saturday evening wondering what to do. The first one said, "Let's go to the whorehouse." But the second one said, "No, I don't think so. We should go to the temple and pray." They debated for a while as they walked, but could not agree. So the first one went to the whorehouse and the second to the temple. However, the fellow in the whorehouse couldn't help but think of the temple all the while. And the fellow in the temple couldn't help but think of the whorehouse while he prayed. So, who had the most spiritual experience?

Here I was on the lake, but I was thinking of church! I might as well find one; one where I wouldn't have a running critique going on in my head. A kind of church that I'm completely unfamiliar with, like a synagogue or mosque.

* * *

I returned to the cabin in time to make lunch and rest before my second riding lesson. Mercifully, this time I would ride only forty-five minutes rather than two hours.

My ride was the big golden palomino, Charley. I asked Barbara if it was named after a Charley she had known? She said she had known several Charleys. I let it drop. Barbara used the first hour showing me how a saddle was put together, and how to clean it. Then she taught me how to saddle a horse properly. She explained the function of the bit and bridle, and how to slip the bit into Charley's mouth, a process that pretty well unnerved me.

Then once again we went over the technique of mounting a horse. The week before, I botched this mounting business so badly that I had Barbara in stitches. This time she found the right analogy, "move confidently and smoothly, Andy, like when you…you know."

As we rode from the stables and corral I was still uncomfortable with the height and was convinced that at some point I was going to fall off. This conviction made me tight and rigid, not the ideal way to ride in the saddle, and it was part of the reason I was so sore afterward.

Another reason was that Charley was, well, as big as a horse! Straddling that wide body put my legs in a bull-legged stretch. I looked over at Barbara's legs; they were so natural looking as she straddled the paint. "I think cowgirls have a natural advantage in sitting on a horse," I said, half kidding. "Your legs are so, so what?"

"Accommodating?" she asked with a smile.

"Exactly, accommodating. I can feel my groin stretch a bit every time Charley clomps."

"I know a stretching exercise for that," she said with a knowing nod. "Remind me when you come over Wednesday -- that is if you are walking again by then."

We rode a trail near the shoreline for a while. Then Barbara gave me a lesson on using the reins and my heels. "You don't have to use much," she said. "Charley will respond to a light touch."

I looked at her. Why was I hearing everything as sexual innuendos? Was it me or Barbara who was peaking?! Or was it the horseback riding itself?

"Andy, you have to lighten up on your two-handed death grip on that saddle horn if you are going to use the reins."

"Right." I pulled the reins to the starboard and surprisingly Charley did a quick 180 degree turn. "Great," I said, a little startled, "It looks like Charley wants to go back." I gave him a pat on the neck, then quickly grabbed the horn again.

"Sure," Barbara agreed. "You're doing really well, Andy. And you're right, let's not overdo it."

We rode back side-by-side and chatted. She told me she had three children: Nathan with her first husband, and two girls with her second. She said she wasn't smart enough to keep from marrying the third time, but at least she didn't get pregnant.

I told her I'd never had any children, but I'd married four times. Was that stupid? Maybe it was just my path, my way of learning about life.

"Yeah, I guess I learned a thing or two," she said. "But there must be some easier way, don't you think?"

"No."

"No?!"

"There are longer ways and shorter ways. But I'm convinced there are no easy ways to learn to love, and be loved, completely."

"Church in a saddle; you may have a new ministry, pastor. And did you notice that you relaxed more when you were preaching?"

"Give me a break, Barbara. After all, it's Sunday," I said as we rode into the corral.

"Yes, Sunday, and you know what that means?"

"We clean the stalls?"

"You're learning real well! By the way, is that guy a friend of yours?" And she pointed to a white car parked up on the road. "And if I'm not mistaken, he's taking our picture."

Chapter 7

Monday I awoke at dawn to the grebes calling to each other on the lake. Their call is sharp but not unpleasant; a high single note that sounds like a question: "Honey?" "Where ARE you?" "Are YOU Okay?"

I answered them as I wobbled to the espresso maker, "I'm still here, but my old bottom hurts like hell." I sipped my latte' and watched the lake brighten. My head was full of thoughts, so before I meditated I picked up my new journal and wrote. I wrote how it felt to stand in the old Mokelumne Hill Church. And the feeling of driving into Riverton again, skirting my old life that was gone, but seemed not that far away, especially as I stood graveside as a pastor and witnessed the Spirit's surprising healing ways.

Then I flipped the pages back to the description of my coffin dream and I read, "I have work to do: acknowledge more deeply the loss of my old life, and lighten up." The events of last week, the wedding consultation and the funeral, were like confusing echoes yet helpful reminders of what was past -- gone, gone, gone. I closed my eyes and pictured the Riverton Church and imagined lifting it, like a photograph, up over my head and letting it go into God's hands. Then I pictured that beautiful place on the Mokelumne River that was the working center for the Foundation. I released that image as well and felt a weight lift from my shoulders.

I gave thanks that there was some lightness in these things as well: the thought of playing the part of Merlin -- how wonderful was that! And every time I recalled the sound of Joannie's female urine gusher, I grinned.

Then I received an inspiration. I opened my eyes and began to write another verse to "Old Bottom Blues":

>   I thought I was hurt
>   As a greenhorn could get.

>   Yes, I thought I was hurt
>   As an Old Bottom could get.
>   But then my baby made me
>   Shovel her horse's shit!
>   I've got those Old Bottom Blues.
>   A bad case of Old Bottom Blues,
>   And it will be a long while
>   Before I can sit.

I spent a good while alternating between playing my harmonica and singing my blues song. Close to noon I took my old bottom for a walk up the long driveway to the road to check my mail box. There I found my newspaper and a letter from Pearl. I opened the letter and found a hundred-dollar bill and a note:

Dear Pastor Andy,
Thank you for helping us bury our Clarise. You are the only pastor I have ever known who truly believes that God is love and, as you once said, we are not punished for our sins; we are punished by our sins.
I know you said there was no charge for your services, but please accept this gift. I know people don't believe you gave all your money away, but I know you did. May God bless you still in the work he has for you now.
Sincerely,
Pearl

I re-read it twice. Did some people really think I kept the lottery money? Who? Church people? That money was the Spirit's doings, not mine. And now it's the foundation's business and I have nothing to do with it; gone, gone, gone.

I began walking slowly and deliberately back down the gravel driveway. I told myself I didn't survive thirty-five years as a pastor by worrying too much about what people thought. Then I wondered about Pearl's blessing for "the work he has for you now."

I'm a pensioner. And I 'm not going to fill up my new-found time with comforting busyness! I'm learning to let life fill me up, drinking deeply of life, like listening to the morning song of the grebes.

I heard Barbara's pickup. Soon she was rumbling down the driveway from her hilltop perch. She reached the fork where her drive joined mine, then slowly crawled to where I walked, and stopped.

"He walks!" She said through the truck's open window.

"More or less," I said.

"Don't give up, Andy, it will get better when we get you broken in."

"I don't like the sound of that."

"Look, when you get more confident in your riding, you can saddle up twice a week, even if I'm not around, and it won't be long before most of the soreness is history."

"That's hard to imagine."

"Don't worry. Anyway, how about giving me some ideas about a costume for Nathan's Halloween wedding?"

"Let's see. How about something really scary, like wearing a wedding dress with a couple of guys in tuxes on each arm wearing #4 and #5.

She grinned, "That's good, Andy. Really good. But it's hard to imagine wearing a wedding dress to my own son's wedding. It might look a little incestuous."

"Right."

"Well keep thinking. I've got to get to work."

"Work? What's that?"

"Honey, it's what I've got for you Wednesday night."

I stooped over and put my hand to my back, "Ooh, I don't know if I'll be ready by Wednesday."

"No problem. I've got a stretch routine for you."

"No, no," I feigned, "Anything but the stretch routine!"

She laughed and pulled away. Barbara was growing on me -- my landlady with privileges. This summer I felt somewhat anxious and cautious that the myth of casual sex would lead to some bothersome romantic drama and a broken heart; probably the same worries Barbara had. I recalled the double-take she did two weeks earlier when at dinner I referred to our arrangement as a relationship. Perhaps we were both learning that there are all kinds of relationships. But I wondered, were there all kinds of broken hearts?

Halfway down the driveway my phone rang.

"Hello."

"Hello, Rev. Shepard?"

"Yes."

"Hi, this is Randy at the Chapel of Peace. How are you?"

A voice from my recent working past. I must have averaged a funeral a month for Randy because most people, especially in California, do not have a church connection, yet sometimes they still want a minister to lead a service. This, even though funerals are going out of fashion. Now more and more people specify that they don't want a funeral. In place of a traditional service, some families just plan an informal get-together in their home, or perhaps a picnic in a park. And some simply ask people to put their thoughts and greetings on a memorial web page and have no gathering at all. Funerals may be going out of fashion, but death isn't.

"Hi Randy. I'm fine, and you?"

"Good. I'm wondering if you would be available to do a service here Saturday morning?"

What the hell was going on? "What have you got?"

"An elderly gentleman who died at the skilled nursing center. His family is from out-of-town, Lodi, and has asked for a protestant minister."

"Possibly; can I get back to you this afternoon?" I needed to think this through.

"Of course. Anytime after one."

"Okay, talk to you then."

The mortuary must have been told that I conducted Clarise's graveside and they figured I was in the burying business again after my year with the Foundation. So they had me back on their list.

But did I want to be on their list, I asked myself as I continued to walk. I pulled the hundred dollar bill out of my pocket and considered how I might spend it. A trip to Sacramento to buy a wetsuit to extend the sailing season? Upgrade my wine selection from the five dollar bottles I've been buying? A pair of riding boots? Maybe harmonica lessons?

On the other hand, I was a pensioner. I needed to learn to live more simply and within my means.

But the mortuary would pay me a hundred-fifty dollars to do the funeral, and my means would be a little higher.

On the other hand, was doing funerals life-giving for me? (Now there's a bizarre thought!) Or was it simply a way to fill my new life with busyness?

But this would not be committing myself for life, only one more funeral. I could try it and see.

I decided to give it a rest and change my focus to my walking. I became aware of each crunching step on the gravel driveway and slowed down my pace. I noticed the blue lake and the golden hills beyond. I felt my body draw in each breath and then let it go. I put the bill back in my pocket and adjusted my posture so I was more upright and balanced. The cabin was still out of sight beyond the downward curve of the driveway and dry grasses.

I let my walking fill me, as if it was everything. God was the road and the landscape. God was the sky and the sun. God was oxygen fueling and energizing my legs. God was looking through my eyes to see its own unfolding mysteriousness. I slowed the pace down even further. I wanted this moment of grace to stretch out for the rest of my life. This was retirement. Retirement was not wading through funerals and weddings to pad my income. How depressing would that be?!

It was then I recalled from long ago the advice one of my teachers gave to a woman who had asked him what he thought about her idea of becoming a psychologist. He said it didn't matter much what she did; it only mattered how she did it. Whether repairing shoes or counseling people, what mattered was if she could bring a spiritual awareness to the doing of it, a willingness to let God's loving presence flow through her efforts.

When the cabin appeared I had decided to call Randy. I could picture him in his dark suit, blue tie and that unique gold tie tack he proudly wore which was shaped like a tiny shovel. I would tell him I would help bury the old gent.

Chapter 8

Like most Wednesday nights, Barbara got home late from Moke Hill as the locals call it. I had been on the phone with my old friends Wade and Josh from the Shepard Foundation. They were bringing me up-to-date on their work with local non-profits.

They gave a major grant to the Calaveras Peace Action organization to fund a documentary film project about the under-reported scope of the wounded vets returning from the Mideast.

And they said the final numbers for the rafting and kayak summer camp that they funded through the Riverton Church were even better than they had hoped for: thirty-five kids a week for six weeks; and half were from low income urban families.

The Foundation also funded the first stage of a redevelopment plan for the Indian Rancheria where my ex lived. The tribe was turning their defunct casino into a Native American Arts Academy for the pacific coast. Later would come a conference center, golf course and condos.

Wade wanted to know if I had read that the California Lottery was preparing to soon start up again? But our call was interrupted by a call-waiting beep. Barbara was ready for the rent. Before we hung up I invited them to come sailing. We agreed on Saturday at one.

I drove up to Barbara's house, which seemed ridiculous, but later I was usually too tired to walk back to the cabin. My mind was still busy with the news from Riverton. I was about to ring Barbara's doorbell when I saw her note to just come in and lock the door behind me. I stepped into the large entryway and heard her mellow massage music playing. The lights were low.

"Hello," I said so not to alarm her.

"In here, Sugar," she said.

Barbara must have had a long day. She was already lying on the table; and the bottle of oil and two small towels were in a bowl of hot water. I walked over to her side where she was draped for warmth with a cover; she had applied a heating pad on her shoulder. I lightly laid a hand on the small of her back.

"How are you?" I asked.

"Thinking about how I could swing an early retirement; or raise the rent to two massages a week."

"Well, that sounds good. As long as one of them was for me."

"Ha! Too bad for you I'm an older and wiser woman than I used to be, and my shoulder is sure reminding me of the older part. I'm taking something for pain most days lately."

I slipped off my sweatshirt, dried off the warm bottle of oil, removed the hot pad from her shoulder, folded the cover down to her waist and stood at the head of the table. In the slowest possible way I let my oiled palms come to rest on her back. Then after several moments I began some long slow circles to loosen up her back muscles from her neck to her bottom. Then I focused on her shoulders, but always extended the strokes down to the related muscles of her shoulder blades. Next, from the side of the table I reached across her back and pulled my hands one at a time toward me in a rhythmic series of strokes that progressively moved from her neck and shoulders to her waist and bottom, and then back up. Then I changed to the other side of the table and repeated.

"You know, Andy," she said softly, "I have some girlfriends who I could line up as clients for you. You seem to be broke and have a lot of time on your hands."

I smiled but didn't say anything. I let the "time on your hands" comment go for another day. Then I thought I would kiddingly call her a pimp, but filed that one as well. Was this some kind of test? Or did she want to get out of our unique relationship?

I went to the head of the table, oiled my hands and gave her a series of long strokes as far as I could reach along her short body, which was down to about mid-thigh, and back up along her sides, then over her shoulders, neck and head.

Most likely she was thoughtlessly giving away her power. Massaging her friends would certainly change our relationship; somewhere inside her she must have known that. She was in the power seat: landlady, riding instructor, exclusive massage recipient, and sexual partner. Is this her way of sabotaging herself in life: giving away her power, then feeling like a victim?

So I moved to the small of her back, laid my hands side-by-side and alternated them back and forth firmly across her sacrum (which comes from the Latin, meaning holy bone). I rubbed faster and faster to create a very warm spot on her second chakra, the sexual center. Then I stopped and held my hands barely above her skin for thirty seconds, letting our energy mix and flow. Next I located her third chakra five inches higher on her spine over her solar plexus, the power center, and again rubbed and warmed this area, and again let my hands hover over this spot.

"Wow, what did you just do to me?"

"Raised your energy to a higher level to bring you back to your senses. That was a bad idea you had."

"Oh, I guess you're right."

"Shall we start on your feet?"

"I thought you would never get there!"

That was more like it. You have to watch these women. They do strange things with their power issues.

I put warm towels on her feet and gave her a drink of water. After I worked her right calf, I sat on the side of the table, brought her foot up to my chest and used the warm damp towel to rub the skin and calluses of her foot somewhat roughly. Then removing the towel I let my wet tongue slip between her first two toes.

"Andy! What do you think you're doing?!"

"Where do you feel it?"

"All over."

"Relax and try not to tighten up. Keep your eyes closed. I'm going to go between each toe. Note how your body responds." I paused, then took my time to let my tongue appreciate each tender space. When I finished I asked, "What was that like?"

"My pussy is dripping."

"Enjoy it," I said and began to massage her feet.

"Andy, you are something else."

"Yeah? I just happen to believe that our capacity for love and joy is much greater than we have yet discovered."

"Interesting thought. But it's better to let your hands do the preaching -- or whatever."

When it was time to have her turn over, I left to use the bathroom. When I came back to the living room, Barbara had spread the blanket on the floor and was sitting on it smiling and holding a shopping bag. She motioned to me to join her, and said, "It's time for your stretching exercise, big boy." I tried to imagine what she had in mind as I untied my drawstring and slipped off my pants and shorts.

"Lay on your back, Sugar. Here's a pillow for your head. Good, now lift your legs and point them to the ceiling."

With a little groan I followed instructions.

"Good. Now take hold of them behind your knees, and little by little spread your legs and pull them gently toward you."

All of a sudden I felt frightfully vulnerable. I nearly balked, but Barbara was now my riding instructor, so I complied.

"And this little guy might need some exercise too," she said, holding the bottle of oil high between my tightly stretched thighs. As the glistening oil slowly dripped between my legs, I felt myself grow harder with every heartbeat.

"Boy, you never cease to amaze me, Andy."

Yes, I thought; I get by with a little help from my pharmaceutical friends.

"Well, this is your basic position," she said. "But before we begin the exercise, would you do me a little favor?"

"Anything."

"Good. Put your legs down for a minute. Do you know who my favorite cowboy is?"

"The Duke?"

"Close, but no. This cowboy knew how to party better than be a president."

"W?"

"Yes!" And she pulled out a rubber mask of George W. himself.

"Oh my God, Barbara," I said and slipped it on. "This is a scary mask."

She shrieked. "To bad you are going to be Merlin; you are a great Bush."

"Your bush isn't so bad either."

"Oh no, not my bush; Michelle's!" and she pulled out a mask of the First Lady, big hair and all, and slipped it on. "Okay, Mr. President, let's stretch and ride."

As I lifted my legs I said, "Barbara, you have gone over the top."

"Over the top is exactly where I'm going. Time to mount this pony. Pull those legs a little more." She turned around on her hands and knees and backed up to my butt and lifted her round bottom, and like a miracle, slid her rose-wet-cave over my erection. I held her hips as she moved up and down on me.

Then the First Lady looked back at me over her shoulder and said sternly, "Now George, you are so easily distracted. Let go of me and hold onto your legs and pull every time I come down so we can get a real nice gait."

She was right. My pull made my hips rise to meet her and penetrate more deeply. It took quite a bit of effort but was exquisite. And the view of her sweet, round, baby-soft bottom in the subtle light, rising and falling to the rhythm of the music helped me get closer and closer.

"Come along now little darling," I said panting. I thought I was going to explode.

My black queen rose up on her knees without losing me and brought her hand to between her legs and began moaning, "George! Yes, George."

"Michelle," I groaned.

She wiggled in my crotch back and forth as if to get the very last drop; then there was nothing but our heavy breathing. At last she ripped off her mask. I peeled off mine and let my legs mercifully cross and sort of fold behind her back. I was slowly shrinking out of her. She looked back at me and smiled, "Now I would call your legs very accommodating."

Barbara liked to have the last word, and she was good at it.

Chapter 9

My baby said I was her favorite cowboy.
What did she mean: I was her favorite cowboy?
Well she rode me so hard, made me cry for joy.
I've got the old bottom blues.
Bad case of the old bottom blues.
Be careful, your old bottom might be
Her ragged toy.

I needed a back-up band. I was getting better at playing harmonica riffs between lines, and solos between verses, but I needed a beat to keep it tight and together.

I got an inspiration. Nathan and Cindy were going to use a local group to play at their funeral, I mean wedding. It was a trio -- guitar, bass and keyboard. They played frequently for the Moke Hill Hotel's Bartini Thursdays, a local ritual every week. The bartender came up with a creative three-dollar martini specialty drink; the cook offered a couple of tasty items for the bar menu, they set up a few more tables in the bar and they packed the place.

The band called themselves the Calaveras Jumpers (a nod to Mark Twain). I knew Bobby, the guitar player. I did his second wedding, but I didn't think he would hold it against me. I got his number from the bar and called him. He liked the idea of a minister singing Old Bottom Blues at the wedding reception. And to keep it a surprise, we agreed to practice Saturday at the Cowboy Bistro where they would be playing in San Andreas. He said to bring my harp (the musicians name for harmonica) -- my debut!

When I hung up I was in an elevated state. The previous night's massage session with Barbara was...I had trouble finding words for it. I had voted for Obama, and I respected how Michelle carried herself as First Lady. Eroticizing Halloween was one thing, but to play out an encounter between George and Michelle was shamefully, disgustingly, hopelessly adolescent, but fun. I had decided to lighten up and be open to life's surprises, and before I could say peek-a-boo, I was George W. playing horsy with Obama's wife.

And now I have my back-up band!

Thursday was the kind of balmy fall day that elicits sweet nostalgic feelings. I was a happy man to just sit on my red brick patio and gaze at the play of light on the lake and play soulful notes on my harmonica for the rest of the morning.

In the afternoon I drove to San Andreas to meet with the children of the deceased at the Chapel of Peace. It wasn't the ideal environment to counsel those left behind. Mortuaries are bloodless and they drip with death lightly disguised. They have coffin showrooms for God's sake! And their Chapels are spirit-free zones.

I have always found the staff to be competent and decent people; but they reinforce dysfunctional cultural patterns of dealing with death, patterns that are intertwined with their vested interest in turning a profit.

But I no longer had a church or a pastor's study in which to do this counseling, so I met with two of Jacob's children, Jason and Debra who were almost my age, in a small, windowless room in the mortuary.

I asked them to tell me about their father. They said Jacob was born in Oklahoma, and as a child his family moved to California in the dust bowl years to work in the orchards of the San Joaquin Valley. He had fought in the Korean War, then married and took over the family owned orchards which he expanded over time. He raised four kids (one had died and one was disabled) and retired seventeen years ago to nearby Angel's Camp to fish and pan for gold. Jacob's wife died seven years ago -- they had been married fifty-one years. Then a year and a half ago his smoking got the better of him and emphysema put him in the convalescent hospital and took his last breath.

As I listened to this neat, abbreviated description, I wondered about the messier parts of Jacob's life; the parts that often end up defining us and our character and our inner work. How did his childhood poverty form his view of life? Did his parents love and encourage him? Did he do anything in the war that terrified him? What was his marriage like, really? And how did he adjust to retired life -- was fishing a love or a screen for boredom? Was his a good death with thankfulness and hope?

It is rare that those attending a funeral, or even a memorial service, are enriched by a story of a real person. I told Jason and Debra that I would help them celebrate their father's life, but they would have to write a eulogy, a tribute to Jacob's journey of ups and downs, and how he uniquely displayed his God-given humanity. What did he love, what did he learn, and what did he reach for? This was not only to create a more personal, meaningful service, but I hoped this exercise would help them in a healing way. They agreed.

And they agreed to no canned music or schmaltzy funeral chapel organ. They said Jacob loved country-western music, so I suggested they call the Calaveras Jumpers and hire them to play a few songs that their dad liked.

I said I would lead the service and offer his friends an opportunity to say a good word about him, and then tie it together within a spiritual context. They seemed to appreciate this even though the family seldom attended church.

The siblings left with their homework assignment, and I put the top down on the yellow bug and drove north on Hwy 49 which snaked in the direction of Hogan Lake and my cozy cabin and my life as a pensioner. I felt strangely good. Somehow this meeting was different, more satisfying than those in the past. I was clear about what I was willing to participate in and what I wasn't. I had spoken more boldly about the kind of service I would be willing to lead -- and if it didn't suit them, I would have asked them to find someone else. There were no church members to placate or alienate, and doing Jacob's funeral was not my job. At the same time I knew that Jacob's life was as precious as anyone else's. It did not need glossing over or covering with false religiosity. I would help this family be real and thankful.

These thoughts and feelings surprised me, and made me feel vital. Maybe my ongoing efforts to create a chasm between my present life and my life as a pastor was futile. And maybe those thirty-five years were not all foolishness.

There were still a couple of hours of daylight left when I got back to the lake. I checked the mail box at the road and found my newspaper and an oversized envelope from the Foundation. Rather than give out my address, they weekly packaged up and re-mailed my personal mail to me. The last thing I needed was a stream of people coming to my door asking for grants.

The package looked like it had been roughed up in transit. I laid it on the seat and slowly drove down the gravel driveway. I stopped at the fork to Barbara's place and considered her opinion that more riding would mean less pain -- an equation that had some merits, and surely some costs. I recalled how Charley and his chums came for a visit to the cabin, and how Charley peered into the window at me. The horse gods seemed to have some plan and I was inclined to play along, so I turned and drove to the horse barn. The horses were in the adjoining corral. I got out and walked to the fence, wishing Barbara was there. Charley led the others over for a greeting and to see if I had a treat for them.

"Hi, big guy. What do you think? Would you let me saddle you up?" I had no illusions about who had the upper hand in our relationship. I walked into the horse barn and got a halter and a handful of grain. I called Charley to the door, offering him the treat. Then bluffing confidence, I slipped the halter under his chin, over his massive jaw muscles and around his tall, soft fuzzy ears, and buckled it.

"Thank you, Charley," I said. "Good boy," and led him near the tack room and tied him to a post. I found a horse brush and swept him down, then laid his blanket over his back. No problem. But then the saddle: anxious not to stand too close to his feet, I kind of heaved it up and toward the beast, and one of the stirrups flung around and slapped Charley on the rear, causing him to take a nervous sideways step, and the saddle fell short and slipped to the ground with a thud. He danced away in one direction and I backed up in the other. I prayed to God Barbara didn't have a surveillance camera in the place. Charley gave me a "What in the hell are you doing?" look.

"Sorry, boy. Sorry," I said as I gently approached him and patted his neck. "I'm a little new at this if you haven't noticed, so can you give me a break and stand still?"

I picked up the saddle and brushed it off. This time I bent the right stirrup up and laid it on the top of the saddle with the belly straps, lifted the whole thing and laid it gently on Charley's back. I walked around to his right side and brought down the stirrup and straps, then back around to his left, and with a prayer I reached under him and took hold of the straps and buckled down the saddle, remembering to keep the rear-most strap loose as Barbara had explained, lest Charley became a bucking bronco.

All right, I thought. Now for the part that most unnerved me: the bit. Getting a horse to take the bit seemed to me an extraordinarily tricky thing. If I were a horse, I would have nothing to do with it. But luckily Charley was trained. All I had to do, Barbara said, was to be confident and take charge (but don't bang his teeth!).

I thought about the previous night. I thought I was taking charge in the massage when I stimulated Barbara's second and third chakras, and then gave her toes a special treat. But in the end, the roles were reversed, and that served both of us well. There is a time and place for taking charge (which I learned the hard way with the Foundation).

I took the bit in one hand and the bridle in the other and offered it to Charley, putting the bit to his sensitive lips. Nothing. I held my breath and nudged his lips with my fingers like Barbara did, and alleluia, he opened up and I pulled the bridle over his ears and the bit slipped to the back of his mouth.

I let out my breath and felt down-right accomplished, like when I served Holy Communion for the first time, stumbling over some words, and forgetting to serve the organist, but I got the job done!

We walked out the side door. I did some stretches and fixed the reins. Then setting my foot in the stirrup and grabbing the saddle horn, I sort of hopped, pulled and climbed, but got myself and my extra forty pounds up in the saddle. Charley whinnied -- to laugh or complain I couldn't tell.

We headed for the lake in a lazy, slow gait; and for an hour I practiced relaxing in the saddle and rolling with Charley's movements. I began, finally, to trust the big guy.

Trust, my favorite word for the over-used "faith". Trust was a key; trust without many expectations except that everything will come out well in the end – and, as they say, if it doesn't, it's not the end yet. The deeper I internalize that truth, the more relaxed and unanxious I experience my days, and the easier it is to practice forgiveness, and love is evermore possible.

In that hour my fear level dramatically decreased. What a day! I couldn't keep it to myself. I fished my cell phone out of my pocket and called Barbara at the hotel. When she answered, it sounded like Bartini Thursday was in full swing.

"Hi," she said without using my name. I still didn't want anyone to know where I lived or my phone number.

"Hi. I'm calling for Charley. He wants to know why you couldn't find a lighter person to rent to?"

"Are you riding!?"

"For an hour. We're heading back from the lake."

"That's great, An... cowboy. How does it feel?"

"Ask me tomorrow. But I'm actually having a good time."

"Well, when you're done horsing around, you should come on over: cheap pomegranate martinis, the Calaveras Jumpers, and Joy."

"What?"

"Yeah," she said in a lower voice, "Your ex is here. We've been chatting."

Oh shit! "What did you say?" I pulled Charley to a stop.

"I said you are getting Nathan and Cindy hitched."

"What else?"

"Not much. She did most of the talking. Joy still loves you I think."

"She said that?"

"No, but I could tell."

"I'm not sure she knows how to love."

"Tough cookie, huh?"

"You could say that."

"You're sure you don't want to come by for a few laughs and stuffed artichokes?"

"Barbara! You know artichokes are our special dish," I said with false complaint.

"That's right, Cowboy; I've got a fuzzy heart for you. But now I have to get back to work. Oh! By the way, I've got an idea for my costume: a karate outfit with a black belt. Joy could lend me hers."

She loved getting the last word. "No, you devil."

"Bye."

The sun was low over the hills, the barn came into sight and I was going over our conversation with Charley. "They were chatting! You know, small towns have their good points and their not-so-good points, Charley. Your Barbara knew it was a heaven-sent chance to tease me, and try to get a rise. But her suggestion to come and have a drink with Joy, that was a test. And the artichoke thing, she was prompting the right answer. This Barbara of yours must not trust men very much -- unless, you know, he's a horse."

By the time I brushed down all three horses and gave them some hay, it was almost dark. The first thing I did when I got back to the cabin was to take two aspirin, and lay on the bed with my legs in the air, and stretch. Then I opened a bottle of good cheap Zin from Lodi and made a chili omelet and had it with left-over cornbread that I had made earlier in the week.

In bed I tried to read but soon turned off the light.

I dreamed the cabin was on fire. I was trying to find the door, but there was too much smoke. I heard someone say, "Sit on the floor, there's less smoke." I did, and then I saw Joy, dressed as an Indian, sitting cross-legged. She said "The fire will not hurt you."

I said, "I can't get out."

"Trust me," she said, "The fire will not hurt you."

"I'm not ready," I said. "I need to get out." Then the fire alarm went off and I woke up to the phone ringing. I felt panicked and disoriented for a moment, then switched on the light. "Hello?"

"Hi, Andy. Thanks for taking care of the horses."

"Sure. Can you hold for a minute?"

"Yeah."

I looked at the clock, ten thirty, then picked up my journal from the nightstand and wrote: The fire will not hurt you. But I am not ready, I need to get out.

"Okay," I said. "So how was your night?"

"It was a good night, just about a full house. But I wanted to apologize. I forget that even though you come off like nothing bothers you, like you have it all together, you still have feelings. I mean that in a good way. Anyway, I'm sorry that I kidded you about Joy. I realized that if you did that to me I'd be mad."

"Thanks, Barbara. I appreciate that. But I'm all right; I had a man-to-man with Charley after you and I talked. He's a good listener."

"I guess I'll have to ask him what you said."

She was fishing. What did she want? "I told him that first you tried to pass me off to your girlfriends, and then to my ex. One might think you are trying to get rid of me. But you see, I didn't jump at either offer, Barbara. I think we have a pretty good thing. And besides, I'm kind of hard to get rid of. Just ask the California lottery. Or ask Joy. She changed her name from Jo to Joy when we were mercifully done."

Where did that come from? And how long had I been sitting on it? There was silence. I just waited. I wrote "Jo to Joy?" in my journal. Finally I heard soft sobs. In my former life I would have rushed up to her house, kissed her and assured her, and asked her to marry me.

Not tonight. Not ever again.

She blew her nose. More silence. Then, "You are hard to run off. I guess I'm stuck with a personal massage therapist for a while."

"Right. And you can still be my riding instructor."

"Okay. And you can be my stable-boy."

"See? Trying to run me off again."

She laughed and blew her nose again. "Thought it was worth a try on a sappy minister."

"Unfortunately for you, those days are gone."

"Damn. Oh well, Sunday at three?"

"If my old bottom heals and the lake don't rise."

"Goodnight, Andy."

"Goodnight, Barbara."

Now I was irreparably awake. What just happened? I got out of bed and made a mug of chamomile tea with a dash of brandy. I sat down with my journal and wrote:

Barbara has tried to show me the door, all the while not wanting me to leave. This is a sign. Another woman not ready for, for... How attached am I getting? Hard to tell. Should I walk away? She shared tears with me -- another level of intimacy.

And what was I doing comparing her to Joy? As if Barbara and I were partners? What message was I giving with the "Hard to get rid of me" line? Maybe she is falling in love with me and wisely knows she can't handle it yet and wants to slow down or break it off, but feels it would now hurt me?

And what about that strange thought of Jo changing her name to Joy-In-The-Morning when she left? That change was prompted by her dream and her new Native American connection and some inner healing; it was coincidental to our divorce -- or was it? I guess part of me feels cheated that I got her bitterness, and now someone else gets her joy.

I put the journal aside and closed my eyes and opened my hands. Slowing and relaxing my breath I reached for an inner stillness. Mindfully I said my take on the Lord's Prayer; "Oh Gracious Creator and Lover of my soul, take up residence in the upper chamber of my heart and flow through my life into the world. Thank you for offering me everything I truly needed today. And thank you for not holding against me all the times I have offended you -- just as I now release everyone who has ever offended me. You strengthen me when tempted, and you protect me from doing evil, for I live in your love and your light in this eternal moment."

Then I pictured Joy standing in golden sunlight, strong and happy. I lifted that image over my head and let it go into God's hands. I felt my shoulders unburden and my spirit grow lighter.

Then I pictured Barbara peacefully asleep in her bed and surrounded by healing light. I lifted and offered this image to God for blessing as well.

Then I sat still for some moments. Was there anything else to let go of? I said my prayer again. Then I asked God what my dream meant? The thought came: Lottery crooks burned your house down two years ago in Riverton, to no avail. It was only a cleansing. The fire can't hurt you.

What fire I asked? "Trust" was the answer. That was all that came. I opened my eyes and wrote: I have a choice; to focus on a fearful image of disaster hanging over my head, or to trust; trust, not brace myself against imagined threats, but to lighten up and Live -- with a capital L.

I finished my tea and turned off the light. The prayer and brandy did their magic.

Chapter 10

I'm not what you would call a morning person. I see fifty sunsets for every sunrise. It's a shame. All that spectacular cosmic fireworks splashing over the sky while I'm obstinately determined to get a little more sleep out of the night. But not on this morning. There was a glorious sunrise going on when I awoke ("Glory" is one of the better words in Christian jargon; it means divine light). The cabin faced east across the lake, and I was certain that the view from the sliding glass doors was among the best in Calaveras County. There were just enough October clouds for the Solar Artist to create a breath-taking orange masterpiece of sky, hills and water.

I scooted out of bed and shuffled my sore butt over to the door to get the full view. The sun was still just below the oak-laden hills and seemed to be waiting there to make its grand entrance; waiting for life to turn its head and welcome its special star, its source, to a new day; waiting for me to open my eyes. Now I waited for the dramatic, dazzling display of its first rays to stream into the room.

I began to wonder who I could share this magic with. Who could I call? Or maybe I could capture it in a photograph and send it to someone. Then I chuckled. I had not even fully received this gift yet and I wanted to give it away. So typical. It was a compulsive habit. I felt if I didn't share the experience, it wasn't very important or significant or real. As if sharing the event was more important than experiencing it. I had been married for thirty-eight years altogether (I liked adding the years together, it made me feel less of a flake) and had believed my happiness, my chance of being loved in return, hinged on what I could bring to the table. Being a pastor was likewise a role in which I no sooner received an insight than I was thinking of how I could share it with the congregation. I was inclined to be so externally oriented that I grossly undervalued my personal, private experiences, as if it wasn't enough to receive and enjoy and value a sunset ride for my own soul's sake. Now something told me to relax and just receive it like a little child.

I watched until the sun peeked over the hill and flashed in my eyes. That sent an impulse to my brain which teased up a memory of an old favorite hymn, and I began to softly sing:

> "Awake, awake to love and work,
> The lark is in the sky;
> The fields are wet with diamond dew,
> The worlds awake to cry
> Their blessings on the Lord of Life,
> As he goes meekly by."

The hymn gave me pause. Love and work? I recalled Pearl's blessing in her note, "God bless the work the Lord now has for you." Yet I am a pensioner and I'm trying to adjust to the fact that my work-life is done.

I walked over to the wall calendar to see what day it was – Friday. What's my schedule today? "Ha!" I said out loud, "Make a latte' and go back to bed!"

I filled the machine and waited for the pressure to rise as the second verse came to me:

> "Come, let thy voice be one with theirs,
> Shout with their shouts of praise;
> See how the giant sun soars up,
> Great lord of years and days!
> So let the love of Jesus come
> And set thy soul ablaze."

I continued to hum as I frothed the milk and mixed in the potent coffee. On the way back to bed I grabbed yesterday's mail and paper and propped up some pillows. Sitting in bed I squinted and let the sun dance and refract on my eyelashes. I sipped my coffee and thought about how far the sun was from our planet. So far that the mystical photons now stimulating my eyes took eight minutes at the speed of light to get here. And the love of Jesus? Two thousand years.

And what about my life, my light? As I cast my bread upon the waters, where will it end up? In God's economy, is love ever truly lost or given in vain?

I sipped my coffee again. A day with nothing on my calendar but to ruminate on old hymns. I tried to recall the last verse of the hymn, but I got the phrases mixed up with the first two verses. So I got up and found my hymnal and brought it back to bed. My third wife hated my singing. Not because it was that bad (I think); she just thought it was so weird that it made her uncomfortable, like watching a movie and all of a sudden the main character breaks out in song and you think, "Come on, get real!" But my song now was for my own ears:

> "To give and give and give again,
> What God hath given thee;
> To spend thyself nor count the cost,
> To serve right gloriously
> The God who gave all worlds that are,
> And all that are to be."

I closed my eyes and meditated for thirty minutes. When I was done I reached for the torn mail package. I spilled the contents out on the bed next to me. There were four letters and several magazines and newsletters and catalogs. I saw right away that each of the letters had been opened; unusual for my forwarded mail. Was there someone new handling the mail at the foundation? But the fact that the big envelope holding the letters had been ripped as well pointed to the discomforting idea that someone was tampering with my mail. There was nothing too personal or important in the four letters, but still, what was going on?

* * *

Attendance at Jacob's funeral on Saturday morning was an admirable fifty. There's an inverse correlation between the length of one's stay in a convalescent hospital and the number of people at one's funeral.

The Calaveras Jumpers set a nice tone with their gathering music, including Hank William's "I Saw the Light." One of the grandchildren set up a beautiful table next to the closed coffin. It was covered with an arrangement of baskets full of fruits and nuts to represent Jacob's work. And on closer inspection it included a worn pair of his leather gloves.

His disabled daughter had found copies of historic pictures of big old cars incredibly loaded down as they traveled from the dust bowl to California. These photos were displayed with a portrait of Jacob. And his son read a quite nice eulogy he had written with his two sisters. It was punctuated with humor and included details I felt many people didn't know.

During the sharing time several people spoke words of appreciation. The best was by a staff woman from the nursing home who said that Jacob had become her friend, cared about her children and never failed to ask after them. He would tell her stories about the big fish he had almost caught, about a wind storm that blew over a swath of trees in the orchard, and about being on a troop transport on the way back from Korea. She said he cared about his roommates and often helped them. And he had given her a beautiful scarf last Christmas which she was wearing.

The band then sang a country version of Woody Guthrey's "This Land Is Your Land." My words were brief. The scripture was from St. John, "All who love are of God." I suggested that our time here was short and precious, but being a channel of love makes it eternal. I said that Jacob's unique way of caring and providing could inspire us to be our best selves today, forever.

On the way home I thought that they wouldn't all be this satisfying, but I could see myself perhaps doing a funeral a month if asked. I decided to call Randy and let him know that I'd be interested in helping out regularly if that worked out for him.

I had to rush back to the lake to meet Josh and Wade. The plan was for them to launch Wade's eighteen foot catamaran at the boat ramp across the lake from the cabin and sail over to pick me up at 1:00 p.m. I almost lost the white car following me when I barely made the traffic light in Valley Springs and turned on to Dam Road. I wondered if the mystery guy had been in the funeral chapel?

As the driveway dropped down to the cabin, I could see Wade's bright red, orange and yellow sails in the middle of the lake. I had just enough time to change clothes, stick some cheap beer and chips in a day pack, and grab my life vest. From the shore I waved so they could see where to beach the boat -- I had now rented from Barbara for over four months and this was their first time at the cabin; in fact, the first time I had invited anyone to my place.

When they approached the shore, Josh furled the jib sail on the bow and Wade let the main sail go slack. The boat coasted nicely into the gravel and sand beach, making a soft landing.

"Hi, Friends," I said in high spirits as I pushed the bow back off the beach and began turning the boat around.

"Ahoy, Andy!" Wade said, "How you doing?"

"Remember, I'm now a pensioner, so the question is 'how you being'; not doing."

"It's been too long," Josh said.

"I know; and I spent the morning at the mortuary, so I have a feeling time is short. Are you ready to launch?"

"Let's go."

I gave the catamaran a shove and hopped on. Wade adjusted the main sail and Josh let out the self-furling jib sail, and in a light breeze we glided back out onto the lake. Wade looked back at the cabin, "You found a sweet spot, Andy. There are just a few lakefront homes on New Hogan. Mostly big ranches out here." As a part-time realtor Wade knew the area well.

We looked at the panorama. Only a few structures could be seen from out on the water. The lake was surrounded by dry, golden grassy hills, and dotted generously with valley oak, blue oak and live oak, as well as grey pines. "Who's your neighbor up there above you?" Josh asked.

"That's Barbara, my landlady. You may know her. She manages the hotel bar and restaurant in Moke Hill."

"Short, long dark hair, nice smile?"

"That's her. Turns out she's a cowgirl and has three horses – she's teaching me to ride."

"Really?" Wade said. "Rev. Andy Shepard, back in the saddle, but this time actually in a saddle? You ought to get one of those black riding coats and present as an old-fashioned circuit-riding itinerant preacher. I bet these Gold Country churches would love that."

"That was a young man's calling," I said. "They seldom lived past thirty-five. Besides, I'm retired."

"Then what were you doing at the mortuary this morning?"

"I need some riding boots."

Josh smiled, "This is great. Here you are, the one-time lion of Calaveras County and the slayer of the lottery; and now you're riding horses, sailing your little boat and living in a small out-of-the-way cabin. What a switch. It's hard to believe. What else are you doing, or being?"

"Not a whole lot. I'm starting to think of the cabin as a hermitage. It's very conducive to meditating and writing."

"What are you writing?"

"Mostly journaling. And I'm working on a blues song."

"You're kidding. You are sitting out here singing the blues?!"

I felt a little embarrassed by that image. Maybe it was too close to the truth. Or maybe it touched my guilt at leaving these guys at the Foundation. Five friends changed the course of their lives to work at the Foundation, then a year later I abandoned ship. For what? I was still trying to figure that out.

"I've always loved the blues harmonica," I said. "So I bought one and have been practicing every day."

"So, what's this song?" Wade asked.

"It's a riding song called 'My Old Bottom Blues.'"

"Oh, I can feel your pain!" Wade said wincingly.

"Let's hear it," Josh said.

"Well guys, if you're free tonight, I'm going to do it at the Cowboy Bistro in San Andreas with the Calaveras Jumpers."

"Sure! I can't wait," Wade said. "This is a side of you we haven't seen."

"That is one of the gifts of being a pensioner," I said. "A chance to reclaim some of those things that one has stored away because they didn't fit an earlier time and place."

"Get ready to come about," Wade said as he took the mainsheet out of the rope lock cleat. Josh did the same with the jib line. All I had to do was make sure the boom didn't hit me.

"Coming about," Wade announced and he pushed the tiller away from him. The bow swung into the wind, the main sail went momentarily slack and luffed noisily. The jib sail caught the wind from the other side and helped pull the bow further around until the main caught the wind from the other side and the boom swung across the taunt heavy nylon tarp that was stretched between the two narrow hulls. The boat tilted with the wind and I scooted to the high side to join my friends and add my weight. Then off we were running on a new tack in a fresh breeze.

Catamarans are among the fastest sailboats because their two narrow hulls give less resistance than one wide hull in the water. Also, the mast is usually higher, and the sails larger for the length of the boat because the boat does not tip as easily. But when the skipper does allow the boat to tip, the windward hull actually comes up out of the water, further decreasing the drag.

"Good work, mates," Wade said. Wade and I had sailed his boat several times on Hogan Lake when I was his pastor, and that's how our friendship was forged. Whereas, Josh and I sailed through ministry together as colleagues for over thirty years, and he was my closest friend.

"So Andy," Wade said, looking intently at me as if this was the question he had been waiting to ask, "Do you think you will be coming back to the Foundation next year?"

"No, afraid not," I said without even considering it, and surprising myself. I didn't know I was so resolute. I could tell Wade was disappointed. "Do you like your work, Wade?"

"It's the best job I've ever had. It feels good knowing we are making a difference."

"I'm glad to hear it. But you should know that I didn't like the work. I was way over-anxious about where the grants were going and how they were being spent. I was getting stressed out."

"And the more stressed you became, the more we all felt stressed," Josh said. "When you stepped down as CEO, it righted the boat. I hate to say this buddy, but honestly, we're all getting along beautifully now. Even John wants to stay indefinitely. But we miss you. There must be a way for you to be involved that works for you."

"I can't think of a way to do that. I know now that fundamentally I never truly reconciled the fact that the money came from gambling,"

"What are you going to do when the new lotto starts back up?"

"When's that?"

"This month."

"Already?"

"Yeah, maybe it's time to start paying attention to your dreams again."

I let that comment sit there. I thought of my disturbing dream of the cabin on fire -- I have to get out! I said. No, I didn't want to be God's point man to stop the lottery again. If commercial gambling is what people wanted, then screw them. I did my part. I gave it my best shot. My four jackpots closed it down for almost two years, and cost me my home, my marriage, my job -- and they tried to throw me in jail.

But Josh wouldn't let it alone. "Have you heard from the lotto people recently?"

"No, not for over a year."

"They must think that with the former managers in jail and the new ones in place, you have no inside connections and can't cheat them again."

"But how could they be sure?" Wade said. "Andy must still make them nervous. They are spending a fortune to start up a state-wide lottery again. I'm surprised they haven't at least tried to scare him off."

My mind went to the white car and my mail. Of course it must be them. I should just call them up and tell them I'm out of the game. Call them?! I bet they have my cell phone tapped. The thought made me angry.

"We have some wind ahead, hold on," Wade alerted us.

"I take it this is not a subject you want to talk about," Josh guessed.

"Right. It's history and I've moved on." I could feel myself getting agitated and I wanted to change the subject.

But Wade said, "Uh, Josh? Did you ever read the story of Jonah?"

"Yeah, poor guy" Josh said, "three days sloshing around in digestive juices. You know, sometimes God gets fairly adamant."

"Maybe free will isn't as free as it seems." Wade added.

I taught him that, damn it.

Suddenly the hull we were sitting on raised up out of the water as the wind forced the mast to tilt. I slid my feet under the straps on the tarp and leaned back over the water. Wade let the main sail out slightly to spill some wind, and the hull eased back into the water.

"You want to use the trapeze, Josh?"

"Sure." Josh unfastened the trapeze harness from the base of the mast and snapped it on himself so that he was tethered to the top of the mast by a long cable. Then he stood up, spread his legs into a wide stance and said, "Ready."

Wade pulled in the main sheet as he also pulled the tiller towards him to steer the boat perpendicular to the wind, which had become stronger and a proper challenge for a catamaran. The windward hull again lifted out of the water with the increased power in the sails.

Josh adjusted his feet to the outside edge of the hull and leaned back over the water, more or less held secure by the trapeze.

Sitting with my feet in the straps I too leaned back as we used our weight to keep the boat from tipping all the way over and to maximize our speed. The mast's side-stay cables began to vibrate with a humming sound. As the wind gusted and varied, Wade moved the tiller slightly back and forth to keep the boat balanced on one hull which was now splashing up water -- mostly on me. Josh and Wade began whooping and hollering and delighting in the drenching I was getting as the wind kicked up swells, making the boat lurch and buck.

It didn't take long to cross the lake at that speed, and soon Wade said, "Ready to come about Andy, you take the jib."

"Okay" I said and reached for the line.

"Coming about," he said and he turned into the wind. The hull I was sitting on came down faster than I anticipated. When it hit the water with a jerk, my feet came out of the straps and back I went into the lake, head and shoulders. I let go of the jib line and was immersed in the startling cold water. When I came up with the help of my life vest, I could see the catamaran streaking away from me, which was a disconcerting sight; but I noticed that Josh's head was turned back towards me and he was pointing. That was standard procedure for a man overboard situation. The skipper has to sail the boat while someone keeps pointing to the one in the water so they don't lose them -- which is easier than you would think -- as the crew maneuvered back to pick them up.

It may have only taken five minutes for Wade to get the sailboat positioned for a rescue, but treading water in the middle of a cold lake made it seem much longer. There was plenty of time to consider Jonah's fate: a guy who said no to God's mission, thus things didn't go well for him. When Jonah finally agreed to speak out against the country's poor behavior, God's resulting grace just disgruntled Jonah further. A funny story unless, you know, you are Jonah.

Wade seemed to be going too fast as the boat got closer. I imagined trying to dive under it with my buoyant life vest on. But at the last moment he turned into the wind with the jib sail furled and the boom loose. I hurried and climbed on board with Josh's help before the breeze blew the boat backward and away from me. I scratched my knee in the process and was shivering when Wade had the boat underway again, but I was aboard.

"Thanks guys," I said with meaning as I worked at releasing the bungee cords holding my day pack to the mast.

"Just doing our job," Wade said with a grin, "which seems to be keeping your ass out of deep water."

"I guess I owe you, again." I unzipped my bag and pulled out my towel. "How about a beer?" and I handed them both a can.

Wade looked at his, "This is what we get? You call this beer!?"

"Old Milwaukee's finest, thirty cents a can." I said.

"How the mighty have fallen," Josh said and laughed. "You have to come back to work."

"Here's some chips. I find they help the beer go down so you hardly notice."

Wade took a gulp. "No wonder you're singing the blues."

Chapter 11

Josh and Wade dropped me at my beach around four, and we agreed to meet at five-thirty at the Cowboy Bistro.

At the cabin I checked my phone. I had a message from Barbara. "Hey, Sugar. The white car was parked up on the road again today. I got a photo of him messing with the mail boxes. So I called my friend at the Sheriff's Department and asked if someone could find out who was stalking us. Turns out the guy is a private investigator and was hired by the lottery people to keep an eye on you. I guess you can't hide from your past for long. So wherever you get your numbers from, be careful -- good renters are hard to find. See you tomorrow."

Can't run from the past; and Jonah couldn't run from his future. Where did that leave me? I wasn't running, I was just saying no. I sat down with a pen and two sheets of paper, and wrote:

To the guy in the white car – tell your clients not to worry. God has lost interest in the lottery and I am out of the game. Now I am just another boring pensioner. So give it up. And for your information, my landlady got a shot of your hand in my mailbox. I didn't know those digital zooms were that good!
Sincerely,
Andy Shepard

The first part was a hope, and the last part was a lie, but maybe it would make him think. I considered including a set of lottery numbers under my signature just to play with their heads, but I knew I would be asking for trouble.

On the second sheet I wrote:

Dear Cowgirl, thanks for the info. But be advised, I believe my phone is tapped. Looking forward to our ride.

Andy

Both notes went into envelopes. After a shower and catnap, I put the top down and drove up to Barbara's and left her note. When I got to the road the white car was parked on the other side (a concession to the Sheriff's Department?). I slowly turned right, crossed the center line holding out the envelope. I stopped at the guy's window. He was about thirty, had a mop of hair and was fit. He reached out and took the envelope. I said, "Would you like a close-up?"

"I already have one," he said without a smile.

I nodded and drove away. Before I was out of sight, he made a U-turn and was behind me again.

The town of San Andreas is spread out along Hwy 49, and the Cowboy Bistro was at the far end. It was a converted old house with a recent addition that now accommodated a band on the weekends. The decor was whimsical. Several parts of every wooden chair were painted different bright colors. There were paintings of cowboys and western scenes for sale on the walls. The tabletops had classic cowboy poems laminated to them, and the menu was eclectic and a fun read, including my favorite: "No time to cook? Try our Rustler's Sushi with hangman's wasabi." If you asked the staff about their spurs, they would tell you they were handy for difficult customers. I got there a little early to see Bobby before the band started up.

"Andy! Hi. Bring your cross harp?"

"Hi Bobby. Thanks for helping me out. It's right here," patting my pocket.

"Dig it out, man. Let's have a look."

Bobby always sounded hyper. I pulled it out, opened the case and handed it to him. He studied it for a moment. "It's in G. Nice harp. You did good." and he handed it back.

"Here are the lyrics," I said handing him a sheet. "I have a tune but I don't really know how to write music."

"No problem. Blues are really easy to pick up on. Play it for me."

I took up my harmonica and felt more than a little hesitant. But I brought to mind how I used to begin sermons: strong and assured, otherwise one could lose the congregation in the first minute. I closed my eyes and played the tune, mildly adding a little flair here and there.

"That's great man. You sound like a pro." I knew he was trying to encourage me, but I was flattered none-the-less. "Now, have you ever played with a harmonica mic?"

"No."

He demonstrated how to hold the harmonica and mic as one unit, then he played a riff through the speakers. Whoa, I couldn't believe all that sound was coming from my little instrument. Then he handed it to me, "Try it."

The amplification made the experience exciting. I got a little bolder. Bobby began a funky rhythm on his guitar behind my song's melody. This was going to be fun.

"Now, Andy, we'll start out with just you playing the tune. Then when you start the second time through, we'll join you, mostly with rhythm. And on the third time, you sing. Then between verses we will all wail a bit. But don't worry, just watch me, I'll bring you in again for the next verse."

Then Bobby read my lyrics. "This is funny stuff. But it's the blues, Andy. So my advice is to do it straight. You hurt. You've been used. And you want to tell the whole world about it. The blues have to have some power behind them. You hurt, but she is not going to get away with it! It's that empowering spirit of the blues that hooks people. So don't be cute with this. Sell it."

"Okay. I'll have my buddies kick my sore butt before I come up."

"There you are. There you are, man. Now, let's put it towards the end of the first fifty-minute set. Have a few beers. I'll introduce you."

When I turned around from the best music lesson I'd ever had, I saw Wade and Josh a couple of tables back from the band. I smiled and joined them saying, "Oh, my Coast Guard rescue unit. I'm glad to see you -- I might need another rescue if I get booed off the stage."

"Oh, you'll do fine," Josh said.

"And when you hit it big," Wade added, "We can say we were there when you first started out."

"Right," Josh continued. "We will chronicle your fall from being a reluctant multi-millionaire and your rise as a soulful blues singer."

I just shook my head, "I'm glad I can keep you so entertained."

The waitress appeared with three pints of local hand-crafted ale. "It's on us tonight, Andy," Josh said and put his arm around my shoulder with a grin, "Remember, no matter what everyone else says, we love you."

"I'll drink to that," added Wade. We all raised our glasses, "To lovable Andy!"

As we drank, a woman at the next table leaned over and asked, "Are you Andy Shepard?"

I just nodded and tried to smile.

"Hey everyone!" She stood and said to the room, "Andy Shepard is here tonight. Let's hear it for the Shepard Foundation."

There was warm applause and a few cheers. I half stood up and gave a wave and sat back down. The woman bent over towards us again and said, "My name is Helen, I live at the Safe Place Transition House. Thank you for helping me get my life back, Reverend." Then she sat down.

Wade and Josh just looked at me and smiled with affection. I leaned over my beer and said, "But it wasn't me."

Wade's eyebrows rose as I heard a familiar voice say, "Who then, grandmother?"

I looked around over my shoulder and there was Joy, my ex-wife. A small electric jolt went up my spine. Josh and Wade stood up and gave her hugs and invited her to have a seat. She said, "Okay, just for a minute. I'm joining these women at the next table."

"Well, hello." I said, meaning: I haven't seen you for a long time and I can't say I have missed you and how strange and unfortunate that we have run into each other here tonight and if Wade and Josh set this up I am going to kill them.

"Hi Andy. Of course it wasn't you. But, you were an indispensable part of the whole thing. We both hated the Lottery, but you were the one who said yes. If I had been in your shoes I would have…well, I did say no, a hundred times no."

"As it turned out, I had no idea what I was saying yes to."

"That's how it works, Love. As I recall, it was you who taught me that."

There was a pause. My brain felt as if it had locked up. But from somewhere, God only knows, I said, "How's your Grandmother, Red Cloud?"

Joy's eyes looked away at nowhere in particular for a few moments, then said, "She says you should know." Then our eyes locked for a very long second as the music started up with "Mommas, Don't Let Your Babies Grow Up to Be Cowboys."

"Well gentlemen, I'm glad we had this little chat," and she excused herself.

Let them be doctors and lawyers and such... the song went along. I looked at my friends and sang softly with the band, "Mommas don't let your babies grow up to be married." They shook their heads at me. Then I asked, "Did you set that up?"

"No, honestly," Josh said.

We ordered food and listened to the music. I was glad my back was to the women's table, and the music was loud so there wasn't much said at ours.

Then the moment came. "You all are in for a rare treat tonight," Bobby said into the mic. "Folks, will you welcome our new up-and-coming blues artist, Andy Shepard doing his latest composition, 'Old Bottom Blues.'"

There was polite applause among a crowd that was mostly talking and eating. I made my way around the table in front of ours. Bobby handed me the harmonica mic and pointed to a mic stand where I could sing. I turned my back on the "congregation" to see if the Jumpers were ready. Bobby said, "Sing us your first line real quiet-like to get your tempo and keep it on the slow side. Then turn around and hit it."

I thought how appropriate the first line was; then I sang it softly to them, "I thought I was ready, but I was wrong."

I turned around, looked down at the worn wooden floor, put the harmonica to my mouth and let my amplified complaint fill the room. As I played the tune I remembered that after my first horse ride I actually felt I had injured myself.

When the band got going on my second time through, it made me sound good, and with more confidence I loosened up with my riffs as they kept a strong beat. Then I stepped to the mic and told everyone how bad it was:

> I thought I was ready, but I was wrong.
> I thought I was ready, but I was so wrong.

> So when I got off that horse
> I had to write down this song:
> I've got the old bottom blues,
> My old bottom blues,
> And I pray I won't have them for long.

The band rounded out the first verse and I could see Wade giving me a fist pump. I glanced at Joy's expression of wonder. I played a riff as the band obviously came to the start of the second verse and Bobby gave me a slight nod.

> My baby she has a sweet round bottom.
> Oh yes, she has the sweetest round bottom.
> But my skinny old butt feels like
> I've been to Sodom.
> I've got those old bottom blues,
> My old bottom blues,
> But please don't tell my baby
> I've got 'em.

I heard some hoots and cheers from the tables. This time between verses Bobby took over the lead on the guitar as I tapped my foot to the beat. I began to get it -- it was their chord progression that cued when I should sing.

> I thought I was hurt as a greenhorn could get.
> Yes, I thought I was hurt as an old bottom could get.
> But then my baby made me
> Shovel her horses shit!
> I've got those old bottom blues.
> A bad case of old bottom blues.
> And it will be a long while
> Before I can sit.

The girl's table howled at that verse; and as the keyboard played the tune with variations, I chimed in echoing his riffs. Bobby got the crowd clapping to the beat. The cord progression came around again to the beginning and I decided to really belt out the last verse.

> My baby said I was her favorite cowboy.

> What did she mean: I was her favorite cowboy?
> Well she rode me so hard
> Made me cry for joy.
> I've got the old bottom blues.
> Bad case of the old bottom blues.
> Be careful, your old bottom might become
> Her ragged toy.

Wade and Josh were laughing and shaking their heads in disbelief. Bobby and the band really let loose on the last time through. I could hardly follow along. When we got to the last note we just let it go all over the place and the room gave us whistles and cheers. I nodded to them once and turned to Bobby and the others and mouthed "Thank you."

Bobby led the band in four more bars while I found my seat. When they came to their second ending, Bobby said into the mic, "I want to go to his church! Let's hear it for the Right Reverend Shepard!" And there were laughter and cheers. I was wet. I took a long draw on my beer.

Josh gave me a big smile, "So, are you Barbara's favorite cowboy now?"

I put on a shocked look, "How could you think such a thing!"

"Right," he said. "I'm getting a whole different picture of the hermitage."

"Speaking of which, does this dinner treat come with dessert?"

Chapter 12

As I drove home from the Cowboy Bistro my mind darted from one surprising or perplexing moment of the day to the next. Once back at the cabin there was no one to talk to, and no TV to distract me. I was forced to sit down with my journal and a cup of tea to sort things out:

#1 Red Cloud -- the Spirit of Joy's medicine woman grandmother. Why would I ask how she was? "She says you should know." What the hell did that mean? Was she mysteriously lurking in the shadows of my life? Was Joy still actively seeking her as a spirit guide? The whole idea of connecting with the dead was unreal to me. But then there were those lottery and casino dreams that changed everything.

#2 Being recognized -- being applauded for the work of the Foundation was painfully awkward. I created Kindom Come primarily for myself because I was repulsed by the lottery money and the greed that powered it; and I needed my friends to be closer, I needed family, especially since Joy was so antagonistic.

#3 Old Bottom Blues -- felt too personal to sing it in public. I should have checked with Barbara first. Though I didn't use her name, Josh got the connection. I doubted the wisdom of singing it at the wedding reception.

#4 Bobby -- would he tutor me in harmonica? Playing in his band was a fantastic experience.

#5 The invitation to return to the Foundation -- now I am very clear, it would never work out.

It had been a long day, and soon the writing put my mind to rest -- at least I knew what the questions were. But when I finally got to sleep I dreamed the cabin was on fire again. The dream gave me the same assurance and the same dismay -- I don't know how to get out! I woke up weeping. I switched on the light, and after I used the toilet I wrote down the dream. Then turned off the light and prayed that I wouldn't re-enter the disturbing dream again.

Early Sunday I again witnessed the sunrise as I made my latte'. There was something about my grand view that made each sunrise and sunset unique. This one was structured in colored layers like a layered cake in grays and pinks.

Back in bed I reviewed my journal writing from the previous night and received an inspiration. If I re-wrote the last verse of my song it would be all right to sing at the reception. So I set about the task:

> Now I've known some women
> But none could really ride.
> You know I've had some women
> But none could really ride.
> So I'm staying in this saddle
> Maybe it's my foolish pride.
> I've got those old bottom blues,
> Painful old bottom blues.
> She said it'd get better
> Before my old bottom died.

It was just the thing to distract me from dealing with my dream, a dream about my anxiety of "getting out" even as I sang about "staying in the saddle."

Barbara phoned in the afternoon when she returned from work. I met her at the horse barn.

"How are you, Andy."

I wanted to tell her about my triumph at the Cowboy Bistro, but I decided to keep the song as a surprise. "Not so bad after my last ride, the stretches have helped. And you?"

"My shoulder is giving me fits. The pills aren't helping much, so I saw my doctor Friday and got an x-ray. Now he wants me to get a CAT scan in Stockton."

We began brushing down the horses. I noticed she only used her left arm. When it was time to saddle up, she asked me to lift hers. We walked the horses out the side door. I watched to see if she needed help mounting the paint, but with one hand on the horn she hopped and in a smooth motion swung her leg over the saddle.

I looked at big Charley, wondering how I could match her technique even using two arms. I stuck my foot up in the stirrup and Barbara said, "Whoa, wait a second, those stirrups are too high for you. Adjust them down some.

As I worked at the buckles I said, "You know, I was thinking of going to Stockton this week to buy some riding boots. How about we go together? And I wouldn't mind driving."

"Always the pastor."

"No, a friend."

"My appointment is Wednesday morning."

"I'll have to check my busy schedule, I think I only have a massage date that evening, so I should be able to work you in."

"Okay, but let's not mention any of this to Nathan until after the wedding. Now let's see you mount that horse without falling off -- like that boat ride yesterday."

I looked up at her with surprise.

"Oh yeah, I was watching with my binoculars. When I stopped laughing I thought I was going to have to call the search and rescue team."

I could feel myself blushing. I didn't have a comeback so I did some stretches.

"Good thing you had your friends with you."

I put my foot in the stirrup again and hopped as hard as I could and it was much easier this time. "That's right, Barbara, we all need to lean on our friends from time to time."

"Follow me; I know a trail down to the Calaveras River below the dam." And as we rode along the driveway together we saw the white car parked up ahead. "That fella's sure persistent. You've got them real worried. You think they will back off after Friday?"

"Friday?"

"The first game."

"Oh. I don't know. After I got your message I wrote them a letter and told them I wasn't playing the lottery any more. I said that God had lost interest."

"You told them that?"

"I just call them as I see them."

"So, God lost the battle?"

"God loses a lot of battles."

"That's not very comforting."

"Think about it, Barbara. Look around, if God was almighty, then God must be either indifferent or unloving. Those options are really discomforting. People with blind faith say that it just looks like God is indifferent or unloving, however we just don't understand God's hidden purposes which are wonderful.

"But the way I see it, it boils down to our free will: God's will is a force but not almighty. We have to will what God wills if the cycle of gratuitous suffering is to be halted. It's a partnership."

We waved as we passed the white car, and Barbara said, "So God gave up, huh?"

"No, God never gives up. God is the God of life and love, which can be postponed, but God is victorious in the end. If almighty means anything, it means that."

"So then, you have given up."

That idea startled me. I asked myself if it was true as Barbara led us across the road and onto a rocky trail that I had never noticed before. The roughness and unevenness of it made me uneasy and I could feel myself tighten up. Then, watching the paint ahead of me, I was amazed at how horses always know where to put their hoofs, even the back ones where they couldn't see. How did they do that? How does one know where and when to take the next step in life?

I looked over at Barbara, "Maybe," I said. "I don't know. It feels like I'm taking some R & R. I know I have limitations -- I crashed into some of them this past year."

"Right, like falling off that boat. That was a hoot. But you got yourself back on."

I smiled at Barbara's humor and wisdom. And I also thought of Jonah again. He was thrown overboard by the crew! He didn't climb back on, and even still he ended up on the right shore.

When we reached the river, the horses took a drink. Barbara looked at me and said, "I'm amazed at how much more relaxed in the saddle you are today."

"You're a good teacher. And Charley's a good horse. I trust both of you."

"Let's walk them for a ways. It's one of the tricks to deal with soreness."

So we slid off the horses and walked back up the trail in the fading afternoon light. "Decide on a costume yet?" I asked.

"Not really. Probably not a wedding dress, or Michelle Obama, or a martial arts master. I thought of coming as a divorce lawyer, that would have fit into the theme, but I couldn't come up with an identifiable costume. You have any new ideas?"

"How about coming as a mother-in-law ready to move in with the newlyweds? You could carry a suitcase and wear a housedress or an apron, maybe some curlers?"

"Great idea! And a feather duster giving the impression that I don't think Cindy cooks or cleans very well for my son!"

"And during the wedding you could throw in a critical comment or two about Cindy's shoes or dress."

"Perfect! Thank you, Andy!"

The white car was still there when we rode back up onto the highway. As we approached, the private investigator opened his door and stepped out, obviously wanting to say something. We stopped as he walked over to us. I reached down and accepted the envelope he offered me. All he said was, "From my clients," then he turned and began walking back toward the car.

"How are the Giants doing?" I asked.

Without turning he said, "They are up four to one."

I stuck the envelope in my pocket and we rode down the long driveway which was planted on either side with young ornamental plum trees. They stretched out in front of us for a couple hundred yards to where the drive forked.

"If you are into the baseball playoffs, you could watch them at my house."

"No thanks. I was just trying to guess how he spent his time up there all day."

"My guess is that he's watching porn on his I-pad or something. Baseball might put him to sleep."

I looked at Barbara and wondered where that comment came from.

"I think half you guys watch porn."

"I think you have dated some jerks."

"I think I have married some jerks."

"Oh," I said and left it there. I opened the envelope.

"Look," she said, "Now he even rides and reads. What a natural."

"It's short and to the point. A Mr. Joseph Raggetti wants me to come in and talk."

"Did he ask nicely?"

"I've seen worse."

Chapter 13

I phoned Mr. Raggetti, the top manager at the California Lottery Center in Sacramento, and agreed to meet him, saying that I always cooperated with them, which was true in a way. However, I said that I had some bad experiences at the Center, so I suggested that just the two of us meet at the picnic area of the Hogan Lake visitor center next to the Army Corps of Engineers' offices. I assured him that our October weather was beautiful and that I would provide lunch. He agreed, and we met on Tuesday.

Looking back, I suppose my hope was to disarm and put at ease the management of the largest gambling establishment in the world. I wanted them to know I wasn't a cheat. In fact, more than anything -- the hassles, the drama, the disruptions to my life -- the thing that bothered me the most about the affair was that many people thought I was a cheat and a crook.

The Lottery was managed an Italian corporation, and Joseph Raggetti spoke with a slight Italian accent, so I made a casserole of cheese tortellini and summer squash with a creamy pesto sauce. To go with it I made bruschetta: artichoke tapenade spread on slices of toasted French bread and topped with diced roma tomatoes and parmesan cheese. To drink I bought a bottle of imported Chianti.

The visitors' center sat on a hill. I had chosen a picnic table in the warming sun that overlooked the expansive blue lake and its dam. I spread a tablecloth, set the table with napkins, forks and wine glasses, then placed the Chianti in the center.

While I waited I studied the view. I have always been fascinated by dams. As a child I loved to construct dams wherever there was a trickle of water. It was a game, pitting myself against the flow, and watching the water rise and backup on the stream until it would inevitably begin to breach my dam. I would rush to fill the breach only to have the stream win in the end.

In that moment I saw my effort to stop commercial gambling as a child's dam-building fantasy. I was ready to concede defeat. I could only imagine the tremendous pressure behind the dam I had constructed by threatening to win every jackpot.

A Mercedes pulled into the parking area and stopped at the curb near the table. A man in his fifties stepped out of the back. I waved and he walked toward the table. We were a study in contrasts. He wore a fine dark suit and polished black shoes and looked to be very fit. I wore short pants, plaid shirt, and worn canvas shoes. I had a ceramic cross – the one I had recovered from my torched home -- hung around my neck on a leather thong. And you wouldn't describe me as very fit.

"Hello, Mr. Raggetti. Thank you for meeting me here in Calaveras County," and I extended my hand.

We shook and he said, "Hello," as he surveyed the Chianti and wine glasses. He smiled and said, "Well, Rev. Shepard, this looks very nice."

"Please be seated, and call me Andy. Would your driver like to join us?"

"That's very kind, but perhaps we need to talk in private."

There was an awkward moment as he unbuttoned his coat and stepped over and sat on the old bench with his immaculate trousers. I pretended not to see his discomfort as I unwrapped the pasta dish and uncovered the bruschetta. "I made us one of my favorite dishes. I hope it is still warm."

"It smells delicious," he said. "Thank you."

"I would like to offer thanks to God," I said and bowed my head. "God of Grace, thank you for this food, it is a sign of your love for us. May your presence at this table help us understand each other and know your will. Amen."

"Amen," Raggetti said.

I motioned for him to help himself as I opened the wine. "A few years ago," I said, "I visited the Chianti Road in Tuscany. I will always remember a small family vineyard and winery we found there. I had phoned ahead to arrange the visit but found it a challenge to find it at the end of a dirt road. The owner was a charming elderly man who spoke a little English and gave us such a warm welcome. He took time to tell us the long history of his winery. We must have spent over an hour there tasting his fine wine and meeting his sons who now do most of the work. It was the highlight of our trip. I hope this wine is half as good. Can I pour you a glass?"

"Please, Andy. And tell me, did you travel with your wife?"

"Yes, although I must confess, she preferred Siena where she shopped for pottery."

"Really? My parents lived for years in Siena," he said with enthusiasm. "There is a famous traditional horse race there in the historic piazza every year. Each of the twelve districts of the city are represented by a horse and rider. The whole town turns out and visitors come from all over to see the spectacle and to bet on the race. My father owned horses and once won the race."

"That must have been some day. You can't visit Siena without hearing about the annual race. It would be fun to go back to see it, especially since I am now learning to ride."

"My father taught me to ride when I was a boy; we were very close -- still are."

"And I bet he taught you how to win."

"Yes, and this is a very fine meal. I admit I was prepared for tuna fish sandwiches. Do you do most of the cooking in your family?"

"Mr. Raggetti, let's be honest today. You must know that Joy and I have divorced."

"Yes, I'm sorry to hear that."

"We had our problems before our battle with the lottery, but the stress -- the accusations and threats and violence -- pushed us over the edge."

Raggetti's face tightened and he was silent for a while. I offered him another piece of bruschetta. "Andy, yes, let us be honest. I have no recording device, so let's put our cards on the table. From your perspective, what happened last year?"

"You may not want to hear this, but God intervened in the California lottery. I have no idea why God picked this battle, but I believe that from time to time people need to be reminded that there is mystery and wonder all around us, and so God demonstrates this with an occasional miracle; then God leaves it to us to start to do the right thing.

"My church has always believed that commercial gambling teaches and encourages greed and is a stumbling block to God's love. But this problem will only be solved by people of good will -- hopefully by people like you and me.

"I am disappointed that the state has not learned and is going in this direction again. My experience tells me that the longer we resist learning our lessons, the harder life gets."

I was on a roll, but Raggetti interrupted. "But maybe God chose to intervene in our lottery because it was corrupt. Among other things, Andy, your battle flushed out a den of thieves in our organization. I suppose we should be thankful for that, and even reward you -- especially since you have refused to take any of the prize money for yourself.

"One of the reasons I wanted to talk is to offer you a position as a consultant. With your expertise you could be valuable to us -- a good six figure salary I would imagine."

I should not have been surprised. I can be so naïve. They will always believe I cheated them, that somehow I had discovered how to manipulate the lottery games. "My expertise?" I asked.

"Well, whatever God has shown you about the weaknesses and vulnerability of our security and our processes."

I couldn't figure out if he was humoring me and my theology, or if he might actually believe God taught me how to cheat. "Mr. Raggetti, thank you for the offer. It's very generous, but I have a pension and I'm getting along very well; actually, I'm starting to enjoy not working any longer. But it puzzles me, you not only have been keeping an eye on me, but you have investigated me as thoroughly as anyone has ever been investigated -- background check would be a serious understatement. So tell me, when you read over my life's story, my interests, my pursuits, my associations, my friendships, my degrees, my work in a half-dozen small rural churches, and my preoccupation with finding the right wife, tell me what gives you any hint whatsoever that I could have some expertise that your staff cannot detect?"

He swallowed his last bite of tortellini and smiled at me. "Andy, really! The hint is there for everyone to see: four successive lottery jackpots. Do you really expect anyone to believe that they were a matter of miraculous luck? Especially after you went on television and predicted your fourth win?! Yes, I read your story, but there are two men who died at your residence whom we could not talk to, so the story is incomplete.

"Of course you dislike the lottery, but I am giving you a chance to at least keep it fair and honest. And you could take your reward and give it away if you like."

"More wine?"

"Just two fingers, please."

I poured and said, "Well, Mr. Raggetti, you're not the only one who doesn't believe that my numbers were picked by God as some divine, playful, miraculous lesson. So I'm not too offended that you think I'm not telling you the truth. And it really doesn't matter much since God seems to be very quiet about the greedy little games starting back up again. I meant what I wrote to you, don't worry."

Joseph Raggetti lifted his glass, "Then a toast, Andy, to your long and peaceful retirement. And for God's sake, be careful out there on that lake."

I drank, but I knew there was a threat implied. And I knew he knew I knew.

Chapter 14

The more complex the organism, and the longer it lives, the more opportunity for something to go wrong with its body. I don't know if that's true, but as a species human beings' bodies seem to need loads of medical care compared to our animal cousins. I wonder how we would fare if we lived healthy life-styles, stopped polluting and quit hurting each other? Trouble is, we tend to be dangerous and sloppy. I wonder how we got this far?

I was trying to put these puzzle pieces together for a sermon I would never preach as Barbara and I drove down and around the foothills toward Stockton in the Central Valley. Our mission was to get a better picture of her shoulder.

"How many times have you been married?" she asked, seemingly out of the blue.

"Four."

"Any of them ever get cancer?"

"No. Good sex prevents cancer," and I turned to her and gave her a smile.

"I hope you're right. My doctor says I have a troublesome spot on a bone in my shoulder."

"Oh? I thought you had an injury."

"Maybe. The x-ray was not conclusive."

"Are you worried? I mean, how worried are you?"

"Let's just say I'll breathe easier when it's ruled out."

In a hospital waiting room we read magazines and waited. They had taken the CAT scan and told Barbara that per her doctor's orders they wanted her to come back after lunch when their staff had a chance to read it. It might save her another long ride for any follow-up.

We went to a western wear store and found me a pair of riding boots that weren't too pointy. I thanked old Jacob and the mortuary, and decided to wear them to start breaking them in. Afterward we grabbed a quick sandwich and hurried back to wait.

As a pastor I have spent more than my fair share of time in hospitals, yet they still make me nervous. Besides the death thing, there is just so much that goes on that I don't understand; much of it hidden behind pseudo-scientific language. Maybe this is why, as I read Newsweek, I was struck by how many ads there were for prescription drugs. They had pictures of healthy, vital people saying I should tell my doctor that I wanted their pills. And on the next page there was always an hour's worth of dreary reading that in essence said they were not responsible if their pills made me sick or killed me. How did we come to accept this practice?

I accompanied Barbara when she was called in. The doctor introduced himself and apologized for our long wait, but it had given their team a chance to discuss her test. He switched on a video screen and showed us the x-ray taken the week before and pointed to a spot the size of a thumbnail that I wouldn't have noticed. Then he showed the CAT scan image. The spot was a tumor, clearly. It was at the end of her upper arm in her shoulder on the bone ironically called the humerus. It had been masquerading as bursitis. He said there was a 50% chance it was cancerous, but they needed to take a biopsy to diagnose it. He said they had an opening and suggested that she have it done that afternoon; then it would take three days for the lab report. It wasn't a pleasant procedure, he said, but they would try to make it as comfortable as they could.

Barbara said she didn't want to wait. The pain had become worse recently and she wanted to get it taken care of. When the doctor stepped out to set up the procedure, Barbara said, "It doesn't surprise me. It has bothered me for too long. I had a bad feeling about it."

"How are you right now?"

She took a big breath and said, "My father died of cancer," and then tears rolled down her cheeks. "I'm not ready, Andy."

"No Sugar, of course you're not. And no one has said you are going to die either. Right now it's just a threat. Tell me, Cowgirl, how do you normally deal with threats?"

"Find out if it's real, then get angry and fight back."

"Good. And when you are tired or overwhelmed, I'll help you." She reached out for me and I took her hand. "Now, what do you need to know from the doctor?"

We made a list of questions and when he returned he took time to answer the ones he could. While she was getting the biopsy, I called the hotel and alerted them that she was not feeling well and wouldn't be in for the dinner shift. When she walked back into the waiting room she was pale and had her right arm in a sling.

As we left Stockton and made our way up through the oaks and hills, I was humming while occasionally glancing at the white car in my mirror. Barbara said that the tune sounded familiar and asked what it was. I hummed some more until I identified it myself: an old hymn that our parents probably sang, "His Eye Is On the Sparrow." She asked me if I could sing it. I said my singing voice might make her feel worse. She laughed and said she would risk it. So I sang the soft and lilting melody:

> Let not your heart be troubled,
> His tender word I hear;
> And resting on His goodness
> I lose my doubts and fears;
> Though on the path He leadeth
> But one step can I see:
> His eye is on the sparrow,
> And I know He watches me.
> I sing because I'm happy,
> I sing because I'm free,

> For His eye is on the sparrow,
> And I know He watches me.

Tears again glistened on her cheeks; she turned to me and said, "I believe that, Andy."

"Then you have already won half the battle."

Torture is truly a horrible word. And because it is still a human pastime that we employ to dominate each other, I will not call insomnia torture. But it's close. Unwelcome wakefulness in the deep, dark night can make you feel endlessly victimized and wondering when it will end as you project a tired and dreary day ahead. In my life it only happens occasionally, for which I'm thankful, and it serves to help me appreciate a good night's sleep. Thursday night was such a night.

I was awakened by my bladder around three and then a low-grade anxiety pestered me for an hour before I surrendered and turned on the light and picked up my journal and pen. It wasn't hard to pinpoint the twin sources of my worries: Friday Barbara would most likely find out the nature of her bone tumor; and the first lotto game in nineteen months would be played in California.

I didn't want Barbara to have cancer. (What a sentence!) I mean, I didn't want anyone to have cancer, but I had a surprisingly deep desire and personal vested interest that Barbara not get cancer. That possibility was painful to me; but pain is what you are in for when you let someone into your life, when you – yes, I will say it – love someone.

That late night thought would have been enough to keep me up. But there was another, and actually scarier thought. I wondered if God was done bothering me with the lottery thing? I knew my pronouncements that God was now disinterested in the lottery were only wishful thinking (as if I could really know what God was up to!) They were prompted by my lack of pointed dreams and coincidences which had driven me to buy the four lottery tickets over a year ago. I couldn't sleep because I was holding my breath, anxiously waiting for the first of the new games to be played without me getting sucked in. And obviously, it's hard to sleep when you're holding your breath.

I set aside my journal, sat up straighter, opened my hands and closed my eyes. I pictured Barbara with the power and light of life around her, and lifted her up into God's hands for blessing and let her go.

Then I struggled to come up with an image to use for my other fear. I tried picturing myself tearing up a lottery ticket and I had to smile. How many people were praying to win the jackpot, and here I was praying I wouldn't.

I tried picturing the Lottery Center which I had visited several times and letting that image go into God's hands. Then I brought to mind Joseph Raggetti, and I asked God to bless him. But after twenty minutes of meditative prayer I was not breathing any easier.

I got up and made some chamomile tea with a slice of lemon. There still was no hint of dawn. I took the tea to bed. I let the warmth of the mug radiate into my hands, and the whiffs of steam flow up and around my face. I sipped slowly the essence of chamomile flowers and the tartness of the lemon. I took pleasure in the flavors filling my mouth, and I followed the warmth of the tea down into my body. Sip-by-sip my shoulders relaxed and my breathing became peaceful. I sent a light prayer of blessing towards those who helped provide the tea and fruit and water.

This mindful cup of tea did what my meditative prayer could not do that night: it coaxed out my willingness to be partners with God. In a soft voice I said, "Lord, you help me deal with Barbara's tumor however it turns out, and I will help you deal with the lottery however you want."

It was not so much a deal as an affirmation that God would be there for me and I would be there for God.

I set my mug aside and turned off the light and slept for an hour before I woke up out of a dream. I was again in my burning cabin trying to find the door in the fog-like smoke. Joy, as a wise older woman, was there urging me to sit down out of the smoke and assured me that the fire would not hurt me. But I complained that there was no way out, and she said that was alright, because the fire was on the outside.

The lake was appearing in the early morning light, and it was espresso time. As I went through my ritual I considered the dream. The cabin stood for my life and its situation. My life had grown smaller, more compact, and simpler – hence, a cabin. I felt as if my life was burning up and being destroyed, and there was nothing I could do to stop it. I identified this as an expression of my feelings about retirement. The fire outside referred to the externals of my life – they come and go, and they constantly change. It is nothing to be alarmed about. But my being, my soul, is a part of a fundamental eternal presence. This Spirit is the fabric of the universe. I need to sit amidst the changes, my dream was telling me, and not lose sight of this reality.

In many ways it was similar to my dream of children playing peek-a-boo in a cheery coffin. But I puzzled over the image of Joy as a wise old woman. Or was it the medicine woman Red Cloud? And why would this message come through her?

Friday afternoon I was brushing and feeding the horses when Barbara came walking over from her house, her arm still in a sling. "I knew you would be a good stable boy."

"Funny, I don't feel too stable since I became a pensioner."

"Miss preaching the good news?"

"Some."

"Well I've got good news. I was tired of waiting so I called my doctor and got him to call Stockton. He just called back. I have an Eosinophilic Granuloma; it means a benign rough-looking tumor that is easily stained with an acid dye."

"Alleluia!" I put my arms gingerly around her.

She held me tight with her good arm. "That was a close one, Sugar. I guess you won't have to do my funeral quite yet."

I let her go, "Oh, I doubt one little cancerous tumor would have been the end of you. It wasn't even on your best part!" and I slapped her rear.

"Spoken like a true man of faith."

"That's right. I knew whatever the outcome, we could have dealt with it."

"Thanks for the vote of confidence, Andy. I'm still looking at an operation and a possible bone graft; but in light of what could have been, it feels like no big deal, especially knowing you're here."

"I'll be glad to be your stable boy, temporarily."

"Good! Then let me show you how to deal with horses hooves."

"What!"

"You can't let them walk around with crap embedded between their shoes and feet. We have a little tool for that. Sort of like what you use between my toes," and I got a big flirty grin. How good to see that again.

* * *

Barbara and her good news made the afternoon fly by. It was only when the sun was setting that I gave the lottery a thought again. Soon the cut-off time for buying a ticket for Friday night's inaugural jackpot came and went, and I had received no prompting to buy a ticket. It was a good day. I spent the evening playing my harmonica and working on a new song: "Will You Be My Winning Ticket, Baby?"

Chapter 15

Saturday morning as I left for the rehearsal luncheon, the white car was conspicuously absent. There had been no winner for Friday's game and evidently I was not the only one breathing easier. Hopefully, Raggetti could drop any contingency plans for me to have a boating accident.

It was the weekend before the wedding. Nathan and Cindy spent the morning at the hotel finalizing plans with Barbara and the cook. Bobby was there to meet with them next about the music. While he was waiting and checking out the church, I had a chance to talk to him about my new song. Bobby was all about music and would play at the slightest suggestion. I played the tune for him on my harmonica. He got out his acoustic guitar and helped me tweak the melody to make it more interesting. We were in full blues mode when Nathan and Cindy walked in. They stood at the back, smiling and listening, as we brought the tune around to the beginning and stopped.

As a joke I said, "I wrote a song for your wedding."

"Are you kidding?" Nathan said, "Let's hear it."

"Okay, just for fun. I call it, 'Are You My Winning Ticket, Baby?'" I turned to Bobby, "It has three verses."

"Fine, keep it slow and throw in a riff between the lines, and follow me."

We played the melody through once and when I sang the first line, "I've been so unlucky, they call me the four-time loser," Cindy shrieked and yelled, "Yes!"

After we finished, Nathan said, "You wrote that?"

"I'm afraid so. But half the tune is Bobby's."

"Perfect; we have to use it in the wedding."

I looked at Cindy. She was nodding. "All right, but of course my fee will go up quite a bit." There was a hesitation as if they didn't know I was kidding. "It's going to cost you, oh I'd say, another $1.50."

It's rare to pull one over on a couple of lawyers. They laughed and said, "Would lunch do?"

"Hey, I'm a pensioner, and Bobby is a starving musician, lunch will always do."

We spent a little time talking about music for the service, then walked across the street to the hotel. Nathan said, "Thank you, Andy, for taking Mom for her test. Typical, we didn't know she had a problem until today."

"If she could have hid the sling you probably wouldn't have known until after your honeymoon."

"She has always been very independent; even more so since her last divorce and the war between my sisters and her.

I raised my eyebrows – that was news to me.

"I don't think they are planning to come to the wedding."

"Sorry to hear that; it's not Barbara's wedding."

"I know, but I've learned not to get in the middle of these things."

The hotel bar was lively when we walked in. It would be a big wedding party: five bridesmaids, five groomsmen, a Best Man, a Matron of Honor and two flower girls; plus there were Cindy's parents and two brothers (Nathan's father was, as Barbara put it, pleasantly deceased), several miscellaneous spouses and children, and me – the reluctant minister.

Soon we moved into the dining room, with its 130-year-old stone walls, which was reserved for this gathering. I sat at a table with Bobby and a photographer who was up and down throughout the luncheon with its toasts and speeches of good wishes. This gave me a chance to ask Bobby what he would charge to tutor me in the blues harmonica, maybe twice a month? He said he would tutor me for free if I could steer some weddings and funerals his way. It sounded slightly unethical, but it was a good deal and I said sure. He suggested that I buy at least two more harmonicas in different keys. Then he spent a good portion of the luncheon explaining blues chord progression theory; and he suggested five good blues recording artists to listen to, and even offered to loan me his CDs.

After lunch we all walked back to the church for the wedding rehearsal. We spent an hour blocking where people would stand or sit. We practiced the procession and recession. And we walked through the order of service and decided where the music would be inserted.

At the end, I had everyone sit in the folding chairs that had been brought in, and I addressed them. "As you have figured out, this is going to be a different kind of wedding. Every wedding is full of symbols, from the white dress, to the candles, to the giving away of the bride, to the rings, to the spreading of rose petals and the throwing of rice. Even the church and the altar are symbols. These familiar symbols are old and traditional, so much so that we seldom stop and think: what do they represent? And do we really buy into their meaning?

"To their credit, Cindy and Nathan have given some thought to the symbols they are using: an abandoned church says something about institutional religion in our world. Perhaps it is an open space to be filled with our own personal experience of spirituality. And Halloween, a night to acknowledge the dead who in some ways hover around us in our daily lives and have more influence on us than we want to admit – influence through memory and teaching, or actual presence; Halloween symbolizes our need to honor and acknowledge them, even gift and treat them, so not to be blindsided by them.

"And spooky costumes symbolize our ability to face and even laugh at our fears, even at death (which is just a profound illusion).

"Perhaps you can see that these unusual symbols are particularly meaningful for marriage, which for many (I would say, most) is synonymous with difficult struggles, with partners who have a monstrous side, with the ghosts of old expectations, and of abrupt death-like endings.

"In the face of this gloom, Nathan and Cindy want us to laugh and celebrate with them. Why? Because love is possible. Every moment, in every situation, with every person, love is possible. And this couple has said yes to this possibility. I believe God will bless their boldness and courage because God is love. So please, come ready to join in this fun and unique love-fest. I ask everyone here to help Cindy and Nathan have a wonderful time next Friday night.

"Now all we need to do is pass the offering plates and go home."

"Not so fast," Cindy said hurriedly, "We have costume fittings for the groomsmen and bridesmaids, and you, Reverend."

For a while there was chaos as people sorted themselves out. Some went back to the bar to have a beer and watch the baseball playoffs. Some headed home. Some brought in boxes of costumes and began laying them out. Barbara moseyed up to where I stood out of the way; she carried a bottle of water to offer me with her good arm. "I think that was the first time I've seen you in action, Rev, you were great. You are so comfortable in front of people. You kept it light, but kept things moving. And at the end you get an E for effort in trying to convince us that a vampire's costume was as appropriate as a white dress!" she laughed, "Nice try!"

"Thanks, I think. How's your arm doing with all this activity?"

"Fine. Having something to do helps me keep my mind off it. Given the fact that they shoved a pencil sized thingy into my shoulder, all the way to the bone, then scraped it on my tumor, I guess it could feel worse."

"How about I give you a foot massage tonight?"

"You know, you're a pretty sweet man."

"Careful Cowgirl, weddings can put a magical, if artificial, glow around things."

Cindy's mother came up to me with two boxes. She was a hands-on, get-things-done kind of person, and very motherly. "All right, Reverend, here you go. I think you've got the best one of all. We found a theater company that was having a costume sale."

As we opened the boxes, Barbara said, "See you later, Merlin. I'd better get to work."

I lifted a green cassock out of the box. The front was appliquéd with gold stars and comets and a shimmering moon covered with sequins. I pulled off my sweater and slipped the cassock over my head and pulled it down. Mercifully, it was a generous fit. Then I lifted a heavy purple robe out of the box and put it on over the cassock. It was open wide in front and the large sleeves were hemmed with ornate trim. A large hood hung down the back and the robe dragged wonderfully behind me as I walked in a circle.

"There's more, Reverend," and she opened the second box and took out a long white wig. I must have looked at it askance because she said, "Come on, this is going to be great," and she had me sit down so she could slip it on and adjust it.

It hung past my shoulders and I complained, "This is getting a little too strange."

"Wait a minute," she said, "there's more." She came up with a headband of golden stars, and she fitted it over the wig. Then she stood back and said, "I see what you mean. Let's try something." She went to her purse and got an elastic band and proceeded to put the wig into a pony tail. She nodded and smiled, "You should take a look."

I walked to the men's room and looked at Merlin. It was a very classy costume, and I even liked the white pony tail with the headband. When I came out I said, "Great!"

She said, "I thought it needed to be accessorized with a medallion, but the only thing I could find at home was this." She handed me a silver peace sign on a leather thong. "It's my husband's. He had it on when I first met him, it's a precious memento, so don't lose it." I hung his chick magnet around my neck and walked around again to get a feel for the outfit. "Oh, there should be a staff. I wonder if it's still in the car. I'll be right back."

Showing off my costume, I strolled past the bridesmaids who were getting their hems adjusted on their witches' robes. I put my hands in the big pockets of my robe and felt a small piece of paper – I pulled it out and stopped in my tracks. I stared at an old faded lottery ticket. I shook my head. Was this a joke? Cindy's mother came in the door and I walked over to her, "Did you leave this in the pocket?"

"No. I never even checked the pockets. Maybe it was the last actor to use this robe? I found the staff," and she handed me a long, silver-painted walking stick with a star at the top. "You think it is a winning ticket?" she said with a grin.

Everyone looks at a lottery ticket with hope. I looked at it again, and read out loud, "December 14, 2008."

"Oh, that's long gone, unless Merlin can do some magic!" Then she stepped back, "You know, Reverend, this costume fits you fine. Why don't you take it home as is."

"Okay, thanks for your help." I was still looking at the ticket when she walked away; or more accurately, I was looking at the date on the ticket. It was the date of the first of my four wins. Impossible. But how could someone find a ticket this old and significant to play a joke on me? I checked the pockets again. Nothing. I began to take off the costume, and as I carefully folded it I noticed it also had two inside pockets. So I checked them and found a folded dollar bill. I looked around to see if anyone was watching and laughing. No one.

I sat down in my cassock and held the ticket and dollar bill together. It was a dream-like moment. I studied the six numbers on the ticket. None of them meant anything in particular to me, but the message seemed clear: here is a dollar, and here are some numbers, get busy. I flashed on my letter to Raggetti, "Don't worry, I'm out of the game."

I put the items in my wallet and finished packing the costume. I picked up my notebook, which contained the outline for the wedding service, and neatly rewrote the order of service as we had adjusted it in the rehearsal. Cindy was planning to have wedding programs printed up with the order inside and a list of participants on the back.

I took out the ticket from my wallet and breathed a sigh; I was out of the game, but maybe others could pick up the ball. At the bottom of my order of service, I wrote: For Those Who Believe In Magic; Here Is A Halloween Treat, 8, 11, 17, 31, 35, 7 (numbers for Saturday's Super Lotto).

Then I just sat and watched Cindy from across the sanctuary. After a while I caught her eye and motioned for her to come over. "Here's the order of service for your program," handing it to her as she arrived.

She in turn handed me a check for $350. "Thank you for everything, Andy." She smiled, then like a good lawyer she looked over the outline. "What's this?" she asked pointing to my addendum.

"Cindy, listen to me," and in a deliberate tone I said, "I don't know anything about those numbers. If you put them in your bulletin it is your choice."

She looked at me and squinted, "Reverend Andy Shepard, you are at it again. What are we going to do with you?"

"I don't know what you are talking about."

She smiled and shook her head and turned around to leave.

"It would be a good idea to throw my notes away when you are done with them."

Without turning around she nodded.

* * *

Saturday evening I got a call from Barbara. She was home and would be glad to collect on my promise of a foot massage. I walked up the drive under the stars toward her house. Like a magnet the lottery ticket pulled at my thoughts. Was I leaping to conclusions? Was I just suspicious of God and over-reacting to anything having to do with the lottery? If it was a sign (and I do believe in signs) did I follow it or did I take a detour by pawning it off on the wedding guests? And if an unusual number of them play, and win, will Raggetti and Company follow the trail back to me? Then what?

I could feel a Jonah-like rant at God rising up in me as I reached Barbara's door. Before I rang the bell I turned and looked back out toward the lake which was hidden in the darkness. I may have had pensioner issues when I moved here, but it was comfortable to be hidden in the anonymity of an out-of-the-way rural cabin. But the action I took today could certainly shine a spotlight on me again.

Then I remembered the agreement: God would help me deal with Barbara's tumor, and I would help God deal with the lottery. How come it always feels like God gets the better end of the deal? Now I know how Jonah felt at the end of the story. Sure, he got rescued from the whale's belly, but in the end he felt he had been had.

I rang the doorbell. When Barbara answered she was wearing a nightgown. "Ah, the best stable boy a gal ever had. Come on in."

She got so much pleasure from teasing me I just played along. As I stepped inside, I said, "You are so kind to your humble servant. How can I ever repay you?"

"Oh, I think we can spread it out with an easy payment plan."

"I am so grateful; you are the easiest woman I have ever known."

She gave me a feigned shocked look and hesitated. I think she wondered how serious I was with that comment, as if a part of her felt she indeed was too sexually available to me; or perhaps it was just the unwritten feminine rule: Thou shalt never make it too easy.

"I'm going to let that comment slide for now, but you may have to pay extra later."

We walked to the living room coffee table where she had set up wine, cheese, crackers, and sliced fresh pears. We sat together on the couch. One of our relaxation CDs for massage was playing.

"This looks great," I said, and picked up the bottle of wine and looked at the label: Seven Deadly Zins, 2007 Lodi Zinfadel. I smiled at the inference and said, "Can I pour for you?"

"Thanks," she said, and gave me a big smile that I couldn't quite read. "So, how does it feel to be back in the wedding business?"

I set the bottle down thoughtfully and handed her the glass. "Mixed emotions, I guess. It's a delight working with your kids, but not all weddings are feel-good occasions; nor so creative."

"You seem so good at it though. Nathan is very impressed."

"Yes, this has worked out well. But I don't expect a lot of couples to beat a path to my door."

"I suppose if you had your own church it would help."

"Trouble is, churches come with congregations, and they're a boat-load of work and heart-ache. I'm done being a pastor, I'm sure of that."

"Not all churches come with congregations." And now Barbara's smile grew more mischievous.

I waited, thinking there must be more to this. She picked up a file folder from the table and handed it to me. I opened it and began to thumb through the pages of a real estate contract; under the contract was a Title Report and Title Insurance Agreement; under that was a Real Estate Disclosure Statement. I turned back to the front of the file and looked more carefully while Barbara ate a slice of pear and sipped her wine. My name was entered as the buyer. The selling price was one dollar.

"One dollar? What's going on here, Barbara?"

"It seems someone has bought you the church in Moke Hill."

"Who?"

"I don't know. My friend Harvey, the realtor who owns it, wouldn't tell me. He said the person who set it up insisted that they be kept anonymous. Harvey agreed. He has been desperate to unload it. All you have to do is sign and notarize this paperwork and pay the asking price, one dollar! And it's yours. And you can't say you don't have a dollar bill."

She grinned. She knew I had found a dollar bill! My mind raced. "You talked to Cindy's mother?"

"No."

"Then you put the dollar in the robe?"

"Trick or Treat!"

I looked at the paperwork again. "Did you pay for the church?"

"Are you kidding, Honey?! I'm terribly fond of you, but if I had that kind of money lying around, these feet wouldn't be so tired every night. No, Harvey told me about the deal this morning and he agreed to let me present it to you. So I sneaked the dollar and the lottery ticket into your pocket for fun. You hit the jackpot, Merlin."

I just looked at her. I felt totally confused. I had to walk through it again. "Someone paid Harvey for the church, and asked him to sell it to me for a dollar?"

"Right."

"And you put the old ticket and a dollar in the robe's pocket to announce the gift to me -- like I had won a jackpot?"

"Right! So what did you think when you found it?"

I was embarrassed. I shook my head and took a big drink of the Deadly Zins. I thought of my wedding bulletin addendum. Barbara was going to find out anyway; "I took it as a sign from God to hassle the lottery again."

She laughed out loud and doubled over towards me and put her hand on my leg. She took a breath and said, "Oh, Sugar. You didn't buy a ticket, did you?"

Now I was embarrassed and a bit pissed. At her? Or at me? I shook my head back and forth.

"Oh good. We don't need the guy in the white car stalking us anymore."

"But I did something better."

"What?"

"I put your ticket's numbers in the wedding bulletin and indicated they were for Saturday's jackpot."

"No!" and she doubled up again with laughter. Then she said, "There are going to be some disappointed people."

That's right! I thought to myself. And part of me felt a great relief -- no more craziness after all. Yet to my surprise there was also some disappointment. A part of me wanted to throw a monkey wrench into the Lottery works again and shut it down for good. I felt so sure that was exactly what was going to happen. Then another question came to mind, "Where did you get that old ticket?"

"I used to be a regular player until you came along saying commercial gambling was a greed machine, and messed it up for everyone. One of my kitchen drawers is filled with my old tickets. At one point I thought I would catalog my numbers so I wouldn't repeat them."

"So you just grabbed one at random?"

"Yeah, sorry. No prayer or anything."

"Nonetheless, you happened to pick the one that you played the very week of my first jackpot, December 14th, 2008.

"Really?"

"That was one of the reasons I thought it was a sign."

"That's weird, Andy. I guess I really messed with your mind. I'm sorry, Sugar," she said with extra syrup, "You still going to rub my feet?" as she wiggled a foot in front of me.

I smiled and said, "Oh baby, you know I live for these toes."

She had the oil and a towel on the end table. I suggested she stretch out and lean back on the arm of the couch. I got her a pillow and covered her with a throw. I sat at the other end of the couch with her feet in my lap on top of the towel. I rolled up my sleeves and oiled my hands and began with a gentle, loving touch. Barbara had not known what her fun little surprise would do to me. It had put me in a whirlwind -- like the bump on her bone that looked like deadly cancer, the old ticket pointed me toward a place I didn't want to go.

As I massaged her feet I let my hands speak words of forgiveness -- both for her and for me. It's all right to be an idiot sometimes. And I suspected Cindy would think I was odd for misleading her with my numbers and my reputation. And I supposed she would think me odder if I now tried to reverse direction.

Fifteen minutes seemed like a long foot massage, but Barbara begged for more. When she finally lapsed into sleepy deep breathing I quit and helped her into bed, kissed her goodnight, turned off the bedroom lights, and carried the dishes to the kitchen. Then, to satisfy one more nagging question, I opened a few kitchen drawers until I found her stash of old lottery tickets. There was a drawer full, maybe several hundred. But how did she happen to pick December 14, 2008? The question still nagged.

I picked up the file folder, turned off the rest of the lights, locked the door and left my landlady sleeping soundly with the rent paid in full.

Chapter 16

I still suspected that my phone could be tapped, so on Sunday morning I took myself to a rare breakfast out at a coffee shop in Valley Springs and used a pay phone to call Harvey.

"Good morning, Harvey Snider Realty, how can I help you?"

"Hi Harvey. This is Andy Shepard."

"Yes."

"Barbara gave me the paperwork last night."

"Good. Does it meet with your approval?"

"It's an interesting offer. But I'm reluctant to accept it without knowing where this gift is coming from. Gifts can have strings attached."

"I assure you Rev. Shepard, there were no contingencies mentioned by my client."

"Harvey, I can keep a secret. Confidentiality is part of clergy ethics. If you can tell me who is giving me the church, I will gladly take it off your hands."

"I can't do that Reverend. In this matter I don't represent you, I represent my client, and I'm bound by an ethical code too. This client was clear that the deal only stands with confidentiality. I could be sued later if I violate that agreement."

I thought of challenging Harvey about realtors who commonly fudge on rules to make a sale; but I decided that in a small community I shouldn't burn any bridges unnecessarily.

"I appreciate that, Harvey. I also appreciate that for over a year you have been trying to market this old building in a little tourist town that has few tourists. So here is how I will help you. I will say a name and you just say no if it wasn't them. This way you will not actually give up the name of the donor."

"Look Reverend, if you don't want to accept a questionable gift from an organization which you do not agree with and have perhaps opposed in the past, why not do what you have done before and just give it away?"

I smiled, "Thank you for your advice Harvey. I will get started on the paperwork. But please tell the seller that I can't buy a church without chairs, one hundred twenty nice, padded, stackable, blue chairs. And the church office is incomplete without a computer, printer and a good copier." That should buy me some time.

"Very good. I'm glad we have an understanding. Talk to you later."

So, Raggetti couldn't give me cash for a bogus job, thus he cleverly bought me a church to hook me; just a little insurance in case I had any ideas to bring his world crashing down around him. He must be a good judge of character since I did jump at the first chance to do just that.

Driving home I wondered what I would do with a church building that nobody wanted. I smiled at Barbara's delight to deliver the church to me, a guy who couldn't afford a modest rental; now he would have his own church. Did she think churches were money machines? Just open the doors and people would walk in and open their wallets? I'd be lucky to pay the utility bills.

But more importantly, what would it mean to take a gift from the lottery? They would have their hooks into me. I needed some help figuring this out, so I decided to call Josh. I invited him to dinner Monday night. He said it was about time, and what could he bring? I said: some good beer.

* * *

I made one of my favorite dishes: enchiladas filled with red peppers, onions, asparagus, cubed polenta and cheddar cheese. The side dish would be avocado and grape tomatoes with a balsamic vinegar dressing.

There was still a little light on Hogan Lake when he arrived. Josh's beer selection did not disappoint, so we sat outside on the patio and enjoyed the beer with chips and salsa. While the enchiladas finished cooking, I brought Josh up to date: the lurking private investigator, the implied threats of Joseph Raggetti, Barbara's old lottery ticket, my Halloween lottery treat for the wedding guests, and the chapel bribe.

Josh listened to this improbable litany with a grin and an occasional nod. Then he took a drink and said, "Very good Andy. The Foundation has been receiving calls this past week from reporters who wanted to interview you for the start-up of the new lottery. They would have loved to have heard this story. You're making this up, of course."

"Of course," I said, then stepped inside to check on the dinner. I came out with the real estate folder and handed it to my old friend who should have known by now that no one could make up a life like mine.

He looked at the first couple of pages and said, "Shit, Andy, you're serious. You said a few weeks ago that you hadn't heard from Sacramento."

"That day on the lake seems like a long time ago, Josh. Life has gotten complicated out here in pensionville, and I don't know what to do."

"Have you had any helpful dreams?"

I took a scoop of salsa on a tortilla chip and popped it in my mouth. I really didn't want to deal with my dreams; but Josh was here to help, and he knew about my active dream life. "Not that helpful, mostly they've been about my retirement. One was about decorating my coffin; another repeating dream is about this cabin engulfed in flames."

"God, Andy! You're going through it, aren't you?"

"I assume we all are."

"Yes, but...? Okay, tell me about the second dream."

I said, "How about we go inside. Dinner should be ready."

We moved to my small kitchen table and opened two more beers. From the oven I lifted the baking dish with half a dozen enchiladas and set it on a pad on the table. Then I pulled out the avocado salad and some sour cream from the refrigerator.

"Excellent, Andy. I've missed your cooking."

"You want to say grace?"

"Sure."

We paused in silence, then Josh began praying the 23rd Psalm:

The Lord is my shepherd,
I lack nothing.
He makes me lie down in green pastures,
He leads me beside quiet waters,
He refreshes my soul.
He guides me along the right paths
For His name's sake.
Even though I walk through the darkest valley,
I will fear no evil,
For you are with me;
Your rod and your staff comfort me.
You prepare a table before me
In the presence of my enemies.
You anoint my head with oil,
And my cup overflows.
Surely your goodness and love
Will follow me all the days of my life,
And I will dwell in the house of the Lord
Forever.

"Thank you, Josh, that was a good reminder for me." I dished out an enchilada for each of us, then passed the sour cream. "The repeating fire dream is short and to the point." I described it and touched on my uncertainty about the Joy figure in it. "I thought it was about the changes in my life this year; but I'm starting to feel the heat (you might say) of the lottery starting up again, so the dream now seems more immediate somehow. And this church gift has got me feeling stuck. It should be an easy decision: laugh it off and reject it. But it isn't feeling that way at all."

"I see that. It's the threat -- Raggetti's implied threat. You're not dealing with someone like Charles Morely two years ago. He was a pathetic embezzler, desperately trying to cover his tracks. You got in his face and he crumbled.

"You are dealing with someone much more powerful who has unlimited resources. So the real estate issue is a big question mark: what happens if you don't take the bait? What's Raggetti's next move? You are a tremendous threat to him; that is why he is threatening you. But if he can set you up with a new ministry, church and all, he will feel more in control. And the door is still open for him to get your secret information of how you unlocked the vault of the California Lottery. If you refuse to play ball, he'll feel nervous and out of control -- then what are his options? Put yourself in his shoes."

"Okay. He believes I somehow cheated his employer -- the Italian company that has the lottery contract. Their investigation last year assumed that I had conspirators inside. They caught their three managers scamming their scratcher's game. One was killed, Charley Morely, at my house. The pressure was on for the other two to implicate me in the freaky jackpots that I won. But of course, they were just as confounded about my wins as was their home office; in fact, it was my wins that put a spotlight on their little scratchers operation.

"Now the previous managers are locked away, so in Raggetti's eyes I shouldn't be much of a threat since I have lost my inside help. My guess is he has been keeping an eye on me in order to see if I have new connections."

"Yes, that makes sense," Josh agreed. "And there are two things that have protected you: they still don't know how you and those imagined inside friends actually manipulated the numbers. That worries them. If they get rid of you, they will never know."

"Get rid of me?"

"Come on Andy, it's not a State bureaucracy that you are threatening. It's a multi-national gambling outfit. Don't underestimate the trouble you are in. Your deep subconscious mind knows -- your house is surrounded by flames."

"You think their next move is to kill me!?"

"Look at you. You have no family, no possessions, no job -- nothing they can use for leverage. Your life is all you have left."

"You said I had two things protecting me."

"Fame. It's amazing how much power fame has. Remember your reception at the Cowboy Bistro? It is a tricky thing to assassinate a celebrity. When the police ask who would benefit from your death, the lottery would be high on the list."

"Yeah, along with an ex-spouse or two."

"That's right. They would have to set someone up to look like the murderer. Or, they would have to really make it look like an accident."

"This is cheery."

"But in spite of yourself you may have helped yourself out with the Halloween numbers."

"What do you mean?"

"If they get wind of it, they may see your losing numbers as the end of your threat."

"Right, it could signal the loss of my powers or something. Using my reputation to tease the wedding guests could indicate it's now all in the past."

"No one won the first game on Saturday, so let's hope someone hits the jackpot this week on Wednesday -- someone that isn't you. That would also make Raggetti breathe easier."

"So you are saying my strategy should be to accept the gift as a sign that I am playing ball; and use the Halloween numbers as a way to say that I am innocent and harmless."

"Possibly."

"Possibly?"

"You seem to be sure that the Halloween numbers are not going to hit on Saturday."

"Right. The whole thing was set up by Barbara."

"So?"

"That's not how it happened before. A dream gave me numbers the first time, and pointed me toward Quick Picks until they shut down the games."

"So?"

"So...what do you mean?"

"You said you were convinced that God put numbers in your pocket; so convinced that you decided to pass them on to the wedding guests."

"Right. But Barbara put them there!"

"So?! Andy, how else was God going to get them in your pocket?"

"She was just having fun with the offer of the church. It had nothing to do with numbers."

"And the date?"

"Okay. Okay! If the Halloween numbers hit, what are they going to do? Put me in a basement and torture me until I tell them how I did it?"

Josh just looked at me and I knew he thought that my disgusting exaggeration was no exaggeration.

"Shit!" I said and conceded, "I guess we need a plan B."

"Yeah, like calling the bride and telling her to delete the numbers on the program."

"Josh, I've been thinking a lot about Jonah, and…"

"All right. Then we need something else."

"You want another beer?"

"Good idea."

We drank all the beer and ate all the enchiladas and were slouched on the couch with our feet up. We were passing the time making up ridiculous plan B scenarios, like blaming my win on a Las Vegas casino conspiracy.

We were laughing when someone knocked at the door. Paranoid, we both jumped. When I opened it, there was Barbara with one arm in a sling and the other holding out a plate of cookies.

"I saw that you had company and thought maybe you could use some dessert."

"Boy, could we!" I said. "Come on in Barbara and meet my best friend. This is Josh," and I took the plate.

Josh offered her his hand, "Good to meet you Barbara."

"Hello," she said.

I closed the door. "Have a seat, and let's see what we have here."

As I unwrapped the plate, Barbara said, "Only store-bought cut and bake cookies. I have to keep it simple with this arm."

"Ah, chocolate chip. Excellent. I'll put on some water for tea."

"So, is there a special occasion tonight?" Barbara asked.

Josh looked at me in the kitchen as I weighed whether or not to tell Barbara about my dilemma. Of course, the longer I mulled over my answer, the more Barbara would be suspicious about what it was.

We had a growing friendship, and she was already a player in this drama (with both the old ticket and the old church) so I decided to let her in.

We had gone through half of the cookies when I was finished telling her about not only the recent events, but also explaining the two deaths at my house on the North Fork of the Mokelumne, and the related drama.

She looked at us, shook her head and smiled. I could tell she did not really buy my version of what she had read in the papers. "That's quite a story, boys. But your problem is simple. Get something on this Raggettti guy so he can't touch you."

"Right," I said. "That would be nice, but what?"

"I don't know. He has a boss I would suppose. Get something on him that his boss wouldn't like. Maybe he's crooked like the ones before him."

"I doubt that; and anyway, how could we find out?" I said.

"But it's a good idea, Barbara," said Josh. "If we had something on Raggetti we could create a standoff."

"But we don't have anything," I lamented.

"It doesn't have to be real," she said.

"Make something up?"

"Why not? If the numbers hit on Saturday, make it look like Raggetti was in on it. He met with you, didn't he?"

"Yes, at the Corps of Army Engineers' visitor center."

"They have a security camera, I bet. So there's video."

"Probably."

"And he wrote you a letter. Was it on letterhead?"

"Yes."

"Then you have proof that he initiated contact with you."

"He could explain it away."

"Yes. But we could copy his letterhead and create a follow-up letter confirming a conspiracy."

Josh then added, "And the church: his gift to you for your help, because you were reluctant to take cash."

"But in this scenario it doesn't make sense that I gave the numbers to the wedding guests. There may be many winners."

"Raggetti could be seen as using it as a smoke screen," Josh said. "Making it difficult to trace several million dollars going to him through one of his buddies."

Barbara summed it up, "All you have to do is hint at the video, show him the letter, and thank him for the church."

"No, not Andy, his lawyer." Josh said.

"Perfect," she agreed. "And to his boss it would look like an inside job. Even without our fabrications, Raggetti would be suspect."

"If we black-mailed him, what would be his next move?" I asked.

"To keep you from implicating him, he would have to pack up the lottery and go away," said Josh. "He would tell his boss that obviously several dozen people were fed the numbers because there had never been more than a couple of winners of the same jackpot. He would say that there was no way to know who did it or how it was done, but it had cast a dark cloud of mistrust on the legitimacy of the games that couldn't be overcome a second time."

"It might work," I said, "If we need a plan B."

"Right, like that is really going to happen," Barbara said. "My kitchen drawer is full of losing tickets, and no matter what date I picked -- your birthday, your mother's wedding anniversary, or the day you first got laid -- that ticket isn't going to win the lottery. And anyway, if it did, your best bet would not be some amateur blackmail scam, but a visit to the Sheriff's Department."

I looked at Josh. Neither of us had considered that option. "I could do a preemptive strike: go to the Sheriff this week and put him on alert. And if we hit on Saturday, we tell Raggetti that the law is involved -- perhaps he would back off."

"Only two things wrong with that plan, Andy," Josh said. "Number one, the Sheriff thinks you're a crook; number two, law enforcement isn't good at preventing murders, just investigating them after the fact."

On that depressing note, Josh said he should be going. As his taillights disappeared over the rise in the driveway, Barbara said that she was going home too. I asked if I could walk her back. She said sure. I grabbed my flashlight and the empty cookie plate, and as we were about to leave my phone rang. I studied the in-coming number; it was from Stockton. It rang again as I showed the number to Barbara.

"It's Nathan," she said.

I didn't want to take the call on my cell phone, so I pressed the button for my voice mail to pick it up. "I'd rather call him back from your phone." I said.

She nodded and we stepped out under the stars. We walked in silence for a minute. In my head I began to review the evening's conversation, but I stopped myself. I wanted to calm my spirit instead. I looked up at the night sky from horizon to horizon. It brought to mind that each star was a blazing life-giving sun; many of them much larger than our own. They were not only warming their own planets, but they were sharing their light with our planet -- and with my body. I then focused on trying to feel each star's light falling on my face, not as heat but as the energy of countless magical streams of photons which had traveled for centuries to bless me.

As I walked in that blessing, Barbara said, "Well, I managed to royally screw things up for you, Andy. I'm sorry." Her voice seemed to weave through the ancient streaming starlight. She sounded discouraged.

After a few moments I said, "It only looks like you've screwed things up, Sugar. We can't see the bigger picture. Don't worry, let it go."

"I shouldn't have come down to your place tonight. That plan we cooked up is bad. It will get you in trouble."

I smiled, "Oh, you are trouble alright. Here I am, in your wonderful cabin by the lake, where I can sail, I can ride Charley anytime I want, and," I paused to consider what word to use, "I can love you." Yes, I had to admit, I was enjoying loving Barbara. I enjoyed letting her be herself, and I delighted in her. May be it was "love lite," but that was only because I was not trying to make her my home, my source of unconditional love – that love was already inside me.

I must have startled her, because we walked along in silence through the star shower. Then I said, "And best of all, you bring me fresh baked cookies."

"You are too kind. You probably know why I came down tonight."

"Let me see, I'll take a wild guess: You thought I might be entertaining another woman in your cozy little cabin?"

"You might as well know, I can be jealous."

"Noted. And next time (you might as well know) my favorite cookies are peanut butter."

She laughed. We walked the rest of the way in silence. When we reached her door she invited me in to make the phone call.

I got Nathan on the line. "Hi, it's Andy, what's up?"

"Cindy and I have been debating (with grace pastor!) about putting the lottery numbers in the wedding program…"

"And you want to know if I am a crook and if I am drawing you into a conspiracy?"

"More or less."

"Before I say more, Nathan, will you agree to provide me with some professional advice if I drop a small check into the mail tomorrow?"

"You want confidentiality?"

"I want to protect you."

"Fine, now you are my client."

"You followed the stories about the lottery a year or two ago?"

"Yes."

"I'm still suspected of fraud. If they had a shred of evidence against me, beside the statistical improbability, I would have been arrested. But as hard as it is to believe, I did not cheat, and I'm not a crook. There's no conspiracy."

"Then tell me about these numbers."

"Nathan, it's just a hunch, yet because of past experiences, I thought it would be worth a try. And since I would rather not have another fight with the California Lottery people, I figured I wouldn't buy a ticket; I'd let twenty or thirty people from Stockton all hit the jackpot -- that might rattle the system enough to get California out of the gambling business again."

"Okay, but where did the numbers come from?"

"Your mother."

"My mother?!"

"It's a long story, but yes, your mother." I pointed the phone toward her, "Right, Barbara?"

"That's right, Nathan."

"So why...?"

"Look Nathan, they could be worthless numbers. You'll probably be razzed by your friends and they will complain that they wasted a dollar. But here is what you tell them: Trick or Treat!"

"So it's all in fun?"

"Oh, I'm having a blast. When your guests see that the infamous Rev. Andy Shepard is performing your wedding, there will be a run on the mini-marts Saturday morning."

"I get it now. Thanks, Andy."

"Sure. And Nathan?"

"Yes."

"Would you please buy your mother a ticket down there on Thursday?"

There was a long pause. Barbara raised her eyebrows at me. Nathan said, "You're kidding, right?"

"Not really; super lotto, please, not mega-lotto. Good night," and I hung up.

"What's with that?" asked Barbara.

"I know you're going to buy one, Cowgirl, and it might be best if there aren't winning tickets purchased near me. I already feel the heat."

Chapter 17

Tuesday morning I remembered no dreams, but as I foamed my latte' I remembered the evening's starlight on my face. Then sitting up in bed with my warm mug, I watched our star's dawn light break over the lake. In that peaceful hour I made a plan C and roughed out this letter:

Dear Mr. Raggetti:
I have received the church building in Mokelumne Hill and the additional equipment. Thank you for the gift. My retirement will now be much more interesting. As for my part, here are Saturday's numbers: 8, 11, 17, 31, 35, 7.
I trust your retirement will also be satisfactory.
Sincerely,
Rev. Andy Shepard
Cc: Lloyd Pettigrew, Attorney at Law
Attachments:
Letter requesting our meeting
Nice video of our lunch

By midmorning I was ready to drive over to the dam's visitor center. When I opened the door to leave, there was something hanging on the outside door handle, a gift: a silk cord with a very small pouch on it. It was obviously meant to be worn around one's neck. I lifted it and got a better look. The tiny pouch was leather with a beaded raven on the front; I loosened it to peer inside. There were three items: a small twig that on closer inspection was a bone – a bird bone I guessed because there was also a black downy feather and a sharp fine claw.

This was a medicine bag. The only person I knew who would give me something like that was Joy. I left the door open, went back inside and sat down. I turned the pouch around a few times. When had she come? What was it for? Why had she given it, and why now? Without knowing the answers to these questions, I debated whether or not to wear it. I decided to give it a try. I unbuttoned the top of my shirt and put the cord over my head. The pouch lay just below the ceramic cross that I also wore. Then I buttoned back up and laid my hand over my shirt at my chest where these two spiritual talismans nestled against my skin.

I closed my eyes and waited, breathing slowly and deeply. I remembered the day I was rooting around in my burned-out house and I found my ceramic cross which was now twice-fired. I took it as a blessing during that difficult and discouraging time. Soon after, Joy left to pursue…whatever. I guessed that this medicine bag represented part of that pursuit. In a way, we both believed in unseen power and mystery in the universe. Now I wore road signs of our two paths toward that mystery. I felt at peace with that, even though I didn't know the meaning of this new gift.

I left and drove to the dam's visitor center and chatted with the woman who ran the office. She confirmed that they had a video surveillance system. It was a digital set-up. I explained my request: I had had lunch with my nephew from New York in the picnic area. I was preparing a special e-mail for him; could I have a short clip of our visit that day?

She said, "You're Rev. Andy Shepard, aren't you?"

"Yes, I'm your neighbor now. I'm living a mile down the road."

"Are you the one with the little sailboat?"

"Right."

"It's a big lake, and the winds can be unpredictable up here, so I hope you are careful and always wear your life vest."

"Thank you. I will."

"What date and time do you need?"

"Oct. 22 at noon."

She called up a program on her computer and tapped in the date and time. She turned the screen toward me and said, "Yup, there you are, Reverend."

I took a look. "Can you stop it and zoom in?"

"Sure."

In a moment there was a clear picture of Raggetti, me and a bottle of Chianti. "Perfect. So, how can we do this?"

"Do you have an e-mail address?"

As I got to my car I vowed to take back some of the bad things I had said about computers. I drove back to the cabin and over the course of the next two hours I ended up saying more bad things about computers as I worked to get the video from my computer to a couple of thumb-drives. By noon time, any benefit I had from my morning meditation had been shot, but I had three copies of Raggetti toasting to my long life.

After lunch I put the top down on the bug and enjoyed the beautiful October weather and the fall colors showing in the black oaks as I drove to Harvey Snider Reality in Moke Hill.

Harvey said his client agreed to my counter offer – the equipment would be no problem. I wrote him a one dollar check. He said the deal could close and be recorded the next day.

My next stop was the post office. Our plan B was to wait and see if my numbers hit the jackpot before having Lloyd visit Raggetti. But I modified the plan. I didn't like the idea of forging a second letter from Raggetti, or getting my friend Lloyd so involved. The new plan had four steps: a) Raggetti initiates a meeting with me, b) he gives me a church, c) I send him a thank you letter with the numbers to the next game, d) my numbers hit with multiple winners.

If my numbers didn't hit, he would think it was a hoax, a not-so-funny joke by a crook who could no longer beat the system. I assumed he would get the letter Friday and would have a sleepless night before the lottery machinery picked Saturday's numbers. I wanted him to know that the hooks he thought he had in me didn't go very deep.

On the other hand, if my numbers hit, and a phenomenal amount of people had the winning numbers, I might be protected by a third party's knowledge (Lloyd's) of his apparent complicity.

I marked Raggetti's letter personal and confidential and sent it registered mail. My next stop was Lloyd's law office in Riverton, thirty miles upriver.

Lloyd was still the lawyer for the Foundation, and he became a true believer after my third lottery jackpot. Sitting in his office he said he had been expecting to hear from me since the lottery had restarted; and he didn't like my plan C. He said that my letter could get me charged with conspiracy and it put me at risk. I said lawyers would be out of business if people didn't take risks or make bad decisions, and then I thanked him for holding copies of my letter and the video.

Driving back to Hogan Lake I was loaded down with memories of my decade of ministry in Riverton. I would still be preaching there if it hadn't been for my dream with six numbers that forever changed Joy's and my life. When I moved to Hogan Lake in June, I tried to accept and embrace the changes. I wanted to be done with ministry and weddings, but now I would be doing a wedding in a few days; I wanted to be done with the lottery, but now I was in a lottery conspiracy; and I wanted to be done with shaman, but now I'm wearing a medicine pouch.

I could feel a blues song coming on. When I reached the lake I had a tune and two verses:

> I thought I was done
> With all my yesterdays;
> I prayed I was done
> With all my yesterdays;
> But they've caught up with me

> And now want me to pay.
> I've made some mistakes
> And I've paid me some dues;
> Yes, I've made mistakes
> And they've cost me some dues;
> But they won't leave me alone:
> These won't-let-me-go blues.

Wednesday came and went, and although there was a state-wide rush to buy lottery tickets for the new games, there was no winner for the top prize which had grown to twenty-seven million dollars. I knew this would be good news and bad news for the lottery officials: as jackpots grew, they became more exciting and attracted more players; however, anxiety would be high until someone, not named Shepard, won.

On Thursday I had my first real lesson on playing blues harmonica with Bobby. Mostly we worked on my songs for the wedding. Bobby also explained a piece of music theory that I could not grasp from my harmonica book. Harmonicas, because of their size and how they are played, do not have all the notes that a piano has. They have only the notes needed to play in a given key. He said to think of a key as a set of notes that sound good together. My first harmonica was built in the key of G and only had the eight consecutive notes that made up that key; then those notes repeated in a higher register or octave. This had the effect of making it much easier to play harmoniously and never off key.

But if one started to play a song five notes above G on a G harmonica, they would be in a different key and that key would be missing some of its notes on the G harmonica. However, in this case something magical happens: the interval of complaint is born. Instead of the melody and chord progression sounding whole and complete, it sounds like a sentence ending with a question mark (like saying, "What's up with that?") the pitch of one's voice usually indicates a complaint. And so it is with blues style harmonica:

you cross over to a key five notes above the instrument's key to get note intervals of complaint – this is called cross harp, harp because the notes are set on the instrument, cross because you cross over to a different key five notes higher than it was made for. This is the Rosetta stone of playing the blues.

"You said you loved me, so why do you treat me this way?" That's the blues, plaintive. And even when a blues song occasionally proclaims something good ("My baby gives me something good at the end of a long hard day") it always sounds like it is only one bright spot in a dreary life. Some days it feels just like that.

* * *

Thursday night I had the dream again. My cabin was filling up with smoke and I couldn't find the door. An old woman's voice said, "Sit down." When I sat, there was less smoke near the floor and I was facing a large raven. I said "I can't get out, where's the door?!"

In a raspy raven's voice it said, "Don't worry, the fire won't hurt you."

I said, "What do you mean?"

"Why are you afraid?" She said.

"I don't know how to get out!"

The raven nodded to the side, "The door is right there."

I looked and realized that the door was where it always was.

The raven began to laugh, "You forgot how you came in here. You are so funny!"

I woke up and shuffled to the toilet in the darkness. As I stood there hoping to hear that I hit the target, I smiled at the raven's words. I knew where the door was even in the dark. I recalled how I got into this place, this life I now lived. I made some choices. I said no to Joy, I wouldn't be a yes-dear husband --

besides, that isn't what she really wanted, and she wanted her real power back. I said no to the church (finally); they wanted a chaplain and I wanted to be a revolutionary leader -- of course, they didn't sign up for that. I said no to state sponsored gambling to fund children's education -- even though nearly everyone liked to gamble. I said no to Kindom Come (aka Shepard Foundation); I was conflicted about living off gambling money, and I became obsessive about how it was spent -- and I didn't want to lose my friends who worked with me. And I said no to making Barbara a soul mate to complete my life; rather I chose to love her from another place – an inner place of wholeness.

Every no is a yes to something else. That's how I got into this place. Every choice was a door I entered. Obviously I was scared that I had hit a dead end and run out of doors at a particularly risky time. But the raven reminded me that I always had a choice -- but she advised me to stay put.

Chapter 18

In my storehouse of memories I have pleasant childhood recollections of Halloween. Most of them have to do with dressing up and trick-or-treating in our neighborhood -- a federal housing project -- then getting carted off to a nearby affluent area to really cash in. Candy, pumpkin carvings and haunted houses: the glory days of childhood. On Friday morning I had to admit that I was looking forward to dressing up as Merlin and having a party to go to -- even if it was a wedding.

I loaded up my costume, harmonicas, music, pastor's wedding book, and the real estate folder.

My first stop was Harvey Snider's Realty to sign the last of the paperwork. He said that the additional equipment I had asked for had already been delivered to the church. This guy had worked overtime to dump this white elephant. Then he gave me copies of the documents and an envelope with the rental agreement and fee from Nathan.

It was a strange moment when Harvey handed me the keys to the old church. In the past, when I was given the keys to my newly assigned church, it was clear that I was only the caretaker of that church and its people; then someday a few years down the road I would turn my keys in and move on. In no way could I say that the church was mine, I was just the pastor. It was the congregation's church. They had built it and supported it. Their family members had been baptized, married and buried in their church. In fact, by church law, the pastor was not even a member of the local congregation.

Now, with a "Here you are Reverend, good luck, and I hope you enjoy it," the keys of my very own church were put into my hand. There would be no personnel committee complaining about the length of my sermons or recommending that I be replaced. There would be no trustees dictating who could use the building and who couldn't. There would be no finance committee wanting to have rummage sales to pay the mortgage or the pastor's salary. It was my church. Of course, it didn't have a congregation, but to me that was the beauty of it! And I could name it any damn thing I wanted: God's House of Blues and Blessing? The Holy Happy Hour Temple? The Church of the Flockless Shepard?

I was laughing as I walked back to the car. I was having fantasies that I never allowed myself to have in thirty-five years of ministry. I pictured a new sign in front of the church:

CLERGY SERVICES

 - Spiritual direction and misdirection
 - Birth and death parties
 - Weddings and divorces
 - Blessings and curses

One stop shopping with Rev. Andy Shepard

When I got to the church at ten to unlock the doors, some of the work team were already there. They were weighting small paper bags with sand and inserting candles in them as temporary lanterns, called luminarias. These were being placed between the dozen carved pumpkins on the low retaining wall bordering the sidewalk.

"Good morning, Andy," Nathan said walking toward me.

"Good morning. How are things going?"

"Great. I don't think we could have picked a more beautiful day for a wedding. We're just waiting for Harvey to show up with the keys."

"Well, I really hate to tell you this, but there have been some changes. Harvey can't rent you this church."

Nathan staggered backwards a couple of steps and his face fell. "What? I signed a contract!"

"Yes, I know. I now own this church and your contract, and a very nice fee I must say." I dangled the keys in front of me.

"Andy, the guru of grace? I could sue you for pain and suffering."

"Ah my boy, you're getting married tonight, your pain and suffering are just beginning." I turned and climbed the four old steps to the concrete walk which divided the small lawn in front of the white church. Then I climbed three more steps to the small porch and front doors. I slid the key into the brass deadbolt, turned it and unlocked a strange new door to my future.

It was a double door. I found the latch that freed the other side and opened them both fully and turned back to the decoration team standing in the October sunshine and said, "I am reminded of the words of Jesus to Peter, 'I give you the keys of the kingdom of heaven; whatever you bind on earth will be bound in heaven, and whatever you loose on earth will be loosed in heaven.' That should give you pause at tying the knot. But you will have to come to hear my first sermon to get an explanation of its meaning and the minimum donation starts at only $29.95."

"No problem," Nathan said. "There is no doubt that $29.95 doesn't begin to equal the value of your wisdom."

"Well said young man. Now let's decorate this place to scare the hell out of people (as weddings should!)"

The team came prepared. They brought a boom-box and switched on some new pop music I had never heard, and for the next hour and a half we had a great time. We hung twenty-five three-dimensional paper pumpkins from the ceiling, together with a colony of bats. Along the four walls we draped strings of party lights shaped like spiders and witch faces. Candles were arranged on the windowsills. We arranged the chairs in a circular pattern, leaving a space for the band and an aisle to the door. Orange and black balloons rose from the chairs in the back rows. A round riser was brought in for the center of the circle which would elevate Cindy, Nathan and me. The florist arrived with two funeral wreaths which were placed at either side of the riser. Each wreath had a banner which simply said In Sympathy. Candelabras, each with a dozen black candles and spider webs, were placed on the riser.

Outside along the walk, six large skeletons were posted, three on each side. A broom rack with several brooms was set up by the door with a sign, Please park your brooms here.

Just inside the door, in the narthex, was a stand with a guest book and a stack of wedding programs. As the team was finishing up I picked up a program and looked it over. On the cover were Cindy and Nathan dressed as vampires, smiling with fangs. Inside, I looked to the bottom right and there was my note and the lottery numbers. Game on.

Soon we all strolled across to the hotel to join Cindy's team for lunch; they had finished decorating for the reception and dinner. Lunch was in the bar where Barbara had arranged a delicious meal of pumpkin ravioli with a nutmeg cream sauce. A salad with cranberries and walnuts and gorgonzola cheese; and fume' blanc from a local winery.

"Dinner will be late, so don't be shy," said Barbara as the first course came out antipasto of artichoke hearts, olives, feta cheese and warm whole wheat sour dough bread. "Rev. Andy, would you care to give thanks?" Then she took a seat next to me.

A bit surprised, I stood and looked at Barbara; the smile I gave her must have been revealing, because she slightly blushed. "I thank God for Nathan and Cindy," I began, turning to the thirteen seated helpers -- a mix of family and friends. "I am beginning to think they have a chance." There was a cheer. "And I want to give thanks for all of you who are doing a great job of helping them have a dynamite wedding (if nothing else)." There was laughter. "And I want to give a special heartfelt thanks for the good news Barbara got from the doctors last week. Her bone tumor gave us a real Halloween scare," I shook my head and swallowed as a tear escaped an eye. "But the damn thing was only a pain-in-the-ass bump that can be removed." There was applause. "So let's praise God from whom all blessings flow, including this wonderful lunch together. Amen."

There were several amen's as I sat down. Barbara leaned over toward me and softly said, "Always the preacher," and she kissed my cheek.

After lunch the wedding couple took some time alone in the bridal suite. Most of the others toured the town or went wine tasting. Barbara finished some behind-the-scenes work then went home to change.

I ignored a series of phone calls and text messages from Joseph Raggetti whom I guessed had received my letter. Instead I took a tour of my new church. I had yet to explore the whole thing.

The main street of town was built on a ridge and the land dropped away sharply on both sides of the street behind the ancient buildings; so under the back of the sanctuary there was a whole other level to the church: a social hall, kitchen, and some offices that had recently been remodeled. My church was bigger than it first appeared.

After a while I walked back to the hotel and sat in the shadowed courtyard that was behind and below the main building. It had a charming garden and pool where they hosted small weddings, mostly in the summer months. On the back of my wedding program I began to outline the homily that I was going to give during the ceremony. I struggled to remember what I had said to Cindy and Nathan the day we met. They had thought it was perfect, whatever it was, and wanted me to say it at their wedding. I paused and let my mind drift.

It was about four o'clock and the courtyard felt like an oasis of calm in this high energy day. All was peaceful except for a raven that cawed from the top of a utility pole in the alley. I touched the medicine pouch. Then Barbara called.

"Andy, the cabin is on fire! The fire department is on the way, but it looks bad."

"You see anyone?"

"No. But there was a boat."

"I'll be right there!"

I swore and cursed all the way to Valley Springs. When I turned onto Dam Road I quit. I just focused on the fact that Barbara was all right, and so was I. I repeated to myself again and again the words from my dream, Red Cloud's words, "the fire won't hurt you."

There was a fire department pickup at the driveway. I was flagged down. I told the firemen who I was and he let me pass. I quickly drove down to the cabin. Streams of smoke drifted out over the lake. There were two fire trucks, and the men were pouring water on my smoldering blackened home.

I found Barbara wearing part of her costume -- a house dress and apron -- standing and watching with a neighbor near her truck. As I got out of the car she walked over toward me.

"I'm sorry, Barbara. It's my fault. I..."

"Wait a minute." She turned toward her neighbor and said, "I'll be back" Then to me, "Let's go up to the house, Andy."

I followed her truck up the hill. We were silent until she closed the door of her house. Then, "How did he find out?" she asked.

"You mean Raggetti?"

"Yes."

"I sent him the numbers. I said it was in exchange for the church."

She just looked at me with surprise.

"I indicated that my lawyer had copies of our letters and the video. I wished him a good retirement."

She smiled and shook her head, "You wished him a good retirement!? You've got some cojones for a preacher!" Then she paused. She was trying to understand. "When did you send the letter?"

"Tuesday, registered mail."

"Jesus, Andy, now he not only thinks you can rip off the lottery, but you're also threatening to get him killed by his boss for scamming the company."

"I didn't think I would hear from him until the numbers hit tomorrow night. Then he would also realize that I fed the numbers to a bunch of people, effectively sabotaging the integrity of the games."

"I can see your thinking, but between now and then -- if there is a then -- can you imagine how mad he is?"

"I know, he has been trying to call me all day."

"Maybe it is time to return his calls."

"I'm so sorry about your cabin, Barbara. It was so stupid."

"To quote an old preacher, it only looks like you screwed up, Sugar, we can't see the big picture. Besides, it's insured. Our big problem now is that we don't know what Raggetti might be up to next. Maybe they expected to find you at home and so they're not through yet."

"Okay, I'll call. I could put my cell on speaker phone; do you have a recorder?"

She shook her head; then said, "Oh, I have a little memo device." She went to her purse and pulled out what looked like a pen. "I use it at work, but it only records a few minutes."

"I have a feeling this will be short." I pushed the button for the speaker phone; then I brought up the recent calls and chose a likely number and then pushed dial.

"Hello?" It was Raggetti's voice. I pushed record on the pen.

"Hello. I think you have been trying to reach me."

"Oh yes. So you finally noticed. Too bad you didn't call sooner."

"I didn't have anything to say."

"I understand. Is that still the case?"

"I think you should know it was only a little joke."

"Very little."

"You seem to have lost your sense of humor. Maybe you really do need to retire."

Barbara put her hand to her forehead and mouthed, "NO, no, no!"

"Look, you little fuck!" He yelled, "I am this close to..." He stopped himself, maybe suspecting that I was recording. Then in a calmer voice, "I'm this close to losing my patience with you."

"Hey, it was a joke, all right? I'm out of the game."

"Well, as you might have guessed by now, this is not a game."

I said nothing more. He hung up. I released the button on the recorder. "What do you think?"

"I'm beginning to see why Joy might have divorced you. You have a way of putting your foot in your mouth."

"Thanks a lot."

"I thought you might have tried groveling a bit, or perhaps using your smooth pastoral tone to calm him down. We have a smoking mess down the hill."

"And a wedding in," I looked at my watch, "two hours. I just wanted to buy some time, make him think I was clueless enough to actually yank on his chain."

"I think he got that message."

The doorbell rang. Barbara opened the door and there was Lieutenant Jim McGuire from the Sheriff's Department -- the same detective that investigated a similar fire that destroyed my home almost two years ago. When he saw me behind Barbara he was surprised and said, "Rev. Shepard?"

"Lieutenant."

"Please come in, Jim," Barbara said. "I guess you two have already met?"

"Yes, we have a history," McGuire said. "Was that cabin your place, Barbara?"

"Yes, but I was renting it to Andy."

"Boy, you picked the wrong renter."

I rolled my eyes. "Hey, I don't smoke, I don't light candles, I don't leave pots cooking on the stove…"

"But you associate with a rough crowd," he said. "We got a call from Wanda who runs the visitor center. She saw the fire and a boat leaving your area."

"I saw the boat too. Did you catch them?" Barbara asked.

"Not yet. So Reverend, do you have any idea who might have done this?"

I had to think quickly. I still felt my best bet was to let my plan unfold and see if Raggetti would stand down and fold up shop.

"The usual suspects," I said.

"Are you playing the lottery again?"

"No, but there have been some strange things happening."

"You mean the private eye that was hanging around here?"

"Right. But this is not a good time to have this conversation. I'm scheduled to do a wedding for Barbara's son in just over an hour. Can we talk tomorrow?"

"Congratulations Barbara." He handed me his card. "Call me at this number."

"Thanks for coming, Jim," Barbara said as she moved to the door.

Before he left he asked for my cell number. Then he said, "You better hurry before the church burns down, Reverend. But I guess you already know about trick-or-treats."

Cute. I was sure Barbara had a better zinger, but she didn't say anything. I hurriedly changed into my costume as Barbara finished putting curlers in her hair and collecting the paraphernalia of a mother-in-law who was moving in with the newlyweds -- a suitcase and a feather duster.

As we left in my car for Moke Hill, we stopped and talked to the fire chief and explained that we were leaving for a wedding. He looked at us in disbelief and asked for Barbara's phone number, then we drove away into the growing darkness. Barbara made a call to the hotel to check on how her staff was doing. Meanwhile my thoughts were on the depressing reality of what I had lost in the fire. My earthly possessions were already meager given the work of an arsonist two years ago (What was it about fire and these lottery guys?) Now, even the stuff I had from my office in the Riverton Church was gone; also gone were my journal, some gifts, books, my wardrobe, and probably the sails to my boat. I couldn't help feeling like I was destined to live like a monk in a cell, living out a vow of poverty. "What the hell," I thought, "Raggetti will probably have me killed anyway." All of a sudden, I felt free as a condemned man.

When Barbara finished her phone call, I asked, "How are things at the hotel?"

"They're a little nervous, but fine. This will be one of the largest dinners they prepared and served. How are you doing?"

"I was thinking of Janis Joplin -- probably a little before your time."

"You think I'm a hick?"

"Sorry, I didn't think you were a fan of '60s rock."

"You kidding? Janis sang my theme song: 'Love Is Like a Ball and Chain.'"

I smiled, "Very good. You remember the song 'Me and Bobby McGee?'"

"Sure."

"Well it has a famous line: Freedom is just another word for nothing left to lose. I'm feeling that kind of freedom."

"That's sad," and she reached over with her good arm and took my hand. "But do you really think you've lost everything?"

She took me by surprise. It was as if she shook me out of my sleep with just the warmth of her hand – the warmth of her heart. I glanced down to my chest where now three powerful charms hung over my starry robe: a peace symbol, a ceramic cross and a medicine pouch. These represented three kinds of power; the power of peacemaking, the power of self-giving love, and the power of unseen forces working on our behalf.

I looked at Barbara, "Cowgirl, you're absolutely right. I've really lost nothing."

Chapter 19

The town of Mokelumne Hill had a Main Street that stretched all of two blocks. When Barbara and I arrived at 6:30 p.m., cars were parked bumper to bumper up and down the dark street. The church looked inviting with pumpkins and luminarias glowing across the front and lighting the way to the door. The hotel was hopping; standing room only in the bar and people spilling out onto the covered boardwalk. I double-parked in front of the saloon, and as Barbara got out I came around and pulled her empty suitcase out of the back seat and handed it to her.

Nathan's best-man, wearing a skeleton suit and mask, recognized Barbara, and with a grin stuck his head into the bar and yelled, "Hey, Nathan, your mom's here and it doesn't look like good news!"

Nathan soon appeared and said, "What's this?"

"Well dear," Barbara said, "I know your little girl is busy, so I thought I would move in for a while and see that you eat right and that the house is kept clean."

Nathan burst with laughter and gave her a gentle hug, avoiding her arm. "You may be the scariest person here tonight!" Then they disappeared into the bar.

The wedding was to start in a half hour. I drove around to the alley behind the church where there was a sign lit by my headlights that warned: Pastor's Parking, all others will be sent to purgatory. However, in my rightful spot was an SUV with a boat and trailer behind it. I managed to squeeze in next to the interloper, then worked at getting out of my bug. The door would only open halfway against the other car; and the fact that I carried forty extra pounds and wore a cassock and robe, made it a challenge. Finally I was out and straightened up when I was shoved hard from the back. I hit the doorjamb and a voice said with urgency, "Are you Shepard?"

Only then did the boat register in my mind. Alarmed, I twisted and swung my right fist back around toward where I imagined the voice to be. My head followed and I saw a man in a black hoody duck. I missed. As I tried to regain my balance I saw his gun come down and wallop me on my head, "Get back in the car, now!" he growled. He shoved me again, once, twice; then when I thought my head would slam into metal on the next push, there was a grunt and the sound of cracking bones. I struggled to stand upright. I heard his body fall onto the gravel.

My dome light was the only light in the alley, but I saw what looked like a person with a cape and raven's mask disappear into the darkness. In between the cars lay a body with its head at an unnatural angle. I stared at it, trying to understand what I was looking at and what just happened. I couldn't see any signs of life. I didn't know what to do. I assumed that it was the arsonist because of the boat. And the raven? Who else, my ex-wife with the black belt.

I looked at my watch: twenty minutes before the wedding. A dead arsonist could wait. I picked up the gun and slipped it into the inner pocket of my robe. I reached back into my car and collected my wizard's staff, pastor's wedding book, musician's harmonica and music, and a confused pensioner's flashlight. I shuffled to the back door of the church's social hall and unlocked it with my new keys.

In the restroom I removed my white ponytail wig and inspected my head: just a bump, no blood. The heavy wig had acted as a hard hat. I replaced my wig and starry headband, then I climbed the stairs and opened the door to the sanctuary and entered a different world. The lights were dimmed, the candles were lit, and several people were already seated. Two guests were coming down the aisle: a dancehall girl and a gunslinger. I walked over to where the band was getting ready. They were all dressed as zombies.

"Bobby, how are you?"

"Great. Hey, you look sharp, man. It's good to see you. I was beginning to get worried."

"Me too, it's been one of those days." (Now that was an understatement!) "Do you have everything you need?"

"Yup. We powered up from that plug over there. I duct-taped the cords to the floor so no one would trip. The speakers are up and working. Your mic is on the riser. We were just tuning up to start with the gathering music. Why don't you check your mic?"

Bobby, as usual, seemed like he just downed six cups of coffee. I stepped up on the riser between the two large candelabras, took my harmonica out of a pocket and the mic off the stand, took a deep breath and let rip a blues riff.

"Good," Bobby said. "All set." He looked at the other guys, "One, two, three, four," and the band took off with a blues number called: Before You Accuse Me, Take A Look At Yourself. It was off an Eric Clapton album.

I walked up the aisle and out the front doors where I took a Merlin pose on the steps, leaning on my star-topped silver staff. The luminarias looked magical and lit the skeletons that lined the walk. People were starting to emerge from the hotel in a steady stream and cross the street to the church. A few cars were still arriving and looking for a place to park. I watched it all with a sense of detachment, wondering about the body in the alley and how close I came to being slumped in my car with a bullet in my head. Part of me was looking for the person in the cape and raven's mask to come up the walk. Instead a couple approached linked with a fat rope tied to each of their necks -- an interesting statement about marriage. I nodded as they entered the church; for a moment they pretended to be choking, then signed the guest book. A ghost gave them a tiny bag of candy with a hand candle as they continued inside to find a seat.

Some came with simple Mardi gras masks, and others wore complete over-the-head rubber masks of one sort of ghoul or another. The band's first number came to an end and they started a Muddy Water's tune, "I Can't Be Satisfied." A couple came up the walk wearing clergy collars and big crosses around their necks, and they were throwing paper money in the air -- the Handlys from the Foundation who recommended me for this wedding. "Wade, Marilyn! What are you doing?"

"Don't you even recognize yourself?" Wade said.

I shook my head in mock dismay and raised my staff, "By the stars I send a curse on you. May your fortunes double and your work be without end!"

"Come on sweetheart," Marilyn urged Wade, "we have to throw the money faster."

We laughed and hugged. When I gave Wade a hug the gun in my robe pressed hard into his chest. "Hey," he said, "Is that what I think it is?"
I nodded.

"Josh told me about your predicament. Tell you what, give it to me. I'll stay close. You don't know shit about guns."

We stepped away from the door and into the shadows; I gladly gave the pistol to him. He gave it a look and said, "Andy! You don't even have the safety on!"

"Neither did the guy I took it off of."

He looked quizzically into my eyes.

"I'll tell you later," I said, and I moved back to the door where Marilyn waited.

"What are you boys up to?" she asked.

"We have to keep an eye on this guy," Wade said. "He attracts trouble."

Marilyn tossed some more fake cash over my head, "Here you go Andy, more trouble," and then they stepped into the church.

Now it was just after seven and the group of witches and skeletons came out of the bar -- bridesmaids and groomsmen – and they began to walk across the street paired up two by two. A car stopped and let them pass while the photographer, whom I had met at the rehearsal, took pictures of the parade.

All at once I recognized the car -- a new Mercedes. Raggetti. I walked quickly toward the street. It was too dark to see who was in the car, but I recognized the two vampires who then came out of the hotel and followed the wedding party. As I got to the street I stopped at the photographer's side and said, "I need a couple shots of this car. If you can get the license plate and driver, all the better."

I took a few more steps to the middle of the street and made a sweeping bow to the vampire bride and groom. Nathan and Cindy stopped in the street, giving the photographer a chance to move about and take several pictures. The flash lit up the street and the Mercedes. I turned toward the church, took a regal stance, and slowly led the couple in front of the car, all the while wondering if I was going to get run over.

Then it occurred to me that I didn't look like a minister who was going to perform a wedding. If Raggetti was indeed in the car, there was a good chance he didn't recognize me.

When we reached the other side the Mercedes began to slowly move forward to pass. The tinted window in the rear door slid down as if someone wanted to get a better view. The photographer turned, not five feet from the side of the car, and took two direct shots of Raggetti's surprised face. As he tried to lift his hands to cover his identity, I waved with a big smile. The window shot back up and the car accelerated. I couldn't believe it. I could never have planned a better scenario. His guy was dead behind the church and his face was caught in front of the church.

"What are you doing, trick-or-treating in the street?"

I turned; there was my friend Wade in a clergy collar looking like a minister. My God, I thought, was he the reason Raggetti rolled down the window? To see if this minister was me? To check if his hit-man, who was now strangely silent, had taken care of me?

"I'm glad you have my back, friend," I said. "That was the CEO of the California Lottery, coming to pay his respects -- only, I'm not dead."

"What's going on?"

"Wait a minute." I caught up with the photographer and said, "Terrific job! I owe you."

"No problem," he said.

"Could you e-mail those pictures to me tomorrow? You may have caught a criminal."

"Really!"

"Really, and when you can, I suggest that you change the chip in your camera and put it somewhere safe. That guy may be back."

Wade over-heard and said, "Criminal?"

"It's a long story," I said, "But I've got to get this wedding started." I reached into my pocket and pulled out Lieutenant Jim McGuire's card. "Would you call this deputy? Tell him please do not interrupt the wedding, but the guy he is looking for is behind the church in the alley; and his boss is driving a big new Mercedes."

"Okay."

"And Wade, this is only between you and me," I said as we climbed the steps to the church doors.

Chapter 20

I caught up with the wedding party in the narthex; they were getting themselves organized for the processional. The band was playing a country-western classic, "Losing You Could Be the Best Thing Yet." As we waited for them to finish, we all had to step aside to let in some late-comers, Adam and Eve, the mythical first husband and wife in chilly-looking costumes.

When the song came to an end I walked up the aisle with my silver staff in hand and my robe dragging behind me. It was a wondrous scene made even more magical by the lighting. The overhead lights were dimmed way down which made the illuminated spiders and witch faces along the walls stand out. The twenty-four candles of the candelabras drew attention to the center of the circle. Family members sat in the first ring of seats in front of the riser, including Barbara who was surprisingly accompanied by her two estranged daughters. The guests were a sight to behold. The photographer was going to have quite a night.

I took my robe up in my hands and stepped up on the riser, then slowly turned to survey the whole congregation. "Tonight the dead are close," I ironically intoned, trying my best to imitate the old wizard from Harry Potter. "On this All Hallow's Eve their spirits are hovering over us, as the Bible says, like a great cloud of witnesses." Then I saw one more late-comer enter through the skeletons and witches gathered at the door. It was someone dressed in a black cape and wearing a raven's mask.

I continued, "You too have come here to witness the courageous act of Nathan and Cindy being joined in marriage. This is a holy and frightful moment. They will need God's help and your help, not only to keep from running out of this church screaming," I let the laughter interrupt, "but to keep them from running away in the years to come. We all need help to love when times get hard. So when they give their vows to each other, I ask you to also promise to be there for them."

This was Barbara's cue. She rose with her suitcase and duster, "Don't worry, Merlin, I'm going to move in with the kids for a while just to make sure everything is going well."

There was more laughter and applause. Barbara took a bow. Then I saw Wade slip in. He gave me a thumbs up.

I turned toward Bobby and said, "Now I believe we are ready." He tapped out a slow beat and the band started in with the processional music: the familiar funeral march, slow and dreary. The flower girls came down the aisle first. They carried baskets of little packages of tissue and tossed them one at a time into the crowd.

Next were the bridesmaids and groomsmen, witches and skeletons paired up with each other and marching to the dirge. When they reached the center they split up and encircled the platform.

Then the music changed. Beginning with a fanfare from the keyboard, the zombies took the dirge melody out of its minor key and played it to an upbeat tempo. The guests rose as down the aisle came the Best Man holding a chain which was tied around Nathan's waist while Nathan walked behind feigning resistance. Then the Matron of Honor likewise pulled Cindy, who walked backwards as if trying to head for the door. Surrounded by laughter, the two vampires finally reached the riser where they were unchained. They stepped up and stood facing me and the music came to an end.

I began, "Let us pray. Oh Great Spirit, as we look around at creation, we know you are not only the God of beauty, but also of laughter. Your beauty inspires us; but your humor helps us get through the trouble in life. Bless this occasion with the exquisite beauty of loving hearts, and with the healing power of laughter. In this way help us be open to your Spirit we pray. Amen.

"Please be seated. Nathan and Cindy, this is a sacred moment in a sacred place. And we understand that you are very attracted to each other; and despite the chains, in reality you would not want to be anywhere else tonight."

Cindy brought Nathan's hand up to her lips and kissed it.

"And yes, we also know you have stood with others in the past and promised to them your undying love; a promise that led to disappointment and heartache.

"But Holy Love has invited you to its table again, and your hunger and joy could not say no. You are here to say yes! So what shall we say about the future? Are you condemned to a frightening melodrama of your love disintegrating again? I am here to say: take heart, this doesn't need to be your fate. I am here to proclaim the power of grace."

I raised my silver staff. "I am here to pronounce God's blessing of selfless love that goes beyond friendship, and beyond sexuality." I raised the staff higher. "I am here with God's help to cast a spell of grace on you -- the grace to live together with kindness, gentleness, understanding and forgiveness." I lowered my staff.

"So I ask you, are you here to say yes?"

"Yes," they said together.

"Are you here to courageously join as husband and wife?"

"Yes," they said.

"I now will ask the witches to add to this spell with blessings and advice." I took the mic and walked to the edge of the platform and held it for the first bridesmaid to speak.

"Kiss each other every night before you sleep."

Then the next, "Tell Cindy her hair looks beautiful."

With laughter I continued around the circle, "Say how you really feel."

"Don't sweat the small stuff."

"Say what you need, (and you may have to say it more than once!)"

I moved to the groomsmen, "Now I ask the skeletons to add to this spell of grace."

"Don't forget your buddies, 'cause one person can't give you everything."

"Count to ten before you react."
"Flowers never hurt."

"Your spouse will change, and so will you -- don't let it freak you out."

"It's the little things that say I love you."

"Thank you, all." Then I looked out into the crowd and said, "Now I need a little grace from everyone, because by special request I have been asked to sing a song that I wrote recently with the help of Bobby."

I took the special mic off a stand and pulled my harmonica out of my pocket. I closed my eyes and hummed softly to myself the first line. Then I took a breath and repeated it on the harmonica, letting my complaint fill the church through the speakers. When I started the second line, the keyboard came in with some rhythm and riffs. Then the full band got behind me on the third line and I gained confidence that I could do this song. I let the band bring the chord progression around to the beginning while I thought of my own weddings -- such hope, such bitter disappointments.

> "I've been so unlucky
> They call me the four-time loser."

I played a four-bar riff.

> "I'm left broke and alone,
> So they call me the four-time loser."

Bobby picked up the complaint on his guitar.

> "When I think I've got a good one,
> I find she's just an abuser."

The keyboard took off on the melody with the bass driving it hard. Between lines I played some licks on my blues harp. When the chords came around again Bobby nodded to me.

> "I bet my heart too much,
> It gets broken right in two."

The rhythm was now getting stronger.

> "I gamble with my heart,
> It's been broken two times two."

I looked at Wade and Marilyn. Marilyn was looking back at me so sadly I thought she was going to cry. I got a lump in my throat. I looked at Barbara and I had to push out a raspy,

> "That's why I'm holding back
> From betting big on you."

Bobby picked up the lead on his screaming guitar while I echoed him some on the harmonica. The standing wedding party began clapping in time. The congregation followed suit. It was building as I started the last verse,

> "As far as I can tell,
> You are one fine lady."

Nathan stole a kiss and the people howled. I walked to the edge of the riser where Barbara sat.

> "But I can't always tell
> Who's a real fine lady."

She gave me a crooked smile, and I played between the keyboard's rhythmic chords.

> "So sweet darlin' tell me,
> Are you my winning ticket, baby?"

Bobby's guitar and the keyboard started going wild. Everyone stood up and clapped. Nathan and Cindy started to dance. Those that could get into the aisle also danced a bit. I tried to stay with the chord changes and watch Bobby. He didn't want to stop; he circled back through the melody three times while the skeletons chanted, "Are you my winning ticket, baby?!"

When we came to a high decibel conclusion, and as people were clapping and hollering, I looked up and there were two sheriff deputies in the back row. Then I searched the room for the raven, but the bird was gone; I guessed she didn't like my song.

I said, "Let's hear it for Bobby and the Calaveras Jumpers." After the applause, I asked everyone to sit down. I waited as people slowly got themselves settled. "It is time for sacred vows. Nathan and Cindy, will you face each other."

Cindy handed her bouquet of wilted, discolored roses to her Matron of Honor.

"Now, will you remove your fangs." There were sighs of regret from several friends. Cindy slipped hers out and handed them to Nathan which made people laugh. Nathan handed both sets to his Best Man who took them as if they were toxic waste.

"Now please take each other's hands, and Nathan, would you begin." I was very interested in what vows they had created.

Nathan said, "Grace: elegance or beauty of form, manner, motion or action."

Then, surprisingly, Cindy spoke up, "Grace: a pleasing or attractive quality or endowment."

Nathan then took a turn, "Grace: favor or goodwill."

Then Cindy, "Grace: mercy, clemency, pardon."

They continued to alternate, and apparently from memory, "Grace: a short prayer before or after a meal, in which a blessing is asked and thanks are given."

"Grace: to lend or add grace; to adorn."

"Grace: to willingly and ungrudgingly extend kindness or other gifts."

"Grace: the freely given, unmerited favor and love of God."

"Grace: the influence or spirit of God operating in humans."

"Cindy, I vow to do my best to be the face of grace to you as your husband."

"Nathan, I vow to do my best to be the face of grace to you as your wife."

Amazing! I thought I almost could not go on. A couple, a pair of fangless vampires, had actually taken what I said seriously. I cleared my throat and asked the Best Man for the rings. He handed me a jewelers ring box. I hesitated, expecting a glow-in-the-dark skull and crossbones or something that would break the spell of their vows. But when I opened it, there were two gold rings with the word GRACE fashioned into each. I smiled at the couple who were smiling at me. I removed the rings and handed one to each.

"Nathan, will you give this symbol of your vow to Cindy and repeat after me. With all that I am, and all that I have, with this ring I thee wed."

When Nathan was finished, I coached Cindy to do the same. I then turned and instructed the Best Man and Maid of Honor to each take a candle and to start lighting the guest's small hand-candles at the end of the rows, and for each person to light their neighbor's candle. The rest of the wedding party came forward and also took candles from the candelabras.

Bobby began to subtly play his guitar. I couldn't believe the song he chose: "Love Is A Ring of Fire" from Johnny Cash. I hadn't once thought of the cabin during the wedding, but now that image came back to me as each candle was lit and with my recollection of the lyrics:

> I fell into a burning ring of fire, I went down, down, down and the flames leapt high...

Other than that, it was a beautiful moment. The bride and groom were surrounded by the candlelight.

When we were set, I laid my hand on Nathan and Cindy's clasped hands, and said, "Let us pray. Oh Mystery, you created us with strength to love, and weakness to fear; and ever since, we have been of two minds, with one foot in heaven and the other in hell. It is hard to dance that way. So with the help of all who have gone before us and who are somehow here on this All Hallow's Eve, and with the help of friends and family, and with a good dose of your Holy Light of guidance, lead Nathan and Cindy into grace upon grace in this dance of life. Amen.

"Now a nuptial kiss."

They kissed well.

I lifted my staff, and over the cheers I said, "Under the authority of the State of California, and with the blessing of the church, I now pronounce Nathan and Cindy to be husband and wife together. And nobody better mess it up!

"Please carefully blow out your candles, and let's dance!" Bobby brought the volume and tempo up on "Ring of Fire." The groomsmen quickly stacked the chairs, and there was twenty minutes of freaky, ecstatic dancing. After "Ring of Fire" the band went right into the old kiddy rock number, "The Monster Mash."

Chapter 21

As the chairs were being stacked Wade came up and said that the deputies had been patient, but now I needed to talk with them. I agreed and told him to slip the gun into the side pocket of my robe; then I motioned them over to us and led Wade, McGuire and his partner to the door that took us down to the lower level away from the festivities. I switched on some lights as we made our way down. The stairs ended in a hallway with doors to the restrooms, kitchen, offices and social hall. We filed into the kitchen where I found some paper cups.

"Water? I'm parched."

They declined.

"I take it you found the body," I said, as I filled my cup.

Wade's eyes widened.

"Reverend Shepard, this is my partner, Officer Mitchell. We must inform you that anything you say can and will be used against you in a court of law. You have the right to remain silent and to have an attorney present. Do you understand?"

"Yes."

"What do you know about what took place in the alley?"

"I got here about six-thirty. It was dark. I pulled around behind the church to park. There was a car with a boat and trailer in my space. I squeezed in so close to it that I had trouble getting out of my car. When I finally did, I was between the cars with my door open when someone suddenly shoved me from behind, knocking me hard against my door jamb. A man's voice asked me if I was Shepard? Only then did I realize it could be the arsonist."

Again, Wade looked astonished. So I said to him, "Someone set my cabin on fire and fled in a boat this afternoon. Anyway, I turned and took a swing at him and missed. He clubbed me on my head with his gun and began trying to shove me back into my car."

I filled my cup again and took a long drink. I decided to not drag Joy into it -- if it was Joy. So I improvised. "I swung my fist back again, wildly, and I got lucky, I hit his face. He sort of slipped to the ground between the cars, then tried to get up. I just fell on his back, his head hit a fender as we went down. I flattened him. He still had the gun. I grabbed him under his chin with both hands and pulled his head back and said, 'Drop it, drop the gun!' He wouldn't, I pulled harder and heard his neck crack. He went limp."

I stopped and took another drink.

"Then what?" McGuire asked.

"I got the gun and stood up and tried to catch my breath. I looked around to see if there was anyone else. After a minute or so I checked on the guy. His head was at a funny angle. He wasn't breathing. I got my stuff out of my car and came in through the back door there." I nodded toward the rear entrance. "I took a look at my head in the restroom over there. I was in a daze. I walked through the church and out the front door and tried to collect myself. That's when I asked Wade to give you a call."

"That's quite a story," McGuire said. "Let's take a look at your head."

"If it wasn't for this heavy wig," I slid it off and showed them, "I would probably be the one dead out there in the alley. But I just have this bump." I bent over so they could see.

"I see. So you didn't black out at all?"

"No. Just saw a few stars."

"And the gun?"

I reached in my pocket and pulled out a heavy black pistol, and I was careful to point it toward the floor. "I think I put the safety on."

I held it out to McGuire. His partner, Mitchell, produced a plastic bag. I dropped it in. "Have you identified this guy yet?"

"No. We haven't moved the body yet. Can you give us a description of his car?"

"It's a light colored...wait a minute. It's right out there." I pointed to the back of the building.

"No it isn't. Only your car is parked in the pastor's spot."

"And the body?"

McGuire looked at his partner and smiled, then after a moment, "Apparently the dead guy climbed into your trunk, Reverend."

I was speechless. My heart started pounding. What was going on?

"We wouldn't have discovered it except the body did not fit, and the VW's trunk lid bulged out a bit."

"Andy," Wade asked, "Shall I call Lloyd Pettigrew?"

The door opened at the top of the stairs. There were some footsteps and then Barbara appeared in the stairwell. "Oh, there you are," she said. "Our photographer was just mugged near the hotel."

McGuire nodded to Mitchell who turned and climbed the stairs. The door closed. I looked at Wade, "I guess you'd better." He left to make the call.

McGuire and I stood alone, looking at each other in the old fashion church kitchen. I didn't know who I was more concerned about: Raggetti and his plan to set me up, or McGuire and the Sheriff's department who now thought they finally had something on me."

McGuire broke the silence. "How did you manage to get that guy in your trunk? There is nothing more awkward and heavy than the dead weight of a body."

"I think there's a better question, Lieutenant. Why did I have Wade call you if there was a body in my trunk?!" I was getting angry. "It doesn't make much sense!"

"No, it doesn't. But if crooks had much sense, we wouldn't catch many of them. My guess? You had a stupid plan and it went bad. Then you started making poor decisions. So here you are, wearing a ridiculous costume, singing some blues song about the lottery at a wedding, with a body stuffed in your Volkswagen Bug on Halloween. I can't wait to tell the guys at the office."

"Silver," I said. "The guy's car was a light silver SUV of some kind; maybe a jeep. The boat had seen better days; maybe fourteen or sixteen feet, outboard."

"Yeah? I thought you told Wade Handley we should watch out for a new, big Mercedes?"

"Yes, a shiny new black Mercedes; probably the best one they make, tinted windows. It belongs to Joseph Raggetti, the new director of the California lottery. He actually works for an Italian outfit, a multinational lottery management firm. He's furious with me because he thinks I'm going to play the lottery again. So he had Barbara's cabin burnt down. And had I been home, who knows what else would have happened. He showed up here right before the wedding."

"Sure, Reverend. The Director of the Lottery was here in Moke Hill on Halloween night. What was he dressed up as, a clown?"

"No. I think it was an Armani suit. But we could check. We took his picture."

"Ha! Don't tell me. The photographer who was mugged took the picture -- and now we will find that the camera is gone."

"Yes, but hopefully not the pictures. I asked him to change the memory chip in his camera and keep it safe."

"Now I know you are shitting me. Why would you bother to do that?"

"Because I needed something to keep him from killing me. The picture ties him to the guy in the alley."

"In your car?"

"Whatever."

McGuire just stared at me, shaking his head, as if he was trying to decide what to do. Then his radio came on.

"Jim, I'm taking a report on the mugging, so maybe you should call for another unit to take Shepard in."

"Do me a favor, ask the photographer if his camera was stolen?"

"Yes, it was, unfortunately."

"Ask if he had a memory chip that he was keeping safe for the Reverend."

There was a long pause. I started to work on a deal with God; something I could promise in exchange…, then embarrassingly I recalled my previous divine deal: God's help with Barbara's tumor for my help with the Lottery. My, my, hasn't that gone well!

"Jim?"

"Yes."

"He said he's got it."

"Thanks. We will be right up."

Thank God, I thought; but then I wasn't sure. (Could anyone really be sure?)

Chapter 22

It was after nine in the hotel's dining room. Wade, Marilyn, Barbara, Lloyd and I were sitting together finishing dinner. The deputies decided not to book me (yet) for John Doe's murder after they saw the pictures and after Lloyd assured them that he would produce me if they changed their minds.

"That was one amazing wedding, Andy," Marilyn said. "I'm just sitting here wondering how I could ever describe it to somebody. It was beautiful, the way the church was set up and lit."

"And the music was awesome," Wade said.

"Right!" Barbara said. "I had no idea my renter was so talented. Andy, you are just full of surprises."

"Uh huh, and wait 'til you hear his song about being in the saddle," Wade said with a grin.

"What song is that?" Barbara asked.

"Oh, the night is still young," I said as a tease.

"You'd better be careful if you want a winning ticket, Baby!" she said.

"Hear, hear," Wade said. "A toast." We raised our glasses. "To winning tickets for everyone!"

"I'll drink to that," said Marilyn with a sly smile.

Lloyd wasn't at the wedding and didn't catch the reference to my song. He asked, "What do you think Andy, are your numbers good?"

"God only knows. I'm just confused."

"Nonetheless," Marilyn said, "I heard on the radio that there has been a stampede to buy tickets. Everyone wants to be the first winner of the new, improved lottery. The jackpot was up to 33 million this afternoon."

I scooted a wedding program across the table to Lloyd. "Here" I pointed to the trick-or-treat numbers. "These are no longer protected by the client confidentiality rule. If it hits, you could plow it into your senior legal assistance agency."

"I don't know, Andy. That could be a slippery slope. Besides," Lloyd paused for dramatic effect and leaned into the table, "I have already bought two tickets for tomorrow!"

"Hear, hear," Wade said. "Let's drink to double-dipping! Leave it to a lawyer to see all the angles."

There was a lull in the conversation. I supposed none of us besides Lloyd had considered the option of buying multiple tickets, using the same numbers, in order to increase ones share of the pie.

There was a cheer from the direction of the hotel's ballroom. It must have been in response to the cutting of the cake; soon a server brought pieces to our table.

"How's your head feeling?" Barbara asked.

"Not too bad," I said.

"You seem to be doing a lot better than the other guy," Wade said. "It sounds like you almost took his head clean off."

"It's hard to picture you doing that," Barbara said.

My four friends looked at me as if I was a sixty year old samurai warrior with understated prowess. I said, "I didn't," and took a bite of the orange and black frosted carrot cake. "That part I improvised for the deputies."

"I knew you were fibbing!" Wade said.

"You lied to the Sheriff's Department?" Lloyd said with concern.

I nodded. "Actually, someone else saved my ass in the alley. When I swung and missed, the guy got real rough with me, trying to shove me back into my car and whacking me on the head. I probably will have some pretty good bruises when I get this costume off.

"Then it happened so fast -- I heard him sort of grunt and bones pop or crack, and his body hit the gravel. When I straightened up and turned around, I saw a person in a black cape and a raven's mask run off into the dark -- a small person."

Marilyn looked astonished, "Joy?!"

"That's my guess," I said. "Her black belt certainly makes her capable. So rather than drag her into an investigation with this improbable story, I told them I did it in self-defense."

"That was poor judgment on your part, Andy," Lloyd said. "You admitted to killing someone and then they end up stuffed into your trunk; then you try to cover for someone who may or may not be your ex-wife."

"Whoever it was, they left in the middle of the wedding when the deputies showed up," Wade said.

"Why would your ex show up at my son's wedding?" Barbara asked.

A little alarm went off inside my head: Warning! Jealousy alert! In a flash I reviewed several possible responses. None of them were guaranteed to get me out of this jam. So I said, "Several days ago I found this hanging on the cabin door," and I dangled the medicine pouch that hung from my neck. It's a Native American spiritual treatment -- I presume for protection. Inside are a feather, bone and claw; possibly from a raven. I can only guess that Joy somehow knew I was in danger."

"Excuse me," Barbara said getting up. Then in a cool tone, "I better check on how things are going in the kitchen," and she walked out of the dining room.

"Are you my winning ticket, baby?" Wade half sang under his breath when Barbara was out of earshot.

Marilyn gave him an elbow nudge. Then she turned to me and said, "Andy, do you have a place to stay? We have an extra bed."

"Thanks, but I have a room here at the hotel -- I think."

"Okay, but if things change, the offer stands."

The band started up in the ballroom and Wade took Marilyn to dance. I looked at Lloyd, "Joy's beloved grandmother was a medicine woman, as you may recall. The story is that her grandmother got into trouble with the law, which created unresolved conflict in Joy's family, and it has been a painful issue in Joy's adult life. I was just trying to keep history from repeating itself."

"I understand. Yet in my experience, trying to protect someone (especially when the law is involved) often makes matters worse. It also makes your lawyer's job more difficult."

"Do you think they can actually charge me?"

"I don't know. Tell me, was your car unlocked?"
"Yes. Who steals a car in Moke Hill?"

"How did you handle the gun? Could the John Doe's fingerprints still be on it?"
I told him about giving it to Wade, who engaged the safety, then passed it back to me later.

"Not good. Did they take a picture of your head?"
"Yes."

Lloyd thought for a while, then said, "To some extent it will depend on how well Joseph Raggetti covers his tracks and how aggressively he is investigated."

My phone rang. "Hello."

"Reverend, this is Lieutenant McGuire. We are impounding your car until we complete our investigation. We need you to surrender your keys. Where are you presently?"

"In the hotel dining room, but I have a change of clothes in the back seat that I would like to come down and get first."

"We can't let you take anything from the car. We will see you in ten minutes." I heard him hang up.

"I'm the one who is being aggressively investigated!" I was on the edge of blowing it. I stood up, I wanted to throw something, anything.

I reached for the vase of flowers on the table, but before I could do any damage, Lloyd said "Come on Andy, let's get some air," and he began to usher me out. His voice was steady and calm. I had seen Lloyd in several sticky situations and he always managed to keep his cool. The man was truly unflappable, and he had the ability to impart that calmness to those around him.

I really didn't want to cause a scene now. So far, I had managed to keep the evening's behind-the-scene drama, well, you know, behind the scene. Nathan and Cindy and their strangely clothed guests were not aware that the Sheriff Deputies at the wedding were not just people in Halloween costume, and most of the law enforcement activity was happening in the alley behind the church.

I had wanted so badly to keep from ruining this splendidly unique and wonderful affair, that I put myself in a bind. If I had immediately reported the death of the arsonist in the alley, I wouldn't have become a suspect. We'd still have his car and boat. And he wouldn't have wound up in my damned trunk!

"Shit!" I whispered furiously as we walked through the bar. When we got outside on the covered boardwalk, I yelled, (not directly to Lloyd, but more to God). "What else can I lose? God damn it! What else can they take away from me, huh!? I don't even have the fucking shirt on my back for Christ's sake!"

My anger sent a smoker back into the hotel. I paced under the porch lights. I was mad at McGuire; I was mad at Raggetti and the lottery system; I was mad at myself; and I was especially mad at God. Tears welled up in my eyes and I literally could not see straight.

"Andy, we'll get through this."

"I was just getting my feet under me, Lloyd. I was beginning to see my way forward. It's gone. Everything is gone."

"You've got to have some faith."

"Ha! John the Baptist got his fucking head cut off. That's what faith gets you." I couldn't believe what I was saying -- I was quoting scripture to a lawyer! I would have laughed if I hadn't been so angry.

Lloyd just stared at me. The corners of his mouth turned up. "Well, well. This is a side of you I haven't seen before. Come here, Andy."

I took a few steps to him and he reached out and took hold of my ceramic cross. He pulled it up and removed it from around my neck, then took my hand and opened my fist and placed the twice-fired cross in my palm. As I closed my fingers around it he said, "It's all right. Be mad, but have some faith."

I took a deep breath. Lloyd was being my friend. He obviously knew me better than I realized, and I was touched.

Nathan appeared at the door near where we stood. "Andy, is everything all right? Someone said you were upset?"

Lloyd said, "I think he needs a beer and a quiet place to sit for a while."

"Sure, we can arrange that," Nathan said.

Lloyd said "Give me your keys, Andy. I'll see that McGuire gets them. We will rent you a car tomorrow."

Without a word I handed him a set of keys: one was to a yellow bug with a bulging trunk lid, and one was to a burned out cabin belonging to an angry, jealous landlady. Then I was handed off from one lawyer to another.

Chapter 23

I walked through the hotel lobby and down the stairs to the garden behind the historic old landmark which was built of stone blocks chiseled into shape by prospectors who had come to California to make a fortune, and ended up simply working themselves to death pounding rock – a futility that I could relate to.

I found a table with chairs and sat until Nathan showed up with a couple of mugs of beer. The first thing I said was that I hoped he had received the ten dollar retainer fee I mailed to him. He laughed and said yes, but this was off the clock. I said maybe not, then as the music of the Calaveras Jumpers filtered down to us, I began to describe to him not only the skullduggery that was going on during his wedding, but how I'd gotten myself into such a mess. I wanted him to hear it from me.

Flabbergasted is a great word, and it perfectly fit Nathan's response. It was hard for him to sort through his feelings of shock, dismay, and concern. The fire would have been worrisome enough, and raised fears about his mother's safety. But the violent death was over the top, and potentially scandalous. When he began to think through my involvement with the CEO of the California Lottery and the numbers boldly printed on his wedding programs, he slipped into his lawyer mode and asked a ton of questions.

I was on my third beer (getting drunk seemed like one of my few options) when Cindy found us. "There you are," she said. "To quote the good pastor, I thought you might have run screaming from the reception yelling, 'What have I done?'"

"I've been thinking about it, but I am still here. Come on baby," he said patting his lap.

She plopped down and put her arm around his neck, "So sweetheart, has Andy been advising you on how not to be a vampire and a four-time loser?"

Nathan managed to chuckle and looked at me. "More or less. But I think I will fill you in tomorrow, unless you want to hear a frightful story on your wedding night?"

That was good, I thought to myself.

"Heavens no! I want to dance with my husband; that is, if this seminar is over?"

"Anything else I should know, Reverend?" Nathan asked, raising his eyebrows.

"I think that was enough, counselor," I said, pretending to pretend grave seriousness.

Cindy got back on her feet, "And Andy, the band is wondering when you are going to sing the blues again?"

In that moment I had so many possible responses, I couldn't pick one. I stood up and stretched. I felt calmer and a little lubricated. "Why not, My Old Bottom Blues it is."

I realized then that I still had my cross in my hand. When I slipped it back over my neck I saw the peace symbol, so I took it off and handed it to Cindy, "Please give this back to your mother; I have reason to believe it played a part in your conception. Tell her I wasn't so lucky."

She just gave me a quizzical smile.

I followed them back up the stairs to the ballroom, which used to be an adjoining building. In the 1800s it was the courtroom for a hanging judge. In those days justice was swift in this boomtown. The jail cell can still be seen on the lower level. They would bring the culprit up to the courtroom, convict him and sentence him, then take him out back (where the pool is now) and hang him from a tree. Then the people would gather in the hotel bar for a drink or two. Mokelumne Hill was a busy place during the height of the gold rush – there was a murder a week. In my mind, it made the ballroom a great place to sing the blues.

Bobby had the crowd on their feet dancing to a fifties classic: It was a one eyed, one horn, flying purple people eater. (Were the fifties really such an age of innocence?) The song somehow worked, people were shaking their stuff in costume.

When the song was finished, Barbara led several servers in with trays filled with glasses of champagne. The Master of Ceremonies announced that it was time for a toast. Nathan's Best Man rose and suggested that we toast to either Nathan's courage or tragic short-sightedness in marrying a prosecuting attorney, and that he might want to brush up on his plea-bargaining skills.

When the Matron of Honor had her turn, she toasted Cindy for a great party, then said Cindy had better enjoy herself because in the morning she would start to serve her sentence of life-without- parole.

The Master of Ceremonies then said "As your glasses are being refilled, Reverend Shepard will sing the blues!"

There was applause as Bobby and the band started off strong even as I made my way to the front. He handed me the harp mic, and I caught Barbara's eye, "This is dedicated to my riding instructor!" I shouted; and then in my lubricated state I let my harmonica fill the room with the complaint of the last line.

Then after several bars, Bobby nodded to me and I started singing the first verse,

> I thought I was ready
> But I was wrong,

As I played riffs between the lines I knew these words were so accurate for my life. So often I get these inspirations, these ideas and plans, and no matter what has happened in the past, I jump right into action, thinking (with St. Paul) that with God, all things are possible!

> I thought I was ready
> But I was so wrong!
> So when I got off that horse
> I had to write down this song:
> I've got the old bottom blues...

I've been writing down my song in my journals most of my life, always thinking I would learn from my mistakes – or at least how I could get myself out of a mess.

> And I pray I won't
> Have them for long!

I turned toward Bobby with my back toward the crowd – my back toward Barbara. I didn't want to see another woman who was angry and disappointed with me. And I wanted to stay up with Bobby – the band wasn't playing Blues 101 tonight, and half of the time I was sort of lost. I just tried to feel it and hear the chord progressions come around.

> My Baby has the
> Sweetest round bottom...

Nathan and Cindy flanked Barbara, and the newly-weds laughed as Barbara hid her face.

> But my skinny old butt
> Feels like its been to Sodom.

There it was: Barbara flashed me a big laughing smile. What I wouldn't do – haven't done! – just to get that smile in my sixty years. Would I always be a little boy all my life?

> I've got those old bottom blues...

I remember Bobby saying the first time we played: sing it straight, you've been hurt.

> Please don't tell my baby
> I've got 'em

Some women say they want their man to be vulnerable and show their feelings, but I never found that to be true; there is definitely a limit. They want to know we have feelings, but the full extent of the deepest, rawest, most humbling and humiliating emotions? They would rather not know.

Bobby led the band in a long instrumental excursion – part blues, part jazz and part funk. I decided to skip the third and fourth verses and just go into my new last verse, which I signaled to Bobby.

> I've known some women,
> But none could really ride…

The double meaning was obvious to everyone; I got hoots and cheers.

> So I am staying in this saddle
> Maybe it's my foolish pride.

Barbara was now nodding and smiling.

> I've got those old bottom blues,
> Painful old bottom blues.
> She said it'd get better
> Before my old bottom died!

Bobby got it: it was a made-to-order snappy conclusion. He motioned to the band, directing the guys with the neck of his guitar to bring it to a sharp ending in eight beats and an extended last note.

In the midst of cheers and applause I yelled into the mic, roughly toward Nathan and Cindy, "Stay in the saddle, kids."

The song (and the beer) pretty much finished the day for me. I was spent. I slipped out of the ballroom and found my room upstairs from the restaurant. It was a corner room overlooking the garden two floors below. I switched on the lights and saw that someone had laid out a new pair of sweat pants, sweatshirt, socks and shorts. There was also a hotel robe and slippers. On the antique dresser was a new razor and toothbrush. I wasn't prepared for this kindness and it almost undid me.

It was good to get the head-band and wig off my head. I automatically began scratching my scalp. I winced when I found the bump – "the fire won't hurt you," indeed! I took a look at it in the round mirror that matched the old vanity. Then I stared into my eyes; they glistened and blinked – I was alive. How many times could I cheat death? Had I truly lost everything? Obviously not. I was alive.

Boy, I hadn't thrown an angry fit like that in quite a while. I had felt so alone and abandoned – old feelings that I thought I had dispelled years ago. Thank God for Lloyd, a lifesaver.

Yes, Thank God.

I took a shower in the common bathroom down the hall. When I returned, there was a note on my bed along with a room service door hanger:

*I didn't get a chance to say goodnight,
but if you would like some "Room Service"
after I finish downstairs, just hang this little
sign on the door. Otherwise, sweet dreams.
The jealous one.*

I was dozing when the door to my room opened and closed. It was either the brief shaft of hallway light or the increased volume of the music from downstairs that woke me. Tired and groggy, I wasn't as enthusiastic to entertain Barbara as when I had put out the door hanger. I hoped she wasn't expecting much, especially without my booster pills. Her footsteps crossed the darkened room to the side of the bed.

"Andy?"

"Joy!?" alarmed, I reached for the table lamp and sat up.

"Yes, but let's leave the lights off." She held my arm and sat on the edge of the bed.

"How come? What are you doing here?"

"Your troubles are not over. Keep your voice down."

"What do you mean?"

There was light leaking in around the window shades and drapes; I could see Joy's silhouette, so I wasn't further startled when she reached out to my chest. She felt for the medicine bag.

"Good; take it off only when you bathe. Listen to me, Andy, its different this time. The stakes are much higher. If they fail this time around, they won't get another chance. You can't wait around for them to come to you, like tonight. You have to take it to them. Here," she took my wrist and put something in my hand. "Take this to the lottery center where Raggetti works. Give it to him, one way or another. Do it tomorrow; it may be too late after the drawing."

"I can't, I'm in too deep already. I'm screwing things up for people."

"Yes you are, old friend, and there is no way out. So you have to go deeper."

"What is this?"

"It doesn't matter. It's medicine."

"Good medicine or bad medicine?"

She didn't answer. We sat in silence for a moment. Then Joy was up and against the far wall. The door opened and a broad shaft of light poured across the bed.

"Hey, Sugar," Barbara stuck her head in and looked around. "You talking to yourself?"

"Some people call it praying." Improvising was one of my strong suits.

"Oh, I'm sorry to butt in. I'll be through in about twenty minutes. Is there anything you want – I mean, that I should bring with me?"

"A bottle of port."

"Sure, and two glasses. See you soon," and she closed the door.

After a long pause, Joy's voice came, "You never did make it easy."

"Neither did you."

"I knew that, but you thought you were easy."

"So that's how I made it hard?"

"You have no idea. But none of that matters. Just start paying more attention and try not to let someone jump you again. You don't even have your door locked for Christ's sake!"

"All right. And thanks for your help earlier."

"How's your head?"

"Just have a small reminder."

"Good." She opened the door, "Have fun – with your Port." And I was alone again. Happy frigging trick or treat! Would this day never end?

* * *

It was more like an hour when the door opened again, but Joy's visit had me wide awake. Barbara had a tray with a bottle, two small glasses, a lit candle and a piece of wedding cake.

"Trick? or Treat?"

"Both," I said.

She laughed and closed the door. "Are you finished with your prayer?"

Without shame (hey, I'm a guy!) I said, "Yes, it just got answered."

"You are quite a bull-shitter for a preacher."

"Ouch. I thought it was a good line."

"Your best lines are when you aren't trying, Baby." She lowered the tray next to the table lamp, then undid her apron and sat at the vanity with the candle and took the curlers out of her hair. I opened the bottle and poured the Port. Watching her back, I sipped as she unbuttoned the front of her house dress, let it slide off her shoulders and then unfastened her bra. I had never seen her undress before. She was always robed when I came to give her a massage.

She stood up, letting her dress and bra fall to the floor. Still facing the mirror with her back toward me, she slowly scooted down her undies and slip and said, "So, your baby has the sweetest round bottom? That was a better line."

"Agreed."

She turned around. "Your reward is the King's dish. Have you ever had the King's dish, Sugar?" she said, dripping with seduction.

"I have a feeling that perhaps I've been deprived. Is it on the room service menu?"

"You can bet on it, but you have to get yourself ready. Here's what you do. It's very simple. Lay on your back kitty-cornered across the bed with your head in one of these bottom corners. Good, and we are in luck because there's no foot board to get in our way."

I adjusted myself to Barbara's satisfaction. When I looked up she backed carefully up to the corner with legs apart and knees slightly bent. It was a tight fit but she was able to slip her bottom over my head and bury my face in her silky, fragrant pubic hair.

I whispered, "Umm, what a good dish to set before the King!"

She took my hands from her hips and lifted them around to her breasts. "This is the proper etiquette in eating this rare dish, my love."

"Rare indeed."

Chapter 24

Friday night's sleep was so deep, and my dreams so chaotic, that morning came like a threatening stranger as I awoke disoriented in the unfamiliar room. I was alone. A vague memory returned of Barbara saying that she had to go. Go where? Her car was at the lake, so I assumed she had her own room in the hotel.

This led me to my new reality: my home was gone. Where was I going to live? The hotel was too expensive. Moving in with Barbara was too...? Complicated? Dangerous? Stupid? And Riverbank Road would be like going backwards. There was the church – my church; now there was a weird idea.

I missed my espresso machine, and I couldn't think of any place in Moke Hill to get a latte`. I tried to go back to sleep and forget about it – all of it.

But it was too late, my mind was on the job, puzzling out how I could make the church work as a residence. It would be in the lower level: the kitchen, restrooms, the two offices and the classroom. That would be more space than the cabin. I'd leave the sanctuary and social hall intact. The kitchen was big enough for a small table. I could knock out a wall between the offices to make a good-sized living room. The classroom would become my bedroom. I would need a shower; the restrooms were adjacent, I could turn one into a shower room and add a door between them.

I got up to get something to write with and start a list. But there was nothing. I had nothing. The anger from last night returned. I marched off down the hall to the bathroom.

When I got back to the room I decided to start the day over. I opened the drapes and raised the blinds to let in some more light. Then I propped myself up in bed and meditated for forty minutes. I spent the last twenty making a thank you list. When I got to

Joy, it hit me – the medicine pouch! Then just as fast – no way! I'm not going to Sacramento to see Raggetti; and for what?

I reached over and opened the drawer in the night stand and removed the pouch. It felt soft and heavy. I opened it up carefully. It was filled with a light grey, chalky powder. What the hell was this? She said it was medicine. It reminded me of something. It was heavy for its size – like cremated remains. Could it be ground up bones? I closed it back up tight and tried to remember her exact words: give it to him, one way or another.

Ridiculous. I got up and dressed in my new sweats and got ready for the day. I still had a life, and I was going to need some stuff. I called Wade and asked him if he still had his truck, and would he like to go saleing, yard saleing, with me. He said sure, if I thought I could hang on this time! (I would have to wake up earlier to outwit Wade.) We agreed to meet in an hour at the coffee shop on Hwy 49, just outside Moke Hill.

I found Barbara doing paperwork in her office. I invited her to breakfast and offered her a ride back to her house in Wade's truck. She said that would be fine if I could give her a few minutes. So in the meantime I walked over to the church and took some measurements of the rooms that could become my home.

Soon Barbara and I were walking up to the highway. In front of the café I bought the county newspaper for the yard sale ads. Then we got a table, ordered breakfast for three (thinking Wade would join us soon), and settled into conversation.

"Did you think I had another woman in my room last night?"

"Things like that happen at weddings you know. And back in the day, there used to be a tunnel under the street from the hotel to the buildings on the other side, to sneak women in."

I smiled, "Come on, why do you think you are so jealous?"

"Oh, I don't know. Why do you think men are such assholes?"

"Could it be that women are fearful and push us away, so we do stuff?"

"Could it be that only stupid women are naïve about what men do behind our backs?"

"Wouldn't it be better to give a guy the benefit of the doubt, at least until you know if he cheats or lies?"

"No. But it would be better if men didn't habitually cheat and lie so we wouldn't have to doubt everything they do or say."

"How can you get the love you want without occasionally extending a little grace to a guy!?"

"Oh, we do extend grace, all the time. That's why we don't usually kill them (unlike the violence that comes our way too often)."

"How about those Giants! You think they will win the World Series tonight?"

Barbara smiled. We sipped our coffee. "I guess I should thank you, Andy."

"For what?"

"For not suggesting that you move in with me. I might have said yes, and we would have been in big trouble."

"Really? You might have said yes?"

"Oh yeah. I might have said yes to anything last night."

"Boy, I missed my chance."

"Honey, I don't think you missed much last night, let me tell you."

"However, I sure miss my espresso machine this morning."

"That reminds me, I talked to my insurance agent this morning. He said that because you and I have a personal relationship you are not classified as a renter, so your losses are covered."

"You actually told him we have a personal relationship? So I can now introduce you as, 'Barbara, my personal relationship?' Great! That would clarify that we do not have an impersonal relationship, like a renter-with-privileges."

"My, you're a little testy this morning. Anyway, the insurance will also pay for you to stay somewhere, like the hotel," she said with a smile, "up to sixty days until you find a permanent place."

"Will it cover room service? I feel like getting personal all over again."

"You are such a bull-shitter."

We were both laughing when Wade walked in. "Good morning," he said as he took off his jacket. "So Andy, how's the old bottom today?"

I looked at Barbara and smiled – a very tempting door had just been opened. She laughed out loud and Wade could see there was a private story.

"Never mind," he said. "I really don't want to know. I was just making polite conversation." He sat down. "So Andy, you have a pistol in your pocket today?"

We busted up again. When Wade was on, there was no stopping him. The waitress brought him some coffee and refilled ours. This was the best place for breakfast in the county. It was run by a family from Greece. The waitress and her mother served up the food that the father cooked with Greek highlights. I never found out why they ended up in such an out-of-the-way place as Calaveras County – and Moke Hill at that! Everyone has a story, an ongoing story, and to some degree they are all intertwined if not interwoven. That's why we were eating breakfast together, and why it was cooked and served by the Greeks.

As we ate, I shared my idea about renovating the lower part of the church for a residence. Since I owned it free and clear, the money I would save on rent would cover taxes, insurance, upkeep, and maybe leave a little left over, stretching my modest retirement income. My plan was to furnish it with yard sale bargains and then use the insurance settlement to pay for the renovation. I would do most of the work myself. Plan "B" of course would be to let the state pay for my room and board, in jail. It was Wade who saw the irony in the plan "A": I would go from not attending a church to living in one.

After breakfast we drove Barbara home and walked through the remains of the cabin looking for anything to salvage. We found nothing except the sad reality that my lakeshore lifestyle, and my four short months as Barbara's massage therapist and renter, had come to an abrupt end. Would Barbara and I continue our personal relationship now that I was gone? I couldn't say. How could she keep a close eye on me now – how would she handle her jealousy?

There were a dozen yard sales advertised in the paper. Four of them were nearby in an upscale subdivision in Valley Springs where there was a country club and golf course. I used to think of yard sales, garage sales and estate sales as junk sales; but this was a different chapter of my life, and like a poor kid on Halloween I headed for the rich part of town.

By eleven we had a truck full: bed, sofa, TV, three end tables and three ugly lamps, a slightly soiled recliner, a braided rug, two small dressers, two boxes of kitchen pots and utensils, and one box of dishes. All for the low, low price of $415.00.

On the way back to the church (or should I say, house?) to unload, I made some calls to some other sales and found a kitchen table and chairs in San Andres for $65. While we were in town we stopped at the thrift store where I bought three sets of clothes, blankets, and linens, a toaster oven and a mixer, all for $28. (Alas, no espresso machine.) Total cost $508 and I was close to having a home, of sorts.

On our second trip back to the church, Wade asked, "Where are you going to watch for the lotto results?"

"I don't know."

"I guess you're going to be doing some homemaking tonight, huh?"

"I don't know."

"So what is it? You have a date?"

"I have a problem."

"You just figure that out?"

"A new problem. I talked to Joy last night."

"When?"

"After I went to bed."

"She called you? When Barbara was there? Oh Boy!"

"No, before Barbara came by, Joy sneaked into my room and…"

"Wait a minute, Andy." Wade pulled the pickup over and parked. "Now I'm all ears."

"She had the black cape on, and the raven's mask in her hand. She checked to see if I was wearing this medicine pouch. She said I was still in trouble and the stakes were now much higher. She said I shouldn't just wait for them to come to me, I had to take it to them."

"Take what? Your now famous flop move that you imagined had laid out the arsonist?"

"You know how to hurt a guy. No, she gave me this," and I pulled out the second pouch from my pocket. "She said to give it to Raggetti before tonight's drawing, one way or another."

"What is it?"

"God only knows," I gave it a slight toss in the air and caught it. "Maybe ground up bones of something – or someone."

"Let's see."

But when I held it out to Wade he took his hand back, "Maybe not. Damn, Andy, you and your strange women!" And he quickly started the truck and drove back onto the highway. He looked at his watch. "We have time to drop this stuff off and get to Sacramento. The traffic shouldn't be too bad."

"It's okay Wade, you don't need to go." I wasn't even sure I wanted to go.

"I'm not about to let you go into the lion's den alone, buddy."

"I mean it. What would I tell Marilyn when they find you stuffed into a trunk?"

"Tell her it was tough luck that I didn't have some raven's guts or something hanging around my neck."

"That's a good one Wade. That will cheer her up."

"All right, smarty; and if it's you bulging in the Mercedes' rear?"

"That's a disgusting image, Wade. But here is what would comfort Barbara: Tell her I was found in the trunk alone – there was no woman!"

We were still laughing as Wade turned down into Moke Hill and Wade said, "Good thing Barbara didn't come in when Joy was in your room!"

* * *

We rolled into Sacramento at four o'clock in Wade's truck. My mind was fruitlessly rehearsing possible plans for delivering the package. Was the lobby safe? Was Raggetti's office safe? Would we both fit in his trunk? Did I have to give it to him personally, or could I leave it on his car, or under a chair in the lobby? Could I give it to a secretary to give to him? How about getting on the roof and dropping it down a vent pipe? How about dumping it in a vase with an arrangement of flowers and having it delivered?

The truth was, if I were Raggetti, I would not want to see me. Not after I wrote him the letter that implied we had a deal, and not today when the numbers were being drawn, and especially not at his office. Certainly last night made it even more problematical.

Then another thought occurred to me. What if the pouch was nothing at all, and Joy was playing a nasty joke on us all? Red Cloud was known for her wicked sense of humor.

When we arrived at the large, lushly landscaped campus of the California State Lottery Center, my only thought was: I'd rather be playing my harmonica out on my little brick patio overlooking Hogan Lake and watching the autumn sunset. We parked along- side a lawn and a grove of liquid amber trees that were dressed like hookers in an arboretum.

"Now what, pastor?"

"I say we appoint a committee to do this job. What do you say?"

"Very pastoral of you, Reverend. And let's make Joy the chairwoman."

"Excellent idea my son."

I made myself touch the door handle. "I'll be right back," I said. "I'm sure I won't be long, so keep the motor running."

"Nice try, Andy," and Wade climbed out on the driver's side. Together we walked past the door of the Sacramento district office and entered the State Lottery Center.

The receptionist was behind thick glass, and the door that led into the main part of the building had a coded lock. We walked up to the reception counter. I became aware of our appearance: I was in sweats, and wore the riding boots that I had worn with Merlin's robes. Wade had on work clothes for our yard saleing. We didn't look like we were ready for business.

"Hello," I said. "I would like to see Joseph Raggetti."

She looked nervous. Maybe she was having a bad day or something? "Do you have an appointment?"

I looked at Wade as my mind did whatever it mysteriously does when I improvise. "Not exactly. But it is quite possible he's expecting us today. We have something of his. Could you please let him know Reverend Andy Shepard is here to see him?"

Now she looked downright agitated. "Andy Shepard?"

"Yes. Maybe you recall, we've done business here before."

"I'll tell him. Please have a seat over there."

We turned. There were a dozen nice chairs and a magazine rack in one corner. As we walked, Wade smiled and said under his breath, "We've done business before!"

We took a seat and watched as the receptionist left through a doorway in her protected space. I took the pouch out of my pocket, put its black silk cord over my head, and hung it next to mine. It was more than twice the size of my light raven's bag. I massaged it with my thumb and forefinger as I watched for the receptionist to return. I could feel the small stick figure of a man which was made of tiny black beads -- the only ornamentation on the heavy pouch.

"What are we doing here, Wade?" I said in a soft voice. "Is this Nineveh?"

"No, Jonah. It's Sacramento, and I don't think Raggetti repents. He isn't any different than Charley Morely or Clyde what's-his-name from two years ago, bless their souls"

"Yeah, all dangerous idiots. Where do these guys come from?"

"Maybe from idiot fathers," Wade whispered.

The receptionist reappeared and gave us a long glance as she took her seat and tried to look busy at her computer. I recalled something Joseph Raggetti said about his father. He was involved in horse racing and gambling in Siena, the heart of Tuscany. I bet he was a piece of work. Maybe he also had his fingers in this sticky pot.

The door opened and out came Lieutenant Jim McGuire. I stared at him in disbelief as he walked toward us with two tall guys in black uniforms with big bold white initials for Department of Justice.

"What a nice surprise," McGuire said. "So glad you could drop in for a visit, Reverend."

We stood up, "Lieutenant," I said, trying to keep the panic out of my voice.

The heavy door swung open again and there was Raggetti, looking as if he was struggling with his own distress. He was flanked by two more officers from the DOJ.

"We were just about to take a drive to the Hall of Justice (I like that name, don't you? The Hall of Justice.) We need to have a talk with the good Director here. I think it would be good if you would join us. And who's your friend here?"

"This is Wade Handly, he drove me here. I don't seem to have a car at the moment." I turned to Wade, "Why don't you hang out in town for a while? I'll call and let you know when to pick me up."

"Wade Handly? You don't happen to work for the Shepard Foundation, do you?"
"Actually, I do."
"Fine, you're coming with us too."

"Just a talk, huh?" Wade asked.

"That's right, unless you want us to arrest you first?"

We paraded out the door. There was a small plaza that we had to cross. Beyond the plaza there were three black SUVs and a Calaveras County Sheriff car waiting. They bunched the three of us together and surrounded us front and back as we walked across the open space. I was shoulder-to-shoulder with Raggetti. This was my moment; I was somehow sure of it. "Joseph," I said as I slipped off the pouch. "I was asked to give you something," and I handed it to him. He took it hesitantly. "Your father's bones."

I could hear him inhale suddenly; his eyes bulged and he stopped in his tracks. He stared at the pouch, "Nooo!" he said in a terrified voice. He said something in Italian and sank to his knees.

I was yanked away by the men in black. They half dragged me to a waiting car. I tried to look around to see what was happening, but couldn't. I was pushed against the fender and handcuffed and patted down. Then the door opened, my head was pushed down, and I was shoved inside. The door slammed shut. One of the officers stood in front of my side-window and I couldn't see the plaza.

Soon someone got in the front of the car and said, "What did you give him!"

"I think it was a leather pouch filled with powdered bone."

"That's all!?"

"That was it."

"Where did you get it?"

"I made it," I lied, despite Lloyd's advice.

Then I could see through the front window that they were carrying Raggetti, feet first, to the car in front of us. They laid his limp body in the back seat, and two officers got in the front. My questioner got out and spoke briefly with them, then quickly, with their wheels squealing, they drove off.

The officer next to my window was on his radio with someone, and there was a conference in front of my car. Wade was surrounded as McGuire grabbed him by the shirt and yelled in his face. Wade shrugged and said something. McGuire yelled louder and I could hear, "You shithead, if he dies you are going DOWN!"

Wade (and this I couldn't believe) turned his head towards me, smiled and waved. McGuire swore all the way to his car and got in. Wade was put in a third car and off we went.

Lloyd Pettigrew entered my locked room at 7:00 p.m. I had refused to talk to anyone and had sat alone for two hours. They moved Lloyd and me to a private conference room. We sat down and Lloyd began, "We got a break. You had losing numbers."

"That's a break?"

"Raggetti was carrying your letter wherein you seemed to be selling him winning numbers; the letter you thought no one would see except you and me. Now the DOJ has it. If your numbers had hit the jackpot, with Raggetti dead, there would have been too much pointing at you, you would have had a nice long prison ministry, Andy. Now it just looks like he was hassling you and you were hassling him. Then he had your place burned down, and then you apparently scared him to death."

"Raggetti is really dead?"

"Somehow you pushed the right button. You care to tell me how you did that?"

I got up, I needed to move. My mind was a confused mess. I walked around the little room. Did I kill a man? For what?

"They were the wrong numbers?"

"You seem surprised."

"Well, we did shut down the lottery once."

"Or, one could say, crooked Charles Morely and his friends shut-down the lottery."

"Maybe. But when I found that old ticket and the dollar in my costume, it seemed like a sure sign: I had winning numbers again."

"Maybe you misread the sign, misread where it would lead you. Maybe this is exactly where it was pointing."

"Here? Being charged with two murders?"

I walked some more. The ground under me seemed to be shifting. Lloyd was suggesting that God, or whatever, had a morbid sense of humor.

"You aren't charged yet. They found the boat at the home of Raggetti's chauffeur. Now it may be possible to show that the two of them put the arsonist's body in your unlocked car and then the chauffeur drove the SUV home with the boat while Raggetti drove the Mercedes. That's why McGuire and the DOJ were at the lottery center when you showed up: to question Raggetti. Which brings us back to the question, what were you doing there and how did you do it?"

"Joy gave me a small mysterious pouch and implied that my only chance out of my dangerous mess was to give it to Raggetti before the drawing of the numbers tonight. It was my guess that it was bone. Did they tell you what was in it?"

"Just bone. That is all they've found so far. But it appears it made his heart stop."

We sat quietly for several moments. Then Lloyd asked, "So what did you tell him when you handed it over?"

I was reticent to say. Perhaps they were murderous words. Lloyd waited, then pushed, "Andy?"

I sighed. "All I said was, 'I was asked to give you something.' And then when he took it I simply said, 'Your Father's bones.'"

"Where did that come from?"

"I honestly don't know."

"Did Joy tell you that?"

"No. She was in a bit of a hurry last night. How is Wade?"

"He is on his way home."

"Good. Now what?"

"Now your lawyer is going to earn his big bucks and get you released by showing them that they do not really have anything to charge you with."

"Sorry about your two tickets; that would have been real big bucks. It was all just a bust."

Lloyd got up and said, "On the contrary, I think you may have won. I wouldn't be surprised if the lottery commission now washes its hands of state-sponsored commercial gambling. The critics' objections have now been proven true: gambling breeds corruption. You may be the real winner tonight, Andy Shepard."

* * *

While I waited another long hour, I tried to finish a blues song I had started earlier:

>Forget about them angels
>And other fancy dancers,
>When I get up to heaven
>There better be some answers!
>'Cause hell no longer scares me,
>The fire's voice just dares me,
>So there better be some answers
>Up in heaven.

Did Joy know that her "medicine" was deadly? Are shaman assassins? Or did I have murder in my heart when I told Raggetti I had his father's bones?

Where is God's love in this?

The door opened and they said I could go. Lloyd walked me out of the building and we were greeted by Ono Park, the reporter who covered the whole Lottery drama. "Okay, who told you I was here?"

"Your friend, John LeFiever, of course. He wouldn't tell me where you've been for months, then today he gave me a call."

"All right, one question, then I have to go. I'm exhausted. We can talk tomorrow."

Ono cued the cameraman. "Reverend Shepard, people know you were a foe of the lottery, did you kill Joseph Raggetti?"

"No, Ms. Park, he died of natural causes: greed and fear."

The cameraman said, "Got it."

"Smart answer, Andy. His father is accusing law enforcement of killing him."

"His father? He's alive?"

"Right. He flew up this evening from L.A. I talked to him at the hospital. Where can I reach you?"

"Uh, reach me? The Mokelumne Hill hotel. Good Night, Ono."

Lloyd drove me back to the grand old hotel, and though it was midnight when we arrived, there were lights sparkling and a crowd of people in the bar. Lloyd dropped me off in front, then drove off to his home in Riverton.

I stepped up on the boardwalk and peered through the ornate gold lettering on the hotel's windows. Surprisingly there was a lively party in progress. People were two and three deep at the bar and the tables were full.

Out of an old familiar place of childhood longing, I momentarily thought they were all there to welcome me home and to shower me with love and honor – the good-boy returns home a hero.

Then I noticed many were glancing at the television. It showed a wild street celebration where people were wearing San Francisco Giants shirts and caps. The home team must have won the World Series, and this bar was the only place for miles around to gather and join the celebration.

Seeing the gathering for what it was, I heard my father's voice, "Son, you be the love you need."

I guess Joy wasn't the only one being helped by their ancestors; and that was a strange thought. It was then I noticed that at one table sat the Foundation's board, Wade and Marilyn with Josh, John and Peter. My heart responded with a flood of affection. I loved them all.

And I loved this old hotel. And I loved Calaveras County. And I loved my life: this crazy dance of Spirit and Spirits, of love and sex, of helping and being helped, of teaching and learning.

I wanted to go in and hug everyone, but I paused to wipe away my tears and blow my nose.

"You going to loiter around out here, Cowboy, or do you want to come in and have a beer with your buddies?" It was Barbara, one arm in a sling and the other holding a bar towel as she stood in the doorway.

I couldn't speak. I just grinned and walked to her and wrapped my arms carefully around her, closed my eyes and felt her warmth. From inside someone led a loud sing-songy chant, "Let's go, Gi-ants."

"What a night," I whispered into her hair.

"I'm glad you made it home," she said softly.

"Yes."

When I opened my eyes again, my five dear friends were filing out of the saloon. Josh came up first and we hugged, "How was it in the whale's belly, big guy?"

"God's a bit of a jokester," I said. "I'm seeing things a little different now."

John LeFiever came up next for a hug. "Nice sound bite on the evening news, pal."

Peter then greeted me with, "Good to see you, Andy. I'm glad I don't have to visit you in jail."

Then Wade and Marilyn, "I don't know about you, Andy," she said: "Breaking people's necks? Giving deadly curses?" She gave me a wink.

"I don't deserve the praise," I said. "It belongs to She-who-must-not-be-named!"

From the darkened street came, "And who might that be?"

My head turned to see Joy and her dog, Jake, walking toward us. How did she pull off these sudden appearances?

"Tell me, Andy," she said as she got closer, "what did you do, stuff that pouch down Raggatti's throat?"

"I wanted to, but no. I just handed it to him," I said, rubbing Jake's head.

Joy raised her right eyebrow at me.

"That was it," I said innocently.

Wade jumped in with glee, "Well, except for that little part that you improvised."

"You improvised? With my medicine pouch?!"

"Not really," I said nervously. Not an argument, not now, I thought.

"You didn't think my snake-bone meal was good enough?"

"It wasn't that. You didn't mention what I should say when I gave it to him; that's all."

"What did you say to him, Andy?" she asked in an even tone.

Softly I said, "Your father's bones."

"What? 'Your father's bones'?!"

Everyone was still and listening. Joy stepped back a pace or two. Her eyes fixed on me. Then suddenly she smiled and said, "Perfect. I wish I had thought of that."

Then Joy laughed and looked right at Barbara, "Keep him, Barbara, this one's got potential."

And to the rest, "See ya, friends," as Joy-in-the-morning and her dog, walked back down the street into the darkness.

Part 2: Limping Into Heaven

Chapter 25

From another world came a voice, an interruption, "Mom, it's Nathan. If you can hear me, squeeze my hand.

I heard him, but I didn't want to squeeze his hand. I would have preferred he shut up.

"Mom, it's Nathan, if you can hear me, try to squeeze my hand. Cindy is here too. We love you."

I felt as if I were floating in space, which was much better than I'd felt before, and I really didn't want Nathan to screw it up. I knew he meant well. He was a smart boy, but he had no idea that I was balanced between very bad pain and oblivion. So I played dead, which wasn't hard since I was nearly in a coma.

"She isn't responding," Nathan said softly over the noise of some machine. I guess he was speaking to Cindy.

Warm hands took a hold of my right foot. They gave it a soft squeeze and a caress, then began massaging it with nice, slow circles. Occasionally the hands stopped at some pressure point to stimulate a linked part of my body – Andy taught me that. It had to be Andy rubbing my foot. He was my massage therapist/pastoral counselor/horseback riding student/lover/former renter/ and sometimes pain-in-the-ass. Like recalling a dream, I vaguely remembered that he brought me to this strange place.

I began to float off into the blue, and I drifted to who knows where for who knows how long. When I returned, Andy was massaging my other foot.

"She looks so peaceful," Cindy whispered.

Great. That's what they say at a viewing in a mortuary. Where am I? I concentrated on this problem. I heard beeping sounds and several voices along with a machine that sounded like a bread maker. A hospital? Yes, my arm, an operation to take off a benign bone tumor near my shoulder. I again tried to focus my attention, but I couldn't feel my shoulder.

"How's she doing, doctor?" I heard Nathan ask.

"She is still not trying to breathe on her own. But her pulse is good, her kidney function is good, and her EEG is normal. We're still working on getting rid of the clots."

Clots? Great, something has gone wrong. But Andy's magic hands didn't even slow down. I could feel his thumbs making tiny round circles as if he was dissolving clots in my feet. I wiggled my big toe (I think). Andy gave my foot a knowing squeeze. I wanted to smile but something was in my mouth.

"We love you, Mom. We'll be back," Nathan said.

Nathan was my first; ten hours of labor. I never wanted to go back into a hospital, so with the two girls I had water births at home. Now I could feel the warm water. I was floating with my coach's hand in mine. "Hey Cowgirl, we're all going to help you through this."

It was Andy. He was holding my hand.

"Your job is to relax and to know you'll be off this breathing machine as soon as possible. It shouldn't be long, you're actually doing pretty good."

I tried to squeeze his hand.

"Okay! I felt that. Now rest, sweetheart. Rest, and don't worry. I'm taking care of the horses – even picking the muck out of their shoes."

I commanded my hand to squeeze again and was rewarded with a kiss on my forehead. "Keep him, Barbara," his ex had said, "He's got potential." Maybe. But right then I wasn't so sure what my potential was.

Chapter 26

I might as well clean out the lottery ticket drawer, I thought, leaning against my kitchen counter, my arm in a sling and sipping my first cup of coffee. It felt wonderful to be home again, but the drawer was bugging me. Why was I so resistant? It was a silly habit: saving my tickets week after week. It was an effort to keep track of my losing numbers so I wouldn't make the same mistake by playing them again. I should have cleaned them out ages ago.

I looked out over the breakfast counter and through the living room windows down to Hogan Lake. It was this view – the best in Calaveras County, California – that sold me on this property. As I stared, not really seeing the blue lake or the hills beyond, it occurred to me that my damn ticket collection was like trying to not forget the faces and names of my old husbands and lovers. I didn't want to play them again either; the right guy had to come along one of these days.

I walked over to the drawer and opened it. I gave a weary look down at hundreds of lottery tickets that I had bought since divorcing my last husband. Look at all those losers, I thought. What a sad collection. Any of them could have changed my life – but no, after playing regularly for four years, here I am. Nothing's changed except I'm quickly getting older.

I ran my good hand through the tickets thinking, all these disappointments, yet they feel light and loose as a cloud of bath bubbles. I stirred them around and lifted a handful, then slowly let them float back into the drawer. Actually, they seemed like ashes, dead useless ashes. What was the real reason I'd been saving them? Was I holding onto a fantasy and not living my real life?

I was hiding in that drawer by thinking: whatever happens during the day, so what. I am going to hit the jackpot! How was I different from those religious people who seemed to glide over their troubles thinking: "Praise the Lord, why should I care, I'm going to heaven." How embarrassing. But no matter, the games were over. The California Lottery had gone out of business thanks to Reverend Andy Shepard who exposed its corruption.

I set my coffee down, brought the recycle bag to the drawer, and started putting handfuls of tickets into the trash, but they didn't go in easily. Each hand full included bitter realities: I was tired of running the hotel, I was tired of living in this crummy little nowhere county, and I didn't want to grow old here by myself! But now I knew no jackpot was going to save me. My tears began to overflow. I let a fist full of useless tickets drop back into the drawer. I walked over and grabbed a dishtowel, sat heavily at the breakfast counter, buried my face in the soft cotton cloth and let go.

Why couldn't I win!? What's wrong with me? Never the right number or the right guy. My grief and misery poured out with convulsive sobs too long denied. The guest house fire and Andy moving to Moke Hill; now the botched operation on my arm.

I covered my face and rocked back and forth. I hated to show the world my embarrassing, unattractive grief. I felt like a weak loser, like I was left standing alone at the dance again. "God damn you, Andy, I miss you!" I said to the empty kitchen.

He had only been a five-minute walk down the hill to the guest house. I have had other lovers in the cabin, but none like the Reverend. And although he now lived near the old hotel where I worked, things had changed.

It was that recollection that brought another wave of sadness. If I hadn't been so stupid, maybe he would have moved in here after the fire. My jealousy got in the way again – typical. Oh hell, maybe it is all for the best. The guy has been married four times –

there's got to be something wrong with him. Screw it.

It had been a horrible month and a half. I was grateful in October when my tests showed that my bone tumor was not cancerous, but my arm operation in November was more extensive than the doctors expected. Then I was mistakenly given the wrong medication and I almost died in the Intensive Care Unit. I spent ten long days in the hospital and then most of December with my son Nathan and his new wife, Cindy, in Stockton where they both practiced law. They lived near the hospital where I was treated daily for the infection I developed. After Christmas I insisted I was coming home – I had had it. I felt too dependent and I wanted my life back.

Now it was only four days to the New Year, and I needed to tackle the drawer. Having nearly died made some things very clear in my life, and one of them was that false hope was false living.

I blew my nose and wiped my eyes, then marched over to the lottery drawer again. I scooped out the rest of the tickets and stuffed them into the bag, then opened a cupboard door and began transferring the fettuccine, rigatoni, spaghetti, macaroni, farfel and lasagna into the empty drawer. "I re-christen you the Pasta Drawer!", I said out loud when I had finished. Though I had been through a long streak of bad luck, I knew my pasta dishes were always winners.

Chapter 27

New Year's Eve day my arm ached. Every day I woke up and expected to feel better. The operation was supposed to not only remove the tumor, but the pain as well; but the infection and the resulting second operation had made my arm feel worse, not better. I gave serious thought to firing my doctors and getting new ones. Still, I was being a good patient: I kept my arm in a sling, changed the dressing regularly, took the powerful antibiotics along with my pain pills, and waited for permission to return to work.

Although I wouldn't be working, I looked forward to being at the hotel for New Year's Eve. It would be the first time since early November. I thought it would be a step toward the way it used to be.

Two dear souls had been covering for me at work. The first was Ray Benson, the owner of our historic hotel in Mokelumne Hill (an Indian name pronounced mo-call-ah-me, but simply called Moke Hill by the locals.) Ray lived down in Lodi where he had a vineyard and winery in the Central Valley. After the crush he was able to leave things to his winemaker and cover for me at the hotel up here in the foothills traditionally called the Gold Country. I couldn't ask for a better boss.

When Ray couldn't get away, my bartender, Sabina, managed things. Like me, she was a horsewoman, and nearly every dollar she made she put into her horses. Her hope was to someday have a horse ranch that would make her a living. The divorce settlement she wrangled from her ex two years ago had helped quite a bit towards that goal.

Sabina at thirty-four was fifteen years younger than me, but people said we looked alike: dark long hair and attractive figures. Even though she was an inch or two taller than me, she was still considered short. We had a lot in common – except that she had married money, and I have been attracted to some poor sons-of- bitches. We were close as sisters, and we loved to have a drink or two and savage men we knew.

The plan for New Year's Eve was for the hotel to serve up a special surf-and-turf dinner until about nine. We had a local band, Bobby and the Calavaras Jumpers, lined up to play at the bar. We were already maxed-out with dinner reservations, and for the first time in a long while we had no vacancies in the hotel.

After nine the band would move across the street to Andy's church (a church without pews or a congregation). He was throwing a dance party for the Moke Hill Community.

Around three I heard Sabina's big, purple, four-wheel drive pickup crunching the gravel as it slowly rolled down my long driveway. I went out to meet her in the cool December air as she pulled in and stopped.

"Hi girl." I said as she stepped down out of the cab.

"Hi Honey. Whoa, I've never seen you with short hair before. It looks really cute!"

"Thanks, it's my one-handed hair style."

"How's the arm today?"

"Let's just say I'm glad you're driving. Do you have time to help me get the horses in?"

"Sure, let's have a look at your sweethearts." She grabbed some apples from her truck and we walked over toward the horse barn. "Why don't you let me take your horses to my place for a while, just until you heal up some?"

"I keep thinking I'll be back to normal any day now."

"Hopefully you will, Barbara, but right now your first priority is to take care of yourself; so why not let me take care of them for a while and give your neighbors a break?"

"I hate being sick, you know? I just don't want to give in to it."

"Right, that's good, don't give in to sickness, just give in to taking care of yourself. You have to do what you need to do to get better, like not being tempted to drag bales of hay around."

We walked into the barn and opened the stalls. They were a mess; my neighbor's boy was supposed to keep them clean. Sabina gave a disapproving little whistle.

"Okay, Sabina, you're right. And thank you for your help."

We brought the horses into their stalls, freshened their water and gave them each a flake of hay.

While we worked together, I asked, "How are we set up for tonight?"

"I think we are going to be fine. We have three extra servers, including Sean who can help at the bar; and I brought in an extra cook. But Ray seems to be more anxious than normal."

"Poor Ray; he worries when we don't have much business, then he worries when we might have too much!"

Sabina laughed. "Right. I think he now understands how much you do at the hotel. This would be a perfect time to ask for a raise!"

* * *

It was a thirty-minute drive from my place on Hogan Lake, through the new town of Valley Springs, to the old boom town of Mokelumne Hill. The hotel was ancient for California; it was first built in 1851 during the gold rush. After it burnt down twice, it was rebuilt with stone in 1883. I could relate to its history; my life was burn down three times – three divorces – and now rebuilt with the stone-like resolve to not marry again. My resolution for the new year would be to renew this resolve.

My greatest regret about my guest house burning down was Andy moving to town. With him at my place it guaranteed my singleness – he was more resolved than I to remain single – and yet, with him there, I was not alone.

"Got a resolution for the new year, Sabina?" I asked as we wove through the hills that were beginning to get their winter coats of green grass.

"Oh yeah," she said with a grin. "I just hope I can wait until midnight to keep it."

Knowing Sabina, I could guess what direction she was heading: "Who?" I asked.

"Sean. He broke up with Trudy a couple of weeks ago and I am dying to find out if he can really ride, or if he's all show."

"Well I hate to tell you, girlfriend, but Trudy says the boy can really ride – for about a minute and a half."

"She told you that!?"

"Yup; made her pretty cranky."

"Trudy takes things way too personally. You've got to work with a boy like that. Tell him how great the first shot was, but that you are a double-shot woman, and that you bet the second one will be even better. A bartender like Sean will understand, and he'll take his time mixing up the second drink just to make you happy."

"Well good luck, I hope your happy hour is all you hope it will be."

"And here's another thing, he's working tonight, so he'll be pretty sober – and we all know sober guys are better lovers."

"He'd better be very sober!"

"I'll keep an eye on him."

"Oh, I bet you will!"

"And how about you, Barb, any resolutions?"

"I just want to stay away from doctors, that's all."

"Good call. I put my ex through medical school – and those were the good years. Then I found out that most docs make lousy husbands; but they are great to divorce!"

"Don't rub it in," I said.

Truth is, I'd be in poverty if Ray hadn't been such a good boss and made me manager. And Andy? He's retired and poor as a church mouse.

We turned off the highway and drove down into Moke Hill. Main Street was quiet and in shadows with the late afternoon's winter sun. I imagined everyone in the little town had their fridges filled with snacks and drinks, ready for a marathon of holiday TV tonight and tomorrow. Hopefully, those who still had some spunk would find their way to the hotel and to the Church of Andy Shepard, the only show in town.

I could hear music when Sabina parked her truck behind the hotel. I always thought it was a shame that the best part of the old place faced the alley instead of Main Street. The main street, which looked like a western movie set, was situated up on a ridge so that the ground fell away behind the buildings. The larger buildings took advantage of this and built a lower level to their structure so they were much bigger than they appeared from the street. Behind the lower level of the hotel there was a charming garden with roses and orange trees and a blue swimming pool.

As we walked the garden path toward the ornate old saloon above us, I could hear Bobby and the boys warming up. I smiled when I heard Andy's blues harmonica playing along. I hadn't seen him since I was released from the damned hospital.

"The Rev is sounding better all the time," Sabina remarked. "I wonder if he's written another song about your 'Sweet Round Bottom' for tonight?"

"I'll wring his neck," I said. "What ever happened to sentimental love songs?"

"He likes the blues, Honey. You're lucky he doesn't sing about breaking up, or how mean you are," she said as we climbed the steps and entered through the back door. To the left was the dining room and bar, and to the right was the kitchen. Sabina went left, I went right.

In the kitchen I found the owner, Ray, huddled with our chef, Benny, and the rest of the restaurant staff. Ray glanced up, "Barbara!"

"Hi Ray, Happy New Year everyone."

"How are you?" Benny asked as he glanced at my sling.

"I'm still on the mend, trying to get rid of an infection. I was getting cabin fever, so I thought I'd come over and pester you tonight. How's the prep coming?"

"They shorted us on the fresh lobster tails, so we're working on a last-minute pasta substitution for the surf and turf," Benny said.

"Do you have any frozen scallops?"

"A couple of boxes."

"How about cutting the tails in half, long-ways, and only using one half per serving, then add two or three scallops nestled inside the curve facing the steak?"

"That sounds better than the seafood pasta dish, and more like what people will be looking for," Ray said, "What do you think?"

Benny smiled, "Let's do it!"

"I'll be back," Ray said. Then to me, "How about something to drink?"

"Sure, but it has to be non-alcoholic, I'm on pain meds."

Ray was a young seventy and stood tall and straight. He was a widower and what I would call a perfect gentleman.

"How about a pot of tea? He asked

"Perfect for an old invalid on New Year's Eve."

"Now don't give me that. Just find a seat; I'll be back," and he headed for the waiter's station.

I walked into the saloon. Bobby and Andy had their heads together over the playlist. Although the place was still closed they didn't notice me as I sat near the window that looked out across the boardwalk and Main Street, with its rickety wooden storefronts.

It was good to see Andy. From the beginning his presence was always comfortable – like an easy chair. Maybe it was his easy smile, or the easy way he carried his body, or the easy and inviting way he spoke and listened. Even his lovemaking was easy and accommodating. Not that he wasn't all male at six foot and over two hundred pounds. It was just that he seemed to be at that stage where he didn't have anything to prove – a stage not many men, in my experience, reached.

Andy had come to the hospital almost every day; he was there even when I was readmitted to open my shoulder back up to treat the staph. Sometimes I'd wake up and he'd just be sitting there by my bed praying, or whatever he does. But I hadn't seen him for over a month while I was at Nathan's and while Andy was remodeling some rooms under the abandoned church to use as his new residence. Yet still he would phone to see how I was.

I couldn't hear what the guys were saying. Andy had his back toward me. Soon Bobby started his band playing a funky blues tune with Andy playing the harmonica. After a while Andy paused and started to sing:

> "She just had one arm,
> But her legs were OK."

Sabina appeared at the bar with a bucket of ice and mouthed to me, "What!"

> "Yes, she just had one arm,

> But let me tell you,
> Her legs were OK."

Ray walked in with a tray and he stopped to listen.

> "She could wrap those things
> Around me any old day!"

Andy turned around with a belly laugh and began walking to my table. The band stopped and Bobby said, "Now that's what I'm talking about!"

"Andy Shepard!" I said, "That church hasn't done you any good at all!"

"What do you mean, Cowgirl. Here you are, my prayers have been answered!"

"You are such a bull shitter!" I said with a grin.

When Ray got to the table, he set down a tea pot, two cups and a piece of tonight's dessert special: double chocolate cake. "Would you like some tea Andy?" he asked.

"What? With seven different beers on tap to choose from?"

"Forgive me; what a faux pas. Sabina, an amber ale for the Reverend, please."

Andy bent down and kissed me. It surprised me. He had never done that so publicly before. Our relationship had been growing cautiously and slowly over the past six months. When he was my renter, we were very discreet. Why? Partly, I suppose, because it started out more as an arrangement than a relationship. And partly because Andy had recently retired from the church were casual sex was seen (if not by him) by his parishioners as a sin. But mostly because we were both sick of failed marriages and didn't want to be seen as partners.

Andy sat next to me and said, "I'm so glad you're here. How are you?"

He looked me in the eyes like it was a real question, and like he was prepared to sit there all night if need be and listen to my real response. Is this love just for me, I wondered, or was it a pastoral skill he had developed over the thirty-five years in the church before he retired?

I didn't want to talk about how my arm was starting to swell, or about how ill I felt. "I've been better," I said.

I could see Andy trying to read between the lines; so I looked at Ray and Sabina as she served Andy his beer and I said, "It's sure good to see everyone again. It's like I've been locked away somewhere." I could feel my eyes tearing up and I tried to will my tears back to wherever they come from.

"We sure have missed you too, Barbara," Ray said, "But you take as much time as you need to get better. Your job will be here when you are ready."

Just as tears were about to fall, Andy said, "But since you're here, the men's room sure could use a good cleaning."

"Your right, Barb," said Sabina picking up his beer again, "He is a pain in the ass."

"Hey!" he said as she took the beer back to the bar and set it down. He got up and gave chase.

Ray leaned over to me, and in a soft voice said, "When you get back, I want to talk with you about a profit sharing deal. I've got some new ideas about this place. And Barbara, don't worry, your health insurance is being paid."

I took his hand and said, "Thank you Ray, you're a real friend."

* * *

It wasn't long before the doors opened and the bar livened up. I stayed planted at my window table while Andy and Bobby walked across the street and then up a few doors to the church to take care of some details for the dance that would take place later in the evening.

The church was a typical white wooden structure topped by a small steeple with a bell. It had closed down about three years ago. Then a realtor bought it figuring he could make some money, but the market soured and he couldn't flip it. After Andy retired from his parish up in Riverton, someone anonymously bought the church for him.

My eyes followed Andy and Bobby in the twilight as they climbed a few steps to the Church's front door; they disappeared inside, and soon the windows lit up and the exterior lights came on. The last minister of the church tried to start up evening services (who the hell goes to church at night anymore?) so he installed outside flood lights on the front and steeple which indeed made the old church look inviting.

I kept staring at Andy's church as I tried to imagine crossing the street after work some day and climbing the steps to the door. I imagined what it would feel like as I opened the door and stepped into the entry way where Andy would take me in his arms and kiss me, then lead me down to his bedroom. I wondered what color it was, and how he had it decorated and how it would feel to make love in a church. Would he greet me in his preaching robe with nothing on underneath? Would he do that for me? I wondered.

"How are you doing, Barbara?" Ray said as he suddenly returned to my table. "Nice to see the church lit up again, isn't it?"

I turned to my boss and smiled, "Very nice."

Chapter 28

The New Year's Eve crowd swelled and by seven we were packed. I couldn't remember the hotel doing such a big business in years past; the dinner and dance promotion was a huge success. The band played thirty-minute sets, and the bar had standing room only as people were either getting a head start on their New Year's headache or waiting for their tables in the restaurant.

From my window seat it would have been funny watching Sabina and Sean try to keep up with serving drinks while flirting with each other – she already had him in a state. But it was frustrating to just sit there and do nothing. I could see how things could be running better, yet I was in no shape to intervene.

Sabina came over and asked, "Want some more tea, or a Coke?"

"Just some water would be fine." I felt clammy and my arm didn't feel right at all. It hurt all the way down to my slightly discolored fingers, and my back didn't feel good either. I thought that perhaps I had just been sitting in one place too long. I began to regret that I was stuck there without my own pickup truck.

When Sabina returned with a glass I took another pain pill and sipped the water.

"You sure you're all right?" she asked.

I tried to say I'd be fine in a minute, but it didn't come out right.

"What?" she said with a frown.

I tried to say I needed some fresh air.

"Honey, you're not making any sense."

She looked blurry. I blinked hard. I could feel sweat dripping. I tried to say that she had work to do, and that I'd be all right. Then I tried to stand up, but couldn't. The last thing I remember was Sabina asking for an ambulance on her cell phone.

Three days later I woke up in the Intensive Care Unit once again. I say "woke up," but consciousness came in stages. I was disoriented at first, but it didn't take long to recognize the ICU – my home away from home. Even in a fuzzy-headed, drug induced fog I could make out the flock of machines that perched around me as they chirped, tweeted and clicked. And of course, there was that antiseptic hospital smell.

My first thought was: I hope they didn't screw up this time.

I watched the nurse grooming one of the "birds" and I tried to scratch my nose. I found that I couldn't move my arms. I craned my neck and saw that my left wrist was tied to the bed rail. And my right arm... What! It was gone.

The nurse saw my movement. "Barbara, hi. You are in the Intensive Care Unit. How are you feeling?"

Her voice was meant to be soothing, but to me it was inappropriate. Soothing wasn't going to happen. My mouth was dry, my nose itched, and I felt groggy, but I managed to slowly say, "My arm seems to be missing. Can I see my doctor?"

"Yes. I will let him know you are awake."

She left. I lifted my head again. Maybe my arm was tucked under the covers. Nope. It was definitely gone. Only a large awkward clump of dressing was attached to my shoulder. I rested my head and closed my eyes. My only thought: I'm fucked.

The doctor came in with Nathan and Andy. He explained that when I was brought in, my whole body was going septic (a cheery word!) and that I had almost died. Indeed, they had brought my heartbeat back twice. They concluded that I would surely die if they didn't amputate. Nathan had given the okay. They removed my right arm flush with my shoulder.

Now my body was finally responding to the antibiotics and they were winning the battle against the infection. I was on morphine, and I could expect to be in the hospital several more days; then perhaps a couple of weeks in a rehab hospital.

There was more, but that was all I could comprehend between the drugs and the shocking news. When the doctor walked out, there was an awkward silence. No one knew what to say.

"My nose itches. Can you untie my wrist?"

Nathan untied me. As he leaned in close he whispered, "We're going to sue. It's clear that this started with the mistaken medication they administered last time. You're going to have whatever it takes to get your life back." He brushed my hair from my forehead and gave me a peck then left the room.

"Well," Andy said as I rubbed my nose, "it seems that the help you gave him in college is going to pay off. And with Cindy an assistant D.A., I expect they will get some speedy results."

"Whatever. But what's important," I said slurring a little, and pausing to swallow, "is that this place didn't kill me. I suspect my very own personal pastor and his prayers got some speedy results."

"That's right, Cowgirl. How can you go wrong: two lawyers in one corner and an old pastor in the other."

Andy took my hand. We were silent for a while. The few pastors I've been around were a chatty bunch. But not my Andy. He had no problem with silence. I winked at him and said slowly with some effort, "How did that song go? 'She just has one arm, but her legs are Okay?'"

Andy smiled and said, "And that's not even mentioning your best part," and he winked back.

"Can you stay a while?"

"Sure."

"Do you have a handkerchief? I'm going to cry."

"Better yet," he said reaching into his pocket, "any horse rider worth his salt carries a bandana."

I took it with my one hand on my one arm, buried my face in it, and wept.

* * *

The next day Andy brought me (of all things) a writing tablet. He called it my journal. On the front he had boldly printed **Barbara's Story**. At first I said in a pitiful voice that I couldn't write with my left hand. He said we all felt that way, but actually we all could write with our opposite hand.

He explained that he had once taken a class in journaling, and that he had learned a technique to uncover the voice of one's inner-child. Then he demonstrated. He wrote a sentence with his right hand:

I am making the church my home which is quite a wonderful thing.

Then he took the pen in his left hand and slowly wrote:

Sometimes it feels big and empty and lonely.

He showed me his writing and said, "Our opposite non-dominant hand writes like a little child, slowly and awkwardly, but often with more emotional truth and vulnerability. And, just like a child, you will learn to do things in new ways (eventually) without awkwardness. The journal will help you record the inner truths that you discover along the way."

Andy had lapsed into his old pastoral role and voice. I could always spot it. In the past I'd say, "Always the pastor!", meaning: get real! But this time I took the tablet and pen, and I just said thank you. I was too dopey to be sassy, and besides, there was a tenderness there that touched me.

Did he really feel that his place was empty and lonely?

Was that an invitation?

Was he here because he loved me? He seemed to love everyone, so did he really love anyone? Was I special, or just convenient? Maybe he drove down here to the hospital because that is what he does, and probably always did.

* * *

January 5
Barbara's Story! I feel my story has ended, not begun.

January 6
I hate taking the pills, I do not trust them, they make me nervous. This whole place makes me nervous, or mad, or both. My youngest daughter is reaching out to me. I see it is not easy. What did I do to her?

January 7
I walked to the toilet at last. I write like a child and I am being potty trained like a child. Ray was here. He is like a father. I cried. I never really had one. I looked in the mirror. Not too bad. I thought it would be worse. But not too good. Hey Lady, what happened to you? I got fucked up.

January 8 – Week 2
Ray bought me an iPad. What a prince. Sabina bought me chocolate, she knows! Andy gave me a real kiss. What a boyfriend.
Nathan and Cindy brought me papers to sign.

January 10
I moved to a rehab hospital yesterday. Stepping out of the hospital made it real. I am a one-armed woman. Maimed. I write better on the iPad, but I am going to stay with this.
I like the little girl inside. And they say it is good practice. I have two therapists and a shrink. Sabine brought me some clothes. She stares a bit, I can tell it freaks her out some. The mirror freaks me out some, too.
The missing arm — I wonder, did they throw it in the trash? My bones, my fingernails — were they still petal pink? Where is my arm now?
Andy brought me another bandana — actually, six bandanas of different colors, "So you can cry about different things," he said. I will get him for that.

January 11
Still have the morphine pump with the happy button. Everyone should have one of these. Fuck the therapists. (My inner teenager.)

January 12
No one visited today. Guess I am old news. No. I guess everyone had their own life. Even I am busy: I am practicing getting dressed. Forget the hooks, buttons and shoelaces — the struggle is embarrassing. Guess it is mostly snaps and Velcro for me for a while. But hey, my new quick release bra has possibilities.

January 13

Brandy, my dear youngest from Oregon, came today. She will alter some of my clothes for my altered body. I do not want any dangling empty sleeves. (Hey lady, did you fight in the war?) Brandy did my nails - hand and feet! Asked her to please tell me what was wrong between us. She said she had told me already and that I had laughed it off! That was sad. I said it must have been that horrible two-armed mother she used to have. Would she please now say it again? I had to ask, didn't I.

She said she heard me say once that having her and her sister was a mistake. She said she thought that was why I did not love her. I gave her the purple bandana. I took the red. A big mother/daughter cry. I think it's better now. At least the door is open.

January 14

I had so many visitors today, don't they know I have work to do! I am exhausted.

And they took away my morphine! But I now know how to safely carve a roast with one arm (with a $200 cutting board and five attachments!) They took away my morphine and gave me a knife; what's wrong with these people?

January 15, Week 3

Andy and I had a heart-to-heart at dinner when he saw me pick up Salisbury steak with my fingers and take a bite. He asked who was going to be with me when I go home? I said no one. My newly married son had his career. The girls? Carolyn never called. Brandy and I still had some things to work out.

Do new parents ever even think about what their adult children will be like? We just assume love will always be there.

Andy said he would stay with me, but...Right, too dangerous, too close, too much like marriage which we both have sworn off. I'll be okay. Always have. Besides, who wants to be someone's fifth wife?

The trick with Salisbury steak? A very sharp knife, and press, do not saw. Anything you have to saw is not worth it.

Note: buy electric knife sharpener. And do not scare off Andy.

Chapter 29

At the time, I didn't see them as miraculous. When you are nurturing your misery and stuck in your fear, you seldom notice the daily miracles.

The First: my medical team destroyed the bacteria that nearly destroyed me as it spread inside my body. And the second: they simply sewed down a flap of skin over the place where my arm used to meet my shoulder – and it all grew together! And quite nicely, actually. When the stitches and the little drain tube came out it all looked pink and smooth and healthy. But at the time, when I was packing up to leave the rehab, I thought it looked hideous. As Nathan and Cindy drove me home they talked about the lawsuit they had filed on my behalf. It had its roots in a comment that Nathan had overheard. A few hours after the operation to remove my bone tumor, the nurses were preparing to wheel me from my room to the ICU. As my vital signs continued to drop, he heard a nurse say on the phone that I had been given the wrong medication. After I was put on a breathing machine, he asked to see my chart, then asked the kind of questions that a lawyer is trained to ask.

Since then, Cindy had gathered medical opinions and statistics showing that complications, and an extended hospital stay, greatly increased the chances of infection after surgery. They also had called in a friend who was experienced in civil lawsuits. Together they mapped out a strategy and came up with what is considered a standard judgment for the loss of an arm due to negligence: two and a half million dollars.

I wasn't ready to think about a lawsuit. My thoughts were mainly on how nice it was going to be to cook my own dinner that night. When I heard them ask if that amount would be acceptable to me, it seemed far off and unreal. I said it sounded fine, and could we stop at the grocery store in Valley Springs. I was preparing my menu in my head: fresh Brussels sprouts with garlic, pasta with pesto, and fresh pears poached in port for dessert – with ice cream? I couldn't decide.

They seemed reluctant to stop and said they wouldn't mind shopping for me after they got me home. I said, "Don't be silly," but when we turned onto my long, tree-lined gravel driveway and slowly crunched along over the crushed rock, I soon saw why: a bunch of cars were parked at my house, something was up.

"Who's here?"

"It's a little welcome home surprise, Mom."

"You stinkers. I should have worn a different outfit."

"Don't worry, you look great, Barbara," said Cindy.

We parked near the back door. Like so many who live out in the country, my back door was the normal way to enter the house. It accessed the kitchen where I normally hung out, and it led to the stables.

People began parading out. First Ray, then the staff from the hotel, several of my neighbors, a couple from the trail riders club, and even my friends from the beauty shop. Finally, at the top of the steps, Andy and Sabina waved. They were wearing big smiles – obviously they were responsible for this little stunt.

As people came forward, some wanted to hug me; talk about awkward! And shaking hands without a right arm wasn't much better. So mostly it was a matter of leaning in and sort of giving neck hugs. Would things ever be normal again? Would people always be different around me, awkward and stand-offish?

Halfway through the impromptu greeting line I glanced up and saw Andy and Sabina still standing together on the back steps. It looked too cozy to me. In a sudden, despairing moment I thought, are they sleeping together?! Shit, while I've been in the hospital getting my arm chopped off, my best friend has been screwing my boyfriend!

My face burned as our chef, Benny, came and slipped his arm around my waist and with the best hug of the bunch he leaned in and said, "Come on back to work, Ray is driving us crazy."

Nathan and Cindy were handing my accumulated stuff to willing hands when Sabina came down and wrapped both her arms around my neck, "Welcome home, Barb. We love you."

I only held my tongue because of the crowd. "Thanks," I said. Slut! I thought.

Right behind her was Andy. He looked different. He had lost some of his extra weight and he had a new dark purple shirt. He was thirteen years older than me, but today he looked younger than that. With both hands he held me around the waist and looked me in the eyes, "You okay?" he asked.

My mind zipped through the possibilities: was it a pastoral gesture? Or was he asking if I suspected something? Could he tell that I was mad? I searched his face. All I could see was concern. Is he that good at lying?

People were watching. I said, "Not really. Nothing is the same. Nothing feels right or normal."

He pulled me closer, and despite my anger, I put my arm loosely around him. He said softly, "There's going to be a new normal for you, and it could be the best one yet. So try to relax, it's going to be fine, even if it is strange right now."

I hugged him tightly, and with a prayer I barely whispered, "You're not fooling around, are you?"

In my ear he said, "Cowgirl, I know you can ride better with one arm than anyone with two."

"You can bet your ass," I said and tried to smile.

He took my hand and led us all back into the house. Inside there was a big banner that read, "Welcome Home." It really did feel like I had been away for a long time. Except for my misguided return in those days before New Year's, I'd been gone most of November, December and January. It felt like a year.

On the table were pink roses and a cake. The cake grabbed my attention. It was made in the shape of an arm flexing its muscle, and the words: "Still Strong – Cowgirl!"

Benny came up and said, "I made it. I hope you like it."

I kissed his cheek, "Perfect. Thank you."

Sabina then handed me a wrapped box. "Everyone at work wanted to give you something."

I set the present down on the table and tried to slip off the ribbon, but it was too tight and I couldn't manage it. How embarrassing, I thought, a gift I can't open.

"There are scissors in the drawer over there, Andy," I said.

When he handed them to me, I fumbled with them, and realized that they were made specifically for the right hand.

"You want me to do it?" Ray asked.

I looked around. All eyes were on me. Do they think I'm helpless, I wondered. My rehab therapists had tried to teach me otherwise. They said there would be times like this – frustrating times. What was it that I had to remember, the phrase they always used?

"No," I said to Ray. "This is a time for 'Creative Options.' A new game they taught me in rehab. I'm to stop, calm down, and create a list of my options; then pick the one that seems the best."

I looked at the gift for a few moments. "Number one: a knife, but handling a knife without holding the object is tricky."

Andy said, "Can't we all play? I say number two: just put it on the mantle and enjoy the mystery of what it could be."

"Number three:" said Benny, "Use a cleaver and give it a few whacks."

"Number four: Use a lighter to burn the ribbon in two." They were laughing and getting into it.

"Number five: Use your teeth."

"Number six: A fingernail clipper."

Then Nathan said, "Number seven: Sue the one who tied the ribbon for violating the Persons With Disabilities Act."

"Wait just one minute now," Sabina said. "Honey, maybe the one who wrapped it tied the ribbon with a simple bow."

I looked at her. She smiled and shook her head as if I had missed the obvious. I pulled the loose end of the ribbon and the bow came apart.

"Creative Option number eight," Sabina said, "Trust your friends." Everyone clapped and cheered.

I looked at her again, trying to decide if she knew my jealous thoughts? She knows how I am.

"I'm sorry," I said to her.

"Not that I didn't think about it," she said under her breath as I handed her the wrapping paper.

I opened the box. There were three one-handed kitchen helps: a special cutting board with clamps, an automatic jar opener, and a compressed gas wine cork remover. I looked up at the circle of my friends wanting to say thank you. I was overwhelmed. I felt bathed in their love. My friends and my family wanted me back at work, back at home, and back in their lives. And they didn't see any obstacles that couldn't be met with a little humor and mutual support and encouragement.

As my tears welled up, Andy handed me a bandana of red hearts. I looked around at the faces and managed to say thank you, then sat down and wiped my eyes and blew my nose.

* * *

Thoughtfully, everyone soon left after the potluck lunch so I could settle in – everyone, that is, except Ray and Andy. They stayed to talk over an idea while Nathan and Cindy went to do my shopping. We sat on the sofa and poured a bit more wine.

"How does it feel to be home?" Andy asked.

"Oh God, it's wonderful," I said. "But I miss my horses. I can't wait until Sabina hauls them back here. How about you, what's it like living in a church?"

"I'm still trying to get used to it. Until a week ago it was a construction zone. Now that the remodel is more or less finished, it's not bad." He looked out the window to the lake like a thirsty man. "I lived on the Mokelumne River for years. Then when I retired last year I moved here to the lake, so I am spoiled. Living in town, in the back of a church, is going to take some getting used to."

"But now that Andy owns the church we have a great business opportunity," Ray said. "The hotel has always attracted and hosted small weddings, but forty-five people or so in our garden is all we can accommodate, and we're limited to the warmer months. If we formed a partnership, weddings could become a major part of the hotel's business. Many couples still want a church wedding: the church holds about a hundred, which is what we can manage for a reception and dinner."

"And you would be willing to do this, Andy?" I asked, a little surprised.

"Six months ago I would have said no way. I was done with marriages and weddings. But now (thanks to good fortune) I seem to own a church. Yet I have no way to afford to maintain it on my pension. So Ray and I have agreed to try it for a year."

"Andy's income will come from the rental of the church and fees for his services," said Ray. "What profit the hotel and restaurant makes on the receptions I will divide 50/50 with you, Barbara. But we need you to make it work. I can do the promotion and advertising, but we need you to book the weddings, staff the events and be the wedding coordinator for the couples. And as for managing the hotel and restaurant, we will get you an assistant."

"I don't know what to say. I was thinking I could do about half of what I did before. Now you're asking me to do more."

"What I'm suggesting is that you shift from a very physical job to a more executive and consulting job. I wasn't aware of how you were filling gaps for the wait staff and bar keeps – even the housekeepers. We have been depending on you for too much. I'm changing that."

"Ray, it's economics. We can't afford more help."

"We can with more business. Your assistant will co-ordinate regular wine-paring dinners, partnering with the local wineries. And I have a few other ideas as well."

They watched me as I thought for a moment. I wanted to tell them to go jump in the lake. They were idiots for asking me to do this. For Christ's sake, were they blind!

Yet they were so good to me through this mess. "I can see that you're enthused about this whole thing; and I wish I could say that I'm ready to grab the bull by the horns. But honestly, I'm feeling more like the bull has run over me. I'm not sure what I'm ready for right now."

"Fair enough. Just think about it."
Right, I thought. They're not listening to me.

Chapter 30

Of all the futures I imagined for myself, a handicapped future was not one of them. I don't remember ever looking at a handicapped person and putting myself in their place, or ever wondering what it would be like to be them. I would, of course, admire how brave and strong and resourceful they were; and I would pity them and thank my lucky stars that it had not happened to me. But to actually fantasize living with a handicap? Never went there.

So the first morning I woke up in my own bedroom without a right arm and with a strangely shaped shoulder, I had a weird feeling that I was in someone else's life. It wasn't really me. While in the hospital, and then the rehab facility, I was a patient, a temporary identity that I could accept although I was impatient for things to return to normal.

My own room, I thought lying in the early morning light. My curtains with blue and purple violets. My bedside lamp shaped like a golden palomino's head. My cranberry chaise lounge with my silk robe draped across the back. Thank God I'm home.

Then I tried to throw the covers off and get up to use the bathroom – awkward, off balance. I walked across the room – a strange new gait. And even tearing off some toilet paper and wiping myself with my left hand made me feel like I was in an unfamiliar body. I was gone, dead and gone, and a wave of grief and anger began to rise again.

Sitting there on the pot, with my elbow on my knee and my face in my hand, I said, "OK, Barbara, hold up just a minute. Do you really want to get mad and cry? You've done that already. I looked around at the unlit bathroom, then out the door to the light filled bedroom. I took a deep breath, "No, I don't."

I looked down, I could have lost my feet, that would have been worse, a lot worse. I wiggled my toes with their pink polished nails and imagined that plight: No more cute shoes and probably no more horseback riding. I pictured myself with my one arm riding my paint, Pomo.

Then I remembered Andy's words, "You can ride better with one arm than most with two." Knowing him, I didn't think he was talking about horses. I smiled and brought to mind his kisses on my breasts, my neck, my lips. Yes, there are worse things to lose, Barbara, I told myself.

Then I got off the pot and decided to shower. I ran the water, and while it warmed up I slipped out of my night shirt and braved a look in the mirror. I ran my hand through my new short hair style and leaned into the mirror to see if there was any more grey in my auburn. I decided that there definitely was.

I stood back and looked at my right shoulder. There was no stump. The whole infected arm had been simply and cleanly removed to save my life. There was some scarring they said would fade with time.

I looked at my sagging breasts. Luckily Andy was an "ass man," as he put it. I turned and took a look – at least it wasn't sagging yet. And although my legs were short, they were okay.

But my eyes were drawn back to my missing arm. This is what people are going to see, I thought. My outstanding feature is no longer my long hair, or my smile, or even my shapely ass. It's what's missing.

Staring, I tried to be objective and imagine how people would see me, and if they would see beyond my handicap. How attractive would I appear? What would be their first impression?

Screw them if they judge me by my missing arm, I thought. I'm more than that. I turned to one side, then the other and studied by breasts. I lifted them with my hand and arm. Maybe if I get a boob job, then where would people's eyes go? Right here, I thought, bouncing them. I could go to L.A.: boob job and cleavage, dye my hair, short skirts.

Luckily the mirror steamed up before I could examine my wrinkles.

* * *

Air-tight canisters, the coffee grinder, and buttering toast provided lessons in patience and creative options as I fixed my breakfast. I started a list – actually, three lists. The "A" list were those things I decided to conquer by practice, like opening a milk carton. The "B" list were those things I could conquer by modification, like grinding coffee beans in the big machine at the store instead of at home, and buying soft spread for my toast. And the "C" list were things I would conquer through replacement, like new easy-open canisters.

I was on my second cup of coffee and learning to read the newspaper on my new iPad when I was surprised to see Andy drive down the driveway. I debated whether to change out of my robe, but decided it would take me too long. Anyway, Andy was used to seeing me in my robe. When he rented my cabin down the hill near the lake, he couldn't afford the full rent on his pension, so we struck a deal: I reduced the rent and he gave me a weekly massage – one of the best deals I ever made because one thing led to another.

I did have time to at least put on some lipstick before meeting him at the door. "What a nice surprise," I said; but suddenly, as I saw him standing there on the porch, I felt unsure. This was the first time since he moved away that he had come to visit. A few days after the cabin burned down I had my first operation. Andy had temporarily moved into the hotel, then into his newly acquired abandoned church.

Why does it feel so different? I wondered. Because he is no longer my tenant? Was he my lover just because he happened to be living on my property, or sleeping in my hotel? Did I expect it to be over now that he has his own place, or that now I am disfigured? But here he is – what does he want?

"What brings you here?" I asked as casually as possible.

"I could say it is your sweet round bottom; but I also happen to come bearing a gift."

I looked at him, and tried to read his mind: how many times in his thirty-year career had Reverend Andy rung some needy woman's door bell, sat with her holding her hand, asking her how she was getting along? Did he give them all happy endings on a massage table? Is that why his wives left him?

"Would you like some coffee?" I asked.

"Sure." He was holding a small box which he brought in and set on the breakfast bar. As I poured him a cup, he studied my three lists. "This is pretty cool. I thought maybe I would find you moping around the house this morning. What are you going to do, wait and get depressed later? Is that your plan?"

"You know, Andy, a lot of people would be more sensitive."

"Sensitive? You mean tip-toe around the obvious and treat you like you're fragile?"

"No, smart ass. I mean let me go at my own speed. Maybe not having a house full of people when I come home looking disfigured. Maybe not trying to reinvent my job when I'm wondering if I can work at all. And maybe not trying to tell me how I should feel!"

"So, Cowgirl," he gently pulled me to his stool, "How do you feel? A little pissed?"

"Yes!"

"A little sad?"

"Yes."

"A little alone?"

"Yes."

"A little unlovable?"

I swallowed and thought of my boob job fantasy, but I didn't say anything.

He put his arm around my waist, took my hand and laid it on his heart, and said, "You know what I think is sexy? Remember our first time? I was giving you a massage, and every time I gave you a long, full length stroke – slowly sliding my oiled hands from your shoulders, down your back, over your butt, and along the back of your legs to your toes – you would slightly raise your ass and give a little moan.

"I thought to myself: damn, this lady is hot. And I wanted nothing more than to pleasure you. Why? Because you really like sex, and you were inviting. One arm or two, it doesn't matter. You just can't help it: you're sexy."

"Hey, guy, you kept rubbing my ass – I think it was you who was giving the invitation. Remember, I turned over and said, 'OK, but if you fall in love with me, I'll have to raise your rent!'?"

"It took a lot of convincing."

"Exactly. You're a man."

"And you're a woman – and always will be." Then he kissed me lightly on the lips. "So when you are ready, at your own speed, I'll take you…" he kissed me, "to church…" he kissed me again, "and I will have a private healing service…," his hand slid down to my ass, "with the ancient rite of laying on of hands."

We had gone as far as I wanted to go. I pulled away and said, "How did you manage to not get kicked out of the ministry?"

"By never screwing a parishioner — seldom even tempted."

"Hard to believe."

"It's true. It would have felt like incest. Besides, I always had a lover."

I had more questions, but I didn't want to get closer. He might talk a good line, but I bet one look at me naked and armless would take the wind out of his sails. Truth is, I didn't like the way I looked, so I couldn't believe he would either.

"So," he said, looking over my three lists again, "which list am I on: conquer by practice, conquer by modification, or conquer by replacement?"

"I haven't decided. Could be I'll need another list or two."

"Fair enough. How about your pickup truck?"

"I don't know."

He took my pen and wrote truck on the second list.

I said, "That's hard to imagine. I'm having trouble even wiping my rear-end."

"Open the box."

The flaps on the box were folded under each other which made it easier to open than the one the day before. I reached in and pulled out a hand sized device that looked like a clamp with a shiny red plastic knob on top that spun. I looked at it from all sides, "Okay, I give up. What is it?"

"It's a Brody knob. They've been around for a hundred years. You clamp it on your steering wheel and with one hand you can turn your truck more easily than with two."

"How's it work?"

"Here," he said taking hold of the clamp with the knob pointing up. He put his elbow, forearm and fist on the counter. "Take a hold of the knob and move my arm making a big circle on the counter."

The red knob fit nicely in my hand with my palm down. As I made a circle Andy's hand followed.

"Your truck's an automatic. You'll have to reach across to put it into gear, but not when the truck's moving. However, opening and closing the door will be a snap because you have your left hand. So will adjusting your seat and mirrors and operating the windows. You will get the hang of one-handed driving in about ten minutes. The hardest part may be getting the key in."

"Handling my big truck with this little knob seems impossible, but thank you," I said.

"Oh, I'm sure there are a lot of knobs and things you're going to handle just fine with one hand," and he leaned over and kissed my neck.

"It's been a while, hasn't it, Andy?" I said, beginning to understand.

"Only 16 weeks and four days. But go at your own speed. What's another few minutes?"

I could have smacked him, but I wanted to kiss him; and I didn't trust him. If I get rejected, I thought, it will be too much right now: One more guy walking out or stepping out or copping out. No, not today.

"Not today, Honey," I said. "I've got to get my feet under me."

"Of course," he said. "I was just kidding – sort of."

* * *

January 24

Home again.

It's horrible.

I feel alone and needy, but I don't want to be touched. No matter what Andy says, I am a freak. Sabina might as well have him. All of those therapists – they really do not know what it is like. My life will never be the same. Never. My life is shit, and a damned Brody knob is not going to fix it. I cannot even walk straight for Christ's sake. And I write like I am mentally handicapped.

January 25
My missing arm has been itching again. Maybe it misses me, wherever it is. If I think it is hard being a person without an arm, it must be worse being an arm without a person.

January 26
The occupational therapist, Maria, was here. She said I needed a hold-bar for the bathtub (list B), a terrycloth robe for drying my back (list C), smaller (lighter) baking dishes (list C).
She taught me the trick of cracking eggs with one hand, and brought with her a dozen for me to practice on (list A).

January 27
I cannot remember ever being stuck at home for this long —
Four days.
Not even a trail ride.
I feel useless. And depressed.
A special driving therapist came today. He said the Brody knob Andy installed was good. He adjusted the position and had me drive him up to the dam and back. He didn't seem concerned, but it scared me. We'll practice again in a few days.

January 28 a.m.
People keep calling and want to come over.
I keep putting them off.
I am waiting for...my arm to grow back.
Or until I wake up from this bad dream.

January 28 p.m.
Maria just left. We practiced balance and walking. She said denial is just a stage, and being aware of it is progress. Progress to where? I asked. She gave me a thin small book entitled Remember: Life Is A Precious Miracle, and asked me, "Do you really think losing a limb should change that fact? Maybe you could reflect on this in your journal." Well, in my head the answer is no, of course not. Life is more than an arm. But it feels so unfair! I do not want to look like this!!!

Life is a precious miracle? So what.

Chapter 31

On the last day of January my life changed. Looking back I can see it. At the time, however, I just knew I couldn't stand myself – my self-pity, my bitter resentments, and my stubborn isolation. I had been building a misery list in my head as if I was making a case, like a lawyer, to prove why my life was ruined.

But there was a voice in me (and there always has been) that said, "I don't have to put up with this." I have no idea how I developed this faithful voice, but it has kept me moving, for better or worse, through forty-nine years and three divorces.

"I don't have to put up with this," I wrote in my journal on the last day of January. But I didn't know how to change things. My arm wasn't going to grow back. So I read the first chapter of my thin little book, fully expecting it to be a sappy, lift-yourself-up-by-your-bootstraps kind of thing. But it wasn't. And it wasn't just fluff about how precious and miraculous life is. It was about remembering to slow down and pay attention.

The first chapter described doing this with walking. So on January 31 at 10:00 a.m. I began a slow walking practice. I stopped building my misery list and focused on the experience of intentionally walking very slowly. I walked in an oval around my living room. I tried different speeds – too fast and I missed too much; too slow and I struggled for balance. I settled on semi-slow motion, an easy rhythm.

When I found myself fretting about the cobwebs that I could see, I said, with my inner voice, It's okay, and returned to my awareness of walking. When I tired of my living room, I put on my raincoat and slowly walked up my long driveway towards the road in the misty rain.

When I found myself planning to prune the ornamental plum trees along the drive, I said, It's okay, and shifted my attention to the wet coolness on my face, the gravel crunching under my feet, and the awkwardness of swinging only one arm.

I saw the mailman pull up to my mailbox while still a long way off. I thought of the get well cards I had received and the ones I wanted to answer until I caught myself. I said, It's okay, but now I'm walking, then I brought my attention back to my breathing, to the muscles in my back that felt tight, to the shifting of my hips, and to my feet in my boots. But as my thin little book had suggested, I just watched these experiences and resisted analyzing or judging them.

When I finally reached the road, I put the mail in my pocket though part of me wanted to open the envelopes. I said, It's okay, I'll open them later, I'm walking.

I turned back toward the lake. As I walked slowly I became aware of the slight difference in walking down the gradual slope. It was then that I could feel that my left side was heavier than my right side. I could tell that my body tried to adjust and leaned subtly to the right. This sometimes caused my right foot to scuff the gravel.

I caught myself adding this to my list of miseries, so I said, Don't worry, Barbara, as if I was encouraging a child I loved, we can work on that later. Let's just walk.

When I reached the house I knew I was on to something. I couldn't remember when I had felt this...what? Solid? Clear?

I made a cup of tea, slowly, and sat on the couch to view the rain which began to fall harder on the lake. After some time I picked up my journal and wrote:

January 31

Remember: slow down, pay attention, do not judge.

*I stared at this left-handed entry. The hand
writing was different, more legible, more adult. I
wrote again. It's okay, just write.
The rain is falling harder now,
I can hear it on the roof.
I drink it, warm and fragrant, from my cup. My
heart serves it to my every cell. I am the rain.*

I listened until my eyes became heavy. I covered myself with a throw, laid down and slept.

* * *

I read the first chapter again in my thin small book, and walked. I found myself trying to work at it, to accomplish something – what, I don't know. To do it right? To be good at slowing down and paying attention? So I wrote:

*February 1
I judge my walking.
That's OK. Now I am writing.
My thoughts in ink,
So I can see them,
Like the wake of a boat
Through the water
That dissipates and is gone.*

* * *

The next day I was walking by the lake when my driving instructor came again. He had me drive toward the town of Valley Springs where there was more traffic. On the highway he said I was driving too slowly. I said I wanted to go slowly to pay attention. As a car passed us and honked, he asked what I was paying attention to? I said, everything, like the smoothness of the shiny red Brody knob in my hand. He told me to pull over and stop. He asked me what medication I was taking as he drove us back to the house.

He had a point: life would be a short precious miracle if I drove as I walked. My new practice suddenly seemed ridiculous. I looked in the index of the thin small book to see if there was a chapter on driving, but no. And to top it off, the next chapter was about washing dishes!

I debated whether to throw the thing in the recycling bag. But for the past three days I had side-stepped the downward spiral of my misery list, and I wasn't going to put up with wallowing in self-pity again. For the moment this practice was the only thing I had going; so I decided to make some soup (slowly) and then read the second chapter during dinner.

I thought I liked to cook. But what I really liked was to feel capable and be efficient in the kitchen and turn out a variety of tasty dishes. Superficially this was cooking. I discovered this by slowing down and paying attention to cubing potatoes with one hand. I wrote:

February 2

I rushed to quickly cut the potatoes.

Where was I going?

The potatoes did not rush to collect sunshine or water, they were not in a hurry to grow. Now they are fat and firm and their earthy skins have protected their moist goodness that slightly sticks to my knife. I will inherit their sunshine treasure which will heat each of my cells.

But first the carefully arranged marriage of flavors to the potatoes - garlic, onion, pepper, salt and cheddar.

With one hand I couldn't hold my thin little book open to read while I ate soup. It's okay, I told myself, just eat, one spoonful at a time. Read the flavors and the textures, and welcome the sun's energy.

* * *

February 3

I must look like an old lady as I slowly and thoughtfully wash dishes. One would think the automatic dishwasher would be a one-armed woman's best friend.

But my thin little book thinks that washing dishes by hand is a nearly perfect practice for remembering to slow down, pay attention and not judge. The book says that if one does not believe they have time for washing dishes, then they do not have time to be fully awake.

My dishes dry themselves.
Their wetness merges with the air
Like every damp breath
From my wet lungs.
The air naturally absorbs,
And then gives back.

February 5

I dreamt again that I was whole, no missing parts. Last time I was dancing, this time I was riding Charley in a parade and waving. Fine, except when I wake up.

Each new day
I must let go again,
Release how it was
And will never again be.

Will a truly new day come?
Will it ever come
Without its load of loss?

Chapter 32

I never considered myself a poet. But on the last day of January my journal began to read more and more like poetry. It was part of the magic of that first week of February when my isolation was no longer fueled so much by the shame of my disfigurement as by my fascination with my new practice. I felt that if I was around people, I would not remember to practice.

But Maria was different. When she came the next week I greeted her with coffee and an apple pie that I had made. I knew there was something surprising and interesting about this woman. I watched her and paid attention to what she said (and didn't say). I noticed how she carried herself with such calmness.

When we sat at the breakfast bar to enjoy the afternoon treat, she asked, "How did you make the crust?"

"Slowly," I said, smiling. "I rolled it without using the handles of the rolling pin. I pressed down hard with the palm of my hand in the center of the pin and pushed it forward. I'm going to have a heck of a strong left arm. I hope I'm not over-using it."

"That's seldom a problem unless you do a strenuous repetitive task. How are other kitchen jobs coming?"

"Everything is different. Mixing is an adventure. I usually give up the spoon and just use my hand directly in the bowl, squishing ingredients between my fingers. You might say I'm into food in a much more intimate way, taking time to experience each ingredient I use."

"So, *Remember: Life Is A Precious Miracle* is working for you?"

"It's the most peculiar thing. This practice would have never made sense to me before I lost my arm. But evidently it's not a book for handicapped people."

"Right; or it's only for those who know they are handicapped – which we all are in some subtle but profound ways."

I told Maria about my driving experience and she had a good laugh. And then she said something that would take a while to understand, "There are two levels of practice. Walking and dishwashing, and others that you will find in your book, are drills: structured, tightly defined activities that are designed to break our habits of mindlessly racing through life. Through these practices we can learn to slow down, pay attention to the more subtle, deeper and profound aspects of daily life, and to open up to life by keeping in check our own judgmental thoughts.

"The second level of practice is not a drill, but a conscious intention to softly apply these three growing skills in all we do."

"But how do you drive like that?"

"You drive a safe, legal speed, without feeling driven, in a hurry, or anxious to get somewhere. You pay attention to driving and to where you are, without being preoccupied – without trying in your mind to be somewhere before you are actually there – and when you find yourself judging or resenting other drivers, or your trip, or your car, or your handicap, let those thoughts go and just drive."

"The way you describe it, it sounds easy – for about thirty seconds!"

"Exactly, Barbara. Then the next time maybe forty-five seconds. Then someday soon, a whole minute! It's just a practice, not a test. And the skills that you develop in the first level of practice which is intense and highly focused, spill over into your more complex daily activities."

"Like being with people?" I interrupted.

"Yes. And interacting with others is the most difficult practice. Let's try something. Please, stand up for a minute. Now, let's pretend we are greeting each other for the first time."

"Hello," she said as she took a step toward me and extended her right hand to shake mine.

"Hello," I said, and with a hesitation I reached out my left hand and awkwardly grasped her hand.

"Many people will make this mistake with you because it is such a habit to shake right hands. Some people believe it goes back to a time when men assured each other that they were not holding a weapon but were greeting the other in peace.

"People will extend their right hand, then realize too late that it is inappropriate. It's not a big thing, but it is an embarrassing moment for them. And if they catch you at a time when you are struggling with feelings of being one-armed, it could be a little painful for you, too. Not a helpful way to connect with people. And they may stumble further by trying to apologize. Then you may compound the difficulty by saying, "No problem," when you both know it was. So, what are some creative alternatives?"

I thought for a moment, then said, "I could stretch out my left hand first before they make a move. That would give them a clue to use their left hand."

"Yes, there will be times when you will anticipate that they will be trying to shake your hand – like during introductions. What else?"

"I could learn to shake their extended right hand more naturally, like nothing is wrong."

"Yes, and if you don't wait to speak but greet them warmly as you reach out, meeting their eyes and not staring at their right hand, their attention will be on you and not your unconventional handshake or whether they extended the wrong hand. What else?"

"Well, I could make light of the awkward moment. I could say something like: I learned the hard way: crocodiles make lousy pets!"

"That's good. Laughter can smooth things over and help people connect. You hit on something else as well: everyone will be naturally curious about how you lost your arm. You will have to come to terms with this. Right now the circumstances of your amputation have an emotional charge, and you will resist having to tell your story over and over. A few people may actually come out and ask you, but everyone will be somewhat distracted with their curiosity. For those with whom you'll have continuing contact, sometimes it will be best to work your story into the context of your conversation.

"But by being mindful, nonjudgmental and not rushing forward, you'll know how to best respond to people; and your ability to do so with grace will increase."

Chapter 33

February 17, a.m.
Today my mind is like a bronco,
over-reacting with fear and bolting here and there.
Ray wants an answer to his offer,
Sabina wants to get me on a horse,
Nathan and Cindy want me to sue the hospital,
and Andy wants a date.
But I cannot even walk
from one room to another without losing focus.
Why do I feel so anxious?
I cannot pay attention to anything!

I put down my pen, leaned back in the couch, and closed my eyes. I repeated to myself: why do I feel so anxious? Then I wrote again.

It is okay, I can figure it out later,
right now I am just feeling anxious.
I am breathing fast. I feel panicky.
I want to run away. My stomach is
a little queasy, like I have lost something
and I will never find it.

That's it: where is my damned arm? What did they do with it? It itches. I held my right shoulder. I squeezed my eyes shut even tighter until I saw all my old two-sleeved blouses hanging in the closet. I opened my eyes and wrote:

My two-sleeved blouses are waiting.
They will wait forever, growing old and dusty.
I have not told them the truth.
What's the truth?

I stood up and went to the phone. I called my surgeon.

"Hello, Dr. Roth's office."

"Hi, this is Barbara Hanson. I have a quick question for Dr. Roth. Is he available?"

"Hi Barbara, just one moment. I'll see."

"Wait, maybe you can help me. I was curious, what happens to amputated limbs, in the end? How are they…or where are they, ah, disposed of?"

"Tissue is incinerated at a special facility. The hospital carefully packages it and it is picked up daily by a service."

"Oh."

"How are you doing, Barbara. Are you all right?"

"Yes, I'm okay. I guess for some reason I am particularly missing my arm today. But the rest of me is fine."

"Would you like to come in and see Dr. Roth and talk?"

"No, but thanks. I just had a hard time picturing where my arm is, or was. You've been helpful."

"Good. Call back if you need to."

"Thanks. Goodbye."

I walked into my bedroom, opened my closet, and looked at all my blouses and riding shirts that still had two sleeves. In bunches I grabbed them by their hangers and brought them to the bed. Then I called Andy.

"Hello Sugar. How you doing?" he asked.

"Hard to say. It's a strange morning. If you're not too busy I could use a hand."

Then I thought, I could use a hand?! How ironic is that. I'll have to scratch that out of my common phrase book.

"No problem. I could leave in about ten minutes."

"Great. Thanks. See you then."

I found an empty box in the garage, and from a kitchen drawer I got my new left-handed scissors. Then I sat on the bed and began cutting off the right sleeve of each blouse and shirt. I tried to work quickly at first, making ragged cuts. But I slowed down and began paying attention, cutting each right sleeve and leaving enough material to someday nicely close the opening – just like the surgeon closed my shoulder with a remaining flap of skin. I carefully placed each severed arm in the small box, smoothing them out as I went. It became my practice. My breathing slowed and my panicky feelings dissipated.

When Andy drove up he found me near the horse barn trying to dig a hole with a shovel – not an impossible one-armed task if the ground hadn't been so hard and rocky.

Climbing out of his car he said, "What are we planting?"

"Burying," I said, and surrendered to the stubborn soil. I leaned on the shovel, "But I think this shovel goes on my "C" list to be replaced with a backhoe."

"Okay." Andy said, taking the shovel and looking at the box. "What are we burying?"

"I want to give a proper burial for my arm. My guess is that you've done a few funerals."

He looked at me with understanding. "Excellent. But what's in the box?"

"Arms. Take a look."

"Do I dare?" He lifted the box as if it held something horrible. He unfolded the flap, peeked inside, then finally opened it fully. He thumbed through the neat stack of perhaps fifty sleeves of many colors and prints. He paused for a moment, then suggested, "You know, these would make an interesting patchwork quilt."

"I don't think I'm ready for that, Reverend. Besides, they cremated my arm, so I want to cremate this box and lay it to rest here where I buried Rusty."

"Your ex-husband?"

"No! My dog, you idiot."

Andy laughed. "Just kidding." He took the shovel and began to dig.

I left and collected some small dry branches, charcoal lighter and matches. When I returned he still had a ways to go.

"I'm amazed Barbara," he said as he worked at some rocks at the bottom of the pit he was digging. "It takes most people about a year to let go of a major loss, if ever. And you've already come up with a good way to symbolize your acceptance of what has happened."

I wanted to tell him about my small thin book and my practice, yet I could feel some resistance – too soon, too fragile – so I didn't. But Andy's observation made me wonder how deep my practice was going. Earlier this morning I was a mess; now here I was calm and feeling I was doing the right thing.

I slowly piled the sticks in the small pit, placed the box carefully on top, then squirted the lighter fluid over it all. I looked across at Andy and waited. He was…what? Looking ministerial I suppose, but in a good way: thoughtful and present.

"These right-arm sleeves have served you well, Barbara. They sometimes have kept you warm and have helped you look your best, always attractive and well dressed. You carefully picked them off the rack at stores and chose them well. But now you need them no longer.

"Dr. Roth saved your life by removing your damaged and infected arm; an arm that I massaged and was very familiar with, an arm that served you well for 49 years. So with gratitude, and some regret, and with hope for the future, we release these sleeves just as we release the arm you no longer need. We give thanks for the gifts of the past and we open ourselves to new gifts in the future from the Giver of All Good Gifts. Amen."

I found myself nodding at the end. Then I lit the pyre. It started slowly, but soon engulfed the sticks and box. It actually gave us a little warmth in this mid-February morning. As the box burned, it cracked open. I watched the colored sleeves flutter and burn, then turn black and ash grey. My arm went up in smoke.

So much effort, I thought, goes into creating things, but it takes little to destroy them. Another reason perhaps to slow down, pay attention and not judge.

With dust to dust, and ashes to ashes, Andy began filling the hole again with dirt and rock. I watched in silence. Was Andy right, was gratitude possible? I knew I should be more grateful for the doctors saving my life. And I should thank my lucky stars that I am as well as I am after being so sick and near death. However, what should have been a fairly routine procedure to remove a benign bone tumor, went bad, beginning with being given the wrong medication after my first surgery. So I felt more victimized and resentful than grateful.

This became clear to me – this conflict – as I heard Andy's prayer. Being grateful, being open to gifts of the future was mostly wishful thinking – or so it seemed to me.

Andy patted down the dirt with the back of the shovel blade, then came to me and put an arm around my waist as we stared at my arm's grave. His warmth and closeness felt good. I just let myself soak it in, like slipping into a spa and feeling muscles beginning to relax. I had kept Andy at arm's length (oops, another awkward phrase) for weeks – months, really. I asked myself if I was ready to be a one-armed lover. The thought made me tighten up again.

"Now what?" Andy asked. "You feel any different?"

Was he looking for an opening? Did I feel more receptive? "Actually, I might be up to going for a horse ride. Do you have the time?"

"I'm retired. I used to have the money but no time. Now I have the time but no money."

"Don't worry. I'll just put it on your bill." My words surprised me. We both knew what that meant. It was a promissory note, like the rent I used to charge him. It was a signal that I would not hide behind my fear and shame forever. I would sleep with Andy again.

He gave me a slight squeeze and said, "Good, but you have to drive us to Sabina's. It'll be a chance for you to show off your new Brody knob skills."

"Really?" I said, pulling away a bit. "I just think you have some kind of weird Brody knob fantasy, Reverend."

"No, no. That's just projection on your part, Cowgirl: like grabbing the horns and wrestling those steers to the ground."

"You mean, grabbing one horn," I corrected him, lifting my one arm.

"That's right, Sweetheart, and one horn is enough," he said with a grin.

I shook my head, "How did those church people up in Riverton put up with you?"

"It's just that you bring out the best in me."

"Thanks (I think). Well, come on then, you throw the saddles and tack in the back of my truck and I'll pack us a lunch."

"Fine," he said as he set off for the horse barn singing one of his made-up blues songs:

> "She said don't worry,
> She'd put it on my bill.
> Yes, don't you worry,
> I'll add it to your bill.

Now I have got those old bottom blues,
And she's got one full till!"

"I heard that!" I yelled from the back door.

Chapter 34

Andy was afraid of horses when he came to rent from me. And rather than cover up his fear (like a lot of guys), he said he liked horses, but from a distance, and he had never been tempted to ride one.

When we negotiated the rent downward to fit with his modest pension, I suggested he could groom my three horses and clean their stables for the rent reduction. He countered with an offer that I could not refuse: He offered to give me weekly massages to help with the pain in my shoulder.

After a few months, and slipping into "happy endings" on the massage table, Andy had a vivid dream in which he gaily decorated his coffin. His interpretation was that his old life of being a minister was over, and he needed to both lighten up and open up to life. So he asked me to give him riding lessons.

I have to hand it to him, after his first time on a horse, I didn't think he would ever get in the saddle again. I had put him on my biggest horse, a palomino named Charley, and Andy was literally scared stiff – he rode with so much tension in his body that he could barely walk for days. But he didn't give up. He began to write funny blues songs about riding, and he continued his lessons. I think this is how we grew closer. He stopped coming off as older and wiser, and allowed me to be in the teaching role.

Now as I drove us out to Sabina's ranch, I felt confused and uncomfortable about our roles. Was I still the teacher, or was Andy now the care-giver minister? Were we still close friends, or was Andy simply feeling sorry for me? Were people going to pity me like a three-legged dog?

When I found myself preoccupied with these thoughts I followed Maria's instruction: just focus on driving. I checked my mirror and saw that I had two cars backed up behind me. I accelerated from thirty-five to fifty-five. I reminded myself where we were going and what would be our next turn. I carefully watched a car approach the highway from his driveway, making sure he was not going to pull out in front of us. I checked my gauges to see if we had plenty of gas. As I took the next curve in the road I focused on smoothly turning the steering wheel with the Brody knob rather than jerking the truck through the turn.

After a long five minutes of silence, I felt that maybe I was being rude by not saying anything to Andy as I drove. I looked over at him and back to the road. He smiled and said, "Life goes on, doesn't it, Cowgirl?"

I didn't say anything. Was that comment about my arm's funeral, my driving, or a suggestion that we could still be lovers? Or maybe his observation was about his own experience: burnt out of his cabin, ironically living in a church and here we were, going horseback riding.

I caught myself preoccupied again as a car began to pass us on the two lane road. I glanced down at the speedometer to make sure I didn't speed up as it passed us in the other lane. I looked down the highway, watching to see if anyone was approaching in our direction from around the next curve.

A deer appeared from below the road on the right and shot across both lanes a ways ahead of us. I took my foot off the accelerator and gently touched the brakes to signal the car behind me. I stared at the place the deer appeared – would a second one pop up? I slowed as the passing car gained ground and moved back into our lane.

Than a fawn appeared on the right shoulder. I braked cautiously, but the car in front locked up its wheels. My heavy pickup would have crushed the sedan from behind, but with the Brody knob I turned the steering wheel to the left and then to the right, swerving through the blue smoke of the sedan's squealing tires. I braked hard, ending up parallel to the sedan and stopped in the on-coming lane. The car behind me screeched to a stop on the shoulder to the sedan's right, and the fawn turned and ran back down the embankment.

I looked over past Andy to the car next to me. The driver sat there just staring straight ahead with her hand to her head. She then turned and looked at me and said, "Sorry."

Honest to God, just as I was about to tell her she was an idiot for nearly giving up her life for a stupid deer, I remembered my thin little book: slow down, pay attention, do not judge.

"You all right?" I asked.

"Yes," she said.

"Where did you learn how to drive, lady," yelled the guy in the car on her right, "in the demolition derby?!" Then he pulled out ahead and turned back onto the highway.

"You were lucky," Andy told her through his window. "My driver was paying attention; probably saved your life.

She just nodded and then started back down the road.

A half mile ahead, a car appeared, coming in our direction. I turned back into our lane and continued to drive. As the car zoomed by I wondered at Andy's comment. Was she lucky because I normally do not pay attention? Or lucky because it was me following her and not some distracted person? I smiled – ironically I was becoming distracted again.

"What are you smiling about?"

"I was 'paying attention'?"

"Well, I was going to say she was lucky that I gave you a Brody knob, but I'm too humble for that."

I looked over and saw him grin. He had dodged the issue as effectively as I had dodged a major accident.

Having been married three times I knew a thing or two about men. The bright ones have learned to side-step certain topics. They knew honesty was usually the best policy, but not always, such as comments about women drivers. I appreciated a bright guy, so I said, "Thank you, Reverend, for saving our lives," and I grinned back at him.

"Any time," he said. Then after a long pause as I again focused on just driving, he said, "I guess life doesn't always just go on, does it?"

Later I would write:

February 17. p.m.
I am a judging machine.
Comparing and evaluating.
Criticizing and complaining.
The more I slow down,
The more I pay attention
The more I see the machine at work.
How little I accept things just as they are.
But today I saw I had a choice,
There was a moment in time, a choosing moment,
And I chose to ask, "Are you all right?"
Let someone else do the judging.

In twenty minutes we arrived at Sabina's ranch. Her place was in a peaceful valley of grasslands and oaks. At the gate we were greeted by Zoro, her Australian Shepherd. Sabina was working and Zoro was very glad to see us. He followed the truck down to the stables which were twice the size of mine: ten stalls and an impressive stack of hay under a shelter. The stables were open to an irrigated pasture where the horses – hers, mine, and a couple of boarders – watched us drive in.

I got out and quickly greeted Zoro, then stuffed some carrots in my pocket, walked over to the fence and called to them. Pomo, the paint, was already on his way. Although Andy had been here riding regularly, it had been almost two months – New Year's Eve – since I had last seen my babies. I rubbed Pomo's face and offered him a carrot. Charley, the palomino, came up to Andy and he produced an apple and patted the big guy's side.

I could feel a wave of emotion rise in my chest and catch in my throat. I wanted to climb the fence, but not with one arm! I went around through the gate and reached up and put my arm around Pomo's neck. I wanted to hug him. He made a soft neighing sound. I kissed him.

"Andy, can you give me a boost?"

He came around and clasped his hands down low. I put my left knee in his hands and he lifted me up until I could swing my right leg over Pomo's back. I grabbed his mane, held on tightly with my legs and gave a nudge with my heels as I pulled slightly to the right. We were off with a slow lope as we followed the fence around the pasture.

It had been a long time since I had ridden bareback. It brought back memories of being a young girl again, and the transformation I had experienced with horses. Again I was no longer small, weak, and vulnerable. On this beautiful creature I was big, strong and fast.

"Good boy, Pomo. I've missed you, boy!" I said out loud.

In a few short minutes we were back where we had started, except I felt I was in a different place. It was as if I had taken a powerful medicine, a remedy for my old neediness that had grown more painful with my new sense of being broken, damaged, and pitiful.

Andy was wearing a broad smile when I returned. I said, "It's going to be okay, Andy."

"Yes it is, Honey."

"And you know what? My shoulder doesn't hurt! First time in maybe a year."

Soon we were brushing down our rides in order to saddle them. I found that it was a perfect task for my first-level of practice. I slowed my strokes way down and began to pay attention to every detail of the experience. I felt my brush move over the contours of Pomo's body, observing his massive muscles and his healthy winter coat and the beautiful patches of color that distinguished him as a paint.

As I ran the brush down his legs, cleaning and smoothing him, I was aware of how I used one arm, and the awkwardness of my body. I no longer could use a hand to brace myself against his weight and to "read" his movements as I worked. I had to bend my knees a bit and take a more solid and balanced stance as I brushed. I had to let go of the frustration of having to use more energy now to do this familiar task.

I'm just brushing. I said to myself. I'm not in a hurry. It's okay. I'm just brushing. I slowed down a little more. I saw that if I slowed too much, the brush couldn't do its job. I had to brush with briskness, but I could move thoughtfully between strokes.

When I was nearly finished Andy had brushed Charley and Sweetpea, and he was beginning to saddle Charley.

I turned to him and said, "I think I'm ready."

"Do you want some help?"

"Yes. I want you to teach me how to give a massage."

Andy finished buckling a strap and turned toward me with a puzzled look. "That will be a switch."

"Won't it," I said with a smile.

"So, you continue to teach me how to ride like a real cowboy, and I teach you how to rub like a real masseuse? Using my body to practice on?"

"Right."

"Well, this is moving in the right direction."

"Maybe, but we don't know how good my massages will be yet."

"I think you'll be great. I noticed what you were doing with Pomo. And he wasn't complaining."

"Yeah? Well then, I'll bring the brush."

"No, no. That won't be necessary."

"Then just my riding crop?"

"No thanks."

"Spurs?"

"You're so thoughtful, but no."

"Too bad. So much for the happy endings."

Actually, I think happy endings are what I had in mind. But a part of me did not want Andy to see me dismembered (as if my clothes were hiding it). I thought I looked hideous, so I assumed he would, too. When I tried to picture myself lying naked on his massage table with my arm chopped off, alluring and desirable were not the words that came to mind. So I pictured Andy on the massage table – much better.

Although I had never given anyone a massage before (except more male members than I wanted to admit), it seemed like a safe way to test the waters and see if they were as cold and threatening as I thought. Besides, after brushing Pomo, I could see that massage -- real massage – might be a good level-one practice.

Andy lifted my saddle up onto Pomo, but I insisted on doing the buckling myself. The bridle and bit were trickier, but Pomo was a sweet and very cooperative horse. Then rather than boost me again, I asked Andy to arrange a couple of bales of hay so I could mount Pomo on my own.

Andy was doing leg stretches when I rode out of the horse barn. I stopped and gazed up to the oak studded hills where Sabina's trail would take us. I tried to pay attention to the moment, to all of it: the cool air, the white clouds, the sunshine, the horses in the pasture, the new grass, the barnyard smells, Pomo's ears twitching, and the sounds of Andy awkwardly mounting Charley.

I also became aware of my inner landscape: once in the saddle, I felt I was in heaven. No matter if I only had one arm, I only needed one hand to hold the reins. And unlike Andy who still relied on the saddle horn for security, I had no need to hold on. My legs and balance and ability to move with a horse's movement were enough. I was a natural, and competent as anyone in a saddle. And still to my amazement, my arm and shoulder, which last year was misdiagnosed with bursitis, no longer hurt. I felt whole and happy.

"Come on, Andy, I want you to ride out in front of me for a while so I can see how you are doing."

From behind me he said, "Let's go Charley, it's a pop-quiz." When he was alongside, he stopped. "This reminds me of last year. There was a while there when the stars were all aligned: your cabin on the lakeshore suited me perfectly, our weekly get-togethers for massage, my horse riding lessons, sailing, playing music. It only lasted months, but in my mind it was a sentinel moment of my life. Then I messed it up."

"Andy Shepard, are you living in the past?"

"I guess so. I'm finding it hard to let go."

"Why let it go? Why not see it as the path that brought us right here, right to this moment?"

"I'm not sure about this moment."

"Honey, you weren't sure in the past either."

Andy looked at me as if puzzled. I had him; a rare moment where I could see him better than he could see himself. "Let's pay attention. This might be a 'sentinel moment' as well," I said.

He nodded and continued to stare. Then he said with a smile, "I love your lips."

"Good start, but I now want you to pay attention to your riding. "Go."

He gave Charley a nudge with his heels, "Come on Charley, make me look good."

I followed Andy out of the pasture and waited as he closed the gate behind us. Then we picked up the trail that led to the ridgeline above Sabina's ranch. I watched him from behind. He rode with much more confidence than he had the last time we were together. He was trusting Charley. His shoulders were not hunched up like before. But he was still too rigid in the saddle.

"Andy, focus for a while on the way Charley moves: forward, sideways, sideways, forward, sideways, sideways. And when he has to step up or around an obstacle, watch how his movement changes."

Riding in silence we passed through a stretch of oaks and grey pines, then crossed a stream. I compared how his body moved with how mine was moving. I became very aware of what was usually natural and unnoticed: my hips and waist were in constant fluid motion, accommodating Pomo's gait, while my upper body kept more of an equilibrium.

I called out ahead, "Now, I want you to do something for me. Let your hips move like a woman's."

"Easy for you to say."

"Come on, give it a try. Play with it. Exaggerate it."

"What if Charley doesn't respect me in the morning."

"Actually, Charley's swinging his ass as he walks. I just want you to swing your hips in tandem with him."

"Like this?" Andy's butt slightly raised off the saddle as he sort of wiggled it.

"Keep your weight in the saddle and let Charley lead. Let your lower body thrust forward and side-to-side while your upper body remains mostly upright."

"You would make a hell of a golf instructor. Am I supposed to think of all those things at once?"

"No. It's mostly just keeping your focus on how Charley's moving, and letting your hips stay loose."

For a couple of steps he did it. "Yes! Just like that Andy. See if you can stay with it to the top of the next rise."

"I don't think John Wayne rode like this."

"Riding tall in the saddle is macho bullshit. Come on now, rock it like your mama and you will feel so much better at the end of the day."

"Come on, Charley, let's swish."

Andy got into it; first in parody, then with more naturalness. After ten minutes I passed him and said, "You're really getting it. Now watch me. Even though Pomo's gait is different, the principle is the same."

Andy watched, then said, "My ass will never swing like that!"

"Maybe not, but you don't have to ride like this," and I stiffened my back and hips and let Pomo jerk me around, which had the subtle effect of changing the way Pomo was walking. "Can you see the difference?"

"It looks like you're fighting each other."

"Good. Now relax, loosen your hips, drop your shoulders, but keep your head mostly steady."

When we reached the ridge we dismounted and walked the horses to give our bodies a rest. I remembered how I overdid Andy's first lesson, and how miserable he was.

"Thank you," he said. "I can tell this lesson is going to be a turning point."

"Yes, for both of us. This has done wonders for me." We looked down at the ranch in the distance. It sat in a shallow valley which opened up as it neared Hogan Lake. Andy was silent as if waiting for me to finish my thought. "I haven't given Ray's offer much thought. I've spent my time practicing some simple exercises that Maria, my occupational therapist, gave me. So tell me, are you still interested in getting back into the wedding business?"

"I've got mixed feelings. On one hand I feel marriage is mostly a set up for heartbreak. Look at us! Between us we have seven divorces. Being the officiating minister makes me feel like a car salesman who knows his customers will crash their new, shiny cars and hurt themselves.

"On the other hand, there's no stopping it; people are going to get married. Couples mostly feel that they are behind the wheel and in control and can keep the car on the road. What was great about doing your son's Halloween wedding was that he and Cindy went in with their eyes open. They knew it wasn't going to be easy. But I know that they all won't be like that."

"There's not a sentimental bone in your body, is there?"

"That's the frightening thing: despite my experience there is still a little voice inside of me that says if I just find the right person I could have a life-long happy marriage."

"I suppose it could happen."

"Yeah? More likely a deer pops up along the road and everything goes to hell despite your best efforts."

"Or a tumor. So, you're not interested?"

"In weddings or marriages?"

"I thought we were talking about weddings."

"Actually, despite my mixed feelings, I am very interested. I can't ignore the signs: I was given an abandoned church, I need a little more income as an old retired guy, you need a less physical job, Ray needs more business for his hotel, and the town needs more tourists to survive. So the answer is yes. And you?"

I paused and I thought about the possibility of becoming a wedding coordinator as we walked along the ridge trail which was also a firebreak. If a grass fire came up the hill from the west and the wind from the coast wasn't blowing much, this bulldozer-scraped road would keep the fire from coming down into the valley where Sabina's and several other ranches were. The firebreak was there to keep small problems from becoming catastrophic – and catastrophic was what I was afraid of with this new job. Most brides (especially first-time brides) have their hearts set on some version of a storybook wedding. That seemed like a big responsibility. Ruining a wedding would feel catastrophic. How could I foresee, or even anticipate problems, and be prepared for them? It would be unmapped terrain – where were the firebreaks?

I finally said, "I guess I don't feel very...very what? Competent? Confident?"

"You mean like I felt before ever getting on Charley?"

"Well, maybe not that scared."

"I hope not. But here I am, swishing my hips. You just need a good teacher."

I looked at Andy. I could tell he had a plan. "And?"

"Her name is Janelle. She's an acquaintance of mine and the wedding coordinator at a large church in Stockton. She said she'd love to meet you and help us out."

"An acquaintance?" I tried to sound nonchalant but didn't.

"Loosen your hips, Cowgirl. She's the pastor's wife."

"Oh."

Slow down, I thought. Pay attention. Don't judge. My breath and heartbeat were perceptibly faster as my anger had flashed. My stomach was tight. My face felt hot with embarrassment. All this reaction just happened on its own.

I focused on the trail crunching under my boots, and I could hear the horse's shoes hitting the dirt rhythmically. My hand that held Pomo's reins was sweaty. I had an impulse to change hands, then realized I couldn't, I was a one-armed woman! I wanted to swear and complain.

I slowed my steps and asked my stomach to relax. I was perplexed: what did not-judging mean in this case? Experiencing jealousy, was that judging? Seeing my jealousy, was that judging? Calling it jealousy, was that judging? Condemning my jealousy, was that judging?

"What's going on Barbara?" There was a softness in his voice.

"What's jealousy?"

Andy's eyes narrowed as if he was thinking. Then, "Mostly it is a fear of loss. But sometimes it is confused with envy: the fear of not getting what others have. And envy is often confused with greed: the fear of not having enough, even in the face of plenty."

Jealousy, envy, greed. Were they descriptions or judgments? They sounded like judgments. But Andy cut through the judgments; they were about being afraid.

"I felt afraid, Andy, afraid I might lose what we have."

He just nodded.

"Soon I'm going to be fifty for Christ's sake, and now I'm, I'm…" don't judge, "I'm a one-armed woman."

He stopped and noticed my tears beginning to puddle. He pulled out his blue bandana and handed it to me.

"I'm afraid, Andy." I covered my face, my private pain.

"Of what?"

"That no one will ever love me." And now I gave in and sobbed.

He took the sweaty reins from my hand and held me. "Who taught you that?"

And without thinking I took a breath between sobs and said, "My father."

"Well, you need a different teacher."

I pulled back and looked up into his face, "But I don't trust anyone."

"I know. I don't either. The job is yours, Barbara. You have to teach yourself that you are loveable. You're not a child anymore, so no substitute father or mother can teach you this. You have to make up your mind to be the good teacher and patiently, with compassion, teach yourself how loveable you are. Then the fear will lose its power over you."

* * *

February 18

If I am the teacher, who is the student?

> *Here I am. Scared and full of tears, a jealous little girl.*

Can I really teach you?

I can't think straight when you are jealous.

> *Then teach me when I am not jealous. Teach me to pay attention to the here and now, the precious miraculous moment. Teach me to recognize the judgmental voices in me, to hear the put-downs that I replay*

> to myself. Teach me to let go of my
> misguided teachers. Teach me to forgive.

Will you be listening?
Can you learn?

> I have to. I don't want to be a jealous fifty-year-old. I want to love myself so just keep repeating. I may need lots of repetition, like kids. I may need to hear it again, but I can learn.
>
> I may forget, but I can learn.
> I may get frustrated, but I can learn.
> I may want to fire my teacher, but I can learn.
> I may feel silly, I may stumble over these baby lessons, but I can learn.
> I can learn. I can.

Chapter 35

March 18th, my fiftieth birthday, was now at a full gallop and racing up to meet me. Until now I had managed to ignore it, although I knew it was coming (as do all women of a certain age). Of course I hadn't mentioned my birthday to anyone. Unfortunately, Sabina always remembers the date, but I'd sworn her to secrecy in exchange for agreeing that she could take me shopping in Stockton on the 20th. And when Nathan called ahead to arrange to come and "celebrate" my birthday, I said that was thoughtful, but no thanks, I had other plans. So we agreed he could buy me lunch when Sabina and I were there. And since I had never told Andy my birth date, all was set for me to have a couple of beers on St. Patty's day and then lay low on March 18th.

But on the 12th my luck ran out. Brandy called. She said that she had to travel from Oregon to Sacramento for her job and she wanted to come and see me for my birthday. In the five years that I've lived in Calaveras County my daughter had never visited. However, we had taken important first steps in the hospital, and since then she had called several times. I couldn't miss this opportunity to strengthen our renewed connection. I would have to open the gate and let my 50th birthday ride in after all; and maybe if things went well, I'd get my daughter back. That would be a dream birthday present and it would truly shrink the significance of my dreaded milestone.

The week leading up to Brandy's visit, I started an ill-begotten project. I spent two days sorting through my big box of old photographs that included Brandy's childhood. I wanted to gift her with a DVD of photos and music of her childhood and youth, so I spent hours trying to pick out the photos I thought she would like.

Many of the photos included her older sister, Carolyn, who was so bitter that I hadn't even heard from her for years. And of course, their father was in the box as well -- I guess I hadn't thrown him out completely. Hour by hour I was transported back to those chaotic years: the drinking, the horrible fights, the cheating, trying to fix things with sex, manipulating with money, and the battles over the kids.

The process set me back emotionally – indeed, set me up, down and sideways. By the time I arranged to have the photos transferred to a disk, I felt sad and alone, and my misery list had lengthened. Yet neglecting everything else, I spent two more days on the computer editing, cropping and trying to pick out music.

Two days before "B" day, I awoke feeling confused, conflicted and exhausted. Why had I indulged in all those old images and memories? What was I doing!?

So I did the only thing I knew to do: My very slow walking practice. I dressed for the cool damp morning air that greeted me outside the back door, and I began, step by step, moving up the drive toward the road. Like a miracle slowly unfolding, it brought reality back to me. It refocused my mind on what is: my breathing, my body, the pleasure of walking, and the trees, lake, and hills.

My reality became the present moment, and the old painful memories faded back into the past. The past became a slightly interesting history including some mistakes, some accomplishments, and some lessons learned.

For nearly an hour I walked and paid attention without judgment.

At the road I turned back and walked all the way down to the lakeshore. I took my time (an interesting phrase in this context, like taking back my time rather than letting it dissipate in mindless distraction). At the water's edge I stopped and soaked in the grand view of the lake rippling in the breeze and the velvet hills far beyond. I let the question come up again: Why did I do the photo project? What was it really about?

A very clear, calm answer came to mind: I wanted to convince Brandy that life had been pretty good back then, and that I had been a good mother. And more importantly, to convince myself. It was about my burden of harsh judgment; I wanted to just erase what had been and to create a different picture – and have my daughter love me.

There it was. I wanted to be loved. The good teacher had some work to do.

It was noon on "B" day when I heard Brandy's car on the gravel driveway. I'd been in the kitchen all morning. I washed my hand and wiped it on my apron, then stepped out the back door. The good teacher said, Now let Brandy be whoever she is. But you don't have to be stuck in the past. And Sweetheart, forget about the DVD. There will be a better time to give it to her.

Brandy pulled up and parked. I waved and she got out of the car and greeted me, "Hi, Mom."

"Hi, Honey," I said, and a flood of emotion filled my heart and tears filled my eyes. We stepped to each other and I put my arm around her neck.

She hugged me and I squeezed my eyes closed to keep from crying.

"You all right?" she asked.

I guess the past will burst in whenever it wants; although it wasn't memories that now possessed me. The tears didn't come from regretful, guilty, angry recollections. It was a release, love's flood gate that had been closed for too long had suddenly opened.

"Yes, I'm fine. I'm just so glad to see you."

We separated and I pulled the blue bandana out of my apron pocket and wiped my eyes. Brandy was twenty-five. She had my dark hair which she wore long, but at 5'6" was two inches taller than me. She had put on a few extra pounds around the middle, yet she was not what I would call overweight.

"Happy birthday! Boy you look great."

"Thanks, Sweetie, you did a wonderful job on this blouse. It fits better than those I had done in town."

"Wait a minute, I've got something in the car." She stepped back to the trunk and brought out a large, flat gift-wrapped present. She was about to hand it to me, then said, "I'll carry it in for you."

"I've got lunch ready. I hope you're hungry."

"You shouldn't have. We could have gone out to eat."

"Actually, as it turns out, I'm a better cook with one arm than I was with two. A lot slower, but better. I'm learning to pay attention, to slow down and enjoy preparing the food."

"That sounds great," she said as we got inside. "It seems I'm just throwing something from the freezer into the microwave half the time. But since Tyler moved in we eat a little better. He's a good cook." She set the present on the table, and in a rush, as if she was more excited about it than me, she said, "You can open it now."

I got out the scissors and carefully cut through the wrapping, exposing a large picture frame. When I pulled it free of the paper I could see that it was a painting. I stood it on edge on the table and was about to say how wonderful it was (a charming picture of a mother sitting in a rocker and nursing a baby). But then I looked closer.

"Is that me!?"

"I gave the artist the photo that you had given me years ago. You said that Dad had taken the shot."

"And that's you!"

"Yup. Pretty cool, huh?"

I stared. I was speechless. I remembered that day. Harry was drinking and though I told him not to take the picture, he took a whole roll just to spite me. Most turned out blurry and were tossed. But one must have been decent. I don't even remember giving it to her. Now the image in front of me was soft and overflowing with maternal love.

I laid the painting flat and hugged my daughter close. "My God, Brandy, it's beautiful. This is the best birthday present ever."

"You're welcome, Mom. And I have another one for you, too (sort of)."

"Really? This is more than enough."

"You are finally going to be a grandmother."

I glanced at her tummy. She hadn't gained weight after all. "You're pregnant!"

"Three months."

With blinding speed the list of response options instantly ran through my mind – some of them were trouble. I sat down at the table.

"I'm going to be a grandmother," I said in disbelief. Different responses and emotions ran through me again. I saw that most of them were about me: about feeling old, useless and unattractive. I put these aside. This news was actually about her.

I looked up at her face, "Are you happy, Sugar?"

"Yes. It's perfect timing. I'm twenty-five, Tyler and I are doing really well together, he's looking forward to being a father, and we both have good jobs."

I stood up again, "Then I'm happy. Congratulations." And for the third time, we hugged.

We talked some more as Brandy helped me put lunch on the table. I had made an adult version of macaroni and cheese, a cucumber salad, and fresh apple pie with ice cream. We talked about her plans which included not getting married – at least not in the foreseeable future. She and Tyler agreed that their relationship would be better without it. She talked about her job – she sold computer chips and things for a big company. In fact she had a work appointment that evening in Sacramento.

And we talked about my rehabilitation. I told her it was turning out to be more encompassing than I had expected. It was challenging me to make changes in how I felt and thought about things. And I told her about my new job offer. She asked about Andy, and I said I still saw him and that he had been a real friend through all of this.

In other words, we danced around a lot of issues. But it was a beginning. When she left, I put the DVD I had made in a drawer and I hung up my new painting – it was everything I was looking for in the old photo box.

* * *

March 18
I held my daughter
At my breast
And rocked her
In my arms.
I rocked her in my arms.
Then she brought
Her swollen womb
For me to bless
With my love.
To bless her with my love.
A grandmother soon
Will look at me
Reflecting love
From my mirror.
Reflecting love to me.

Chapter 36

I was on the shore of the lake and lost in my slow-motion walking practice when Sabina and the horses turned off the highway and headed down my driveway. I had let the sound of the small lapping waves at the water's edge set the pace of each mindful step, and the rhythm of my breathing kept time with the raising of each foot. My body shifted weight from one side to another as each wave withdrew from the gravelly shore and the next one approached.

As my thin small book had suggested, each time a distracting thought came to mind I carefully placed it on an imaginary shelf behind me and told it that I would consider it later, and then I focused again on walking. But the sound of Sabina's truck brought conflicted feelings of regret and happy expectations. I regretted that my peace was interrupted – as if I could not experience peace unless I was engaged in one of my intentional practices. My happy expectations were that now my babies were home (and life would be like it was before I lost my arm.)

Were these feelings a form of judging? I was puzzling over this as I walked more normally up the slope past the foundation of my old cabin and toward the horse barn. This graphic reminder of the fire that had driven Andy to move to town brought up different feelings: anger and disappointment. I became aware and amazed of the contrast between the peace of mind I experienced in my walking practice and the assault of emotions tugging at me in the matter of a single minute.

When I reached the barn, Sabina had the corral gate open and was backing the trailer toward it.

"Hi," I said as I came alongside her pretty purple pickup.

"Hi Barb," she said through her open window. "You sure you're ready for these three?"

"Absolutely. I can't tell you how much I've missed them these past three months."

"Has it been that long!?"

"It seems like a lifetime."

We got the horses out, but there was no way I was going to manage closing the horse trailer doors and ramp with one arm, so I left that task to Sabina. When I tried to latch the corral gate however, the bolt on the gate didn't line up with the hole in the post. I remembered that I had to lift up on the gate with one hand and slide the bolt with the other.

"You want me to get that?" Sabina asked when she saw me try to force the gate up with the bolt.

"No. I'm going to have to learn to do this when there's no one here to help." I stuck the toe of my boot under the gate to give it more lift, but the bolt still didn't match the hole.

As I tried again Sabina said, "Reminds me of an old boyfriend; he had the same trouble – just couldn't find the right hole. Then when he did, his bolt shrunk."

I let go of the gate and my struggle, leaned against the post and laughed.

"Then what did you do?"
"Just like they taught you in rehab: Creative Alternatives."

I looked at the gate, "I'm going to have to make a new hole."

"That could work."

"But until I get my drill out, I have another idea. Watch the gate, will ya?" I walked into the barn and came back with a block of wood and a short board. I put the block under the center of the board, and one end of the board under the gate. Then I stepped on the other end of the board to lift the gate and match the bolt with the hole. That did the trick.

"Yep, I think you're ready, girlfriend." As we walked to the house she put her arm over my shoulder and said, "You're doing so well, I'm proud of you."

It was an unusual moment. Outside of the doctors, no one had touched me where my arm once hung. For an instant I wanted to move away, but I let that pass. I would later write this poem:

March 20

She touched me

And my shame met her love.

Her love won.

In between the barn and the house

I began to walk lighter.

As we washed our hands, she asked how I survived my birthday. I proudly showed her my new painting and told her about the healing visit I had from Brandy. She smiled and said it was about time.

We locked up the house and climbed into my truck. It was going to be a serious test. I had an appointment with the wedding coordinator down in Stockton, an hour away in the Central Valley, and I would have to drive in traffic for the first time.

But it was not just a driving test. It was also testing the notion of becoming Andy and Ray's wedding coordinator in Moke Hill. If it wasn't for my arm I would be looking forward to the change and a new challenge. But as I drove the two lane road that wound down through the Gold Country, I felt weary of changes. My life was moving through heavy traffic, and the stress of facing daily adjustments and detours made me want to postpone this whole thing. Yet I wasn't getting any younger, and getting my former life back was a fantasy.

It was difficult to put these disturbing thoughts on the shelf behind me and just pay attention to driving. Indeed, it was driving toward this appointment that was stimulating these thoughts and feelings. My anxious thoughts kept falling off the shelf. Could life – real life, messy life, unpredictable life – really be lived with peace of mind, experiencing each moment as a miracle?

"What are you thinking?" asked Sabina.

I hesitated and searched for a way to summarize these thoughts, then surprised myself and said, "I'm too worried to be happy. And I wonder if worrying is a habit that can be unlearned?"

"Shit girl, it sounds like you need a shrink."

I smiled. "You know any happy shrinks?"

"Oh, I bet they're happy when they deposit your check."

"No, really, do you think psychiatrists are a happy bunch?"

"Would you be happy if you listened to people's misery all day? At least when you tend bar, people usually change the subject after their second drink."

"Maybe that's why shrinks put so many people on medication."

"Yeah, just another way of saying 'stop your bitching.' So tell me Miss Barbara Hanson" she said in mock seriousness, "What are you worried about?"

"Me? What do I have to be worried about? Here I am with my best friend who is helping me learn to drive with one hand. Heck, they could have really screwed up and cut off both of my arms and I would have had to learn to drive with my teeth!" I let go of the Brody knob and tried to grab the wheel with my teeth.

"Hey! Knock it off!"

I took the wheel again, laughing.

"Now you're making me worried!"

"Oh, don't worry, be happy!"

That started us singing one of our favorite songs that we sang at the hotel to keep things light. Putting on a Jamaican lilt we sang:

> "Every life we have some trouble,
> When you worry you make it double.
> Don't worry, be happy.
> Cause when you're worried your face will frown,
> And that will bring everybody down,
> So don't worry, be happy."

Then we made up verses until we got to the outskirts of Stockton:

> "Missing some fingers and missing a thumb?
> So driving a truck makes you feel so dumb.
> Don't worry, be happy.
> Guy at the bar is sloppy drunk
> When he burps he smells just like a skunk.
> Don't worry, be happy."

Then I came up with this one:

> "You turn fifty and want to faint
> Cause your mirror says,
> 'Honey, a chick you ain't!'
> Don't worry, be happy.
> Then your daughter says by September
> You're gonna be an old grandmother!"

"Wait, wait! Really?" Sabina stopped me.

I nodded and tried to scowl.

"Holy shit, we might as well eat lunch at the Senior Center."

It was mid-morning when we met Andy's friend, the wedding coordinator. Her office was in her husband's large, attractive church on one of Stockton's main boulevards. She was a four-plus woman named Janelle who greeted us warmly. She had words of praise for Andy, and I felt we would get the royal treatment because of their friendship. I extended my left hand, and without blinking she did the same, and we shook. I then introduced Sabina who seemed confused and started to extend her left hand as well, then her right hand as she laughed nervously.

Her office walls were hung with framed wedding pictures, and there were shelves of wedding stuff. Wedding gear, I thought, like the tack-room in my horse barn which is full of horse gear, but getting "hitched" in this place is much more serious. The shelves displayed a basket full of small bundles of rice, several ornate table decorations and centerpieces, a small white satin pillow with wedding rings tied to the top, and guest books.

Someone from another planet would not guess that this paraphernalia was associated with one of the greatest risks humans take. Did I want to work with these risk-takers, managing their hitchings, dealing with their fears – and my fears?

As we sat down, Janelle said, "I suggest that this be the first of three training sessions together." She spoke with soft authority and confidence. She seemed totally comfortable with her weight the way some women are, as if it was completely normal. I would have felt conspicuous in her place; more so than with a missing arm. I put this thought on the back shelf for later.

"Today," she continued, "I would like you to sit in with me as I work with a new couple. We've already had a get acquainted time where I showed them the sanctuary, took down some information and gave them some homework (things to think about). Then in our second training session you can shadow me during the day of a wedding, but there won't be a lot of time to chat that day. But at our third meeting we will debrief how the wedding went and answer any further questions you may have. How does that sound?"

It sounded like Janelle was used to being very directive, but just short of dictatorial. She also spoke as if she had a clear outline that she followed, which was probably helpful in her job. She seemed to invite my input, but I got the feeling she would push, in her gentle way, for me to see that her idea was best. She was not going to be my friend or my servant;

she was the expert. This was my first lesson in how to be a wedding coordinator.

"Fine," I said.

"Good. And while we wait for the couple to show up, let's look at what I call The Wedding Coordinator's Ten Commandments." She handed us each a typed page, and for the next twenty minutes we went over the list.

1. You do not have to agree to do every wedding. Know your boundaries.
2. Let the couple know that drunk people, whether guests or members of the wedding party, will be shown the door.
3. A church wedding is a church wedding — joyful but with Spirit — and the building must be treated with respect.
4. Photographers cannot distract, delay or alter a wedding ceremony.
5. No children participants younger than seven years old.
6. Weddings never go perfectly, so everyone must keep their sense of humor.
7. There will be a rehearsal and everyone in the wedding as well as the musicians and photographers must attend.
8. Groomsmen will play no pranks during the wedding.
9. Mothers are not in charge.
10. Payment is always up front.

My initial response was that the list was too authoritarian, but by the end of twenty minutes I had a hunch that Janelle had just saved me a lot of headaches.

She ran the meeting with the couple just as efficiently. It was over in thirty minutes and the couple left with more homework and an appointment to meet with the minister. Afterward Janelle answered questions we had and gave us a flow-sheet that outlined the tasks of a wedding coordinator in a rational, chronological sequence. She had been doing this job for fifteen years and it showed.

At the end Janelle assured me that if I could run a hotel, I could do this job. And if something needed lifting or moving, I could just ask the groomsmen, they were always looking for something to do.

When we left, my mind was made up to take the job and was jumping from thought to thought. I felt it would be better (and safer) if Sabina drove. She agreed. But we had only gone several blocks before she pulled into a shopping center.

"What's up?" I asked.

As she found a parking spot she said, "Big Janelle was great, but she never told us what shoes a wedding coordinator should wear. A serious omission, don't you think?!"

I grinned and nodded, "A very serious omission. I guess this is a good place to do a little research?"

"Yes, but I think we should call it essential vocational rehab."

"Perhaps we can find some creative alternative here. Maria would be so proud of me."

"Settled. My girlfriend has had a birthday, let's shop!"

* * *

We met my son for lunch downtown at a very nice Chinese restaurant near his office. After we were settled and had ordered, I handed Nathan a file folder that contained several letters relating to my arm and the suit we had filed. The correspondence was from the hospital and their lawyers and insurance companies. There were also copies of my latest medical records.

"Thanks, and pardon me for mentioning it, but happy birthday." He quickly thumbed through the file and said, "Surprisingly things are moving along. I think they want to settle this without a trial. They are not disputing that you received the wrong medication. But, of course, they won't want to link your infection to that mistake and the resulting ten days in ICU.

"Cindy thinks it is being expedited because of the increased competition between the three hospitals here in Stockton and the ambitious building project that the hospital is involved in – some say they are over-building. She said if they get some bad publicity about dispensing the wrong medication and post-surgery infections, it will cripple their business plan. Usually, even if they plan to settle out of court, they stall for several years so the lawyers rack up a lot of hours and claimants will lose patience and settle for less. And in the meantime, if the claimant dies, the hospital is off the hook for pain and suffering money."

I was relieved when our food came. I wasn't sure why, but I was feeling increasingly uncomfortable with talk about the suit. I didn't say anything. Rather I just noticed that my body felt tense, my good mood over picking out two pretty pairs of shoes was gone, and I felt irritable.

"So Nathan," asked Sabina as three delicious smelling entrees were set in front of us, "How quickly could it be done?"

"If Cindy is reading the signals right, maybe a year or so." He passed the Chicken Chow Mein to me.

"One of the great things about Chinese food," I said, wanting to change the subject, "something I never noticed before: No need for a knife."

"You're right Barb," said Sabina, "But the trick is, how will you manage chopsticks with your left hand?"

I tried to position the chopsticks in my fingers and get the ends to pinch together as they watched. For a minute I took it as a challenge. Then I announced, "It's time for a creative alternative," and I signaled for the server to get me a fork.

As we ate, Nathan explained that soon I would be asked to give a deposition where the lawyers would ask me questions under oath. They would be looking at how strong our case was and where the weaknesses were. "The more we can show how profound the effects of your disability are, and how it is directly tied to the hospital's actions, the better the settlement will be."

"Well then," Sabina said with a smile, "We should get videos of Barb trying to use chopsticks, that would be worth another million itself!"

"Something like that," said Nathan. "We would show how important horse riding was to mom and the investments she has made in horses and stables, for instance."

"But I am still riding," I said.

"What?"

"Yeah, started a few weeks ago. And I'm still giving Andy lessons."

"Don't underestimate your mother, young man," Sabina said half in jest.

Nathan turned my file over and made a note – a lawyer's habit. Then he took a bite, obviously thinking. "Well then," he said, "perhaps we could suggest to their counsel that the Stockton newspaper could do a story on how a horsewoman learns to ride again after a hospital's mistake caused her to lose her arm. Maybe a Sunday section human interest story, with photos."

"Your son's a natural," said Sabina.

I didn't say anything, I just watched a new set of feelings come up inside me.

"We will also want to show how your disability impacts your ability to do your job," Nathan continued.

I looked up from my plate and caught his eyes, "I have a new job."

"Really?" he said with the sound of disbelief.

"Yup," Sabrina said, "and she already has new shoes to go with it. Too bad she didn't lose a foot. Now that would have been a real sad story!"

I look at her, not believing what she just said. Then she started to laugh. That made me laugh, so she laughed harder. I knew what she was doing: she knew that I was feeling resistant to go forward with a lawsuit. She knew it better than I did. And she was supporting me.

Nathan shook his head and asked, "What's your new job?"

"I'm going in partnership with Andy and Ray. We're starting a destination wedding business. I'm going to be the wedding coordinator, Andy is going to offer his church and be the one who ties the knots, and Ray is going to use the hotel for receptions and lodging and do the promotion. And he is hiring me an assistant to do the more hands on running of the restaurant and bar and hotel.

"When would you begin?"

"I had my first training session today as a matter of fact. We're going to gear up for June."

"How will this affect your income?"

"Hard to say, but think of how much you and Cindy spent on your wedding last year, then double it because I know Ray and Andy gave you a deal, and you two did a lot of the work yourselves. I'll get half of the profits with a guarantee to match at least my present salary."

Nathan made some more notes.

"How are you two doing?" I asked him, changing the subject again.

"Fine."

We all ate in silence again. Then he said, "Harry called."

Harry was my second husband and the girls' father. "Oh? What'd he have to say?"

"He had heard about your operations and wanted to know how you were."

"Right. What did he want?"

"I'm not sure. He had already talked to Brandy; I had the feeling he was pumping me for information."

"What'd you say?"

"He knew we were handling your lawsuit, but beyond that, of course, I didn't say anything."

"He can smell money."

"That's my guess. I know he's Carolyn and Brandy's father, but you wouldn't do anything, would you?"

"Anything?"

"Like loan him money or something."

I stared at him for a moment. Already he was worried about what I might do with my fantasy fortune. "I don't have any money, Sweetheart, just a mortgage," I said with more feeling than I wanted.

"Wait a minute, wait a minute. No family fights in front of friends," said Sabina. "Go back to a neutral corner and count to ten."

"You're right, Sabina. I'm sorry Mom, I was out of line. It's really none of my business."

I was so close to reminding Nathan that I had spent a small fortune on his education. Sabina had saved me. It would have been unkind, and it would have been defensive. He was right, I tried to buy love, with his father and the girls' father. And everyone could see it.

* * *

March 21
I hate myself for being so stupid.
I let men walk all over me.
It has made a mess of my life.

> Oh? If you were a smart girl could you always see through guys and know when they were telling you the truth and when they were lying?

Not all the time.

> No. But you always gave them a chance to do the right thing. You did not give up on love; that would have truly been stupid.

I gave them too many chances!

> No, you gave them chances until you had enough. Then you tried someone new. That is what smart people do. That is what people who don't hide in fear do.

Boy, I had enough of Harry!

> Indeed. And you do not have to let him back in. And you do not have to make yourself unhappy by hanging onto the past. That, dear one, is loving yourself.

Chapter 37

Spring came to the foothills with its cool mornings, sunny afternoons, and its bouquet of wildflowers. I rode every day, and for a week I saw no one. I also continued to practice intentional walking, brushing and cooking even though there were times when I now felt somewhat resistant to slowing down and paying attention. My little thin book anticipated this and suggested that one welcome the feelings of boredom or impatience with the practice, and that these feelings would lead to some jewel-like insights.

April 8

Yesterday I wanted to rush ahead and get things done.

Today I read, "What is more important than savoring life? And where else do you need to be than right here? And when is a better time to wake up than now?"

Oh, to hold lightly
Today's nagging concerns,
So to hold closely
Bright light-hearted life.

The next morning I sat at the breakfast bar drinking my coffee and making a list of things to get done. As I stared at my list I became aware of my feelings, as if suddenly noticing the music in the background of a movie. I began to list them:

Urgency and impatience – I need to get started;
Worry – I will not be able to get it all done;
Anxiety – I am not sure how to accomplish some of these things;

Happy anticipation – I am hoping some things will be a pleasure.

It reminded me of my old misery list, so I tore up the list and threw it out. Then I took a shower, as if to wash away those feelings. I coaxed myself to shower slowly. I enjoyed my body so much I got wrinkly fingers.

After I dressed I started another to-do list, but at the top I wrote: Nothing to do that's very important. Then I listed the same things I had written earlier. Again I stared at my list to see what feelings would come up. I noticed my left-handed writing was more pleasing than it was earlier in the morning. I felt lighter, emptier maybe.

I poured a fresh cup of coffee and spiked it with chocolate syrup. As I lifted the cup I paused to catch the delicious aromas. Then when I drank I noticed the beautiful partnership of the bitter dark roast beans and the sweet rich chocolate, followed by the warm pleasure flowing down into my body. So at the bottom of my to-do list I added something Maria had said early on in my rehab work, "It is not what we do, but how we do it." I was beginning to see.

On the heels of that thought I picked up the phone and called her. Maria had left a message to confirm our appointment for the next day. When I got her on the line, we agreed on the time. Then she said it would be her last visit, that I was graduating, so if I knew of anything that I needed to work on I should jot it down. Before we hung up I invited her to stay and have lunch as well.

Nathan had generously arranged for her home visits. Although I didn't want to run up his expense, I immediately felt sad, and scared at Maria's news. I tried the best I could to welcome these feelings. I was slowly learning that as a gracious host to what Maria called "emotional energies" I could sidestep the habit of over-identifying with them. Rather than being taken over by fear and sadness, I would just be a person who now had fearful and sad feelings.

Then I asked myself where these feelings came from? My first thought was I would never see Maria again; but I reminded myself that she didn't actually say that. I would ask her what was possible.

Then I realized that I attributed the progress and changes I was experiencing to Maria. She was my guide, and I was afraid that without her my misery list and my self-hatred would drag me down again. Yet a part of me knew that this too need not be the case. I resolved not to let that happen.

* * *

The next morning I made ramen noodle soup with fresh vegetables and small shrimp, and a side of diced cucumber, beets and balls of mozzarella cheese with balsamic vinegar dressing. Lunch was ready at ten when Maria rang the bell. I opened the door and was greeted with a surprise: Maria held a bouquet of daffodils and tulips.

"Good morning, Barbara. I picked these from my yard to celebrate your graduation."

"Maria, they're beautiful. Thank you," I said and took them. "Come on in."

We walked to the kitchen. "Something smells good."

"I've made some soup and salad for lunch. I thought we would talk for a while, then eat," I said, filling a vase with water and flowers. I carried them out and set them in the living room. "Let's sit in here."

Ironically, now that I knew that Maria would not be coming anymore I took notice of her as if for the first time. She appeared to be my age; and her features and coloring were such that I couldn't tell if her background was Asian or Hispanic. In fact, I knew very little about her, just that she was always focused on teaching me something.

As we sat down on the couch she asked, "So did you think of anything to work on this morning?"

I pointed to the hummingbird feeder hanging outside the window. "Got any tricks up your sleeve for cleaning and filling those little devils?"

"Anything is possible. But again, you've got to ask yourself how much is it worth in time and effort? I don't know of any hummingbird feeders that are easy or convenient for one-armed people. It would be an interesting project to build a special holder that would enable you to take it apart, wash it out, fill it and put it back together. Is it that important to you?"

"I miss watching them. Hummingbirds are so small, yet so feisty – a little like me."

Maria smiled and got up and looked out all three living room windows that faced the lake. Then she looked at me and said, "Sometimes it is helpful to take a small step, a partial solution, and see how it goes for you. In this case you might try feeding different kinds of birds with easy to fill birdseed feeders. In the meantime, plant some flowers and shrubs that hummingbirds are attracted to."

"Good," I said. "I could try that."

"And another thing," she said as she came and sat down again, "Having one arm will tend to push you into some rich experiences that you wouldn't have otherwise."

"Yeah, like massage."

Maria hesitated for a moment, then said, "Tell me."

"I mentioned to you before that I have this boyfriend, Andy."

"Yes."

"He sort of came into my life through the backdoor. He was my renter; and to save money he paid part of the rent by giving me massages."

Maria smiled, "Nice."

"Even though we both didn't want to get too involved at this stage of our lives, one thing led to another."

"Uh huh."

"Well, this arm thing sort of put our love making on hold."

"That's not uncommon. Is he out of the picture?"

"Oh no, he says he is still raring to go. I'm just afraid to let him see me like this."

Maria nodded her head.

"So, as you just said, I have come up with a small step, a partial solution. I am going to start by giving him a massage and see how that goes. However, I've never given anyone a massage, so it's going to be a new experience for me. Whether it will end up, as you say, a rich experience, I don't know. I'm supposed to give him a massage tomorrow. He said he will teach me as I go."

"Barbara, nearly everyone is shy to some degree about being seen with all their so-called flaws. And when someone loses a limb, their shyness is sometimes off the charts. Now, obviously, I've never experienced what you are dealing with, but I've known many more limbless people than you, and some have sex lives that I am jealous of. The fact that you've already taken this step (and it's not a small step, Barbara) is commendable. I could give you some massage pointers if you would like."

"That would be great."

"First, I think you want to give a relaxation massage rather than a therapeutic massage. This means long, slow strokes – but not painfully slow; enjoying touching him. No deep tissue work or slapping or pounding. And be generous with the oil, slippery, but not drippy.

"Second, ask him if he has any sensitive or ticklish spots so you can avoid them. You don't want to break the mood or make him tense.

"Third, remember some of his moves when he massaged you, what really felt good. He most likely gave you what he himself likes.

"And most importantly, don't stress your own body. Spread your feet and bend your knees; stay balanced and move like a dancer." She stood up and demonstrated the correct posture, massaging someone on an invisible table. "When you're receiving a massage you never get a chance to see correct posture which can make all the difference. Let's practice at your dining room table."

We moved to the table and again she demonstrated as if the table was someone's body; and this time she put her right hand behind her back. "When you begin each section of the massage, it is important how you lay your hand on his body; not suddenly, but as if you are setting down a full, hot cup of tea, gently and carefully. This communicates caring, builds trust, and encourages him to relax. Here, you try it."

I massaged the table for a while as Maria corrected my posture and perfected my slow strokes. When we finished she said, "And Barbara, if you only want this massage to be a small step, have Andy lay on his stomach and only massage his backside."

"Right," I said, but my imagination immediately jumped to possible medium sized steps. I pulled the reins on this fantasy and said, "Let's have lunch."

Maria helped me set the table and serve up the soup and salad. When we finally sat down I brought my notepad with my Maria-list and laid it next to me saying, "I jotted down a few other issues that have been coming up."

"Right," she said, "But first let me tell you, your ability to prepare a meal like this with one hand is extraordinary. You are so far ahead of the curve. How have you done it?"

"It's not hard since I let go of the habit of hurrying. But this practice of slowing down, paying attention, and not judging has had other weird effects. It's made me notice how my feelings just sort of pop up automatically. And I find myself studying them before they take over. It feels strange, like standing on the outside looking in. I've noticed that most of the time, no matter what the feelings are, there is a fear driving each one."

"What has happened, Barbara, is that you have found the secret to rehabilitation. As we heal physically and learn the practical aspects of coping with our disabilities, there is an opportunity for a much more important area of healing and growth: a chance for the emotional and attitudinal handicaps that are acquired over a lifetime to be healed as well. It is as if a door opens for ones inner light to shine out."

"It sounds noble, but all I wanted was to stop feeling so miserable."

"That's how this practice works. Your new awareness will, in time, make you less susceptible to your fears. You've practiced fearfulness for a long time, so it will take a while for that peace you experience while doing your intentional practice to be a part of your everyday life. But believe me, you are moving right along, quite quickly actually."

For a while we just ate as I thought about what she had said. Was I really moving along? I felt like I was barely crawling. Then it occurred to me: Thank God that I don't have to deal with something really tough, like Janelle. So I mentioned to Maria about my meeting with Janelle, and how thankful I felt that I didn't have to deal with obesity.

"So you think it would really be harder?" she asked.

"Much harder. Or what if I had lost both arms?!"

"It would have been the same. You take the same steps for the same healing and find the same wholeness. It is mostly your fear that makes it look harder. Consider a person who has lost a thumb, you might think that they had it easier. But it is not so easy, and for some it could feel harder. Yet everyone can work for the same wholeness, much as you have."

"The same wholeness, with no arms?"

"Rehabilitation is a more complex word than most people think. It has very old roots. Its root, habit, refers to clothes; and not just a nun's clothes. It refers to the customary and appropriate garb of a profession. So rehabilitation is like getting dressed, or redressed, appropriately for life. Rehabbing a house is getting it dressed back up so it doesn't look so shabby and you can live in it again.

"But you are not a house, you are a person of sacred worth. Luckily there is a second root meaning to rehabilitation: ability, to be capable, to have what it takes, to be fit. So rehabilitation is to make able again. But then what does it mean when we say that someone is permanently disabled? Is there no rehabilitation for them?

"The confusion (your confusion) is about the external versus the internal. No matter how many limbs you have, or how fat you are, you are always capable of being a person, a whole full person of sacred worth, even if externally you may now have slightly fewer options. And this life, Barbara, is not about how many options we have, it is about how we use our options. When you get that, you are rehabilitated and capable for living."

The doorbell rang, surprising me. I hadn't heard a car approach. When I answered it, Andy was standing on the porch. "Oh hi, Andy. Come on in. I have company. What's up?"

He hesitated, then asked, "Are we still doing massage today?"

"It's tomorrow, Andy. But come in and meet my occupational therapist."

"Tomorrow? Figures, I've lost track of time this week. What time should I come?"

"Two."

"Well, thanks for the invitation, but I think I'll just take the boat out for a sail. See you tomorrow."

"Sure. See you then."

When I got back to the table I said, "It was Andy, he was confused about our massage day. Unlike him."

Maria nodded. "Maybe he's as nervous about it as you are."

* * *

As I prepared for bed that night I decided that as a one-armed woman, one of the things I missed was washing my face with two hands. This task, once refreshing and satisfying, was now a drippy awkward ordeal. Two hands nicely match the symmetry of one's face. And it takes two hands to scoop up enough water for a thorough rinse. Then drying one's hand and arm is a lovely conundrum, like one hand clapping. When my head finally rested on the pillow I felt irritated that I had not asked Maria for advice about this problem.

This thought led to the recollection of Andy's mistaken appearance. My mind began to review other little things that I had noticed lately about Andy – little absent-minded behaviors that didn't amount to much, but now I wondered if they were part of a pattern? Maybe this move into the remodeled church in Moke Hill had stressed him more than it appeared. Add to that, the stress for a man newly retired, and the fact that he lost all his things when the cabin burnt down. He probably is dealing with as much loss and adjustment as I am. On top of that, he has been dealing with my struggles as well. The poor guy probably needs to get laid. Maybe I'll take a big step tomorrow.

Chapter 38

"I'm sorry for my goof-up yesterday, Barbara," Andy said as he came in and followed me to the living room. "I seem to be kind of scattered lately."

"No problem, Baby. Maybe you just couldn't wait to see me." I slipped my arm around his waist and smiled up at him.

"Yes, that was it. Gosh, you're so perceptive," he said with mock sincerity.

"Uh huh. You know, we handicapped folks develop very sensitive awareness with our other, um, faculties."

He looked at me not knowing how to take that comment. Then he noticed how I had set up the room. "Very nice! You got the table up; I could have done that for you."

"No, no, Sugar. You are on the receiving end today."

He continued to survey the room. "And my favorite massage music, candles, a pitcher of water, you're warming the oil, and no horse brushes or spurs in sight. I'm relaxing already."

"That's the idea. Now, the bathroom is that way, you may remember. When you are ready, come out and lay face down under the flannel sheet."

He smiled at my act. "Well, I feel I'm in the hands of an experienced massage therapist."

"Just one hand, Baby. But that could mean a massage that's twice as long."

"I guess you could start by helping me with the foot that's in my mouth."

"No problem; we'll get you straightened out."

While Andy was in the bathroom, I turned the furnace up a bit and pulled off the sweat shirt I was wearing over a short-sleeved tee with a purple cotton jumper. Earlier I had decided not to wear underclothes, but now I felt unsure about that decision. I still didn't know where I wanted this massage to go. I closed the drapes and was wiping off the bottle of massage oil in the kitchen when Andy came out and laid on the table.

"All set," he said.

He pretty much filled the whole table at six-foot one and about forty pounds overweight. It suddenly looked like a big job.

"Tell me, Reverend Shepard, do you have any sore or tender spots that I need to know about?"

"Yes, where the saddle meets my old bottom," he said from the face cradle affixed to the head of the table – a table that he'd bought when he first moved into the cabin.

"Okay. And any ticklish areas?"

"No."

"Good," I said, oiling my hand from the pump bottle that I had transferred the oil into this morning. "So, since I'm pretty much working in the dark here, you'll have to tell me how to do this, starting with the basics: faster, slower, firmer, softer."

"Right. We'll keep it simple and basic. I sure didn't learn to ride Charley on my first day."

The sheet was at his waist, and as he took a deep breath and slowly let it out I could see his body begin to relax. I felt tense so I did the same as I stood with my belly near his head, my arm extended over his upper back, and my open hand an inch from his skin. Remembering Maria's words, I very slowly and lightly let my hand make contact with his back between his shoulder blades. I leaned into my hand as I moved it down his spine to the small of his back, then slowly circled back up his right side to his arm, then over to his neck and up over his scalp, and finally, letting his hair slip through my fingers with a little pull. This was the beginning stroke Andy had used on me a dozen times.

"Oh, I can see you are going to be an excellent student. Nice touch. But instead of rubbing directly on the spine, go down on either side, that's where the muscles are."

"Okay." I pumped more oil on my hand, took a step to my right, gently placed my hand on his upper back again and then pressing, I slowly slipped down the long muscle just next to his spine; then I drew my hand firmly back up his left side, ending with the top of his head and hair.

After one more set of these I moved to the side of the table and began making large circles on his back with the heel of my palm.

"Good pressure," he said as I moved the circles down to his waist and back up to his shoulders. Then I moved to the other side of the table to repeat these strokes.

"Try using your forearm instead of your hand, starting near my spine and moving down and away to my side, then circling back to the spine." Andy must have guessed that with one hand, I could overwork it and tire. The use of my forearm rested my hand.

After about ten minutes I decided I liked doing massage. I liked the rhythm the slow repetitions with the music, and I began applying Maria's dancing technique, shifting my weight from leg to leg.

After working circles on Andy's lower back with my hand, I covered his upper body and uncovered his butt and legs. I switched back to using my forearm and massaged his rear like kneading two loaves of warm bread dough. By the sounds he was making, I could tell he liked this as much as I used to. I switched from one side to the other using plenty of oil, then with my elbow I gently nestled it down where his legs came together, then ran it slowly up his crack, slightly parting his cheeks.

"Okay," he said, "Where did you get that move? It wasn't from me."

"You know what they say, mothers are the invention of necessity."

"I'll have to think about that, but do it again."

After a couple more times he was starting to enjoy it a little too much (too soon). So I pulled the cover down over his butt and placed a chair near the foot of the table. I sat – as much to rest as to massage his feet. By the time I finished both feet Andy was breathing like he was asleep.

This would be a good place to stop, I thought; a successful small step, Andy is relaxed and not terribly turned on. I let my hand spread the excess oil that was on his foot up over his ankle and calf. Moving slowly I felt his coarse hair under my hand – so nicely male. I moved my hand higher and reached the soft warm place behind his knee. Then again, from his toes that hung over the table I slid up his calf and continued as far as I could reach while seated, which was barely to his lower thigh, and slowly back to his toes, giving each of them a slight pinch. I was taking pleasure not only in touching his body, but also the warm thrill building in my own.

I stood up and pumped some more oil and with my little finger I lifted the front of my jumper and nuzzled up to his toes as my hand laid oil all up the back of his thigh. I spread my legs so as I leaned into his foot it pushed deep between my thighs as I reached up and over his ass and then, ever so slowly, brought my hand sliding back down his leg. I felt his toes curl a bit, letting me know that he was indeed not asleep.

I let my hand slip up his inner thigh as high as it could go until it softly touched something that was not leg. I wiggled my fingers. He wiggled his toes.

"I could use a ride," I whispered.

"I'm so glad," he said.

"Can you turn over?"

"Thought you would never ask."

I pulled the cover completely off the table, and Andy turned over, a bit like an old man. But when I saw him I said, "Lord, how could you lay on that thing?"

"I was being polite."

I pumped another squirt of oil and said, "Now I know its been a while, so don't do anything too quickly," as I gave him a glistening, slippery coat of lotion. Then with the help of the chair I climbed onto the table, lifted my jumper and straddled him. I reached under the skirt and guided him in. I bent over and kissed his lips, then sat up straight and asked, "How close are you?"

"Depends on the kind of ride you have in mind. A few minutes, maybe."

I looked deep in his eyes and sat still and smiled. He was breathing noticeably, his face a little flushed. "Let's try to take it slowly."

"Okay," he said, looking back into my eyes.

"Tell me Andy, what do you see?"

He took a couple of breaths, then said, "I see my lover, spirited, fun, loving, beautiful, and full of surprises. I see a friend who shares her fears and victories, and who accepts me as I am. I see a brave person who is healing from a difficult blow that life has dealt her."

As he talked I could feel him inside of me beginning to get softer, so I began rocking my pelvis slightly. "How's that Honey."

"Yes, just like that Cowgirl. He reached down to where we were connected and searched with two fingers, "Tell me where, Baby."

"A little higher. Yes. Now a little harder. Just like that." His touch was perfect, like heaven. Our eyes were still locked.

"Slow down those hips now, I'm getting too close," he said.

"Okay." And rather than rock up and down, I moved them side to side. Soon I noticed that this intensified what he was doing with his fingers. I closed my eyes as the pleasure mounted.

"Open your eyes Barbara. Your turn. What do you see?"

"I see…someone…hard to believe…doesn't judge me…doesn't run from me…"

"Slower, Baby."

"Doesn't…does…don't stop Sugar…who pleasures me…faster, Honey…who pleasures me," my voice was rising. "Who loves me!" Almost unbearable pleasure exploded and I rocked harder on him.

"Barbara, Barbara…" he said urgently and grabbed my hips and pulled me tight to him. I bent over, breathing too hard to kiss. I buried my face in his chest.

* * *

It wasn't long before we had to move our bodies off the small massage table. We stood and hugged a long time, but didn't say much. I think we both knew we had experienced something wonderful and new and deeper in our relationship, yet didn't have words for it.

Andy got in the shower. I opened a bottle of wine and poured us a couple of glasses, I took them into the bedroom and sat on the bed. As I listened to the shower I thought about how intense love making can be after a long dry spell; almost worth the wait.

I could hear Andy softly singing. It was something about love and grace, probably one of his old church songs. I sat with a grin for a minute, then set the wine down and undressed. Naked and exposed, I walked into the bathroom and stood there, trying to decide if I was ready to have Andy see me. Or was it too big a gamble?

"Andy, can I join you?" I said through the frosted glass.

"Love to, Baby."

I rolled the door to one side and stepped in. Andy rolled it closed again and took me in his arms. The warm water washed over us for a long while.

I broke the silence, "Honestly now, Andy, what do you see?"

Andy stepped out of the spray and looked at my shoulder. "I like it better than a stump. And the surgeon did a superb job, smooth and clean. But if you're asking me if I think you look unattractive with a missing arm, you're crazy. You are sexy and beautiful and delightful."

I nodded as the hot water drenched me. I wanted to believe him. I said, "Come here, Sugar." He stepped back into the water with me. I reached down and took his amazingly responsive member. "Now, say those last three words again."

"What?"

"Sexy," I said, giving him a nice squeeze.

"Sexy," He said with feeling.

"Beautiful," I coached with another squeeze.

"Very beautiful."

"Delightful," and a squeeze.

"Delightful," and he reached and took hold of my nipples.

"Okay," I said, "Let's say it again."

"Sexy," he said, giving me gentle squeezes, and I returned the favor.

"Beautiful." I could feel I now had more to squeeze.

"Delightful."

I stretched up to kiss him and gave him my tongue and a long squeeze. Then I looked down. Halfway there. I knelt and after a dreamy five minutes in a tropical storm, I decided I believed him. Afterwards I was a little worried about the Reverend as he had a bit of trouble getting out of the shower; he half-heartedly dried off and flopped on the bed. He was still there when I had finished drying my hair. I came and sat on the bed next to him.

"Did I pass the test?" he asked.

"I wasn't testing you, Andy, I was testing me."

"So you really base your lovability on a guy's erection? That's pretty iffy."

"It's a pretty direct indicator, I'd say."

"I say it's problematic."

"It's foolproof. Anyway, you had me at halfway. I just felt it would be fun and fair to finish what I had started."

"Oh, it was definitely fun and fair. But I think in the spirit of full disclosure you should know that I take Levitra, and have since I turned sixty."

"No!"

"Yes."

I got up and walked out of the bedroom. "Shit!"

I suddenly stopped in the living room. I asked myself what I was feeling? I was pissed. Why? I thought Andy loved me, and now it was just a pill!

That sounded silly. I was confused. I marched back into the bedroom and picked up my glass of wine and took a drink. I looked at Andy. He motioned me to come and sit by him again. I sat down.

"So, what does the pill do?" I asked.

"Sometimes my body plays tricks on me. Sometimes I want to make love but I can't get a full erection. That does not make me feel very confident as a lover. So I take the pill for a guarantee. But (and this is a big but) if I am not turned on by someone the pill will not work."

"Really?"

"Really, Baby. You are sexy, beautiful, and delightful."

I picked up Andy's glass and handed it to him. Then I took mine and raised it: "Well Sugar, here's to Levitra. I hope you have a good supply!"

* * *

April 12

He saw me:

My missing arm,

My foolish fear,

My small step,

My need to connect.

He didn't run,

Even when I started to.

What kind of a man is he?

Chapter 39

As I held my bright red Brody knob and accelerated up the gravel driveway toward the road, my mind was flying way ahead to my meeting with Ray and Andy. Up ahead two rabbits bolted from the trees on one side of the drive, ran wildly ahead as if racing my truck, then turned sharply toward the trees on the other side and disappeared. I took it as a sign and stopped. I began to chastise myself for forgetting my practice. Then I criticized myself for judging and chastising. At that I laughed out loud and gently forgave myself.

After my training with Janelle I had told Ray and Andy that I would accept their offer to be their wedding coordinator. We had set up this lunch meeting to do some planning. My mind was trying to play out the meeting in advance. So I put the meeting on the get-to-it-later shelf behind my head and took a couple of slow breaths.

There was more. I had awakened that morning full of energy. My breakthrough with Andy the day before, after months of physical distance, seemed to change everything. I was done hiding out. I felt more like my old self. And I felt like I had some catching up t0 do.

I reminded myself of the new attitude I had adopted: "what is more important than savoring life; is there any place better to be than right here; is there any time better to wake up than now?" I thanked the bunnies, took my foot off the brake, and as I slowly rolled up the drive I found pleasure in the flowering plum trees that I had planted all along the way. At the road I stopped, looked left and turned right.

Only once before had I driven one-armed by myself; that was last week to the grocery store. This would be the first drive to work. To work! I tried to put that one on the back shelf, but for miles as I watched my speed, checked my mirrors and paid attention to traffic, I repeated the refrain: I'm driving to work!

* * *

I parked in front of the Mokelumne Hill Hotel. It looked like an artifact from the past life; like visiting the home of my childhood. So much had happened since I last worked in early November. I walked to the big double doors on the corner and into the saloon. Sabina was behind the bar and Andy was sitting at one of the old oak tables. Sabina saw me come in and said "Hallelujah! The dead has risen!" and she came around and met me with a hug.

I just grinned through watery eyes, "Hi, Sabina. Boy, it feels like it's been a hundred years."

I looked around and spotted one of the regulars who smiled and said, "Welcome back, Barbara."

"Hi, Jake."

Andy got up and walked over saying, "She has risen indeed." He gave me a kiss. "Well, I'm glad to see you Cowgirl. I was hoping I had the time right."

"Watch out Rev," said Sabina, "Your age is showing."

Andy slightly bent over, put a hand to his back and feigned a shuffle back to the table saying, "I can still outride you, you little whippersnapper."

"Yeah, right Andy, if you remember where you put your horse."

"Horse? I wasn't talking about horses, sweetheart," and he gave me a wink.

"You better rein him in Barbara," said Sabina with a smile. "He's getting a little frisky."

"What am I going to do, Honey. He's a stud."

Sabina gave the dozen or so customers a sweeping glance and said, "Okay everybody! Barbara is back."

"Yes she is," said Andy, and we sat down just as Ray came in.

"Howdy, Ray," Sabina shouted out.

We waved him over and stood up.

I gave him a hug around his neck and Andy shook his hand. Sabina came over as we sat down; she handed us menus and asked, "What would you like to drink?"

"Coffee for me," I said.

"Me too," said Ray

"And you, Stud?"

"That's Reverend Stud, if you please. And I'll have another Amber Ale."

"How are you Barbara?" asked Ray.

"I'm good. And I'm ready to work."

"I'm glad to hear that. How did your training go?"

"Fine, but it will be a long while before I can master weddings like Janelle. She runs them like an old hand at a roundup." I looked at Andy and added, "I can see why you lined her up for me. The pastor there hardly has anything to do; Janelle organizes the whole thing and the pastor doesn't even show up for the rehearsal."

"Imagine that!" he said with a knowing smile. "That's great. We old guys need all the help we can get, right Ray?"

"Indeed. Barbara, you are going to be the key to this thing. But let's order lunch first and then see where we are."

During lunch they surprised me when Ray showed me a brochure they had printed up. It featured attractive photos of the church and the hotel, a map and directions to Mokelumne Hill with a short history of the town, a list of services we could provide, and pictures of Andy and me on the back.

I'm not sure where they got my photo, but in the picture I had two arms. I couldn't decide if I liked that or not. It was like seeing an old movie of New York with the twin towers. I couldn't exactly describe the feeling – something like tragic sadness. But would a photo of me without my arm be better?

Yet the brochure was well done and it had been distributed to many places where brides might be looking. Also, Ray had a website set up where the same material could be found. He had me take out my iPad and proudly showed me where it was in cyberspace. He was also able to get us in the spring bride supplements of three newspapers in the Valley. The boys had been busy.

I was working on my Portabello mushroom sandwich when I asked them when they thought we might start getting responses. They looked at each other and Andy called out to Sabina, "Could you bring the cell phone?"

"Gladly, it's all yours." She came over and handed me a smart phone. "Thank goodness you're back, it's going to get a little crazy around here."

She poured us some more coffee and walked back to the bar.

I looked at Andy quizzically.

"That's the wedding phone with its own number; and this is a list of couples who need a call back; and these are the appointments you have with couples on Saturday," Andy said handing me two sheets of paper.

I watched my emotions flare up. First there was my anger. Why hadn't anyone bothered to check with me? They are scheduling my life. Who do they think they are?!

Ray must have seen my reaction, "Of course, Barbara, if Saturday won't work for you, we can reschedule."

Then I saw my fear: How can I possibly do this? What will people do when they see me? This is out of control. But under these feelings and thoughts was my now familiar slow down, pay attention, don't judge. I took the two sheets without comment and stared at the names – people who would expect that I knew what I was doing.

I looked up at the two men who now looked anxious. They had worked hard and probably thought that they had set things up perfectly for me, yet now they knew I was not taking this well. There was an awkward silence. I had thought I was ready to work. I was so happy to drive to the hotel, but now I wanted to tear up the lists in my hand – and God damn it, I'd have to use my teeth!

"Excuse me, I have to use the restroom." I walked to the hallway and out of the room. Tears began to run down my cheeks. In the women's room I used my new phone to call information and then was connected to Maria's office. I got her answering service and hung up. I sat down on the toilet – what would Maria say?

"What you are feeling is normal. It's all right. But look at you, you've worked so hard to get here, to get back. You are able again. You can do this if you just take it one step – a small step – at a time."

I wiped my eyes and calmed down for another minute. Then I walked back to the table. I noticed Sabina watching, but she didn't say anything.

I sat down and just said, "I'm scared."

Andy asked quietly, "What is it that scares you, Barbara?"

"That I will fall on my face and be humiliated, and I will let you both down."

Andy nodded, then said, "Did I ever tell you the time I did my brother's wedding? I was a young pastor and it was my older brother's second marriage. It was a very nice outdoor wedding with lots of family and friends. My wife sang a beautiful wedding song, and then I led my brother and his bride through their wedding vows; in doing so I mindlessly called his new wife by his old wife's name – just as I had always referred to his wife. The name was barely out of my mouth when I realized my mistake. I must have turned three shades of red.

"But here's the thing: everyone laughed, not at me but at the humanness of the situation. After all, my brother had made these same promises to his first wife, and here he was saying 'Until death do us part' with another. Weddings are never perfect, and they are set-ups for hilarity. So here is the question, Cowgirl: not whether you are scared, but do you still have a sense of humor?"

I smiled, wiped my eyes, and said, "Andy Shepard! You didn't."

"Yes, and they still speak to me."

"I know you are going to be excellent at this, Barbara," Ray said.

"Maybe, but no more surprises." I lifted the phone, "Call me. Let's talk things over, okay guys?"

They nodded. "Of course, Barbara, you're right. I'm sorry," Ray said.

"So, what else should I know?"

"I have Alzheimer's," Andy said.

"Right, that's nothing new!" I said. The tension was broken as we all laughed.

Chapter 40

April 25
I looked in the mirror again.
The two-armed woman is fading.
Was she so temporary?
And what will come of this one-armed woman?
Will I fade away tomorrow?
Then who will Barbara be?

* * *

My thin small book had seven chapters; each ended with exercises and questions for reflection. The forward suggested that the reader thoroughly work through each chapter before moving on to the next. I had read, worked and reflected on four of the seven chapters so far. Several times I had to go back to the earlier ones and try to apply them again with new understanding.

The fifth chapter was shorter than the others. It simply gave guidelines on how to practice gratitude – a chapter I wouldn't have had any use for a few months earlier, but I took it as a challenge. The first difficulty with the chapter was sorting out whether one had to feel happy about something to be grateful about it.

I was thinking about this when I was waiting in the lobby of the law offices belonging to the lawyers of the hospital where I'd been treated in Stockton. Was gratitude a feeling? Did I have to learn how to feel grateful about things? Would I have to feel happy about facing the hospital's lawyers as they tried to deny me any compensation for the hospital's negligence? Should I be happy about submitting to an examination by their doctor?

I turned to Nathan, who sat with me (along with his friend, Tony, who was a trial lawyer specializing in medical malpractice), and I asked him, "What is your definition of gratitude?"

"Gratitude?" He thought for a moment then said, "Sincerely acknowledging a gift. Being thankful I suppose."

"What if you don't like the gift?"

"Even if you don't like the gift, you could find it valuable; or if you can't see the value, you could be grateful for the giving of it rather than the gift itself."

Tony leaned towards us and added, "The gift could be good for you even if you don't like it, such as a difficult lesson or bad tasting medicine."

"Are you happy to take the medicine?"

"Only if I'm phony."

That was it. Putting a layer of syrupy gratitude over everything seemed phony. The practice of gratitude had to be more than that.

"I hope you're not thinking about saying you're grateful for any of this in your deposition," Nathan said frowning.

"No, Honey. I was just thinking about something I read recently: 'Without gratitude, life is mean and loveless.'"

Tony leaned back in and said, "Without justice life is mean and loveless."

That sounded good, but it bothered me. As Nathan answered his phone, I mulled it over. Did it mean that kindness and love were impossible without justice? How much kindness and love would there be if these depended on life being fair? Maybe in spite of injustice, gratitude could be practiced – and maybe my world would feel less mean and loveless. So what could I be truly grateful for, if not happy about, in this legal game that I am in?

Before I got very far with this question, the receptionist said we could go in. Then for an hour I was asked questions about my hospital experience and my recovery. The big issues seemed to be first of all, had I been informed of the risks of surgery; secondly, how had I followed my doctor's orders; and lastly, how had my amputation affected my life.

Afterward, any gratitude that I was able to find earlier was shot. Although the lawyers had not been unkind, I left feeling irritated or resentful – maybe both – but at who or what I wasn't sure.

That morning Nathan had picked me up at home and driven me to the deposition. Now the plan was for him to pass me off to Cindy while he finished up some things at his office. Cindy wanted to take me shopping at her favorite dress shop, but I asked her to first take me to see Janelle. My first encounters with marriage-bound couples (the ones Andy had set up for me) had raised some questions that I wanted to talk over with her.

What if a couple decided that they couldn't afford what we were offering? Should we try to pare down the package to meet their budget? No, she said. The cost could go up, but not down. It's a business, not a ministry. The couples see it that way and so should we. They could easily get married somewhere else.

What did she do if the couple wanted to use their own minister? Another minister should have a very limited role; Andy must be the main officiant, otherwise we could end up with some unpleasant surprises.

Did she put a limit on how long a wedding ceremony could be? Yes. Music, special readings and sometimes a homily could make the length vary, but shoot for twenty to thirty minutes, forty-five maximum. We don't want a hundred people leaving our church feeling bored and exhausted; that's bad for business. More importantly, to be fair to our staff, be clear on the time guests must leave the reception.

I thanked Janelle with a box of chocolates – I was grateful.

Afterward, as we drove across town to the dress shop, we chatted and I realized that this was the first time Cindy and I had been together, just the two of us, since I stayed with her and Nathan after my first operation in November. This came to me when she said, "You know, Barbara, it's amazing to see the difference in you now."

"How do you mean?"

"Well, I hope you don't take this the wrong way, but you are more self-assured somehow; calmer perhaps. I can't put my finger on it. After what you've been through, I find it surprising that you're actually in a better place. I don't think I would be."

I wanted to reject her appraisal but caught myself. Although I knew I was making big changes, I wanted to keep them private, if not secret. To see what I was becoming required acknowledging what I had been, yet obviously this was not much of a secret. So instead I said, "Thank you Cindy, I appreciate that," although it tasted like unpleasant medicine. "This rehab experience has been quite a journey. Still, I must admit, I feel apprehensive about being on trial with the lawsuit."

"Barbara, you won't be on trial, they will."

"It didn't feel that way today."

"I can imagine; but anyway it's not going to trial. They're moving very quickly. They want it to go away. It's a bad time for them to have any negative publicity – and we certainly can make it painful for them."

"How so?"

"You are not the only one who has been injured because of medication mistakes at this hospital. We have uncovered a disturbing number of cases. They know you could be the poster-girl for a much more damaging suit."

"They didn't seem on the run today."

"That's their normal bluff. But once they concede the proven connection between your extended stay (the result of their mistake) and your staph infection, we will just be talking numbers. Nathan said you presented wonderfully today, so I'm predicting we will reach a settlement by summer."

"Why don't they figure out why the mistakes keep happening and fix the problem?"

"Exactly. You would think they would have a vested interest in doing that, but it's a complicated problem, and many hospitals are plagued by it.

"Basically, it's all about money. Healthcare is one of the country's largest industries, and it's not only very competitive but there are several financial pressure-points on hospitals: nurses and other staff salaries have gone up the pay scale; cutting-edge equipment has become outrageously expensive; complicated insurance and billing processes now demand their own large departments; and most hospitals are now private for-profit institutions. So to save money, staffing is usually at a minimum. They ask staff to do more with less.

"Government regulators see this problem and are encouraging hospitals to change their recordkeeping and charting procedures. They're nudging hospitals to become computer centered and paperless. That could eliminate the majority of these kinds of mistakes.

"But to ask an already stressed-out staff to go through such a major shift, and to provide the training and equipment, is difficult and expensive. So a tired, harried nurse gave you the wrong pill that triggered blood clots and nearly killed you."

"I feel grateful to be alive."

"Right; or you could have been a stroke victim. That would have been grand."

"See, that's my resistance to all this. On one hand they screwed up, but on the other they saved my life, and more than once I gather. Maybe all's well that ends well."

"Except all's not well; not with you, and not with the hospital. The suit will help you deal with life with one arm, and maybe nudge the hospital to fix its problem."

Maybe, but I doubted it. I wasn't clear how money would help me be well – the same wellness Maria talked of. It would be nice, like hitting the lottery. I could do things and buy things that I otherwise couldn't, but I would look the same in the mirror, I would still have to meet new people and get past their distraction over my arm, and buttering my toast would still be a pain in the ass. And what could money do about my jealousy and fear, my inattention, my judgmentalism and ingratitude?

When we got to Cindy's favorite upscale dress shop I put my doubts aside and decided that I was grateful for her help. We picked out a charcoal dress with red trim, and a light blue pantsuit together with a white blouse for my new role as Wedding Coordinator for Mokelumne Hill. The shop also did tailoring and could alter the right shoulder and sleeve on each. Cindy said she wanted to pick up the tab, calling it a late birthday present. I didn't want to be dependent on my kids and was about to protest, but instead I saw it as another chance to be grateful.

***

April 26
The more grateful I am,
The less I want to hurry and the
More natural it is to slow down.
The more I slow down,
The more I can pay attention.
The More I pay attention,
The more I notice when the

Judging voice comes up.
And the more I let go of judging.
The more I can see through
Grateful eyes.

Chapter 41

My two daughters live in Oregon where they were born and raised. The oldest, Carolyn, had made it painfully clear that I needn't call any longer after our last argument about her father, Harry, my second husband. I still sent her Christmas and birthday cards to keep the door open, but never received a response.

When Sabina poked her head into my office and said that a couple of folks were waiting to see me, we both thought they were interested in a wedding. I followed her down the hallway and out into the saloon. My heart stopped when I saw Harry and Carolyn standing in the middle of the room. Was it really them? Carolyn looked so different. She was still thin, but looked older, and now had short blond hair. Harry was a little paunchy, but surprisingly dressed up.

For a few moments my mind froze up like a balky computer – too much input, incompatible program, cable in the wrong port. Then anger flashed across my inner screen and a commentary began scrolling down: she never even called to say she was coming; and why is she here with him? And what are they doing coming here where I work? I hit the key for withholding judgment.

"Well," I said. But up popped several of my favorite swear words to choose from. I hit the key labeled slow down. "What a surprise," I managed to say, hoping it sounded noncommittal.

"Hi, Mom," Carolyn said.

"Hi, Barbara, we just came by to see how you are doing," said Harry. "Nice place you've got here."

What the hell did he want? I pushed the key that said pay attention and turned to look at Sabina who was now back behind the bar and staring at them.

"Sabina, this is my daughter, Carolyn, and her father, Harry."

"Good to meet you," she said. "Can I get you something to drink?"

They hesitated, so I said, "How about bringing us a pitcher of ice tea down in the garden." Then turning back to these family ghosts I said, "It's a nice day out and I've been in the office all morning, so why don't you follow me."

As I led them to the hallway, then down the stairs, I recalled Nathan's comment about Harry having phoned to ask about me, and pumping Nathan for information. I wanted to tell him to get lost, but this was a rare opportunity to see Carolyn, so I reminded myself to slow down again.

I led them to a small table in the sun, between the pool and the orange trees. I pulled over a third chair and said, "This should give us some privacy. Have a seat."

I caught Harry looking at my shoulder. "This is great, Barbara. How long you been here?"

"Five years." I glanced at Carolyn's eyes and tried to read what this was all about. Not for a moment was I going to believe that they just came by to see how I was doing. It had been four long months since the doctors had to remove my arm, and not a peep from my daughter. But here she was, sitting at this table with me, and a surprising tide of affection washed over my anger. I willed back my tears and said, "It's sure good to see you again, Honey."

She looked away and didn't say anything. Did she want to pick up again on the argument we had years ago? When we last spoke she wanted me to know how horrible I was for leaving her father when she was thirteen.

She looked back and said, "So, how are you?"

There was a hardness in her voice which made me feel defensive. Did she come with Harry as if to say she loved him and would never love me? I wanted to grab her and shake some sense into her.

Don't judge, I told myself. She is angry. It is what it is. I said, "If you mean how I'm getting along with one arm, better than I thought I would. Of course I'm still adjusting, but I'm doing fine and I've had some wonderful help."

"You always were a strong woman, darling," said my ex.

Trying to ignore him I watched as Sabina delivered our tea, then I asked Carolyn, "And how are you doing?"

"Fine."

I just nodded and waited. I wanted to hear more. But in the awkward silence Harry butted in, "Nathan said you've got your little ranch fixed up real nice."

"Harry, I would like to talk with Carolyn alone; if you wouldn't mind, could you wait in the bar for a bit?"

He looked at Carolyn as if she would protest for him, then finally he said, "Sure, darling."

"And Harry, don't call me darling. If I were your darling you wouldn't have fucked half the women in Eugene."

"Now that's not true."

"That's right, my mistake, most of them told me that they turned you down."

"How many times do I have to say I'm sorry?!"

"I'm sorry too, we had a sorry-ass marriage. So I am asking you real nice-like, please don't call me your darling."

"Anything you say." He stood up, hesitated for a moment as if he expected Carolyn to get up and leave too, but she just stared down at her hands. So he picked up his glass, turned and walked to the stairs.

We waited until he reached the top and disappeared through the door. Then I said, "I know he is your father, and that you love him. That's good. He will always be your father, you are connected by blood. But he was my husband – connected not by blood but by promise. Harry made a habit of breaking that connection and breaking my heart. Someone can have bad parents, but they are still your parents. However, a bad husband is no husband at all, just someone you used to love."

She didn't say anything. She just sat looking at her hands. I couldn't tell what she was thinking. So I said, "Brandy told me that she had once heard me say that I regretted having the two of you. That was horrible of me, and not true. What I regretted was having children with Harry, and not giving you a better home. You both should have been surrounded with love and understanding, not with what we put you through.

"I love you, Carolyn, and I always will. I'm grateful you are my daughter. Now please, tell me how you are, really."

"Not too good, Mom."

"What's the matter, Sweetheart?"

"I married this guy two years ago. I'm so embarrassed…" Her voice began to break as she tried to hold back tears. "He beat me and threatened to kill me, so I moved into Dad's apartment. Then the guy took my car and all my savings." She wiped the tears from her face.

"I'm so sorry, Sweetheart. Were you injured?"

"Just bruises and a black eye. He was so sweet in the beginning, then he just changed and became someone else."

I wanted to put my arm around her, but I wasn't sure it would be welcomed. "You never know," I said. "Believe me, I understand."

We sat in silence. I pictured her most likely on Harry's couch in a run-down place. I asked, "Is your dad working?"

"He was driving truck, but he got a DUI and was laid off. Now he wants to buy his own truck."

"How is he going to do that?"

Carolyn paused as if deciding what to say, then she simply said, "I don't know."

Immediately I got the picture. The truck, that's what this was all about. He brought Carolyn as leverage to get to me and my hospital settlement. Now a wave of new anger flowed over the wave of affection that had flowed over the old anger. I needed to push those keys that said slow down and don't judge, but I couldn't find them.

I stood up, "Tell me the truth, Carolyn, I need to know," my voice sounded like I was talking to a ten-year old. "Did Harry mention that I was suing the hospital?"

"Brandy told him. What's the problem?"

"What's the problem?!" I turned and walked over to the pool. What was the problem? Harry's an asshole, that's the problem. But I already knew that; no surprise there. So what's the problem?

Better yet, what am I afraid of – that's usually the question. I thought I was getting my daughter back, but I am afraid it's just about money. They are just trying to use me. How come she doesn't love me? I'm afraid she'll never love me. Never.

I was about to turn around to complain, and ask why she just couldn't love me; but a thought struck me: there is no promise that your child will love you – not even an obligation. Maybe they will, maybe they won't. I don't have any right to expect her to return my love. I am her parent, not her friend. That thought didn't come from me. It was like a butterfly landing on my shoulder, and it instantly got my attention and, surprisingly, calmed me down.

I turned back and saw my twenty-seven year old daughter watching me. She said, "I thought you might be able to help him. What's wrong with that?"

"There is nothing wrong with that, Carolyn." I gave her a slight smile, the kind that said I knew she was struggling and that I hoped she would figure it out some day. "I just misunderstood why you were here. Let's go back up stairs."

Climbing the steps was like rising out of the lowlands of the self-inflicted pain of longing and guilt, and reentering my rehabilitated highlands of patience and compassion for myself and those around me – a land that I was beginning to access. At the top of the landing I opened the door and walked in.

Harry was at the bar and had exchanged his tea for something stronger. I took a stool next to him. Carolyn slipped in or his other side. "Harry," I said, "I'm sorry if I sounded a bit harsh. And I am sorry to hear that you are out of work."

"Yeah, well, I got my eye on a beautiful tractor-trailer; it's a repossession and a real steal. I think I could do better as my own boss."

Now sitting close to his face, I couldn't help but see what life was doing to him – or what he was doing to himself. He had become wounded and sad. It was hard to believe that I had chosen to marry him. I tried to remember what it was that I had seen in him, and for the first time it occurred to me: Harry reminds me of my father! Oh my God! Why would I marry my father, the selfish, cruel bastard?

The thought was so disturbing; I shut the door on it. Instead, I forced myself to see the changes I'd made and who I was now.

There had been a long pause. Sabina jumped in, "That's an interesting plan. You know what they say about old truckers, don't you?"

"They don't die, they just change gears," Harry said and grinned.

"Well Harry," I said, "You are going to have to put in a different gear to finance that truck. I have a feeling there isn't going to be much of a hospital settlement."

There was a moment of loud silence, then Harry said, "Why's that?"

"The hospital has problems."

"What do you mean? We've all got problems."

"Isn't that the truth. Hell, I'm still waiting for your eighteen thousand dollars in accumulated child support."

"Oh Harry," Sabina said in mock surprise. "Don't tell me you planted the seeds but didn't feed and water the crops?"

Harry's face turned a deeper shade of his ruddy red. "Come on, Honey," he said to Carolyn, "It's time to go. Your Mom's got her hand out again. Thank God she's only got one now."

Stunned, I just watched as they headed for the door.

"Oooh, I do believe we've seen Harry's true colors, Barb," Sabina said loud enough for them to hear.

I was thankful they were gone.

* * *

May 3

How much pain
Can a mother absorb
And still be a mother?
Does pain obliterate the love,
Or in a strange alchemy
Reinforce the love for her own
Flesh and blood?

Chapter 42

Ready or not, my first wedding was in early May. It was planned on short notice, but I was thankful that it was to be a small affair with about eight in the wedding party and fifty invited guests. (And Janelle had said we could count on roughly half the number of guests that had received an invitation.) Andy must have been nervous as well because in the morning he had twice asked how many chairs to set up in his chapel.

I learned on this first go around how busy I would be on a wedding day, how fast things would happen, and that a big part of my job was about being an island of calm in a sea of nervous energy and unpredictable feelings. It was obviously a skill I would have to grow into as I gained more experience.

Our first mini-crisis was about the marriage license. I knocked on the door where Jason, the young groom, and the best man were getting dressed.

"Yes?" I heard through the old, thin hotel room door.

"Jason, I need the marriage license please," I said from the hall.

"Just a minute," he said. As I waited I could hear him rummaging around; then "Shit, Brad, where did you put it?"

"I handed it to you, at the rehearsal dinner, Jason. Didn't you give it to the priest?"

"You didn't give it to me!"

"Yes I did. Remember, right before I gave a toast?"

"Shit, shit." Then there was more rummaging. Finally the door opened and Jason, with his pleated shirt untucked, said, "I think I gave it to the priest."

"Reverend Shepard wasn't there last night."

"Oh. Then I guess I left it on the table downstairs."

"Those tables have been cleared and we are all set up for the reception. But I'll go down and see if someone put it aside."

"Thanks, Barbara."

I went downstairs to the restaurant and found my new assistant hotel manager. She hadn't seen the license but would ask the other staff. Meanwhile I searched around the lobby and saloon, any place where it could have been laid; but no luck.

It was just an hour before the wedding and we had no marriage license; so I crossed the street to the church where Andy was showing the florist where to put the flower arrangements.

"Andy, remember we need space for three bridesmaids and groomsmen, so you have to move those flower stands up a step."

"Okay. How are you doing?"

"We've got a slight problem. Jason has lost the marriage license."

"Ha! That sounds like something I'd do – lose the license, or the ring, or my shoes – a subconscious message. So he didn't give it to you last night?"

"No, and I forgot to ask him for it. We've looked everywhere. Maybe it was thrown out when they cleaned up after the rehearsal dinner. So now what?"

"Well, they can't get married without a license."

"Can't we go ahead and do the wedding and have them get a duplicate next week for you to sign?"

"Barbara, I can't say, 'I now pronounce you husband and wife…' if they're not legally married, and they're not married until I sign the license and mail it back to the courthouse."

"But it will only be for a couple of days."

"What if they change their minds and don't show up with the license? Everyone will think they're married when they're not, and we would be a part of a hoax."

"I don't think they would do that."

"Probably not, but it would be a mess, one that we couldn't undo. And what if Jason didn't really lose it, and for some reason they don't want to be legally married?"

I looked around at how nicely the chapel was dressed up; and I thought of the bride and bridesmaids and their new dresses, and the guys' rented tuxes, and the guests that were making the trip to Mokelumne Hill. Our first wedding was going to be a disaster.

Then Andy said, "Maybe we can do a blessing of their relationship instead of a marriage ceremony. Have the couple meet me in your office as soon as they can."

I wasn't sure what Andy had in mind, but he had officiated at weddings for over thirty years and I had to trust him in these matters. So they conferenced, and a half hour later in the narthex I was helping the bridal party arrange themselves in the right order for the processional. While music played, I cued one of the groomsmen to light the candelabras; this signaled that the wedding – or blessing – was beginning. Then I sent the parents down the aisle to be seated, ushered by the other two groomsmen. When the young men returned, the wedding march and little parade began.

These few intense minutes which start the ceremony are the main reason to have a rehearsal. The most important part of my new job was to smoothly pull off a wedding procession. As I watched from the back of the chapel and saw that indeed everyone took their proper places in front of Andy, I smiled and began to breathe more easily. Now it was in Andy's hands for a while.

He gave an invocation and had the guests take their seats. Then he said, "On behalf of Jason and Patricia I want to welcome you and thank you for being here today to share in this holy and joyous moment, a moment of sweet love and sacred promises.

"In our culture there are three important stages or seals to getting married. The first is when a couple discover in their hearts that they have found their life's partner, and then pledge themselves to each other. This is perhaps the most profound event that seals their marriage.

"The second is when on a day like today they tell their social circle to now consider them to be husband and wife and to treat them as such. Here the couple invites their friends to support them in both the happy and inevitably difficult days to come. This too seals their marriage, for marriage is a social agreement as well as a heart agreement.

"Then, finally, the couple registers with the state to make their partnership legally binding. Today we are celebrating two of the three seals – the first two. This morning we discovered that the marriage license was misplaced and apparently lost. So the seal of a legal marriage cannot be made today; that will happen when Jason and Patricia return here with a new license. But today we are going to bless what has been sealed in their hearts and ask you to support their loving and enduring relationship."

I was thinking, nicely done, Andy, as he paused. There was quite a bit of murmuring, and then Patricia's father stood up. "Reverend, is this what you were looking for?" He was holding a large brown envelope and he took a few paces from his front row chair toward the wedding party. The groomsmen parted and he climbed the three steps up to where Andy stood.

Andy took the envelope, opened it and pulled out the license. He held it high and waved it to a cheering church, saying, "the third seal!"

As the father turned to step down, he said, "Sorry Jason. Guess you will have to make an honest woman of my daughter after all."

Everyone laughed except Patricia's mother and me. Older married women seldom laugh at their husband's irritating jokes. As for me, I wondered if the dad had pocketed the license on purpose, or had he just tried to be helpful when he saw it neglected on the table last night. However, I knew I wouldn't forget to ask for the license again at the rehearsal.

* * *

Andy made a brief appearance at the reception, then disappeared. Late in the afternoon, after the bride and groom were showered with birdseed and the D.J. had packed up and left, I found that Andy had returned and was having a beer at the bar. The thought of sitting down sounded heavenly and I took the stool next to his.

"Where'd you disappear to?" I asked.

"I don't like receptions, especially with strangers – and I've wandered through way too many of them. They make me feel lonely."

"Too bad. You missed a good lunch."

"I bet. Maybe if I'd had a date, but she was working."

"That's an understatement," said Sabina as she brought me a glass of white wine.

"I'll tell you," I said, "I was ready to chuck this whole wedding coordinator thing when the license came up missing."

"Come on Cowgirl," Andy said and put his arm around me, "You did great. And besides, that was minor. You haven't seen anything yet."

"Yeah," said Sabina, "I bet we'll get some couples in here that will inspire you to lose their license."

"Save it, guys. This is not the time to tell me horror stories."

Sabina was drawn to the other end of the bar and Andy said, "Well then, what time is it?"

"You've never shown me your new digs. I'm curious, what have you got going on under that church?"

"Really? Don't you know? Upstairs, the chapel is the holy of holies; but downstairs is the den of iniquity."

"Ooh, sounds exciting."

"When do you finish up here?"

"Well, since I'm now a professional (not to mention, a poor handicapped person) I don't have to stick around to make sure the bathrooms are clean. So I can be over in about a half hour."

"Wow. Then I better get over to my bachelor pad and clean my bathroom."

I leaned over and whispered, "Forget the bathroom, just make sure you take one of your magic pills."

Andy's eyebrows raised and Sabina, watching from the other end of the bar, grinned and nodded as if she could hear me. Then Andy stood up and walked toward the door.

"And where are you off to, Reverend?" Sabina asked.

"Honestly, Sabina, weddings are hard on my heart. It's time to take my medication."

"Really. I thought I just poured you your medication."

"Yes, and I appreciate that. But for what I've got, alcohol is contraindicated."

"Contraindicated? What's that supposed to mean?"

"Remind me to tell you sometime. I gotta go."

"Yeah, well you sound like my ex husband."

"Oh Sabina, and on such a day."

* * *

When I got to the church the door was locked. I could feel irritation bubbling up. The last thing I wanted to do is walk down the block, around to the alley, and then back to the rear of the church were the door to the lower part of the building was.

I told myself to slow down, then knocked on the front door hoping he might hear me downstairs. God, he's probably taking a nap, I thought.

Then the door opened and there was Andy, again wearing his preacher's robe! "May I help you, sister?"

"Why yes, Reverend. I was just at a wedding and I'm looking for a honeymoon."

"Good timing, my child," he said glancing up to the early evening sky. "I believe one is on the rise. Do come in."

I stepped into the narthex; Andy closed and locked the door. Then he began to slowly unzip his robe, saying, "Let's have a look and see."

He had nothing on underneath. How did he know this was my fantasy from months ago? Before he reached the bottom of the zipper, I reached down and took hold of him. That really got a rise. "Andy, Sweetheart," I said, "You are an amazing man." He bent down and kissed me for a long time – him in my hand, my tongue in his mouth.

I wanted to have him right there on the floor, but he coaxed me down the stairs to his bedroom. He helped me off my new charcoal dress with the red trim. He tried to find the hooks on the back of my bra strap and I had to show him my special easy fasteners on the front. I laid down and he kissed my neck, saying softly, "To have and to hold."

He kissed my breasts and said, "From this day forward."

Then, "For better or worse," as he kissed my right shoulder's pink healed wound.

"For richer, for poorer," he kissed my bellybutton. "In sickness and in health," he kissed my right thigh. "Until death do us part," he kissed the left.

With each tender kiss I said, "Yes," and yet I wasn't sure what was happening. Was it all a part of this playful fantasy? Andy seemed so sincere. When he began pleasuring me in earnest I smartly put these thoughts on my back shelf and began to let him know how good his lovemaking was.

* * *

As our breathing returned to normal, I noticed the warm golden afternoon sunshine that came through the windows of Andy's new bedroom. The light brought to life the bold colors he had chosen for the walls: contrasting burnt umber and creamy yellow. The colors complemented the light, billowy Indian print bedspread he had pinned to the ceiling, hiding the fixture to give the room indirect light. He had used the same material for window curtains that hung to the floor. The only thing hanging on the walls was a picture of a beautiful horse running through water in a sunset.

"God, Andy, this is a very seductive bedroom."

"Do you like it?"

"I love it. And if I didn't know you better I would say you were gay."

"That's funny. I had a parishioner who once asked if I was gay. She had assumed that was the reason I was getting a divorce."

"What did you say?"

"I said I had never sucked a cock, and did she think I would like it?"

"No!"

"You're right, but that would have been a good comeback. No, I said that unfortunately I wasn't gay, otherwise I might have avoided all my women troubles."

I laughed and rolled to my side and kissed his cheek, "We are a bunch of bitches, aren't we?"

"Yes, but women don't have a monopoly on intimacy problems. I'm afraid it's a human thing."

I kissed him again on the earlobe and give it a nibble, "This is a human thing too, isn't it?"

"Uniquely human. Not sex per se, but wanting to pleasure each other, satisfy each other, and be one together at least in that one moment of bliss."

"Do you think Patricia and Jason have a chance?"

"For what?"

"For this, until death do us part or something." He lay silent for a while, thinking. I knew it was a bad question. Four times divorced and now he was roped into a wedding business. What old memories I must have conjured up.

I could feel I had broken the spell of our afterglow. Finally he simply said, "Maybe if they just have as fine a honeymoon as this, it would be enough."

I snuggled up and softly said, "Thank you, Andy."

* * *

May 11
Maybe.
Maybe it would be enough.
One fine honeymoon.
Being desired – supremely.
Giving myself – totally.
Satisfied – satisfying him.
One fine honeymoon,
Heartfelt – heart filled.
A touchstone experience
To remember – to savor.
Forever – eternal.
I was loved – perfectly.
Maybe it is enough.
Thank you.

Chapter 43

I slept a long, sweet, restful night at home after my first wedding and my personal tour of the Church of Andy Shepard. It was after nine when I finally awoke, but it seemed earlier. The sky had clouded over and was trying to rain, which made the light in my bedroom dim and soft. Lying there, in a dreamy in-between land, I began to think: It's Sunday, and I don't have to go to work. So what do I have to do? I have no appointments. I don't have to go anywhere. I don't have to call anyone. There are no house chores that have to be done except feed the horses. So what shall I do today?

That is when I realized how full my days had been for weeks, especially since I began to climb the learning curve of my new job. But more than that, how absorbed I'd been for months with my rehabilitation. In no particular order I tried to make a list in my mind of what I had accomplished: relearning so many things like driving, cooking, caring for the horses, washing my face and countless other daily tasks that needed creative alternatives; learning to use an iPad, learning to give a massage, learning to greet people in a new way, adjusting my wardrobe, adjusting the corral gate, adjusting how I walk – God, even walking.

Then to this list I added: preparing for the lawsuit, learning how to write poetry, learning to see my fears and let them go.

Learning to be a lover again.

And in all this, learning to slow down, pay attention, withhold judgment and be grateful. It seemed amazing.

I adjusted my pillows and sat up against the headboard, then reached over to the night stand for my thin small book. I stared at the title, *Remember, Life Is a Precious Miracle*. I thought of my first reaction when Maria gave it to me: ducky, a sappy motivational book. I didn't want anything to do with it. But as I discovered, the book wasn't about convincing me how precious life could be; it simply instructed me how to experience life more deeply.

An urge came to open the book and finish the last chapters, but it felt like rushing, and I was learning not to rush through life. So what shall I do today? The question seemed off and somewhat compulsive, like I was trying to push myself; there was a hidden, frantic quality to it.

I said it again slowly out loud, "So what shall I do today?" Then I rephrased it, "So what would I like to do today?" Then I closed my eyes and pictured myself as a young girl – the girl I have been helping and loving. I asked her, So, what would you like to do today?

Boy, she said, we've been so busy? I would like to just hang out today and rest.

Good idea, I told her.

Thank you, she said.

My eyes still closed, I slowed my breathing slightly. Her response came back, Thank you. That was a first. I let it float in my mind: Thank you, Barbara. Thank you. Thank you for rehabilitating me. Thank you for quitting your misery list. Thank you for staying open to Andy, for not letting jealousy and fear muck up your life. Thank you.

Thank you? Who was saying thank you, and who was being thanked? Interesting. Then I just sat there and felt quiet and calm. I found myself enjoying breathing. I smiled, What shall I do today? How about enjoying breathing?! Who would believe that? It was so strange but so natural at the same time. Then the strangest thought of all: was this a prayer? Did I just pray?

After some time I got up to use the toilet and then without thinking I picked up my iPad and sat up again in bed. I tapped an e-mail:

From: Barbara Hanson

To: Janelle Parker

Sent: May 7, 2009

Subject: Gratitude

Warmest thanks, Janelle, my first wedding went well, mini-crisis and all. You are a good teacher. And you were so right: Andy is great and I am in good hands.

With gratitude, Barbara

Then a second one:

From: Barbara Hanson

To: Maria Santiago

Sent: May 7, 2009

Subject: Gratitude

Maria, thinking of you this morning and how grateful I am for you.

I am still "becoming able" with your book. And I thought you might want to know: the massage turned into a big step. Also we got my first clients married!

Many thanks, Barbara

This was fun.

From: Barbara Hanson

To: Sabina Cullerton

Sent: May 7, 2009

Subject: Gratitude

We did it, Sabina! We are a good team, I am so glad to work with you.

Your grateful Fross,
(friend and boss)

P.S. Let's ride soon. When are you free?

And finally:

From: Barbara Hanson

To: Andy Shepard

Sent: May 7, 2009

Subject: Gratitude

Sugar now that's a honeymoon. But I am not sure it is enough.

Your Cowgirl

I didn't send this one. It sounded like a confused message. Last night was not just good sex, but "honeymoon" implied marriage – I shouldn't kid around with that word. And "not enough?" What was I trying to say?

What did I want to say? I deleted it and tapped out a new one:

> Dear Andy, thank you for your love.
>
> Barbara

Delete. Sounded almost trite.

> Andy, from the bottom of my heart, thank you for loving me.
>
> Barbara

Delete. That didn't sound like me. Too artificial.

> Sweetheart, hope this honeymoon lasts a while. I will let you know when it is enough!
>
> Barbara

I liked it, and I almost sent this one. It spoke the truth about our past relationships, and I liked being sassy (and I think he liked it too). But it wasn't what I really wanted to say. How could I say I really appreciated him? What's the difference between loving and appreciating someone? Writing a guy and saying that you appreciate him sounds like the beginning of a Dear John letter: I appreciate you, but...

Delete.

> Dear Andy, last night meant a lot to me. How did I get so lucky?
>
> Love, Barbara
>
> P.S. Your bathroom was not half-bad either.

I smiled and pressed send.

* * *

It was eleven when I got up and made the bed. I did it as a practice: slowly smoothing out the bottom sheet with my hand, noticing its texture and its creamy rose color. By turns I slowly walked from one side of the bed to the other to pull up the sheet, blanket and comforter, noticing the softness of the carpet under my feet and the inlaid pattern of wood on the headboard. I gave each pillow a good shake to fluff it and then carefully arranged them.

I looked at my work with satisfaction and thought of the good night's sleep I had had, so without feeling too silly, I prayerfully gave gratitude for my bed.

I stayed with this practice as I fed the horses and showered. I continued as I fixed and ate my lunch. I had never had a half day like this before. Slowing down and focusing on paying attention for more than an hour or two usually began to feel like hard work and caused me to rebel. Then I would shift to "light-duty": the more casual practice only required me to not hurry and to stay present to what I was doing. I could plan for, but not be preoccupied with the future. I could reflect on, but not be obsessed with the past. I could be discerning, but not judgmental about things and people. And more recently it meant raising gratitude to a more intentional level, but not manufacturing it.

* * *

After lunch I got a call from Nathan. "Hi," I said. "How are you doing Sweetheart?"

"Hi Mom, fine. How are you?"

"Now don't tell the lawyers, but yesterday I pulled off my first job as a wedding coordinator."

"Did it go well?"

The thought flashed through my mind: did part of him hope I had struggled just to strengthen my lawsuit? "Yes, very well."

"Great. Speaking of the hospital's lawyers, they offered a settlement. It's lowball, but it's another signal that they don't want to go to court."

"What's the offer?"

"One million, but the loss of a limb, if it was not gross negligence, most always starts around two and a half for someone your age. So with your agreement I want us to counter with three."

"Someone my age?"

"Yes. Someone who is still working, and who is single with a reasonable expectation of marrying."

"I think we both know I think marriage is very unreasonable."

"Doesn't matter, Mom, it's statistical"

"Right. Three marriages, three divorces."

"Doesn't Andy have four divorces? So who knows, Mom?"

"You're starting to meddle."

"Sorry. Just say yes. We still think we can get this done by summer."

"How much of it do my lawyers get? You've never said."

"Come on, Mom, what do you mean, I'm going to charge my mother?!"

"Well, you and Cindy are putting in some time. You should get something."

"That's thoughtful, but no."

"What about Tony?"

"He's just a consultant. I consult for him, he consults for me. It's a wash. So, Mom, is three million acceptable?"

"That makes the pill they gave me very expensive, doesn't it?"

"It makes their mistake very expensive."

"Tell me Nathan, you were there that day, did they keep my chart and the doctor's orders on paper or on a computer?"

"Both. I saw your chart, hand written; but I also saw doctors doing reports on computers. However, I think they just use the computers for word processing and create hard copies."

"Cindy said hospitals are starting to move completely to computers and it should reduce the mistakes."

"Let's hope so," he said.

"Okay, Nathan. Ask for four million and settle for three."

When we hung up, the kernel of an idea, planted by Cindy, began to grow. Now I needed to know if a couple of million would significantly help the hospital convert completely to computer charting.

My iPad signaled that I had mail.

> From: Andy Shepard
> To: Barbara Hanson
> Sent: May 7, 2009
> Subject: Jamisons
>
> Hi, glad to hear from you. To tell you the truth, I thought I might have scared you off with the marriage vow thing. As for being lucky, I think people are more lucky when they are not running with fear. And you have been very brave.
>
> By the way, when is my appointment with the Jamison couple? Today? I think I wrote it down, but where??
>
> Love, Andy

I fixed a cup of tea as I thought over his e-mail: marriage vows, overcoming fear, staying open to good things? Was Andy tiptoeing toward a proposal?! Would he tiptoe? No, I don't think so. I suppose he was saying that our growing relationship was a gift made possible by letting go of fear.

I sat down with my tea by the living room windows and watched the gentle rain fall. A May rain meant the hills would remain green through June providing a nice backdrop for our June weddings.

That made me think about Andy's Jamison appointment. I went to the calendar on the wedding smart phone and then called Andy.

"Hi Cowgirl."

"Hi Baby. You dressed?"

"What have you got in mind?"

"Not what you are thinking. The Jamison couple should be there in twenty minutes."

"Shit. I thought it might be today. I couldn't find where I wrote it down."

"I wrote it down for you on a hotel memo."

"You did? Well I better get married – I mean ready." He laughed.

"Very funny." I guessed he was joking.

"What's their date?"

"June 21. A hundred to a hundred twenty guests, eight attendants plus two flower girls and a ring bearer. She's Methodist, he's Jewish and wants his cantor involved."

"Thanks. I better change clothes. Talk to you later."

Chapter 44

My saddle weighed a ton, and I was only five feet four. After the doctors took off my arm (I still refused to say that I lost my arm – it sounded ridiculous) saddling up called for a creative alternative. I drilled a hole through the saddle horn and threaded a cord through it; then I tied the cord into a short loop. I asked my neighbor to rig a pulley and rope from a rafter in the barn so I could attach it to the loop on the saddle.

The only tricky part was getting the horses to stand still underneath this contraption as I tried to lower the saddle slowly with one hand on the rope. Sweetpea, my bay, took to it the best, and today I had her groomed and saddled by the time Sabina trailered her ride down my drive.

"Hi," she said as she stepped down out of her truck. "Turned out to be a nice day."

"Any day on horseback is a nice day."

"Yes, it's been too long."

"I packed some trail food and water. How about we take the riverside trail today?" I said as she opened the trailer gate.

"Sounds good, Barb. I'll get Smoky out then help you saddle up."

"Thanks, but I'm all ready to go. I used the pulley."

"Really? I've got to see this thing." She backed Smoky out of the trailer and walked him to the barn. I showed her the set-up, including my modified saddle on top of Sweetpea."

"I guess there's not much you can't do with one arm."

"As it turns out, Sabina, in some ways I can now do more than before. My therapist said I might find that I'm pushed into new, rich experiences."

I stepped up on a bale of hay, put my boot in a stirrup and mounted. As we rode out of the barn and were going up the drive toward the road I said, "You want to hear something strange? I feel so different that I woke up the other morning and I had the weird feeling that I didn't know who I was any more. Even Cindy told me that she thought I had really changed. Have I, Sabina?"

"Changed? You are so different, it's spooky."

"How?"

"Well, Fross, since you asked, you used to go from zero to bitch in three seconds. Now I see you counting to ten and coming back with a load of understanding. And your jealousy thing hasn't ridden through town in some time. And you are quieter; you used to be hilarious in how you could rip people, but that old gal is gone. Instead you seem – I don't know – maybe more grown up."

"Is that good?"

"It's different."

I didn't know how to take that. We rode in silence to the highway, crossed over and headed left for a short distance. We found the path that led down through oaks, pines and scrub, and would take us to the stream coming out of the dam.

It's different, not good or bad? I wanted assurance. Did my friend still like me? I was afraid she didn't, a fear which I recognized more frequently now. Funny, I used to be the one who found reasons why I didn't like somebody.

I reminded myself that Sabina had made the effort to come and ride with me today, and that she was evidently still my friend. I struck up our conversation again when the trail widened and we were riding side by side.

"I have a decision to make, and I'm not sure how to make it." I told her about my phone call with Nathan and my idea to use most of the settlement to get the hospital to change.

"That's a mighty big bite to take; what's your plan?"

"First, I've got to know how much money it would really take for them to convert to computers – and don't want to ask my kids to find out, they will just try to talk me out of it. How would you do it?"

"If you were going to build new stables, you could ask what someone else paid to build stables of a similar size. So find a hospital that has recently completed this conversion and ask them. Then when your hospital comes up with an estimate you will know if they are using funny numbers."

"That makes sense. I don't want to give them money that isn't used for this project."

"No. In fact, the standard practice is to schedule a number of partial payments to be made as stages of a project are completed."

"That's good. Then after I figure out how much it will take, I'm thinking of chatting with the hospital administrator to see if they are likely to deal."

"You are going to talk with the hospital while your son is horse trading with their lawyers?"

"I guess so."

"He's not going to like that. And it could change what the hospital is willing to settle for."

"Up or down?"

"Hard to say."

"So I should wait?"

"I would get your ducks lined up, then let your son do his thing. After you have your dough, then be the hero."

"Sounds good."

"How much are you going to keep?"

"I'll figure out what my expenses and losses have been since November and add an amount for future costs for things like tailoring and hiring help for things I can't do any more. Then I'll add an amount for expenses I can't foresee. I'm thinking two or three hundred thousand."

"How about a consulting fee for your bartender?"

"Do you need money, Sabina?"

"See, that's what I mean. The old you would have cut my legs out from under me."

"Okay, let me rephrase that: boy, you really know who your fucking friends are when you get some money! Was that better?"

She laughed. "I really love you."

"Even if I'm a little spooky?"

"Yeah."

When we reached the stream we followed the fisherman's trail for a ways looking for a sunny spot to have a bite to eat. With Sabina leading, we rounded a bend and came upon a cougar with a deer kill just fifty feet in front of us. It let out a startling yowl. Smoky reared and turned to bolt into the stream causing Sabina to lose her balance and fall into three feet of cold water. The cougar bounded toward us on the trail, closing the distance to twenty-five feet, and it stopped and yowled again. As Smoky disappeared back up the trail, I got Sweetpea to stand between Sabina and the cougar. I raised in the saddle and yelled at the cat, "No! No!" Its tail swished snakelike, and for a long moment we locked eyes.

Sabina got to her feet and picked up a heavy waterlogged branch for a club. She waved it yelling, "Get! Get!"

Sweetpea danced, I pulled the reins, "Whoa, girl." Just then the cougar bounded up to the right, between the trees, and stopped, still in sight. Then it turned and crouched, swishing its tail again.

"You all right?" I asked, keeping an eye on the cat.

"I think so."

"Let's get out of here, slowly. You first, back up the trail."

After a few minutes, Sabina said, "That cougar isn't going to leave the deer kill. I think we're fine. And besides, I think you put the fear of God in him when you stood in your stirrups and waved, letting him know that you still have one good arm! That wasn't too bad for a granny. I know I'll never forget that picture."

"Very funny. Where do you think we'll find Smoky?"

"He might run all the way back to the trailer. He's such a big baby. The worst part is I'm freezing."

"Well, get up here. Sweetpea and I will help you warm up a bit." So with some little struggle and ingenuity, Sabina got on behind me.

"Careful now," she said. "I don't want to fall off twice in one day."

When we reached the place where the trail left the stream and began to climb toward the road, Smoky was there waiting. Sabina slipped off Sweetpea and began talking softly to Smoky as she approached, calming him down. "It's okay, Sugar. That big, bad kitty is not going to bite you. And I'm not mad that you dumped me in the river and left me to be mauled." She took his reins and stroked his neck while still talking sweetly, "And thanks a lot for running a mile up the trail while I was back there freezing. Yeah, you big baby, you're a good one."

She mounted Smoky and led us up the trail. In forty minutes we were crossing the road to my driveway with its long row of purple trees leading down to the house and the lake beyond. As we rode side by side I said, "Andy is sure getting the hang of riding. You should have seen him last summer. He was scared stiff. But he stuck with it; he said retirement was the time to try to learn some new things. Now he's looking pretty good in the saddle."

"My guess is that he was thinking of you, Sugar, when he said he wanted to try something new."

"Could be; he's a lively guy."

"I never think of Andy as older, except when he forgets things."

"Right, I think he has had a stressful year. I guess as long as he remembers who I am, it's no big deal."

* * *

May 20
The lion protects her dinner
And fends off the competition.
There is just so much food to go around.
And hunger is an ever-present companion.
I know hunger – hunger for love.
I know the hunt for affection and acceptance.
I know the threat of losing the connection,
The fear of abandonment and starvation.
I would have bared my claws
Until they were dull and useless.
But I awoke: I am not a lion,
And there is love enough to go around.
I'm a woman, beautiful and delightful,
And given half a chance
Love flows from me,
And returns.

Ray's idea to advertise a 20% discount to celebrate our new service turned out to be very effective, and I booked seven weddings through June, and a possible six more in midsummer. And to keep business flowing I even offered couples gift certificates for a night's lodging and dinner if we booked someone that they recommended to us.

On the night of the cougar encounter, I had a rehearsal for our third wedding. At seven, the wedding party gathered in the chapel. I collected the wedding license and had them sit in the first two rows. With my notes in hand I stood in front and welcomed them. Then I gave them "the talk" that I mostly put together from Janelle and Andy:

We are going to have a joyful time.

It is going to be a beautiful wedding.

Tomorrow, everyone please help the bride and groom and relieve them of any unnecessary concerns and details. It is their day.

No jokes or pranks during the ceremony.

Photographers, I ask that you not wander around during the ceremony.

No one participates tomorrow who is not sober, period.

Now I am going to talk you through the ceremony, then we will walk through it. And remember, although it never quite goes as planned, the wedding will be perfect. So keep your sense of humor.

I turned to my next page which was Andy's outline of the ceremony as he had worked it out with the couple. It was fairly straightforward except for the fact that the bride wanted her three fathers (biological and two step-fathers) to walk her down the aisle.

After I explained each step of the ceremony I had them stand and take their positions for the start of the wedding. When the pianist began the wedding march we soon had a hitch. It was obvious that the three fathers and the bride could not walk abreast down the aisle – it was too narrow.

We stopped and as we tried to decide on other possibilities, it became clear that the pecking order was an unspoken issue of the fathers' participation. Then I noticed Andy standing at the stairway door, watching and smiling. I raised my eyebrows as if to say, "Help."

As he approached he greeted everyone, "Good evening. I've got an idea that would work very well. Each of you gentlemen had a hand in raising Kimberly at some stage of her life. So this could be symbolized beautifully by helping her down the aisle in stages."

Andy arranged the men and had the music begin again. Kimberly came through the door with her biological father and met her first step-father about a third of the way down who took her to her second step-father, who brought her to the front where the groom took her arm and stood before Andy. This met the approval of the family.

"Thank you, Reverend Shepard," I said. "I think this will make a delightful procession."

"Yes," he said. "Now I will say, 'Let us pray,' and give the invocation, then ask the guests to be seated. Then,"

I interrupted, "Thanks Reverend, I'm sure you have other things you need to do. I can finish the rehearsal."

"Other things?"

"Over at the hotel," I said not really knowing what Andy was doing that night. He looked puzzled. "And before you go, let me give you the marriage license," I held it out to him. "Don't let us make you late."

He stepped out of his position in the wedding party and I walked him partly up the aisle. Softly he asked, "Where am I going?"

"Andy, this is my job," I whispered. "Why don't you go bless some beer and see if the San Francisco Giants are playing?"

Then he got with it," Good idea, Cowgirl. Sorry."

For another half hour I walked the group through the rest of the wedding service. Then I closed down the church as they moved across the street for their rehearsal dinner.

I caught up with Andy who was indeed at a table in the saloon watching the game. I sat down across from him, "Hi, I see you found your way over here. What was that, a senior moment?"

He looked at me, studying my eyes, then took a sip of beer. I sensed that he was trying to decide on how to answer me. He glanced at the TV and said, "I guess you could say that."

"Are you feeling all right?"

"Why do you ask?"

"Recently, you've been forgetting things."

He just nodded. I got up and went to the bar and got a glass of wine from Sean who was on duty. When I sat back down Andy said, "Lately, if I don't write things down I'm liable to forget them."

"Maybe you should see a doctor?"

"I did. She ordered some tests. I go back in a couple of weeks."

Why the hell didn't he tell me? I reminded myself to not judge. "What did she think was the matter?"

"In her office she gave me some simple cognitive tests. It looks like," his voice dropped, "early signs of dementia."

"Dementia?!"

"I know, but she said dementia is a symptom, not a diagnosis."

"A symptom of what?"

"Many things evidently, but most commonly Alzheimer's."

We looked at each other, silently connecting in our fear. This couldn't be right. He was in his early sixties, he couldn't have Alzheimer's. "Did you tell your doctor how much stress you've been under this past year?"

"Yes, we talked for quite a while. There is no specific test for Alzheimer's, so they test for and rule out other diseases that cause dementia. But at this point I don't have any other symptoms that would point to another cause."

"But you're just forgetful, not nuts."

"Right, not nuts yet. But that's where Alzheimer's goes: short-term memory loss, then confusion and repeating my questions, then anxiousness and manic behavior and wandering, then personality shifts and inappropriate behavior, then profound memory loss and insanity, then finally physical disability and death. No cure."

How could he just sit there and say those things? This was a nightmare. Besides, I've known other forgetful people – they didn't have Alzheimer's!

"Come on Andy, get real. It's probably just diet and exercise, or stress, or blood pressure, or some medication you're taking. Hey it's probably those little magic pills! Does she know you're taking them?"

"Yes, and I had a complete physical; I'm apparently healthy. But the cognitive tests show I'm definitely having a problem tracking and remembering things – I know you and Sabina can see it. I'm going to get a CT scan and some more blood work. We'll see. There is an outside possibility it could be some other delightful disease."

"Andy, you don't have Alzheimer's. My aunt had it and she didn't even know her own sister half the time."

"It is a progressive illness, Love. It begins subtly, and then…, In fact, it's usually mucking up your brain for several years before you have any symptoms at all."

"Okay, but you remember when they discovered that I had a bone tumor on my shoulder? And I was sure that I had cancer, and I had to wait for the biopsy report? That's what you are doing now, Andy. Let's not jump to conclusions."

"I know, the waiting is the hardest part."

"When do you see your doctor again?"

He pulled a note pad from his shirt pocket and studied it for a second, "A week from Thursday."

"I'd like to go with you."

"That would be nice. Thank you, Sabina."

I held my breath for a moment; then he couldn't keep a straight face. "Andy Shepard! You do that again and you won't live to see anything progress."

He laughed. I shook my head and thought: no way he has Alzheimer's.

Chapter 45

I felt emotionally derailed after Andy told me about being tested for dementia. My feelings were scattered all over the place and I couldn't pull it together to practice. Thank God I had the distraction of a wedding the following day. Seeing Andy perform the ceremony with his usual grace and wit helped me pretend that everything was fine.

Yet as soon as the reception was over and I was driving home, my mind was again a jumbled mess. The one guy who knew how to love me, why! Why did he have to get some fucking disease? "Goddamn him," I said out loud. Then louder, "Goddamn him!"

I imagined him looking at me and not knowing who I was. It isn't fair, we were just starting to really get close. Tears began to blur my vision, so I looked for a place to pull over.

Between Mokelumne Hill and Valley Springs I stopped on the side of the road. I tried to cover my face with one small hand, and I cried thinking of all the men who let me down and pulled the rug out from under me. Shit, I just can't get a break. I cried in anger, but I also cried in grief. He was here tonight, but when it really gets a hold on him it won't be Andy any longer. I'll lose him, and there won't be anything either of us can do about it. It's a Goddamn train wreck.

I was startled by a tap on my window. I jerked my head and saw Andy standing next to my truck window, looking in. I glanced in the rearview mirror and saw his little yellow VW parked behind me, then found some tissue and wiped my face as I let down the window.

"Hey, Cowgirl, looks like your radiator's leaking."

"Yeah," I said and blew my nose.

"You got away before I could tell you what a good job you did. Everything seemed to go well."

"Thanks. You too."

"So, what's the deal?"

"You're the deal, Honey."

"Yeah, well, last time I looked, I was still here. Aren't you getting a little bit ahead of yourself?"

I nodded.

"Hey, listen. I'm going to San Andreas to play a few songs with Bobby and the Calaveras Jumpers at the Cowboy Bistro. I could use some help carrying my harmonica case; could you give me a hand?"

I smiled but wasn't sure, "I don't think I would be good company."

"Great, and I'm not a very good singer, so it will be fun. Come on."

"All right."

We left my truck on the shoulder. Andy drove us to San Andreas with the top down on his convertible Bug. San Andreas was a main street town of about three thousand, and the county seat. The Jumpers played at the Cowboy Bistro most Saturday nights. It was a favorite local bar and grill, and had cowboy themed décor including cowboy poetry laminated into the tabletops.

Andy had a table reserved near the band. He asked me to order him a beer while he conferred with Bobby. Bobby had encouraged Andy to develop his blues harmonica playing, and occasionally Andy would sit in with the Jumpers and play some blues and sing a song or two he had written.

The Bistro was already quite lively and loud as I waited for Andy to come back to our table. Soon my spirits began to lift and I thought of Nathan's wedding last October on Halloween. Andy had presided, and Bobby's band had played for the wedding and reception. The thought made me smile. It was the most unusual, but joyous wedding, with everyone in costume. Andy sang a song he had written: "They

Call Me A Four-time Loser, Are You My Winning Ticket Baby?" And at the reception he surprised me with a sing about teaching him to ride called: "My Old Bottom Blues."

When Andy finally returned to our table, I had our drinks and was looking forward to the music. "All set," he said as he sat down.

"Have you written a new song?"

"Yup, the blues just seem to pour out of me," he said with a smile that said hold on, this is going to be another wild ride!

"What's it about?"

"I don't want to ruin it for you, but let's just say it's about not taking ourselves too seriously."

That got my back up. "You mean we should pretend that nothing is wrong? That if we lose something valuable and irreplaceable that we shouldn't care?"

"That's one way to put it – but not a very good way. It's more like keeping things in perspective and not pretending that something is more valuable than it is; it is the perspective that takes in the long view."

"Is that why you think I was crying?"

"No. I think you were crying mostly because you love me."

"And?"

"But part of you has come to assume that love is rare. You have a hard time trusting that love flows to you forever; so if what you love is lost, you've lost it all."

"Always the preacher."

"Well, you know what Isaiah said."

"Repent, the end is coming?"

Andy laughed, "No. The Spirit of the Lord is upon me to preach good news…."

The band began to play, and unless we shouted, we couldn't continue to talk. So as I listened to the first couple of numbers I tried to make sense of what Andy had said: taking things too seriously, the long view, trusting that love is eternal. But for me this love is rare. And now I will have to watch Andy change into something else, something broken and distorted and hideous. I felt the sadness come up again and I tried to remind myself: slow down (we don't know what the tests will show), pay attention (we are here at the Cowboy Bistro, listen to the music), don't judge (will the future be hideous? It will be what it will be), and be grateful (for what?). I held that question in my mind: for what? Where is the gift in this?

"Okay folks," Bobby was at the mic. "Tonight we have a special guest. Give it up for Reverend Andy!"

There was a cheer and some enthusiastic applause. Andy had been in Calaveras County for over a decade, marrying and burying, giving invocations and blessings at community events, and preaching in Riverton. But he was best known for his extraordinary involvement with Kindom Come which did battle with the California Lottery and set up the Shepard Foundation which gave grants to local non-profit organizations. So as Andy took his place with the band on the low platform, there were the usual hoots and whistles!

Then Bobby said, "The Old Rev said he was in the mood for some Bob Dylan," and he counted to four and the band began to play a long intro with a slow, moody beat, featuring Andy's blues harmonica.

I was taken aback when Bobby began singing "Knocking on Heaven's Door." It was even more disconcerting when Andy joined in singing the refrain, which over and over repeated the ominous title.

I knew what he was doing, he was saying things were changing, but take the long view. Every time the chorus came around I had to press back the sadness. Then Andy sang the last verse about a dark cloud descending.

It felt like the slow song went on forever; a lot of knocking, and the tension of whether or not the door would ever open. When it finally ended, Bobby announced that they were now going to do one of Andy's originals, "The Senile Blues." Andy began with his harmonica, setting a real bluesy tempo and style. The band came in and took some time building up to the first verse. Then Andy sang:

> It seems like only yesterday
> My pop taught me to drive.
> Can't forget that sky blue Chevy,
> I felt I had arrived.
> Now I wander down my street,
> Feeling dumb and really beat,
> Can't find my car and that's no jive.
> Got those old senile blues.
> Got those old senile blues.
> Now don't you laugh, I'm still alive.

I had to laugh with the crowd, but I knew it was a true story, and he had made a song out of it; so this is what he meant about not taking oneself too seriously. After the band followed the harmonica's riffs for a while, Andy started the second verse:

> My first girl's name was Evelyn,
> That I still remember,
> Like when I first kissed her sweet lips
> At school in September.
> Now my new babe's mad at me,
> And she is looking sad at me,
> Can't recall her name, just her gender
> Got those old senile blues.
> Got those old senile blues.
> So I picked a name to lend her.

I laughed again. But I remembered I didn't laugh when he called me Sabina. Is he trying to prepare me? Before the last verse Bobby showed off his guitar playing as he led the band in some variations on the song's melody. Then Andy sang:

> It makes you laugh, it makes you cry

> As this thing progresses.
> Try to fight it, try to hide it,
> Your mind still regresses.
> But consider this my friend:
> Life is precious to the end,
> Though, with your best plans, it messes.
> Got those old senile blues.
> Got those old senile blues.
> I sing so it won't depress us.

I clapped, but I didn't laugh at this verse. "Life is precious?" Had I talked to him about my thin small book? Where did he get that? I was puzzling over this when he came back and the band took a break.

"I have to say, Andy, that was pretty brave of you. 'The Senile Blues'? Does anyone else know how real that is for you?"

"No."

"I guess you've been thinking about this for a while?"

"And it gets a little more real all the time."

"And the good news?"

"Life is a precious miracle."

"Okay, where did you get that?"

"Isn't that the book you've been using for your recovery? I saw it at your house."

"Maria gave it to me. It's been a big help."

"I think it's been more than that."

I looked at him closely. What did he know?

He continued, "It's become your path, hasn't it?"

This was my private life. I hadn't invited him into it yet. It was my secret, a powerful secret that was giving me a new kind of life. I didn't know how to answer him.

"I'm not asking you to talk about it, but I want you to know that I've been using that book for twenty years. It was one of five or six books I used to keep on my desk – when I had a desk. It's been a big help for me, too. So if sometime you want to talk about it, that would be fine."

Still I didn't say anything. How many of us were walking in slow motion as a practice? I wondered. Or paying attention to the smell of potatoes as we cut them? Or learning to withhold judgment toward a careless, frightened driver? How many? I had never thought of that. I never pictured anyone else reading the book. I felt that no one else needed it like I did. Nor would anyone take it seriously like I was. Now those thoughts seemed...naïve, the least judgmental word I could come up with.

"Thanks, Andy," I said finally. "I appreciate that. And thanks for the song. I felt you wrote it for me."

"Maybe I did, I can't remember." And we both laughed.

Chapter 46

On Friday, June 5, Andy and I were scheduled to see his doctor and discuss the test results. I had two appointments in the morning with new couples; the first at 9:00 a.m. I wanted to be at my office early and get organized for the day which included an evening rehearsal for Saturday night's wedding, but I was struggling. I hadn't slept well and I had tried on three different outfits – a slow process with one arm. I had half-heartedly reminded myself, No hurry, no worry, but then essentially said screw that.

I looked in the mirror without satisfaction. My white pants could have used some ironing, and my flowered blouse didn't seem to fit right – none of them fit, no matter who did the alterations.

There was no time to do any "slow down" practice. I got to the hotel at 7:00 a.m., parked at the back and hurried up the stairs, but found the door still locked – I usually didn't come to work this early. I dug out the key from my purse, slipped it in and turned. I realized that I needed to keep pressure on the key, turning it to the right as I pulled on the handle with my other hand, which of course wasn't going to happen. I tried to pull the door open with the key. No way.

I knocked, but there was no response. I knocked harder, but there was still no response. Why didn't we have a doorbell back here!? I was getting mad. I was going to have to walk back down to the garden and over to the side street, then up to Main Street and try the front door. At least there would be an intercom that I could yell into.

But I stopped myself. What was going on? What was happening with me? I noticed that I was huffing and puffing. I put my purse down on the landing and leaned against the railing and closed my eyes. I asked myself why I was so impatient and irritated.

I run this hotel and I can't even open the door!

What else?

I woke up in a bad mood.

What else?

I feel anxious. I guess that means I'm scared. I'm scared about Andy's doctor appointment.

Why?

It seems obvious, there are a hundred reasons.

Why, really?

Alzheimer's is going to take him away. First my arm, now this. I feel cursed.

Ah, the old misery list. It's back. Is that what I want? Do I want this list to define my life?"

I was still breathing hard. I willed myself to take deeper, slower breaths, yet my mind jumped from one problem to another. I watched it, observing its panic. I called up an image of myself as a six year old. I asked her how she felt.

I 'm going to be left all alone! Who's going to help me?!

I will. I am a grown-up. And I am a delightful, beautiful woman. What do you need right now?

I'm locked out. I'll always be locked out.

No you won't, I won't let that happen. I'll start by getting this door open for you. It's going to be fine. I'll see that you get inside and are safe. I love you.

I took my cell phone and speed-dialed the night clerk.

"Hello?"

"Hi Margaret. It's Barbara. This sounds silly, but I can't get in the back door. Could you help me?"

"Be right down."

We hung up. As I waited I noticed that I felt calmer. I even smiled that I hadn't used my phone earlier. The thought came to me to call Andy. It was early but still…. I pushed the button for his cell.

"Good morning, Cowgirl, how are you?" He seemed amazingly awake.

"Hi Honey. I'm spinning out a bit. How about you?"

"Hard to say, but it's a good day. We'll know what we're dealing with."

"You still want to drive?" I asked.

"Sure. I'll pick you up at 12:30."

"Okay. And Andy?"

"Yeah."

"No matter what, I love you."

There was a pause on his end, then he said, "I don't know if that makes this easier or harder, Barbara. But I love you too, and we'll find the grace to deal with whatever."

My nine o'clock was a pretty thirty-five year old with professional quality makeup and boutique clothes. She came with her girlfriend rather than her fiancé. (I realized this would be the norm for first appointments because brides were so much more into weddings than grooms). Before I offered to show her around, I asked if she had set a date yet. Janelle had taught me not to waste my time if I couldn't accommodate a couple's date; nor should I set a date without a deposit – dates change more often than one would think. This wedding business was one drama after another.

"Saturday, July 23," she said.

I brought up July on my iPad. "I'm sorry, that date isn't available. Would another day be possible?"

"Another day? Certainly not. Ray said you would take care of us. He's a friend of my fiancé."

"I wish I could help you."

"Are you saying someone else has reserved that day?"

"Yes, and as a small destination wedding venue, we can only accommodate one wedding a day."

"I would be willing to pay a premium if you could move the other people off that date. What would it take?"

"I couldn't do that. I'm sorry."

"You mean you won't do that. What if we doubled the price for your top-drawer wedding package?"

"That's a generous offer, but how would you feel if I bumped you off a reserved date?"

"And how would you feel if Ray bumped you out of your job? All you have to do here is call the other couple and say you made a mistake and offer them a half-off deal on another date. I will make up the difference."

Her friend jumped in, "Yeah, how hard could that be?"

I looked at the glamorous women sitting in front of me as if they were never going to budge. Slow down, I reminded myself. Obviously they were used to getting their way, even if it meant bullying and threatening. I had a choice: I could get into a power game, call them names and show them the door; or I could withhold judgment and accept them as they are, sadly self-centered. I chose something in between. "You know, often when a door won't open, it is for the best."

"Oh, you're wrong. This isn't for the best, this is crap."

"I meant for me. But I hope you do find a wonderful place for your wedding." I stood up, thankful that I would not be their wedding coordinator. As for Ray, I had no doubt that he would be on my side.

My ten o'clock couple didn't show up, so I spent some time on the internet learning more about Alzheimer's. At noon I sat at the bar with a salad and a glass of wine and talked with Sabina. She had called her ex-husband, the doctor she put through school. He was connected somehow with the Methodist Hospital in Sacramento which now had a computer on a rolling stand in every room. He said he would check into the hospital's cost of fully converting to computers.

I wanted in the worst way to tell Sabina about Andy's tests. Not only could I use the support, but she had suggested that he see a doctor. However, it was Andy's business, and if I was honest with myself, I wasn't ready to talk about him possibly having Alzheimer's – after my internet search I felt it was a more frightening word than cancer.

Andy was on time, normally he was, but recently I couldn't count on it. As we drove out of town and headed down toward the Central Valley to Stockton, I asked him, "Do you think your memory has gotten better or worse lately?"

"Well it hasn't gotten any better. I can't tell you how many times I've search for things I've misplaced; thank God I don't have many things to lose since the fire. A few days ago I looked for the milk in the refrigerator and was surprised that I was out, so I bought some more. This morning I found a carton of spoiled milk in the cupboard. I've definitely got a screw loose. The only question is whether the screw can be tightened again, or are the threads stripped and the damned thing is going to fall out. Then I guess my brain comes apart. But let's not talk about what-ifs until we see the doc. Do you have any questions about the rehearsal tonight?"

"Three solos seems like a lot."

"It is a lot, but I couldn't talk them out of it. I know that when they are just standing there in front of everyone while the songs go on and on, they will wish they had taken my advice."

"Tonight I'll have the songs sung all the way through. Maybe they will see that it is too much."

"Or maybe we should charge by the minute; that would get them thinking."

"Right. And too bad you weren't paid by the minute when you were preaching; you would be a rich man."

"That was different, Baby. Every word was gold, nothing but profound truth."

"Oh? I've heard that twelve o'clock noon on Sunday is the happiest hour in America. That's when church is out."

"Not in my church. When I finished a sermon they would applaud until I gave an encore."

"Now I'm really concerned about your memory, Sugar."

We walked into the medical building where Andy's doctor had her office and I was reminded of when our roles were reversed. Last fall Andy had been insistent that he go with me for my biopsy on my shoulder. I remember how scared I was that I might have cancer. He was a wonderful support.

Was Andy scared now? If he was he didn't show it. Was he that good at hiding his fear? The only time I'd seen him afraid was when he pushed himself to ride Charley. Even then, he stuck with it until he was comfortable. Then there was the time he did Nathan's wedding, the same day an arsonist set fire to my cabin with all of Andy's things in it. That night the deputy sheriff almost threw Andy in jail. He seemed unruffled through it all.

We stepped into the elevator and he pushed the button for the third floor. As the doors slid shut he said, "You know, I've never spent a night in the hospital, never had an operation or even a broken bone. I've been blessed with a healthy life. I've been so lucky."

I didn't say anything. I waited for him to finish that thought. But that was it. I thought he was leading to the bitter irony that after his long run of good health, his life might now end with a lengthy dreaded disease. But there was no bitterness in his voice. It sounded more like gratitude. Could he really walk into Dr. Kendra Pai's office with gratitude? Is this how he dealt with his fear? Was it real?

He signed in at the reception counter and we took a seat. I heard him take a deep breath and let it out as if trying to relax. Then he said, "Thanks for coming with me today, Barbara. It means a lot."

Again, gratitude. "Sure Andy, but there was no way I was going to let you come down here alone. After all, how many times as pastor were you there for others?"

He thoughtfully nodded. Then an image came to my mind. "Just imagine the many people you sat with in hospitals, all those facing uncertain futures, some of them in their last days. Imagine them here in a big circle, smiling and wishing you well."

I guess that did it. Andy's eyes glistened. He smiled as he wiped a tear rolling down his face. "Yes," he said and took my hand.

"Oh yeah, I have something for you." I reached into my purse and pulled out the blue bandana he had given me in the hospital after my amputation. "This might be a good time to give this back to you."

He gave me a knowing smile, then wiped his face with the bandana. I took his hand again as he closed his eyes and sat still. I knew he had started praying or meditating or whatever he did. And that's how we spent a long fifteen minutes before a nurse opened the door, "Mr. Shepard?"

Rather than an exam room with a table, we were shown into Dr. Pai's office. She greeted us, and Andy introduced me as his close friend. She was a thirty-something Asian woman, and she wore a white lab coat over her black dress.

"And how are you today, Reverend?"

"I'm doing well, thank you," he said and we took a seat.

"I've taken some time to review the results of your tests. They rule out concussion, stroke, brain tumor, malnutrition, vitamin deficiency, thyroid and metabolic disorders, and infections – all of which can cause cognitive impairment. Your neurological exam has also ruled out DLB, FTD, CJD and Parkinson's – diseases that may also bring on dementia. And I haven't detected any signs of depression. Tell me Barbara, does Andy seem depressed to you?"

"No, not really."

"But when we review the history of your symptoms, Andy, and your cognitive testing, you still present early stage dementia."

"Isn't there some normal memory lapse and a little confusion as we all grow older?" I asked. I was suspicious whether this young doctor really knew the realities of seniors.

"Some, but not much. And Andy is very intelligent and aware, so he is capable of hiding his symptoms. To your credit, Andy, you got yourself in here and have been very forthcoming about the changes you have noticed.

Things like your recent need to ask someone at the bank to untangle your checkbook; showing up on the wrong day for an appointment; walking out of a store without your purchase; and needing to make reminder notes for many things. In and of themselves, these are not a big problem. But because these are fairly unusual for you, when you add them up as changes you have noticed in the last eighteen months or so, it is very significant. I suspect these symptoms played a role in your sudden retirement from the foundation where you were Chairman of the Board."

Andy nodded, "So what does that leave?" Then, almost matter of factly, "Alzheimer's?"

"Yes, Andy, it all points in that direction. Right now you definitely have mild cognitive impairment. Now, some people with this early stage dementia never go on to develop full-blown Alzheimer's Disease. But most do. And unfortunately you are sixty-three, and people who have symptoms before 65 for some reason advance more rapidly. AD patients normally survive from four to eight years (some much longer). I would expect that you have less time."

Dr. Kendra Pai paused to let us respond, but neither of us could. Andy nodded slowly and looked like he was trying to get his mind around this information. She went on about the telltale signs that Alzheimer's leaves in the human brain, signs not readily detected in tests. Again she paused and gently asked, "Do you have any questions?"

"What do we do now? What do you recommend?" Andy was able to ask.

"First of all, this has been a difficult thing to hear. You probably will need a few days to absorb it. It's like taking a blow, you may feel out of sorts for a while. Then you might want to get a second opinion of my diagnosis and of what you are facing. Also, even though there is no cure for AD, there are a few drugs that can slow down the progress for a while in the beginning. They do not work for everyone, and they have some side effects; when you are ready, come back and I will go over those options.

"I understand that you have no family that will be caring for you, but if Barbara or other friends will be involved in your care there are resources that can help them learn what to expect and what to do – this will be important. And there are issues, financial, legal, placement, and end-of-life issues that should be settled sooner than later."

"When," Andy started, then paused. "How will I know when I reach the point where I cannot practically make informed decisions?"

"That's a problem. It will sneak up on you. Most people struggle with denial, then their memory and reasoning powers fail them; then their perception of reality will wane. And it's different for different people. You have some decisions to make; make them in the next month or so."

Then Dr. Pai reached over to her desk and picked up some printed material. "Here is a booklet on Alzheimer's Disease, and this is a helpful article for caregivers of people with AD. And I have included a list of nearby long-term care facilities that offer memory wards."

"What's that?" I asked.

"A special lock-down ward for those with acute dementia. Usually the staff have specific training for these patients."

My mind summarized it – a loony bin. This was a disability that went from bad to worse to unthinkable. The young doctor talked with us for a while more – something about research, clinical trials, relevant websites, and Andy taking advantage of the good days he still had.

When we left we drove directly back up the two lane highway that snaked through the Gold Country to Moke Hill. Andy was quiet and didn't seem to welcome conversation. I wanted to cry and swear, but the last thing I thought Andy needed was for him to feel that he had to be a pastor to me. When we reached Valley Springs I asked "What do you want to do, Andy?"

"I think I'll go sailing while you get ready and do the rehearsal."

That was the last thing I expected to hear. He still kept his small sailboat on the beach at my place, but hadn't used it much this season. Now what did he think he was going to do? Sail off into the sunset? Chaos and heartbreak were coming and had to be faced. We drove the rest of the way in silence.

It was late afternoon when we arrived. Andy pulled up in front of the hotel and turned the engine off. He looked at me, searching my face for something, maybe trying to read my state of mind which even I could not describe. I said, "We need to talk."

"Tomorrow. After the wedding."

"Okay."

He pulled out his little notebook from his shirt pocket and wrote it down. Then he said as he tucked it away, "This is where the practice gets really interesting."

"Practice? Is practice still possible?"

"We are always rehearsing something, our fears, our distractions, our misery list. It might as well be our awareness, our gratitude, our peace of mind. It's our choice, Cowgirl."

"Is it?"

"I'm going sailing. We'll talk tomorrow."

He leaned over for a kiss. I put my hand to the side of his face and search his blue-grey eyes, and it wasn't fear that I saw. I saw that he was loving me. My hand slid to his ear and I caressed it as I gave him a soft smile. I let my hand slip around the back of his neck and I slowly leaned to him until our lips touched. His hand went to my waist, then to the side of my breast. I pressed into his lips a little more. I had never noticed before how alive and hungry his lips were. Like a tableau, we held this position as if we wanted to preserve it forever, trying to press it into our memories where it would not get lost or fade away, to establish this memory deeper than any disease could touch.

* * *

June 5

She said, "I'm locked out!"

"I'll always be locked out."

Exiled.

Estranged.

Soon I'll be locked out

Of Andy's memory.

"I can't open the door!"

I'm dis-abled. But I knock.
Knock, Knock, Knocking
On heaven's door.
Knock, Knock, Knocking
On heaven's door.
I've come to heaven's door limping,
Limping all the way.
Why won't it open?

Chapter 47

I had a difficult time sleeping the night after our time with Dr. Pai. My anger and fear kept me awake until 2:30 a.m., so I switched on the palomino table lamp and took up my thin small book and read chapter six. It was on compassion: feeling someone's pain and responding. Unlike early chapters, there was no practice given, just the suggestion of looking for compassion and discovering it, like gratitude. I wrote in my journal:

June 6, 3:30 a.m.
Compassion.
The sixth chapter is on Compassion
Like gratitude
I can encourage it
But not manufacture it,
They must naturally arise
From the practice:
Slowing down
Paying attention
Withholding judgment.
I can choose to practice,
But Gratitude and Compassion
Simply arise.
All I have to do is
Encourage and welcome them.

Then I decided to close my eyes and again call to mind the image of myself as a little girl: my hair fixed in two ponytails, and wearing my favorite blue polka dot dress and my first pair of cowboy boots. I asked her how she felt. She said she was disappointed with Andy and wanted to run away. She said she didn't have to put up with him and his hideous disease. She needed someone to care about her! Someone who would not leave her.

She was being a little shit.

That thought shocked me. Evidently I not only had no compassion for Andy, I didn't even have compassion for myself. Where was the good teacher that this child needed? The voice of the needy, wounded little girl had taken over. How could compassion arise?

I lay there in despair. I knew that I had let this wounded part of me be in control most of my life. I felt hopeless, trapped. My mind raced. I wanted to get really drunk. Or maybe get on a plane to somewhere, anywhere, and tomorrow let the damned bride and groom figure out their own stupid wedding.

And then I had a fantasy of shooting my horses and then shooting myself.

That's when I said out loud, "Whoa, Barbara, show down." I made my breathing slower and deeper while I watched my belly rise and fall. After a bit, I again pictured Pomo and his beautiful coat of milk chocolate patches on white. I could see his big brown shiny eyes and wonderfully long eyelashes. I imagined running my hand over his massive muscles and patting the side of his neck.

I brought to mind the day I first rode Pomo after my amputation; I was at Sabina's and I rode bareback – the joy, the feeling of strength and speed and wholeness. And I remembered back to when I bought Charley, the palomino I had dreamed of as a girl, bringing him home, walking him out of the trailer, and knowing that he was mine, that somehow I had made my dream come true.

"Sweetheart," I whispered to the scared girl who believed she would never get what she needed, "I love you, and I know you are frightened about Andy. But look, you have a few more days to love him and then he will be gone. Don't miss out on this chance. It's a precious gift – for you darling, and for him."

* * *

The RSVPs had come back heavier than expected, so this wedding was to be a little larger than our stated limit of one hundred and ten. We could accommodate the additional guests in the chapel by utilizing the chancel area for seating, thus effectively making it a wedding in the round. For the reception and luncheon we set up some tables in the garden and hoped the late spring temperature would be comfortable.

The mini-crisis began when more than a dozen people without RSVPs showed up as well. We weren't going to turn them away, so at 11:00 a.m., just before the ceremony was about to start, I made an announcement to the guests to please scoot together to make room for people who needed a seat. The groomsmen set up chairs in the narthex. We left the double doors open at the back so these latecomers could see; and we opened the outside doors for fresh air in the crowded church. I hoped that the fire marshal wouldn't make a surprise visit.

The candles were lit, the parents seated, and before the procession Andy gave a formal welcome and his standard introductory remarks. Then the first solo began, an old John Denver song about his lover filling up his senses "like a night in a forest, like the mountains in springtime...." As the soloist sang the second verse, "Come let me love you, let me give my life to you, let me drown in your laughter, let me die in your arms...," I stared at Andy and I began to choke up with tears. I was standing next to the bridesmaids and wanted to step out and compose myself, but I soon had to help the procession begin. As the piano played by itself before the last verse I tried to inconspicuously dab my eyes.

Then a curious thing happened. At least two uninvited bees decided to attend the wedding as well, and evidently they thought the soloist smelled like sweet flowers and they tried to land on him as he sang the last verse. He subtly swatted at them as he sang, but this only seemed to make them mad. Yet he would not stop singing. He tried walking to another spot, but they followed.

His singing began to suffer. The guests began to murmur and I surmised that they were scared he was going to get stung. But at the same time they found it comical.

At the final phrase, "Come love me again," he took one more futile swat. There was laughter and applause while the soloist made the bold decision to leave and walked cautiously up the aisle past me and out the door.

Andy broke in with, "Obviously a very, very sweet song. However, none is more sweet than the wedding march. But before we begin, ah" Andy looked straight up the aisle to where I stood at the double doors and said, "Would Miss Barbara Hanson (our Wedding Coordinator) please come down here for a moment. I need to confer with you."

A shock went through my body. Had it come to this already? Had Andy lost his way in the middle of a wedding ceremony, a ceremony which he had done countless times before? As I hurried down the aisle I found a little thankful place in my mind: At least he hadn't just blundered ahead but had caught himself.

As I got closer to where he stood on the third step of the chancel, he broke into a smile which quickly made me reevaluate what he was up to in front of our overflow crowd. He must want me to close the outside door to keep the bees out. Didn't he think that I would have already figured that out? When I reached the first step I looked up at him and whispered urgently, "What?"

In his regular voice, which was amplified by his lapel mic, "Barbara, I think I might have something of yours." And he held out something in his closed hand in such a way that I had to climb the three steps to receive it.

What had I lost? And why did he think this was a good time to return it? As I took the steps I checked for my earrings, then looked at him with questioning eyes. He opened his hand, it was a ring.

"Barbara, will you marry me?"

My eyes went from the ring to his face, he was serious. And as surprising as this question was, even more surprising was a place inside of me that wanted to say yes.

I took the ring out of his palm and studied it to stall for time. It was an old gold wedding band, but it looked familiar. It couldn't be! I looked closely, then checked for the inscription inside; it said "I'm Yours." It was my old wedding ring, the one I threw in the lake. Speechless, I looked at Andy again.

"I said, will you marry me?"

I looked around at the crowd which had grown very quiet, then said to him, "For how long?"

There was scattered laughter. "Until death do us part, Sweetheart."

Those words stung. I shot back, "I suppose that would include mercy killing."

"That would be better than a divorce."

"I'll have to think about it," and I handed my ring back to him.

"For how long?"

"As long as it takes, Andy!"

There were a few hoots. I suspected that some of the guests thought this was a part of the ceremony – a California psychodrama wedding.

"Well then," he said to the crowd as much as to me, "That's a good start, I think."

I turned and walked back up the aisle.

* * *

Andy and I had decided to meet in his apartment under the church after the reception and luncheon that afternoon. But I was able to catch him sitting in the chapel before the reception as the wedding party was posing for photographs. The bride and her mother and father were being arranged when I sat down next to Andy and asked in a low voice, "Where did you get my ring?"

"When I was launching my boat yesterday I saw something shining in the water. What were the chances? I took it as a sign."

"And you thought you would marry me with my old wedding ring!?"

He fished it out of his pocket so we could see it again. "It's not a bad ring; it's just that the wrong man gave it to you."

"Are you all like this? Let me see it." I was curious if it would still fit, but jewelry in general, and rings in particular, were difficult to manage with one arm. And I sure as hell wasn't going to have Andy slip it on me – not in a church at a wedding. "Didn't you imagine that your little stunt just might distract from the couple's wedding?"

"I imagined them wondering, as they signed their divorce papers, if we did any better than they did."

"Andy Shepard, they are going to hear you," I hissed. "We'll talk when this is over. Did you write it down?"

He looked at his note pad and nodded. I got up and walked back across to the hotel.

* * *

It was five p.m. when I was able to return to his place. When I walked in I could smell spaghetti sauce. He greeted me with a kiss and we walked into the old church kitchen. He had tried to transform it with trendy paint colors, a wine rack, and posters of artichokes, ripe sliced tomatoes and pears, but the line of old cabinets and the linoleum floor still gave it away.

There was a skillet of sauce simmering on the stove, and he had set the small kitchen table, which he had picked up at a garage sale, with a bowl of salad, a basket of bread, a candle and flowers that looked like they were recently part of a wedding.

I guessed we were going to have dinner.

"Would you like something to drink?" he asked as he walked to the stove and gave his marinara sauce a stir.

"Some wine would be nice."

"Red or white?"

"Whatever you're having."

"I have a nice Italian Barbarra, my favorite."

"Fine," I said and I sat down at the table. As he chose a bottle from the wine rack there was an awkward silence. My mind raced through possible ways to start our conversation about death and marriage. His charming dinner preparations had detoured the heavy conversation I assumed we were going to have.

I had to remind myself of all three of my new guidelines for living and just sat and watched his personal ritual of uncorking a bottle of wine, selecting glasses, and carrying them to the table. He sat them down side-by-side and poured a dark, rich-looking wine. He set the bottle down, took his seat and handed me my glass. I followed his lead as we lifted our drinks and lightly touched glasses. I thought he was going to offer a toast, but instead he took a sip and stared into his glass – I suppose he was savoring and evaluating the vintage.

I took a sip. It was velvety, complex – Andy had stretched his budget for this wine. I took a second sip. The fruit and alcohol and oak seemed to be perfectly balanced. Andy looked up, smiled and nodded. A thought jumped off the please-wait shelf behind my head: What was this ridiculous marriage thing about? I told the thought I would get to it later and I put it back again where I couldn't see it jumping up and down for attention.

Then I looked for compassion. I had no idea what Andy was thinking or feeling. He had heard a horrendous prognosis and gone sailing and found my old wedding ring. Now he appeared to be thoroughly enjoying this great wine. I wanted to drag his feelings out of him – feelings I assumed he had, feelings I would have had if I were him. Then maybe I could be compassionate!

At that I began to chuckle out loud and shake my head as if to say: unbelievable. Andy somehow seemed to understand and laughed too. For a moment we just smiled at each other until he said, "You want some salad?"

"Sure."

He drizzled some homemade looking dressing over it and tossed it. I handed him my salad plate (a grandmotherly thrift store item among his mismatched dinnerware). He served up the mixed green salad and took care to top it with a slice of avocado. Then he passed the bread basket and cruet of olive oil and said, "I have heard that sometimes an acute sense of one's mortality can heighten their experience of the wonder and joy of life. That's what I feel today."

He waited for me to pass the bread and oil back to him; then as he poured olive oil in his old granny saucer he continued, "When the bees were buzzing the guy who was singing, I was transported into a magical realm and saw the wedding gods take command where you and I had failed to limit the idea of three long solos. The guy never came back in the chapel and that was that!" Andy laughed as he broke bread and dipped a piece into the oil.

"No, no," I said. "What the wedding gods were doing was keeping me from melting down as I listened to that John Denver song, 'Like a walk in the rain, you fill up my senses.' It's not good when the wedding coordinator can't see through her tears."

"Then that proves God is a multi-tasker, a choreographer of an intricate dance who accommodates the spontaneity of the dancers. And speaking of multi-tasking, I should put on the pasta to cook."

Andy got up and went to the stove. I thought about his comment about death: sometimes the gift of death's nearness is a heightened awareness. He was not grieving yet. At least, not today.

I flashed on the day after I returned home from the rehab hospital. Andy showed up and he noticed my "A, B, C" to-do lists and said that he was surprised. He had expected me to be depressed and moping in self-pity. The truth was that sometimes I was and sometimes I wasn't.

"I'm surprised, Andy. I thought you would be struggling with grief and fear around the Alzheimer's diagnosis."

For a few moments he didn't say anything. Maybe I shouldn't have used the "A" word. It had such a bad sound to it, and it didn't feel like a compassionate thing to bring up. But was conspiring with a person's denial compassionate? Then he turned his head toward me and said, "A close friend taught me to allow myself to go at my own speed."

"Good advice."

He smiled and came back to the table and carefully took a bite of salad and was obviously enjoying it.

"How was sailing yesterday? Find any other treasures?"

"Yes. The wind gave me a gift. Sometimes it stops and leaves you stranded – but not for long. You just have to wait, and trust, and it comes back again and you are on your way. So I asked myself, is death just a time when the wind stops (or as we say, dies down)? In death do we just stay forever in the middle of a placid lake – RIP? Or does the wind come back and the dance continues? In my experience, the wind always comes back." Here he looked into my eyes, "I've always wondered how deep my faith went. Is love forever? Dr. Kendra was a good test. And amazingly, on the lake, I felt no fear, only curiosity: where will the wind take me next?"

As we finished our salads, I knew that I've never had that faith. Long ago the wind drove me out to a stormy sea, and ever since I've just been trying to hang on to my boat.

Then it hit me: this was not entirely true. Recently I had learned to calm the waves. Was that faith?

Andy got up again and drained the spaghetti and fixed two plates of pasta and marinara sauce. When he had served us, he sat down and asked, "More wine?"

"A little."

When he had finished pouring he held the colored bottle up to the light to see how much was left. He seemed to look at it for a long time. "That's the main issue, I think. How much is left in the bottle?" he said, tapping his head. "I want to err on the side of some left, rather than ran out."

"What do you mean?"

"I mean I want to take my last boat trip before I forget why."

I still wasn't sure what he was saying, except that we both knew there would come a point where he could not remember enough to function on his own. "What about the weddings?" I asked.

"As long as I have the service in front of me, printed out and inserted in my worship book, I shouldn't have much trouble for a while. But I was thinking, as insurance, let's get a wireless communication system. You know, a small, hand-free headphone and mic for you, and an earpiece for me. Then if I start to sail off in the wrong direction you can talk me back. Plus, it could help you talk with your staff back at the hotel without running back and forth."

"Okay, that could work."

"How do you like the spaghetti?"

"It's delicious. But you might want to limit your wine drinking tonight. I hear alcohol is contraindicated for your special medication."

He smiled and nodded. "Now, you're not going to say anything like that into my new earpiece, are you?"

"Not unless you want me to."

"Barbara, about the ring."

I interrupted, "What would you have done if I had said yes?"

"Well, I guess we would have had to set a date."

"Bullshit. But let's talk about that after my rehearsal."

"You have a rehearsal? Tonight?"

"Yes, Sugar, and you've got another wedding tomorrow. Check your note pad."

He slipped his pad out of his shirt pocket and studied it for a bit. "Right. Do me a favor, will you? Give me a heads-up call in the morning?"

"Sure. And you do me a favor. No more pretending to forget, like when you called me Sabina for a joke. If I'm going to be in your corner I can't be second guessing you. Deal?"

"Deal."

"I've got to go. Thanks for the dinner, Sugar. It was the first time you've cooked for me. It was very good. I could get used to this kind of thing.

"I guess dessert will be later," he said with a knowing grin.

"I'm sure it will." And with that I got up and gave him my best promise-kiss.

Chapter 48

The saloon was already doing a good Saturday evening business when the folks for the rehearsal began showing up. My assistant, Jody, was preparing to host a wine pairing dinner for sixteen with a winemaker from Black Sheep, a local Calaveras County winery. They would be pouring a different kind of wine with each course while their party dined at a line of tables on one side of the restaurant. Jody's party was gathering in the saloon with several regulars, some tourists and most of my wedding party, including Carlos and his four groomsmen, Gloria and her four bridesmaids, some family members and three musicians. Sabina brought Sean in to help at the bar.

At 6:40 p.m. I asked the best man to round up the wedding party in about ten minutes. I walked across to the Chapel carrying my tote with everything I needed for the rehearsal. I turned on the lights and checked that everything was cleaned up and rearranged. One of our busboys took care of this on the weekends when we had weddings and rehearsals.

As I looked over Andy's notes on the ceremony I couldn't help thinking of his proposal that afternoon. Had he really decided to ask me to marry him after he found out he was going to die? Was that sweet or cynical? Did he see it as getting a caregiver for when he started being confused, wandering off, and acting (as Dr. Kendra so nicely pit it) inappropriate? I didn't want to think that. I forced myself to study his notes again. He had written that the couple wanted to kneel for a prayer of blessing near the end of the wedding, so I put out our kneeling cushion on the top step of the chancel.

Soon people began coming in, led by the bride's aunt who was shooting the whole rehearsal with a video camera. I got a couple of the groomsmen to set up three chairs where the musicians were to play, and to rearrange the standing candelabrums. Then I showed another family member where to set up the guest book.

By 6:55 p.m. everyone was present and ready to go except a bridesmaid, two groomsmen and the groom. The groomsmen were found outside having a smoke. I waited ten more minutes, then asked Gloria where her fiancé was. She didn't know. She tried his cell, but no answer.

There was to be a dinner after the rehearsal and I wanted to keep things moving, so I took the best man and we walked across Main Street to get the late comers; we were followed by the aunt with her camera. We didn't see them in the saloon. So I sent the best man into the men's room while I checked the ladies' room. Still no luck.

Next I asked the best man to check downstairs in the garden. The movie maker followed him, while I found Jody to see if she had seen my missing groom or bridesmaid. She leaned toward me and softly said I should check room Number Six; Carlos had arranged for the room rather hurriedly.

Outside the door to Room Six I paused. Should I be discreet? I listened and could hear Carlos and what was surely the voice of the missing bridesmaid. While Gloria awaited her loving, loyal, until-death-do-us-part husband to be, he was screwing one of her friends. Are they all like this? Is this just male behavior? I had been married three times and none of them could keep their pants zipped up. I started to knock, but didn't. Maybe I should just go back and wait. It's none of my business; or rather, it is just business, let it be. Practice compassion.

Then I pictured Gloria holding hands and kneeling in prayer with this asshole. I know, don't judge, but she trusts him and will have kids with him and then surely it will blow up in her face. It made me mad, but I was about to turn around to leave when the best man and the video aunt spotted me and came walking down the hall. As Andy would say, it was a sign.

"He wasn't in the garden," the young man announced to me and the camera.

"I think he might be taking a nap," I said to them in a conspiratorial whisper. "Let's take a look, shall we?" And when the camera was ready I opened the door with my pass key.

Oh my. The look on the bridesmaid's face was worth a thousand words. But we couldn't see his face; it was buried between her legs – but his young bare ass was prominent.

We stepped in and shut the door amid shouts of, "get out!" and, "Turn that camera off! And, "I told you we were going to be late?" and, "Carlos, Carlos, how could you!"

But the best man had the best take, "Carlos buddy, you are screwed."

* * *

There was no need for a rehearsal, of course. The wedding was called off. The good news was that there was no violence. The dinner was already paid for so most stayed for the postmortem except Gloria and her parents, and Carlos and his best man.

I shut down the church and called Andy as I drove home. I told him he had Sunday off and that I was sorry but I was in no mood for dessert; I would gladly take a rain check though.

Soon I was in bed writing in my journal:

June 6
Andy once said
God was all about love
But God had no opinion about marriage.
Andy once said
Marriage was a religious fetish,

Embraced for security and heirs.
He is so romantic.
I say marriage is
Signing your name to a promise,
An impossible promise.
I say marriage
Is a big gamble
And few have a winning hand

I put my journal down on the nightstand and took up my iPad. I started this e-mail:

> To: Andy Shepard
> From: Barbara Hanson
> Sent: June 6, 2009
> Subject: Promises
>
> Dear Andy,
>
> What are we going to do, Sugar? Life seems so cruel. The couple tonight surely proved that broken dreams and unhappiness is what people can expect most of the time.
>
> You found my old wedding ring and said it was a sign. You read it as a signal to promise me your love – that you could give me what someone else could not.
>
> I read it as a reminder of promises broken, people being too wounded to love very much, and of life being too hard to sustain love.
>
> In the face of Alzheimer's, how can we promise to love?
>
> Barbara

I sent it.

June 6 (cont'd)
There will come a time
When a difficult stranger
Who does not know me
Will wear Andy's face.
What will love mean then?

A tone said I had a reply.

> To: Barbara Hanson
> From: Andy Shepard
> Sent: June 6, 2009
> Subject: Until death do us part
>
> Dear Barbara, that was a great e-mail.
>
> Yes, life seems so cruel. Yes, life is hard and people are the walking wounded. Yes, promises to love are both brave and foolish.
>
> And yes, Alzheimer's will rob me of the ability to keep a promise to love you – unless. Unless I don't live that long.
>
> And why would I? Would you? Would you choose to live your last days out of your mind? (or with your mind out of you?) I'll just help old Alzheimer's finish the job. As the song goes, "I can't love you forever, but I can love you for as long as I live."
>
> So marry me Barbara Hanson, until death do us part.
>
> Andy

I read and re-read this e-mail. Then sent this back:

> To: Andy Shepard
> From: Barbara Hanson
> Sent: June 6, 2009
> Subject: What's the point
>
> Dear Andy,
>
> You are right. I wouldn't choose to live like that either. Yet I'm not clear about what marriage means as a short-term deal? You know I love you. And the honeymoon has been divine. Why pretend we will someday sit together in our rockers on the porch remembering the great life we've had together and looking at pictures of the grandkids?
>
> Barbara

I sent it, then added to my journal.

June 6 (cont'd)

Suicide,

Euthanasia,

End-of-life management.

Giving up, giving in, letting go,

"Let go and let God,"

Or help God and get going.

Life is a precious miracle,
But what kind of life?

Andy's reply...

> To: Barbara Hanson
>
> From: Andy Shepard
>
> Date: June 6, 2009
>
> Subject: Home Sweet Home
>
> Dear Barbara, I can't say what our marriage might mean for you, but for me it's about home, feeling at home; not a place but an experience.
>
> You've heard me put marriage down. That's because it hasn't worked for me (or for you). But I know we can be at home together for some good days ahead; and home at the end.
>
> Love, Andy

My last e-mail of the night:

> To: Andy Shepard
>
> From: Barbara Hanson
>
> Date: June 6, 2009
>
> Subject: Come Home
>
> Dear Andy,
>
> When was the last time you had breakfast at home? See you tomorrow, I'm cooking.
>
> Barbara
>
> P.S. Write it down, 9:00 a.m.

Chapter 49

Sunday was an all-day dessert. Maybe other people have loads of days like this one – I hope they do – but Sunday was a first for me. A romantic movie kind of day with a French toast breakfast, a horseback ride along the lakeshore, exchanging massages, making love, and making dinner together; after dinner we sat in candlelight for two hours talking about our past, present and future. Then with a ring on my finger we actually slept together for the first time.

It was still dark Monday morning when a noise woke me up. Andy wasn't in bed. I heard something in the living room hit the floor and break; the clock said 3:45 a.m.

"Andy?" I called out, but no answer. I thought I heard the front door open, "Andy, are you there?" Still no answer.

I switched on the light, fumbled with my robe, then walked cautiously into the living room, "Andy?" With the light from the bedroom door I could see the floor lamp tipped over.

I switched on the overhead and looked around and saw that the front door was standing wide open. I went to the door, turned on the porch light and called again, "Andy," and listened. I heard someone walking on the driveway gravel.

I slipped into my flip-flops and walked quickly up the drive where I saw him walking in the light of a half moon that was low over the hills. He was naked.

"Andy, wait."

He turned his head, "Carol?"

"Wait a minute, will you?"

He stopped and I caught up. "Where are you going, Sugar?"

"I'm lost, I think."

Wandering, this was supposed to show up later, and I hadn't read what to do when it occurred. "I know the way home, Honey. You want to walk with me?"

"I think it's this way," he said and started up the drive again. So I walked along. He was not only naked, but barefooted too.

"This is kind of rough on the feet, isn't it?"

"Yeah, hurts like hell."

"Come on, Andy, let's go back to my house and get your shoes."

He stopped again to look at me. I could see him trying to figure it out. He looked around at the house with all the lights on, then made a pained face. He took a big breath and gave a sigh, "Sorry I woke you up, Cowgirl, I thought I'd get some air."

"Sure you did, Nature Boy."

That's when he realized he had no clothes on. "Shit!" he hissed.

There would be no clever covering it up this time.

As we started back I said, "You know, if you had invited me, this could have been a pretty sexy moonlight walk," and I opened my robe and did my impression of a one-armed flasher.

"I'll try to remember that," and he put his arm around me.

"And who is Carol?"

"Carol?"

"Yeah, you thought I was Carol."

"My second wife. She divorced me."

"Uh-huh. It was probably your naked night hikes."

"Who knows."

"And the name of your first?"

"Georgie. Georgie, Carol, Jonna, and Joy. I'm sorry, Barbara. This thing is a little worse at night."

"You okay now?"

"Okay as I can be walking naked on gravel and thinking of things to come."

"Slow down, Honey."

"I know. And pay attention, and don't judge. Thanks," he said with a smile.

We walked the rest of the way in silence. After we cleaned up and were back in bed, I snuggled close to warm us up (and I suppose, to give us both assurance that for now everything was all right).

Soon the image arose of Andy's eyes staring at me as he tried to understand where he was, what was happening, and who he was with. It scared me. What was it like for him? He seemed lost in time, like when I push the wrong button on the remote for the DVD machine. The movie jumps in time, out of sequence and disjointed. Then I don't know exactly what happened – I goofed up. Andy wouldn't know what was happening – that his brain had short-circuited and jumbled his memory. This time he was able to connect the dots and reorient himself fairly quickly. But it was going to get harder.

* * *

June turned out to be a very busy, full month. Andy recruited Rev. John LaFiever, an old friend and retired pastor who worked for the Shepard Foundation, to be on call. John agreed to officiate at our wedding ceremonies when Andy couldn't. Hopefully then, we would have no disruption to couples' weddings.

With John in place we scheduled a meeting with Ray to alert him about Andy's condition, and to introduce Ray to John. We also called a meeting with the hotel staff to let them know what was happening with Andy and how to handle his memory lapses. Ray and the staff became like guardian angels for Andy: respectful yet watchful.

By the middle of June we had already worked ten weddings and I felt, if not like an old pro, at least more comfortable and confident. And on June 16th, a

Wednesday afternoon, we had wedding number eleven – ours.

We decided that we wanted a private wedding in Andy's church; just Andy, me, and Reverend John. This was in part because we didn't want anyone's emotional baggage filling the room ("Oh, those poor dears, they've been through so much and now what future do they have," sigh.) And partly because of our own baggage: seven weddings between us ("This all seems so familiar?!") And partly because, well, neither of us really liked weddings – or marriage for that matter. So without announcing an engagement (outside of Andy's peculiar public proposal) or a wedding date, we asked John to meet with us at the church at 2:30 p.m. without saying why.

We had agreed to bring something which for us symbolized home. At 1:30 p.m. we met at the church; me in my everyday clothes and an apron, with a freshly baked apple pie in a glass dish; Andy wore his gardening clothes and brought a trowel, gloves, and a pot of petunias. Most of the chapel chairs had been stacked and put away. Only a small table with two chairs remained. Thoughtfully, without hurrying, I draped a tablecloth over the table, then Andy set down a candle, our marriage license and a pen. We set our symbols of home on the table, lit the candle and sat down.

Our plan was to sit together for a while before John arrived. I looked at Andy looking at me. I smiled at him smiling at me. "You know," I said, "Getting married might be a sign that you don't have anything left in the bottle."

"You have a point there, Cowgirl. And not only that, you once threatened me that if I fell in love with you, you would have to raise my rent."

"Oh yeah, this is going to cost you."

"You'll probably make me stop sleeping with Sabina for starters."

"You betcha. And don't you think I haven't caught you looking at Jody, too."

"Darn. I'm so sorry, how can I ever make it up to you?"

"You could teach me to pray."

He studied me, wondering if I was still joking. "You mean like: Oh God, please take this license away from me; but not my will but thine be done?"

"Not my will, but thine be done? Where does that come from?"

"It's in the last chapter of that book of yours, but it's from Jesus' prayer in the Garden of Gethsemane."

"Andy Shepard! Marriage as crucifixion? What would your congregation have said?"

"While they sat there in stunned silence, I would have reminded them that St. Paul (who by the way counseled his parishioners not to get married) said that husbands should submit to their wives like Christ gave himself up for the sake of the church."

"Really? Breakfast in bed, a massage every day, and naked moonlit walks at night?"

"Something like that, until death do us part."

"Oh yeah, the fine print. Andy, before I'm a widow could you teach me to pray like you do? I want to learn to do that."

"It's Flora's prayer. She was one of my teachers thirty years ago. It's like a house with seven rooms. You walk in the back door and you take twenty minutes or so to walk from one room to the next, then you go out the front door ready for the day. It's pretty easy and I'd be happy to teach it to you."

"Okay," and I put my hand in my lap and closed my eyes.

"You mean right now?"

I opened my eyes and asked, "You have something else you want to talk about?"

He took out his little note pad and flipped a few pages. After a moment he asked, "Are you legally divorced?"

I didn't expect that. "Yes, are you?"

"Yes." Then he flipped a couple of pages and asked, "Is Hanson your maiden name or one of your ex's?"

"It's my maiden name.

He stared at his notebook some more, then finally said, "Oh yeah, before we get married I have to know: when you replace the toilet paper roll do you have the paper coming off on the front side or back side?"

"Is it a deal-breaker?"

"Afraid so."

"Then I think we should pray about it."

He smiled and said, "All right Miss Hanson, enter the back door by sitting as relaxed and comfortable as you can; eyes closed but not tight; hand relaxed and open, not clenched; mind focused on watching your breath rise and fall. Relaxing is the first room." Andy spent a couple of minutes suggesting that I relax different parts of my body in a slow sequence.

"Now as we enter the second room continue to relax each part of your body as you repeat silently this affirmation in rhythm with your breath; I am whole, light-filled, and free. If your mind strays, without judgment just gently return to the room."

Andy waited for a few more minutes, then he continued in a quiet voice, "Step into the third room and let any concerns you have today come to mind. They can be big or small. Let three or four simply bubble up into your awareness without you looking for trouble."

I thought of Andy's disease; then whether I put enough flour in the pie for a thickener; and then what our friends would say about our marriage. Then

I was concerned that I wasn't concerned about getting married.

After a couple of minutes he said, "Now enter into the fourth room, bringing these concerns with you. It is a room where it is possible to give these concerns to God. Here's how it works: picture your concerns one at a time – let's say you're anxious if John is going to understand our wedding request – imagine a photo of John as best you can, and lift it slowly over your head, offering it to God. God will always take it from you and bless it in the most perfect way. As you let it go feel the lightness-of-being on your shoulders. Likewise, release your next concern."

Andy gave me time to do this. I pictured him standing tall with bright eyes and a smile, and I lifted that picture up with my left arm and hand and held it there. I waited, but nothing. Then as I let go of my grip, it was gone. I indeed felt lighter. Then I pictured and released my pie and our friends in turn.

"Now enter the fifth room. Stand in the center where a beam of golden light is coming down. Allow it to enter your subconscious storehouse of memories; the light touches and heals anything in there that is ready."

After a short time he said, "Now enter the sixth room. Here's where you can ask God a question. Think of an area of your life where you need guidance. Formulate a question and ask it directly to God, whom you may not see, but who is listening with interest. Pay attention to what comes back as a thought, image or feeling."

This wasn't hard. I asked if marrying Andy was the right thing to do; and before I could settle in to wait and pay attention, the thought (a recollection actually) came to me: Maria had said, "it isn't so much what you do, as how you do it." I began thinking how to do this marriage, how I wanted to relate to Andy, how I wanted to respond to what was going to happen to him, how I could bring my practice to our marriage.

But soon Andy said, "Finally, step into the seventh room. When you enter you will go through a wonderful fountain of light that is energizing and healing. It will penetrate and cleanse every cell of your body. Take as much time as you need. When you are finished step out the front door and gently open your eyes."

I can't say how long I spent in the fountain of light, but at some point I heard Andy get up and walk across the room. So I opened my eyes again to see the familiar chapel of Reverend Andy Shepard and the table that was set with the candle, petunias, garden trowel and gloves, and an apple pie. There was also a marriage license and pen. It all somehow looked different. It looked inviting, it looked right, and it looked like enough.

I turned and looked toward the door. Andy and John were standing there looking at me. "When she's praying, John, it's like seeing a sleeping child, so sweet and innocent; then when they wake up, all sass and trouble."

"Come on, Andy, you get a little bored without some sass and trouble around," John said.

Andy smiled, "Some say I bring it out in them."

I laughed and stood up. "Hi, Reverend John, you ready for a little work?"

"Sure, what's up?" he said, walking over with arms out to hug me.

"A private ceremony," I said, leaning into him.

As he let me loose, he noticed the table. He leaned over and squinted to read the names on the license. "Good Lord."

"We would like you to officiate. Just the three of us," Andy said.

"Seriously? You are losing it day by day and sliding toward lockdown ward, and you want Barbara to marry you? Why?"

"That's not the only scenario, John."

John searched Andy's eyes, "What else?"

"Until death do us part, John," I said.

"So, the plan is to help things along? I wondered if you had considered that."

"John, I have tried all my life to be profoundly at home with a loving partner. I want to have that with Barbara and go out with a smile on my face rather than have my last words be, "Oh well."

"And you, Barbara?"

"He's loved me like no one else. I'll take however many days he has left." Andy looked at me like…there are no words for that look. It made me feel like I was his Christmas, birthday and the last day of school altogether. He took me in his arms and kissed me like he had been away from home for a long time. When we parted we looked at each other. I said, "I love you, Andy."

"I love you, Barbara."

"Okay then," John said. "By the power vested in me by the state of California, and by the authority of the church, I pronounce you husband and wife together. And what God's love has put together, let no one attempt to divide." He held out his hand and shook with Andy, "Congratulations."

John turned to me and I said, "We are going to have a dinner party reception Sunday night at the hotel. Can you come?"

"I wouldn't miss it," and he gave me a sweet kiss.

"One more thing, my friend," said Andy as he held out the pen.

John sat down and dutifully filled out and signed the pastor's part of the license as Andy and I stood by, arm in arm. Andy whispered, "Sunday night?"

I nodded, "With Bobby and the Calaveras Jumpers," I whispered back.

"Oh yeah."

When John finished he stood and said, "So, am I free to tell the rest at the Foundation?"

"Yes, of course. And tell them we expect to see them Sunday night. Bobby and the boys will be playing. But John, the part about helping things along is a pastoral confidence, okay?"

"Sure. However, you should remember the Board wanted to kill you more than once."

"Right. But you know what people say. 'It just wasn't my time.' Like in most things, timing is everything."

Chapter 50

We mailed this announcement to family and friends:

*Home is where we slow down for each other
and make time, an open place,
for them to enter our lives.*

*Home is where we pay attention to each other,
noticing and listening, trying to understand.*

*Home is where we respond to each other
without judgment,
where acceptance and forgiveness
are sacraments of love.*

*Home is where love softens the harsh side of life,
and with compassion
someone walks with us in our pain.*

*Home is where we can catch our breath
and nourish our spirit with gratitude
So we can be our best selves.*

Dear Ones,

We have decided to make home together. We were married in a private ceremony on June 16, and we invite you to a dinner and dance reception at the Mokelumne Hill Hotel this Sunday at six o'clock.

No gifts, please. If you insist a donation may be given in honor of this occasion to the Grace Project in San Andreas – a respite program for Families of Alzheimer's patients.

Joyfully,

Andy & Barbara Shepard

RSVP

Sunday, June 20 - midnight
I love my husband.
And he knows how to make love to me,
Perfectly. I hope he doesn't soon forget.

* * *

I didn't realize how few possessions Andy had until we moved his things to my house – our house. When I suggested that we could use my pickup, he laughed. He packed two small duffel bags with all his clothes, two small boxes with books and music, a shopping bag with things from his desk, and an espresso machine. It all fit easily in his VW Bug. He left his garage sale treasures: old furnishings and kitchenware. We thought we might upgrade a few things and offer his place as one more lodging option but that would come later. Our first job was to upgrade our ability to live together – accommodating each other's personal rhythms, communicating our needs, and sharing household tasks.

Also, there were the little surprises about each other that took time to digest. For instance, it took a while for Andy to get used to how I cooked with one arm: letting me take my time, and how I mixed ingredients in a bowl with my bare hand.

And there was his wedding ring which the goldsmith finally finished. For Andy it was an in-your-face reminder of his somewhat embarrassing reversal about getting married again. And the ring, which had my name across the face of it in bold relief, also reminded him of the reality of his faltering memory.

As for me, I had to learn to make a quiet time during Andy's morning practice of meditative prayer. And I had to accept that he farted out loud – often.

I also found out that he not only played pinochle at the senior center twice a month, but he met his ex-wife, Joy, for lunch each month. Every jealous bone struggled with this one. "Why?" I had asked. "I buried my blouse sleeves that I no longer needed, so why haven't you buried your last marriage with your others?"

He said they exchanged custody of Jake, their dog; and he was also interested in Native American spirituality. Joy was in training as a shaman. He said if it was a problem for me, he would give up the lunches.

But I said that if the lunches became a big problem, I would let him know, but for now I would practice letting them go and spend a little more time in the fourth room of my prayer house. Jealousy and demands had never helped in my marriages; in fact, quite the opposite. And if I found that Andy wasn't trustworthy, well then, we didn't have a marriage and that was that.

One of the gifts of our marriage was that I gained a real ally in my plans to use my settlement with the hospital. Early in July, Nathan and Cindy came to see us. They had been at our wedding reception, and although they didn't understand why we got married, they liked Andy. They appreciated how he had conducted their Halloween Wedding, and how he had helped me through my surgeries; and they trusted him in regards to my coming settlement – after all, he had given away his tremendous lottery fortune to the Foundation, so he couldn't be a gold-digger.

Whether they knew Andy had AD, I didn't know. The people who casually knew him hadn't picked up yet that he had a problem. Surely some had heard from those who knew, but had my kids heard about it? I didn't think so. They didn't say and I didn't want to tell them – I didn't want them butting into my life, and I couldn't guess how they would relate to Andy's plan for his early end.

It was hot, over 90 degrees at Hogan Lake, and the grasses had long since turned brown (or golden, as we like to say in California) yet the rolling hills surrounding the lake were still beautiful with their dark green oaks sprinkled over the landscape. Two boats, perhaps fishermen, left wake patters in the inviting blue water.

I had made flan the night before, and when Nathan and Cindy arrived for lunch we were preparing the tacos, Spanish rice and avocado salad. Cindy was carrying a nicely wrapped gift. As she handed it to Andy she said, "I know you said no wedding gifts, so consider this a house warming gift for you, Andy. And maybe you'll want to share it with Barbara."

"Thanks," he said, and he set it on the table. "What would you like to drink? We have, ah, water and..."

"He looked over at me. "Sparkling water, cola, and Andy made some sangria."

Cindy went for the sparkling water and Nathan chose the sangria. While Andy poured our drinks, Nathan asked, "So, how's the wedding business."

"Ray and Andy obviously found a big un-met need and did a great job marketing to it. We've been busy for two months straight." I picked up a photo album and laid it open on the table. "Here are our happy customers." Each page had a photo and the names of the bride and groom; they were posed with either Andy or me or both.

"Wow," said Cindy as she flipped the pages. "You have this thing down pat."

"Not really," I said. "Each one is unique, and I've discovered that there are a thousand things that can go wrong at a wedding. We could write a book."

"Look at this, Nathan," Cindy said pointing to a photo. "Two guys! Is that legal?"

"They can't get a license yet, but they can have a wedding or a holy union service," Andy explained.

"Yeah, the word's out that Andy will do a church service for gays and lesbians. We have three more booked already."

Nathan flipped a few more pages, "Where are the photos of your wedding?"

I hesitated. There weren't any. Neither of us was anxious to have photos taken that day. I have thrown out more than my share of photos picturing happy days that were supposed to usher in marital bliss. And the act of throwing them out (or using the scissors to cut out the offending son-of-a-bitch) always made for a bitter experience.

But more than that, I suppose I wanted to protect myself. Since that day in Dr. Pai's office, death has been our companion. And ironically, in the face of AD, death was a welcome guest – we knew there could be worse things. Part of me wanted to take loads of photos because Andy wouldn't be around for very long. But the thought of me lingering over photos of our wedding and reception seemed somehow masochistic or morbid.

"We didn't bother," I said. "Been there, done that."

"You're a pair," Nathan said, looking back and forth between us. "You are the most reluctant, jaded, pessimistic married couple, yet you are running the hottest new wedding venue in central California. You, Andy, a minister of a church without a congregation, tying the holy knots, and you, Mom, a wedding coordinator when you were trained more as a divorce coordinator!"

Andy started to laugh just as Cindy said, "Nathan! That's awful!"

"No, no Cindy. It's not awful," said Andy. It's grand. Life is grand. It's messy, it's surprising, it's inconsistent, and Nathan is right, it's ironic and funny as hell. A toast." Andy lifted his glass and we followed. "Love trumps our folly. Life is grand!" And we all drank to that.

"And I have something that could make it more grand," Nathan said as he pulled a folder out of his briefcase. He opened the folder and handed a document to me. As I began to read it I realized that it was a settlement agreement.

"Let's sit down," I said. They sat as I read over the three page agreement that awaited my signature. When I finished I said, "It looks like this took a lot of work. And I appreciate it very much. But it's not enough. Two million is not enough. We need three million."

Nathan chuckled, "Right, Mom. How would you possibly get by with two million dollars?"

But Cindy could see that I was serious. "What do you mean, Barbara?"

"There is something that needs fixing and its going to cost at least three million dollars."

"Mom, we've already got them to double their original offer and we think it's fair." Nathan had a hint of pleading in his voice. "What could possibly cost three million dollars?"

"I know it seems like a lot, Honey, but I've checked it out and for a hospital this size, that's what it will take for them to convert to digital charting, orders and records. But if we think about it as protecting people and perhaps saving lives, it's a deal."

"You want to pay the hospital to buy computers?!" Nathan sounded exasperated.

"It's much more than that," Andy said. "It's software, consultants and training. And the doctors are the biggest blocking force in the hospital's need to switch to computer orders and charting. Like most of us, they don't want to change how they do things, even though it will significantly reduce mistakes like what happened to Barbara. They shrug it off as someone else's mistake. But Barbara has figured out the leverage she holds. Not only does her case point to the vulnerability the hospital and doctors have in continuing to make mistakes and fighting malpractice suits – a vulnerability that you yourself said could be exploited in the media – but she also has the leverage of a lot of money."

"Mom, we've been fighting for you, for your future and your needs. And we have been working to hold the hospital accountable. Do you really want to throw all that out the window?!" Nathan's voice was rising.

"Look at me, Honey, does it look like past malpractice and gross negligence suits have helped? If punishing hospitals hasn't fixed the problem, then maybe we haven't understood the problem."

"Nathan," said Cindy, "Let's calm down and look at this, all right? Let's hear what Barbara has in mind."

"Andy, is this your idea? Just because you gave away your lottery fortune doesn't mean Mom won't need this settlement. She's lost an arm for Christ's sake, and she is going to need some help as time goes by."

"Nathan, stop!" Cindy said fore forcefully. "Now, tell us everything."

I assured my son that I had started investigating this idea before talking to Andy. But I didn't mention that Cindy gave me the inspiration. Then as Andy got up to put the lunch on the table I told them about meeting Sabina's ex-husband at the Methodist Hospital in Sacramento and his description of how they recently made this digital conversion.

Then I shared how Andy and I had talked to the chaplain at the Stockton hospital where I had been treated. The hospital had talked for five years about computerizing the charting, orders and records, but the project wasn't going anywhere. The hospital administrator was for it, but he met strong resistance in those who rationalized that there were more urgent needs that were waiting for money. I suggested that Nathan, Cindy and I have a meeting with the administrator and tell him that if they upped the settlement, I would place it in an escrow or trust account that would pay for the conversion as each stage was completed.

When Nathan again said I wasn't thinking about my future, I gave him my notes on my extra expenses for the last nine months, and the estimated annual cost of hiring some help occasionally. I said that two hundred thousand would be more than enough for me.

He rolled his eyes. "There is no way you can anticipate what you will need in the future, when you get older."

Cindy nodded, "Have you considered long-term care insurance? Your ability to care for yourself in old age (if Andy passes first) may be more problematic with one arm."

"About a hundred dollars a month," said Andy from the kitchen.

"Okay," I said, "and I added twenty thousand to my expenses."

"This is crazy," Nathan said. "It's like trying to blackmail the hospital. These guys are going to do what they are going to do; and meanwhile they will tie up our suit for years."

"Nathan," said Andy as he brought tacos and rice from the kitchen, "Isn't lobbying, politics, union negotiations and lawyering usually one form of blackmail or another? When Cindy prosecutes a criminal, how does she get him to plead to a lesser charge? By holding something bad over his head. Blackmail."

"I wouldn't call it that," she said. "It's leverage. And mom has one more piece of leverage. Their new wing will be completed next year. They could run an ad campaign when it opens, stressing their state-of-the-art computer system that flawlessly tracks patient care, treatment and medications from start to finish. Or, they can deal with a media campaign stressing Barbara's long recovery from their tragic mistake."

Nathan turned his irritation toward his wife, "Cindy, we can't count on them doing the rational thing, or even the thing that is in their best interest. An extra million dollars is something their lawyers will fight against."

"We'll tell the administrator that if they throw in one million, we'll throw in two. And it's for a project that is already on the books. Then we will let him talk to his board, then the lawyers. Chances are the administrator will fight for our two million."

Nathan thought for a moment, but before he could say anything, I laid my hand on his and said, "Honey, it's a part of my healing."

Then Andy said, "Let's say grace." He bowed his head and said, "Thank you, Lord of Life for this food. You are the source of all good gifts. And thank you for this family that I am now a part of. May we be a gift to each other, and together may we gift the world. Amen."

I noticed that Andy forgot to set out the avocado salad. I got up and got it and brought it to the table saying, "We made your favorite, Nathan." In the end, my son agreed to draw up a counter offer along the lines of my proposal, and to set up a meeting for him and me to meet with the hospital administrator.

After lunch Andy opened the present they had brought. It was three bottles of massage oil of different kinds. Lawyers, the good ones, always do their homework.

Chapter 51

July 15
How did things change so quickly?
Who hit the fast-forward button!
Who am I now?
And when will I catch up with her?

* * *

Andy's hardest time was not the small, frustrating lapses of memory during the day, but early evening restlessness, a symptom we were told might develop but was expected much later – months, or a year or two. This restlessness was a low grade agitation when the sun went down, a mild symptom that only promised to get worse as his brain became more gunked up. Andy said it felt like he was supposed to be somewhere but didn't know where.

Dr. Pai was surprised that Andy seemed to be racing forward with his AD. She wanted him to take another test, a new PET scan technology. And he tried two different medications she had prescribed which promised to slow down the progress of his symptoms, but he couldn't tolerate the side effects.

Dr. Pai did, however, give him pills to calm him mildly in the evenings, which seemed to help. He was cautioned to not take his booster pills together with his calming pills; so we usually made love in the afternoons, which was actually our favorite time. Then in the long warm summer evenings we would often take a drive, sometimes up to the quaint town of Murphy's for dinner, and sometimes higher up into the Sierras.

It was during dinner at Sorrenson's Resort in Hope Valley, just beyond the Carson Pass, that we had our first real conversation about what Andy wanted to do between now and the end. I asked him, "Is there any place you want to visit or travel to while you can?"

"Travel? No. I used to have a list of countries that I wanted to visit some day. But now? I don't think so. It made more sense when I could anticipate collecting experiences and memories which I could reflect on over the years to come."

We enjoyed our dinner at a table on the restaurant's deck. Andy pointed to the evergreens covering the mountains and the small but lively Carson River flowing toward Nevada, "I soon may not remember this place, but it wasn't hard to get here and it didn't cost thousands of dollars. More importantly, I'm with you." He looked at me with a heart-felt smile. "Would there be more love if we were sitting along the Seine in Paris?"

"No, Sugar, not a bit more." I took his hand. "So there is nothing you particularly want to do with the time left?"

"Just be at home with you, like now. I don't know if it's the tranquilizer, but I feel eternally at home in this moment. And it wouldn't be so if you weren't here. I know that I am a child of the universe, and in some way I belong in this beautiful dance of the stars and galaxies. But when you look at me like that, I know it and feel it in the best of ways."

What could I say to that? It was the best thing anyone had ever said to me. I wanted that message to just sit there between us for a long time as I studied the features of Andy's face, noticed the cooling air of the high country, and listened to the soft sounds of the river and some far off ravens calling.

"And I want a party," he said finally.

I laughed. "What? A going away party?"

"I don't know. Not a wake; not so much a going away party, but more of a hello-again party. It's been over a year since I left the Foundation. I've kept those five close friends at arm's length while we all adjusted to me not being in charge. They were at our reception but there was a lot going on that night.

Let's have John, Wade and Marilyn, Peter, and Josh over for a dinner party.

"That sounds good."

"And I want to ride the horses with you more often."

"Okay."

"And I want to rent all of Bill Murray's movies, eat popcorn and laugh together – a lot."

"Great."

"I want to plant some trees and flowers."

"Dinner parties, horseback riding, watching movies, gardening; it sounds an awful lot like being home."

"You've got it, Cowgirl."

* * *

I didn't understand why a nudist couple wanted a church wedding. Why not get married out in a beautiful forest or a nudist beach? But they were determined, and we were the tenth wedding chapel they had called. They wanted an all nude church wedding for about thirty people, and a nude reception.

Andy said he had no problem with it, so I worked out an agreement with them: no nudity in view of the town people, or in the hotel. The reception/pool party would be in the hotel garden where they would pay to screen off the section visible to the neighbors. Also, even though Andy decided to not wear clothes, I would be dressed, and so would my staff serving food and drinks in the garden.

At one o'clock the guests walked over from the saloon. As they arrived I greeted them at the door of the chapel and gave them instructions. They undressed in the narthex where I had clothes racks in place. They also hung their robes which they had brought to use later. Most were seasoned nudists, but there were a few who were newbies to this practice and a little hesitant. Each in turn signed the guest book and walked into the chapel as naked as when they were born.

Inside, my bare-assed husband wearing only his preachers' stole and his tiny earphone, greeted the guests. The chapel itself seemed undressed with the chairs stored away. But there were twelve tall white standing baskets filled with fragrant Asian lilies. The baskets were spaced apart to form a large circle. Andy had the guests fill in the spaces between the baskets. As I peered through the small windows in the swinging doors, I could see that this arrangement actually made a striking picture – a ring of bodies and flowers.

I turned on my mic and said into Andy's ear, "Okay, Hon, I don't see any more guests coming over. Time for your intro; and I hope to God you didn't take your Lavitra this morning.

There was stifled laughter in the crowded narthex. Not only were there three full clothes racks, but now a nude couple with a guitar, and the bride and groom who were in their forties and fully dressed – her in a nice slender pearly wedding dress, and he in a tux. After the laughs I cracked open the doors so we could hear Andy.

"As we stand naked before God, having shed some of our pretenses and inhibitions, perhaps we are more prepared for marriage." He paused, looking around at the guests. I couldn't tell if it was for effect, or if he was trying to remember something. Dr. Pai had remarked that Andy had the self-awareness and ability to hide his memory lapses. But he continued, "Those of us who don't make a practice of this have sometimes wondered if, during our marital fights, we took off our clothes and became more real and vulnerable, would our fights become more…what? Softer? Shorter? And maybe compassion would be more readily available. So I am pleased to be asked to officiate today for Tonya and Brian. And just as you have made them feel comfortable in their nakedness, may you continue through the years ahead to help them feel comfortable in marriage. Let's welcome the bride and groom."

I opened and fastened the doors for the nude musicians who began to slowly walk the circle singing the old John Denver song, *Sunshine on My Shoulders*.

Following them were the bride and groom. There were surprised looks when everyone saw that they were clothed. From the narthex I could see that a few didn't look too happy. Andy broke the circle and took a place in the center. The bride and groom followed him, and the singers took Andy's place to close the circle again as they sang a second verse about how being exposed to the sunshine makes us feel happy and high.

The musicians were able to get most of the people to join them in singing the chorus again. Most knew this old John Denver song. When it came to an end, Andy began from his notes in his wedding book, "Friends, marriage is designed as a safe place to be ourselves."

Brian took off his coat and handed it to a guest to hold. Tonya took off her shoes and handed them to another guest.

"It is designed as a place to be honest and transparent."

Brian took off his shoes and handed them off to others. Tonya, her veil.

"It is designed as a place where we are loved and cherished just as we are."

Brian removed his cummerbund and pants and passed them to other guests. Tonya turned to have Brian unzip her dress which she stepped out of and handed to a guest.

"It is designed to be a place where we are honored and affirmed and accepted."

Brian untied his bow tie and peeled off his socks and distributed them, Tonya, her slip.

It is designed to be a place where we will be forgiven for our faults and failures."

Brian unbuttoned his shirt and took it off. Tonya unhooked her bra and tossed it to a friend which got some chuckles.

"It is designed to be a place where our true beauty can be seen."

Brian stepped out of his shorts and gingerly handed them to a willing hand. Tonya worked her pantyhose off, compressed them into a ball and handed them off. Nearly everyone around the circle held a piece of the couple's clothing as if they had helped and encouraged the couple's disrobing.

"Now I ask you both, will you take each other as husband and wife, creating a safe place to be yourselves, loving and cherishing each other as you are striving to be honest and transparent; will you honor, affirm and accept each other, forgiving faults and failures, and above all else, delight in each other's beauty?

"Brian?"

"Yes, I will."

"Tonya?"

"Yes, I will."

"Then by the authority of the State of California and of the church, I pronounce you husband and wife together. What God's love has joined together, let no one try to separate (or clothe). You may kiss."

As they kissed I glanced at my copy of the service, then turned on my mic. "Andy, is there going to be a prayer of blessing?"

He looked over at me and mouthed, "Oops." People were clapping and it took a bit for Andy to get their attention. But when he did he said, "There is a very old custom of sealing a marriage by symbolically tying a knot. So if Tonya and Brian would hug for a moment." Tonya's breasts flattened against Brian's chest. Andy slipped off his stole and wrapped it once around the couple and tied the ends, then began, "Oh Great Spirit, may Brian and Tonya be bound together in love yet free to learn and grow. Bless them this day and all their lives. Amen."

* * *

In room Number Ten we lay in bed, spent and quiet in the warm summer evening before sunset. It was becoming a tradition for us to make love after most weddings – and after the nudist wedding we felt particularly inspired. Now in the stillness with Andy on his back I lay facing him; I ran my hand over his shoulders exploring them slowly and thinking what he must have carried in his life, the burdens of being a pastor – heavy with deaths, and births, adoration and rejection, joys and sorrows of a thousand parishioners.

My hand investigated the muscles and bones of his arms as I thought of the women he must have held and loved and lost. Then I softly held his hand that had just pleasured me, and I pictured the cups of wine and plates of bread he must have lifted to bless Sunday after Sunday for over thirty years.

I let my fingers play in the hair on his chest. Then I slightly pressed my palm to feel the rising and falling of his breath and wondered at how precious each breath was – he wouldn't breathe forever. I tried to imagine him as a newborn, gasping for the first breath of his life – the beginning of this man's unique story. My hand went to his soft belly and I began to slowly make large circles there like when I was giving a massage – a regular activity we now both enjoyed. And with every circle my hand was drawn lower, brushing his pubic hair, then barely touching his oh-so-male point of pleasure. I gently took hold of him and gave it a subtle squeeze as if to say hello darling.

"Whoa, Cowgirl, I doubt if I have another go in me."

"That's fine, Lover Boy. Anyway, I sometimes like it when it's small and soft. It's cute, like its sleeping."

"So this isn't a test?"

"Tell me, what's my name?"

"Sweet Barbara Shepard."

"You passed," I said as I scooted down and began what I couldn't do for years after my first husband demanded it in the rudest terms. Some men are so aggressive in that way that I think their real fantasy is to make another man suck them off – however, I'm sure they would never admit it.

I didn't really want Andy to give an encore. I wanted to see what it would be like if I slowed down and paid attention to the sensations of caressing his sleeping little darling with my lips and tongue and mouth; to envelope his total maleness and savor it. But my sucking meditation was short-lived.

"Andy Shepard, can't you just relax and think of baseball for a minute?"

"I guess my booster pill's second stage just fired."

"Boys and their rockets!"

"My guess is that it's one of those unarmed, short-range rockets."

"A dud?"

"A dud!? Now those are fighting words."

I laughed as I let him turn me over, and though it wasn't the hardest of erections, he did get it in.

"Dud or stud? What do you think now, Cowgirl?"

"It's a good start, Dudly, but you have a long way to go."

"Oh? But I know a shortcut." And he slid a hand down between us and suddenly it wasn't just fun and games. I kissed his neck long and hard as I pulled his head tight to me. It didn't take me long and soon I tightened every aching muscle in my body and moaned too loud for the thin walls. I came before he did, so with effort I rocked my hips to his thrusting. He slid his hand out, straightened his arms and lifted his chest off of me and began a rhythm that I didn't think he could maintain. His breathing was heavy. I wanted to help. I dropped my knees to each side and dug my nails into his butt and began talking him toward his pleasure. "Come on Baby, that's right. That's right, give it to me. Yes. Give me your love, Sugar. Good. Good. Harder."

He quickened his pace like a race horse heading for the finish line. "Come on you stud. Give me all you have. Now. Now. Come on big boy." My own body was now becoming beautifully warm again with his every deep thrust. "Oh Andy, God, you feel so good, don't stop."

Funny how laughable these words are at a distance, but how urgent they felt at the time. When my sixty-three year old lover finally collapsed in a heap of sexual saturation, I began to laugh, "I'm so sorry, Sugar."

Andy began laughing too, "I was hoping for a heart attack," he said as he tried to catch his breath. "That would have taken care of things in the best way possible."

"Oh sure, and it would have left me with quite a reputation."

"That's right: Barbara the man-killer, watch out for her, you'll be lucky to survive with just scars on your ass." We laughed together and rolled our sweating bodies apart.

"Well, too bad, Honey. It doesn't look like it's going to be suicide by sex. You'll have to keep thinking."

"How much cheesecake would it take?" he asked.

"Make it chocolate cheesecake and we'll have a double suicide."

"Two chocolate cheesecakes and a big pitcher of margaritas."

I laughed, "Well officer, obviously he forgot that he had just eaten a cheesecake when he started on the second one. He had a bit of a short-term memory problem."

We laughed some more, then finally Andy said, "I think you should book some more nudist weddings."

"Yeah, Sugar. You know, the naked truth isn't so bad."

Chapter 52

July 24, a.m.
My thin small book says to practice
three things, open three doors:
slow down
pay attention
don't judge.
Then three things will bubble up,
three graces will enter in:
gratitude
compassion
humility.
If they don't bubble up I may
be stuck in:
resentment or jealousy,
blind insensitivity,
selfishness or arrogance.
If so, the practice must go deeper,
but without pushing.

* * *

It had been a difficult week.

First, Andy got disoriented and stubborn while we were on a trail ride. We trailered the horses past the dam and parked five miles down the highway. After a few hours, without the lake or creek as references, Andy insisted that the wrong trail was the way back to the truck. I told him that I was familiar with the area and that he was heading the wrong way. He dismissed this in a manner that I had not seen before and he just rode off in the wrong direction. Finally I shouted at him to stop and I demanded that he look at his ring and try to remember why my name was boldly on the face of it. Only then did he follow me, silently, back to where we began.

Secondly, Nathan called and said that the hospital administrator would not meet with us on the advice of their lawyers. And again Nathan pushed for me to sign their offer before the door closed and the case dragged on toward a two year court battle.

And finally, despite my warnings, on the day of a wedding the groom's brother, who was also the best man, showed up drunk. I had to ask him to leave, and everyone was mad at me. The wedding went on, but we discovered that the brother had left with the ring! I wrote in my journal:

> With all three events I believed I was right and I had insisted in my way; and each time I ended up feeling upset, perturbed, irritated and generally pissed. What I didn't feel - what didn't bubble up - was gratitude, compassion and humility.
> Gratitude? Well, maybe a little. My wedding ring ploy worked with Andy, and we made it home. And the drunken brother didn't stay and make a mess of the couple's wedding. And Nathan tried my idea despite his reservations.
> Compassion? Maybe, but it only went so far. Does compassion trump doing what is right? And how do I really know what is right.
> And Humility? What the hell is that? Is it doubting that I know what is right? Should I humbly doubt myself at every turn? Should I defer to everyone's stupid ideas?!

Andy finished his morning meditative prayer, walked into the kitchen and poured himself a cup of coffee, then joined me on the couch in the living room where I was writing, I looked up and asked, "All right, Pastor Andy, tell me, is humility doubting myself and just going along with everyone else's stupid ideas?"

"That's so humble of you to ask, Sweetheart. So if I give you my stupid opinion of humility, are you prepared to adopt it?"

"Nice try. I asked first."

"Well, as Forest Gump might say, humility is what humility does. You can't define it very well, but you know it when you see it."

"That was a stupid movie. I don't know what everyone saw in it."

"They saw a very humble guy."

"Does one have to be stupid to be humble?"

"If you know you are stupid it helps. Smart people can be very arrogant."

"Okay." I reached out to my writing stand and began to jot down a thought. Then I asked, "How do you spell 'arrogant?'"

I was surprised when he laughed and said, "Wow, I have never seen someone get it so quickly!"

"Lucky, I guess."

"There you go again! You're a natural."

"Oh, love has just blinded you, Honey. I have been an arrogant jackass this week."

Andy took a sip of his coffee and looked at me thoughtfully. "Barbara, if you've been arrogant I haven't seen it. I think you may have to go deeper. There is a kind of arrogance that is just a cover up for fear."

Andy's words, like a scalpel intent on excising a cancerous tumor, sliced through my defenses with shocking efficiency. I wanted to leave the room or at least change the subject, and I didn't know – didn't want to know – why. We sat there in an awkward silence. I looked at him, but he wasn't going to help me out. I decided to pay attention to my feelings. "You scared me on the trail, Andy. Sometimes I feel that I am in this way over my head. I got scared, then angry." I swallowed back some tears. "And I cursed myself for getting married." The tears fell. "I know, that sounds horrible, but I did."

Andy pulled out the familiar blue bandana that I had returned to him in Dr. Pai's waiting room. He handed it to me, "It's okay, Baby. Go on."

"Oh, Honey, I don't think I can handle this." I began to sob into the soft fabric.

"Handle what?"

"Alzheimer's."

"Of course not. Nobody can. It has its way and it wins in the end. I will say things and do things that you can't control, can't handle. It's not a horse that needs training. It's a progressive disease. You're afraid you can't keep my symptoms in control. But that's not your job. I don't expect you to do that. And you are afraid you can't keep me alive. That's not your job either."

"Well, I can't just let you ride off and get lost!"

"Why not?"

I could think of a hundred reasons. What did he mean? I searched his eyes.

"Why not?" he said again. "We are on an adventure here, Love. But trust me, before it gets too wild, it will be over."

"How will you know?"

"There will be a sign."

* * *

That afternoon I tried to call Nathan, but I didn't get him; so I called Cindy on her cell. She sounded busy but glad to hear from me. I was going to tell her that perhaps my idea was a foolish dream, that Nathan was right and I would reconsider the generous two million dollar offer.

But before I could start, she said that she was going to call me that evening. She had caught the administrator in the hospital cafeteria during lunch. "I introduced myself and told him that I respected his decision, but that this wasn't a meeting. I said I just wanted to give him a two million dollar gift from my mother; then I handed him an envelope with our counter offer."

My mother? Sweet.

"Then I said that you would be very disappointed, heartbroken, if he did not accept it because you were so grateful that the hospital had saved your life."

"Do you think he will read it?"

"Absolutely."

"Will he take the bait?"

"I expect the jury will be out for a couple of weeks. We'll see."

My lesson in humility wasn't over. That evening I got a call from Ray in Lodi. His ongoing role in our wedding enterprise was to promote it and keep our web site current and attractive. Our customers' on-line comments have mostly been glowing. But he said that the bride of our latest wedding posted some very critical feedback. It seems that I was a "Little Nazi, inflexible and uptight." Ray said he was going to call the client, but wanted to know what went wrong?

"What went wrong? I was inflexible and uptight, Ray. I'm afraid I wasn't at my best. I had to deal with a drunken best man, and I could have been more gracious. I'm sorry."

"How drunk?"

"I caught him peeing in the church shrubbery. I thought he would embarrass us all, so I sent him home, or wherever."

"Good. I would have done the same thing, Barbara."

"But you would have been charming; me, not so much."

"Don't worry. You're doing a terrific job. There'll always be those days."

"And how about Andy? Any comments there?"

"She said he did a beautiful service, and amazingly, it was all from memory."

July 24, p.m.

Being right

Being pushy   Being patient

Being arrogant   Being a listener

Being ugly   Being gracious

Fear is the difference.

Fear aborts humility.

Chapter 53

On August 29th we gave a party that was not a "Going-Away Party."

Andy thought of it as a "Make-up Party" for the year that he purposely had little contact with his friends on the Foundation Board. They were friends I had met, but didn't know well.

Three were old colleagues of Andy's: Dr. Peter Dow who had quit the ministry early on and became an educator; Rev. John LaFiever who had a career as a college campus minister; and Rev. Josh Thomas who was perhaps Andy's closest friend and who had served a church in the next county until he came to work for the Foundation. Marilyn and Wade Hampton were members of the Riverton Church where Andy had been pastor until the California Lottery had derailed him. And Lloyd Pettigrew was a local lawyer who served as counsel for the Foundation.

Andy had once confessed that his effort to set up the Foundation was in part a selfish one. He had hoped that working closely with his old friends would be like having a family and the home he longed for. But it didn't work out that way. The work had gotten in the way. At least when he left, they parted as friends. In the invitations Andy had asked them each to bring a lawn chair (for sitting near the lake shore where we would have dinner) and a stone of about a pound that told a story of gratitude.

As it turned out, Wade and Marilyn came in the afternoon, arriving on their catamaran. And Josh also came early to sail with Andy. I said no to the invitation to sail; swimming was one thing I had yet to attempt as a one-armed woman. Rather, I took Peter and John, who also came early, for a horseback ride along the lakeshore.

It was a fun afternoon, and when Lloyd arrived at five we were setting up the shade canopy over the picnic table and carrying the food and drinks down from the house. Finally, we set up our chairs in a semicircle facing the lake and sat and enjoyed Andy's sangria and my guacamole.

Josh had brought his guitar at Andy's request. After we all settled in and were chatting, Andy said, "I've written something for this sweet occasion. You may remember the classic cowboy song 'Ghost Riders in the Sky'… well, I've added a few new verses for it."

He handed a sheet of music to Josh, took his harmonica out of his pocket and began the soulful, driving tune. Josh began strumming cords and keeping the beat. Then together they sang about a cowboy on the range who sees a herd of cattle thundering through the cloudy sky, chased by exhausted riders who could not catch them. It seems that they are doomed to pursue the cows forever.

As Josh played, Andy said, "You can help out on the chorus, yipp-i-a, yippi-i-o."

After three verses Andy added two of his own:

> As cowboys searched among those clouds,
> I've tried to find a wife,
> To have and hold and feel at home
> This long and lonely life.
> It's hard to find a good one who
> You know will love you true.
> I've roped some troubled, angry ones –
> Found heartache and the blues.
> Yipp-i-a, yippi-i-o.
>
> Now time is short, the end is near,
> And soon I'll have to go.
> But finally I've found a gal –
> Oh man, she loves me so.
> In these last days I feel at home,
> At last I'm satisfied.
> No longer need to chase a ghost
> Nor heaven be denied.
> Yipp-i-a, yippi-i-o.

I glanced at John as we all clapped. Although they knew about Andy's diagnosis, only John and I really knew what Andy was pointing to with the line "the time is short, the end is near." Yet, as I looked around at his friends' faces it seemed they all knew that short meant short. And afterward, no one spoke.

What could be said that was neither shallow nor blunt? Yes, we all knew that everyone would someday die, but maybe people are not built to live with an expiration date. It was an invitation for melancholy. It made denial almost impossible. And hope? What does hope mean with a short expiration date?

I caught this last thought and realized that I had slipped into building my misery list again. Slow down – I shifted my attention to my breath and deliberately slowed its rate. Pay attention – I observed Andy, he seemed to be doing the same thing I was doing in the silent moment. Don't judge – I was blaming myself for regressing into my old misery-listing habit, so I told my wounded inner child that there was nothing to be afraid of today, that I had brought her to a party, so let's enjoy it.

I got up and walked over to Andy and sat in his lap with my arm around his neck and said for everyone to hear, "Okay, Cowboy, so the ghost riders are endlessly cursed to frantically chase a herd that they cannot catch. Maybe it's because if they caught them they wouldn't know what to do with them."

"Yeah?" he said, smiling. "Or maybe they always end up being more trouble than they are worth."

"Really? So then why chase them? Why not eat beans instead." I raised my eyebrows and grinned.

"Beans?" He looked over at the table, "Did I forget the beans?"

"Focus, Honey." I wiggled my butt a little. "I am sitting in your lap and I am asking what the cowboy would do if he actually caught a cow?"

Josh jumped in, "I don't think we all want to know, Barbara."

"Really!" John said. "Anyway, if his ass felt like mine after horseback riding, he couldn't do much of anything." Now the group was laughing.

"Well, I would start with those big black quivering lips," Andy said slowly as if anticipating the pleasure of it. "I would kiss them – first the salty top one under her wet nose…"

"eeyoo," Wade said.

"Then the fleshy bottom one scented with alfalfa."

"Nooo!" pleaded Josh.

"I would kiss those huge lips until her long talented meaty tongue flicked out to clean our nostrils."

"Andy Shepard!" I said, rolling my eyes.

"Yes! Then I would bury my face in her fuzzy ears, nuzzling in there nice and deep-like, and whisper that I really wanted what she had, and I wanted it really bad."

"Okay, Andy, enough already," Marilyn said, putting her hands over her ears.

But Andy continued louder with urgency, "Then I would slowly move down her body, rubbing my palms under her big beautiful belly and taking hold of her sensuous warm udders and feel their heaviness filling my hands. Then slowly and rhythmically pull and squeeze them; I would work her teats so lovingly that only rich glistening white cream would squirt out into my bucket."

"Andy, you're sick!" said Wade.

"Or very hard up," said Peter.

He continued as if uninterrupted, "She would softly low and swish me with her tail in appreciation. And when she had given me her all, I would make the best ice cream in the west!"

I smiled and shook my head, then stood up. "And that, folks, is Andy's unique way of announcing that we will crank homemade ice cream after dinner."

"We're having ice cream?" he asked.

Was he kidding? I wasn't sure. He wasn't supposed to pretend. So I just continued, "But right now I could use some help getting the tops off of these containers and setting up our tostada bar. And don't be shy, we have plenty of sangria."

Soon we all began to make and eat our first round of tostadas. The conversation turned to weddings. I described our recent motorcycle club wedding which included the bride's bouquet cleverly made of a variety of flattened beer cans. It was quite a sight when she tossed it to the assembly of single girls in boots, short shorts and small leather tops.

This got Andy's friends talking about unusual weddings that they had attended or officiated.

During this lively interchange Andy went back up towards the house for more ice and the cold ice cream mixture. I glanced in his direction as he made his way up from the lake, past the foundation of the cabin; then unexpectedly he veered off toward the horse barn and disappeared inside.

It seemed like he was in there quite a while when I got a phone call on my cell. Andy simply said, "I'm in the horse barn," but by his tone I knew it was a question.

"You took a wrong turn, Honey. Go to the house and bring down the ice cream mixture and more ice."

"Right. Thanks."

Josh was sitting next to me and had overheard. "How often does that happen?" he asked softly.

"Some days are worse than others, but I can't figure out why."

"Isn't that true for all of us?"

"Yes, I suppose so."

"If you need someone to hang out with him while you are away, please call me."

I thought to myself that Andy had said he wouldn't let things get too out of hand; certainly not to where he would need constant care. However, I was sure that we had different ideas of what out of hand meant. I didn't want to say that to Josh. Andy had only expressed this to John and me, and asked that we keep it to ourselves.

"I will. Thanks, Josh." I said as I watched Andy reach the back porch of the house.

Then Josh said, "I've heard that folks with Alzheimer's really connect with music that's familiar. It's going to be very interesting to see the songs Andy comes up with as time goes by."

"I think you're right. And please feel free to come over anytime with your guitar and play with him. I'd like that."

"So would I."

After we all took turns cranking the ice cream maker, we enjoyed delicious blackberry sundaes with berries Andy and I had picked along the creek below the dam. At one point, Andy got people's attention and said with mock amazement, "This is the best sundae I can ever remember eating." We knew that wasn't saying much and it got a laugh.

We had another hour of light and it finally felt cooler. Andy cleared a circle on the ground in front of our crescent. When he straightened up and faced us, he said, "I would like us to build a small gratitude altar in this circle with the stones we brought. And as we each in turn prepare to lay our stone, tell us what the stone reminds you of – what blessing is written in its features." Then he returned to his chair and said, "Who would like to go first?"

"I will," said Wade as he searched to the bottom of his day pack and came out with a palm sized stone. He lifted it up for us to see and said, "This is a pretty smooth river rock with some sparkly flecks in it. But right here there is a nasty little chip, a flaw. When Andy confided in me that he was thinking of buying his first lottery ticket, I was a bit shocked. I had heard him preach against gambling and the lottery. And I confess that I was disappointed in him; he was going to violate not only his own values, but his interpretation of God's word, as well. In my mind he was definitely teetering on the pedestal where I had put him.

"But as it turned out it was the beginning of the end for the crooked California Lottery. It was a surprising blessing. And look, it has put us all to work helping Calaveras County. Thank God for chips."

Wade got up and set his stone in the circle, and I thought of another of Andy's inconsistencies – he had vowed to not marry again.

Marilyn then held up her stone. "This stone looks nice and smooth, but when you look closer you can really see that it is dull and roughed up. When you and Joy separated, I was saddened and shook up. I loved you both, as spiritual leaders and friends. I couldn't understand why you couldn't obviously, work things out. Then I came to see that your marriage wasn't so much polishing each of you, it was roughing you up. It wasn't a good match at all. Now I am so thankful for you and Barbara. You are perfect for each other."

I smiled as Marilyn got up and placed her stone, arranging it to touch Wade's. My mind went to the jealousy I felt when I learned that Andy was having lunch with Joy once a month. What an unfounded fear.

Peter said he wanted to go next. He reached under his chair for a stone weighing considerably more than a pound. "I found this by the Mokelumne River." He held it out for us to see. "It's a nice egg shape, and I thought it would do because Andy is a good egg. Then I looked at the underside," he turned it around, "and I found this surprising white quartz ring on it.

"Three Christmases ago I was struggling with depression over my prostate cancer diagnosis and how the treatment was going to affect me. Andy twisted my arm to join them for Christmas dinner. I slept over, and on Christmas morning the three of us had Christmas stockings to unpack. Well, amidst the candy and nuts and other treats in my stocking, there was a box of condoms! Andy said it was a gift of hope.

"So this is for you, Andy," he said as he held up his stone, then turned it around. Indeed, the ring resembled a rolled-up condom. "A good egg who knew that someday I would get it up again."

I laughed with the others as Peter nestled his stone next to the first two, and I gave thanks for Andy's booster pills.

"Well, I guess I could go," John said next. "I, too, brought a handsome river stone. You know, they say a rolling stone gathers no moss, and obviously, this stone has been rolling. God knows how high up on the mountain it began. But we are not stones. And like it or not, we pick up a huge amount of stuff as we roll from birth to death. We try to jettison some of it from time to time – we change jobs, we get divorced, we move, we drop old friends and make new ones, we find God, we lose God – but a part of everything we touch stays with us, even if only subconsciously, even if only in spirit. We may not be able to recall most of our experiences, but as spirits our living, growing experience (our moss) will always be a part of us." He paused and looked at Andy, "You will always be a part of me and I will always be a part of you, my friend, no matter what. And for that I am thankful."

I watched John place his stone with the others and I made a mental note to follow up with John on his stone's story. It touched on a question I had been storing away on my back shelf for weeks: did Alzheimer's destroy memories or just mess up our access to them? And how much moss do we take into the next life (whatever, wherever it is)?

Now Josh retrieved his stone that he'd set on the table. Returning, he sat in his chair, shifting the weighty stone from hand to hand, thinking. Then finally he started, "It is unbelievable how old these rocks are. Shit, it is unbelievable how old we are!"

We laughed as we all agreed.

"Andy, we've been close friends for thirty-five years. That's a long time. I am so grateful for that. I wonder if I would have stayed in the ministry all those years if we hadn't taken off to ski and hike together, sharing the difficulties and heartaches of our jobs and our lives."

"Me too, Brother. Thank you," Andy said as Josh put his stone in the circle.

And where would I be, I thought, if Andy hadn't seen me through this past year. Yes, just one year, but it seems like a long, long time ago when he asked to rent my cabin.

Lloyd was next. "Yes, Josh, these river stones are old. And I would add: they are also solid. There are stones that are flaky, crumbly or soft. But I think these are mostly granite, and very solid. Andy, when you came to me and said that you wanted me to set up a foundation to give away all your millions, I thought you were exercising bad judgment, and that you would sooner or later regret it. But now seeing you and Barbara and the life you have, I think your judgment was solid and very wise."

Lloyd rose and set his stone on top of the others and in a flash of insight I saw Andy as the gift he was. He had wonderful friends, and yet in the past year he had invested so much time with me. And after his time became so precious, he wanted to be with me even more. What an extravagant gift.

I fought back the nagging thought that I was not worthy, picked up my rock and said, "My rock isn't from the river. It isn't smooth and round and easy to carry. It's hard and jagged and pointy, like my experience of having my arm amputated. I think we dug this one up when we had the burial for the sleeves I cut off my blouses – an experience that I wrote about in the journal Andy gave me. He said if I reflected on my journey of recovery it would teach me and I would be enriched. And that is what happened.

"He encouraged me and I found my courage. He taught me and I found my inner wisdom. He loved me and I learned to love myself. And now I am grateful to limp into heaven with one arm rather than spend my life in fear."

I stopped and stared at my rock. Everyone was still. I wasn't sure I had really said what I wanted to say. I wanted to say that I was now a better woman. I wanted to say that I knew I could now let Andy go though it would be difficult. I wanted to say that I believed.

I looked at Andy and saw his tears. I pulled our soft blue bandana out of my jeans and handed it to him. Then I placed my rock on the pile.

We all waited for a minute, then Andy walked to the circle with his stone, the eighth. He stooped down and examined each stone as he arranged them in a neat pile which he called an altar. As he worked he said, "The Old Testament says that the ancient Hebrews had a custom of setting up small stone monuments like this to mark where they had witnessed God in action – a reminder of God's help. I guess we all need reminders: despite appearances, we are not alone; despite experiences, divine help is offered; and despite occasions of feeling like a stranger in a strange land, we are at home.

"As I was listening to your stone stories, I had a funny thought. What if stones floated in water. I hear that some volcanic stones, pumice, will actually float.

Well, if all stones floated, the seas would be covered with stones and our weather would be very different, probably making life impossible. But although a few things float, most things sink – so much so that Hogan Lake will someday fill in and be a meadow. Same with memories. A relative few float near the surface and are accessible; but most sink down into the deep subconscious. If they all floated at the top, our minds would be chaotic. If too many sink into forgetfulness, well, that brings chaos as well. So my stone is in gratitude of the floating recollections I have today of my friendships – of all of you. And as for the sinking, I'm grateful for that as well."

In that moment I knew what Andy's plan was. The heavy, sinking stones – he would load his pockets with his friends' stones of gratitude and sail to the middle of the lake and let their love accompany him to the bottom.

Horribly perfect.

Chapter 54

Soon it was dark. The party had been fun, poignant, and in the end, sad – how could it not. Josh stayed after the others had said their good-byes and left. Andy invited him to take a walk together.

I showered and then tucked myself into bed. I wrote in my journal until I got sleepy.

August 29

Things to talk about with Andy:

Do not worry about me. I can "handle" it now.

"Faces gaunt, eyes blurred, shirt soaked with sweat?" you kind of poured it on a little thick, partner. Looking for a good woman could not be that hard, could it?

Or are there things you have not told me?

Did you really give Peter a box of condoms for Christmas? Would Santa approve?

Josh and I were going to time your detour in the horse barn, but you figured it out too soon.

Did you really have to separate yourself from your friends for so long? They really love you, you know.

You said we all need reminders about three things: divine help is always offered, we are at home, and the third thing?

You were not very subtle about the stones and the "sinking."

And it is not nearly as good an idea as the two cheesecake plan. And certainly, I think we should

try the sex-induced heart attack a few more times.
Can you wait until our grandchild arrives?
Oh yea, the third thing we need to be reminded of: we are not alone.

I turned off the light and fell sound asleep.

* * *

When I woke up I was still alone. The house was quiet. I looked at the clock. It was almost seven in the morning. Next to the clock there was a card that said Cowgirl on the envelope. My heart stopped. I slid my legs over the side of the bed sat up and opened the envelope. The card pictured a distant sailboat on a lake. Inside Andy had written:

I got lost yesterday in the barn,
Even I couldn't miss that sign.
I kiss you with this card.
You taught me to ride again...
On the awesome power of love.
You gave me a place
To feel at home again...
On this beautiful Earth.
And best of all, you helped me
Limp into heaven. See you there...
I'll always love you,
Andy

Tears blurred my vision. I wanted to read the card again, so I set it down and with my hand wiped my eyes. Then I saw our blue bandana had been placed on the night stand next to the clock. I picked it up and felt it between my fingers. I brought it to my face. I could smell him. His words from a few months ago, the day he was diagnosed, came back to me: "This is where the practice gets really interesting."

Perhaps. But first these tears.

Postscript

Andy's boat was found capsized, his body was never recovered. It was reported as an accident.

Ray threw a celebrative wake for Andy at the hotel. Bobby and the Calaveras Jumpers sang his songs.

It took another year, but the hospital finally settled and converted to digital records, charting and orders.

A part-time Unitarian minister took over for Andy. I trained a new wedding coordinator, and Shepard's Chapel continued to hitch up couples.

The Shepard Foundation granted Sabina and me the money to start a non-profit riding school for special needs children and youth. We quit our day jobs.

Note to Readers

The historic hotel in Mokelumne Hill, referred to in this story, is based on the Leger Hotel that is still there doing business. However, the characters in this novel associated with the hotel are fictional.

I have been asked about Barbara's "thin little book" *Remember, Life Is A Precious Miracle*. There is no such book (as far as I know). But there are books that describe walking meditation and other Buddhist-like practices that facilitated Barbara's rehabilitation. I recommend the books by Tich Nhac Hanh.

And finally, you may be interested in my earlier novel, *The Way Home*, which tells of Rev. Andy's adventures (written from his point of view) that precede the events of this story.

D.E.

Made in United States
Orlando, FL
02 August 2024